The Fovean Chronicles

Book Two: Indomitus Vivat

By Robert W. Brady, Jr.

Start every adventure as if it is your last. The person coming back from it is not going to be you.

The Fovean Chronicles
Book Two: Indomitus Vivat
© 2012 by Robert W. Brady, Jr.

ISBN: 9780979367960

Cover art: Boris Vallejo

Second Printing

10   9   8   7   6   5   4   3   2   1

Known Fovea

Prologue

The Almadain

A white stallion that Men called 'Blizzard' stood with a Man on his back on a street made of stone, in a city made of stone, where arrows flew around him and magic crackled the air. Screams from warriors and lesser horses tore his ears; blood and smoke and the acrid stink of fear filled his flaring nostrils. He stomped a metal-shod hoof and brought sparks up from the ground, bobbed his head and snorted in anger while the Man debated with its mate on a lesser horse next to him.

It hadn't always been this way, the white stallion remembered. He'd been free once. He'd been *the Almadain* – first stallion and protector of his kind. He'd run with the wind in his mane on the Wild Horse Plains, guarding the Herd That Cannot be Tamed, sacred to the goddess Life, the sun or the moon hanging over him, thick grass at his hooves, mares to breed with all around him, his sons and daughters as far as his brown eyes could see.

But then the man-god Steel had come to him, and sent him south to the lands where Dwarves and Uman and *Men* dwelt, to find the one with hair light like his own, and blue eyes, and to carry that one forward on his back into a future unknown.

The Almadain could have refused. He had no love for Men. Men had hunted his kind, come to steal his foals, his mares. Men stank of the flesh they consumed; they made things that cut and stabbed, hard bits that pinched the gums and thick leather that chaffed the back and sides. Men were killers no better than the loafer wolves that weeded out the sick and the weak from the herd, except that Men preyed on the strong.

But Steel had shown the Almadain a future where this one Man ran free, with no horse to guide him, hunting where he would, feeling detached from the world. In that future, the Man killed with a hunger worse than all of the loafer wolves that the Almadain had ever seen. In that world, Men and Uman came by the hundreds and took the plains where the Herd ran, and enslaved or killed the Almadain's kind, driving them under the lash in homage to the god War, sweeping out encased in armor to conquer and destroy.

The Almadain could not really understand that hunger. It wasn't *horse-like* to want more grass than the herd could eat, to want to see farther than the edge of the plains. These were man-thoughts. But not understanding them didn't make them unreal, and the Almadain needed no convincing what were the vices of Men.

So the Almadain had left his herd, his mares, his foals, and turned south. He'd found the Man and befriended him, borne him on his back, run with him into sharp steel and screaming men and horses. Where the Man was strong, the Almadain had been strong as well, and together they had protected the Man's herd.

More importantly, in the quiet times after the battles, after the blood that flowed and the voices that screamed, while other horses stood trembling and fearing the next day, the horse called Blizzard and the Man called by many names had come together. The Man had curried him with soft brushes, picked the dirt and worse from his hooves, stitched his wounded sides sometimes and run his fingers through his mane and tail.

Sometimes in the dark of night, the man with white hair had taken the Almadain's head in his arms and held it; and shook with grief and let the tears run from his strange, blue eyes. Sometime the man spoke softly to the horse, going on for a long time, not really saying anything with his words, but conveying with his scent and with the sound of his voice that the things he saw, that the things he *did* were as terrifying to he himself as to the Almadain and to the other creatures, the Dwarves and Uman and *Men*, whom they together visited these things on.

In the quiet in the night and after the battles, the Man had come to love the horse, and the horse the Man in some ways. The sacrifice had proven its worth – the Man might be a conqueror, a killer, a predator but, thanks to the love of a horse, not a monster.

Steel heels touched the horse's sides. That meant start forward. Blizzard bobbed his head and obliged, leading hundreds of horses not quite like him into the heat of battle, the smell of blood, the chaos of the worship of the god War.

And before the violence wiped all other thought away, the horse called 'Blizzard' reminded himself that, in fact, the Man had not become a monster *yet.*

Chapter One

Welcome to a Brand New Day

My daughter came into this world screaming on the twenty-fifth day of Life in the eighty-first year of the Fovean High Council. Children born in Life are supposed to be robust and healthy. Lee, named after my mother of all people, made no exception. Her Andaron name would be "Grip Like Steel," which suited her and which would change from time to time throughout her life.

King Glennen and his wife, Queen Alekanna visited the estate in Thera regularly, as did my Free Legion ally Nantar and his wife. Thera was considered the military center in Eldador and we trained in the open with both the Free Legion and the Eldadorian armies - occasionally with foreign generals who paid to learn from *The Conqueror*, also known as 'me.' All of the Eldadorian Dukes recognized me as the heir apparent to the throne even though nothing formal had been declared. Unlike the feudal systems of Earth, it seemed that Eldadorian nobility wanted anything *but* the throne. Quite frankly I could see why.

On the third day of my daughter's life, Alekki (Glennen's pet name for his queen) held Lee in the crook of her arm as Shela watched from her recovery bed. Shela's maids had wrapped her hips tight with bed sheets, to the point of strangulation, to guarantee her some portion of her figure back. Once again, as ever, I felt glad to be a man. Glennen and I drank brandy with Nantar after a light dinner. I hadn't seen Nantar's wife.

"Well, I see I will be having another one," Glennen complained amicably. Alekki looked sideways at him and smiled to herself. She stood barely five feet tall, thin and graceful with brown hair past her shoulders and green eyes that sought the soul. Her lips, when she relaxed, formed a perfect bow – Alekanna had been born to the job of queen. "You make claim to these great things, but you do me no good, Duke Mordetur."

"He has offers from other nations to do *them* no good," Nantar challenged him. His black beard bristled in a smile. "I even hear that the Trenboni want to offer him a Duchy outside of Outpost VII."

I'd sent a letter to an Uman-Chi ambassador, asking why they wanted an audience with me, and the idea had worked. I had not yet responded.

"Pah!" Glennen spat. Glennen stood almost as tall as I, muscled but with his share of fat from soft-living in his capitol, his jowl starting to sag and his long, black hair shot with gray. His eyebrows naturally formed a single line over a hawk-like nose. "Outpost VII indeed," he said. "They probably just want to give him enough land to blame their Scitai problems on him." He clapped me on the shoulder with a meaty hand.

"I think the Duke is staying right where he is, Nantar," Glennen added, just the slightest bit of warning in his voice.

I just smiled at Shela, who beamed back at me. Motherhood seemed to suit her. Her long, black hair framed the reddish tint of her face, her brown eyes followed her baby. I had known this woman for thirteen months – I might have celebrated her birthday in that time if she had known it. She guessed her age at seventeen – a mother of one when most of her childhood friends were weaning off their second. Women twice her age where I came from had not done so much living.

"There is word of the Confluni massing on the Volkhydran border," Glennen mentioned nonchalantly. He stretched and yawned, following me through the corner of his left eye. "I don't suppose you will be going back there next year?"

His ultimate worry, I thought to myself. Many speculated that Eldador grew too powerful too fast. Her own population and armies swelled, her own economy booming under the rise of capitalism, the only such economy on Fovea. Glennen and I had a project going on in my shipyards to build Eldadorian Tech-Ships that would rival those of Trenbon, then to wrest sea power away from that nation. A punitive strike against Eldador now seemed imperative to keep all of the power on Tren Bay from shifting radically.

"Your heavy lancers would be an asset," Nantar added, also eyeing me. Nantar was called 'the greatest warrior alive.' A Volkhydran of the Volkha side, he was of the race of Men, shorter than I but more heavily muscled. Nantar was lethal with any weapon, yet carried with him an infectious smile that never seemed to leave him. He had been spending more and more time here. His wife liked Shela and Alekanna's company and he studied the Wolf Soldiers intently as he built his own version: the *Sarandi*. Also derived from desperate men (and women), they were his version of my version of the French Foreign Legion mixed with the Navy Seals.

Only the Free Legion and the Wolf Soldiers had lancers. Even the Eldadorians were unwilling or unable (ok, unable) to adopt the fighting style, mainly because we wouldn't teach the simple rudiments of lancing. Without knowing how to couch the lance, how to pick a good lance, how to train the horses appropriately, lancers were like Nantar, Thorn and I had been in Conflu – guys with long sticks that broke after the first pass.

Lancers had to charge in a line and slash the enemy diagonally, or they were engaged and then had only the advantages of men on horseback. They had to turn in the same direction for a fast second attack that didn't turn into an equine mob. Barding had to be built to add momentum to the charge, not hold back the horse using it. The mounts had to be strong enough to bear a knight but fast enough to be useful in the hit-and-run battle that made lancers *so* devastating. They required constant training, specialized armor and continuous upkeep specific to an elite troop of men who did essentially nothing else. It was all hugely expensive, even if you knew what you were doing.

My Wolf Soldiers with this training were called 'Theran Lancers,' and Two Spears excelled among them. Kills with a Glance complained bitterly to me to send back his son, my blood brother, so that he could glean that training, but Two Spears seemed perfectly happy with me (and a bevy of female admirers willing to do anything to wed the brother of Rancor the Just). For his performance, he had been rewarded with the Mark of the Conqueror. Two Spears wasn't a Wolf Soldier, but he commanded them, and they loved him.

"I'm doing new things with them," I said, feigning as much false indifference as they were, "and I'm not ready to commit them to campaigns yet. Besides, I am a daddy for the first time. I think I want to enjoy that."

Alekki sighed, bouncing Lee lightly in her arms. Neither Glennen nor Nantar looked happy.

"What if Ancenon calls you?" the latter asked.

I shrugged. "I will deal with that then," I told him.

"Is that fire-bond thing still in effect?" Glennen asked, *way* too personally. A sour look bristled Nantar's beard.

"It is never not in effect," I answered him truthfully. Not until we spent all of the gold from Outpost IX, anyway, therefore as good as never. "But it doesn't commit me to every Free Legion campaign."

Nantar straightened and so did Glennen, and I saw the storm on the horizon. Who I felt committed to remained a sore-spot for both the Free Legion and Eldador – more-so because I felt sure that there had been offers to act *against* Eldador recently, and Ancenon couldn't be sure which side I would be on if he dared to accept one of them. Quite frankly, I couldn't be sure, either. I loved Eldador in-as-much as I spent a huge portion of my life, but I owed that life to the Free Legion.

Right then the door burst open and Nantar's wife, Lanette, burst in, her dress torn and a scar on her shoulder. I stood up with Nantar and Glennen, the Sword of War in my hand before I realized it.

She flew into Nantar's huge arms. He wrapped her in them like a cloak of muscle and bone. Her lower lip trembled and she looked up into his eyes.

"Drekk is dead," she told him.

***

Drekk liked to hang out at the estate in Thera because of its central location that let him go back and forth between other nations with the goods and information that he pilfered. I let him have the run of the estate, the wharves, Free Legion Shipping and the warehouse that I had given him. We kept it all hush-hush as an integral part of the Free Legion Intelligence Branch that consisted solely of him.

Or so I had thought.

Two hundred Wolf Soldiers ringed the warehouse where he and Lanette had met to discuss some trinket that she wanted for Nantar on his upcoming birthday. According to her, ten men had dropped out of the rafters and attacked the both of them, for what purpose we did not know. Drekk had laid down his own life to back her out through an alleyway door to safety. A *very* subtle sooth-saying by Shela confirmed that she told the truth and hadn't been involved in the killing in some way.

The warehouse covered three thousand feet square, one of the smaller ones but entirely adequate for Drekk. He had stacks of crates against one wall that had been broken open and a desk that had been rifled through. His body had been stabbed at least a dozen times, although blood puddles on the floor around him where he lay by that one door showed that he had not died alone.

Yet Drekk had never been a warrior – anything but. His weapons involved stealth and secrecy and knowledge only guessed at, the shadow in a shadow and the dagger in the night. He didn't fight and he didn't raise armies, but he knew more of the facts about what actually went on than any of us could guess at.

He didn't look like he had seen this coming.

Shela had come with Glennen, Nantar and I, borne on a litter with Lee. Arath and Dilvesh were in the Lone Wood, and fast riders were on their way. Shela had already informed Ancenon and D'gattis, and they were going to find Thorn. The Wolf Soldiers were marshalling. I already suspected what I would find out here, and this would be expensive for someone besides me.

"Murder, plain as it gets," Glennen said. He looked at Nantar with brown eyes softer than they normally were. "I *am* sorry," he added.

Nantar nodded, then looked at me, then Shela, then back to me. Lanette had stayed with Alekanna, but we obviously needed Shela's unique talent.

"Can she do anything?" he asked simply.

I turned to Shela.

Giving birth had done nothing to weaken her magical reserves. She'd told me that her power derived from the desires of men – if such men were involved in this murder then she'd know. Otherwise, it became a matter of how well they had protected themselves.

Looking down at the dirt floor with a tight grip on Lee, Shela incanted something low in her throat. The baby lay quiet and oddly inactive while her mother performed her casting, reaching out with a chubby hand. I didn't know that much about babies but for three days old this one seemed to make her presence known pretty well and to react to what went on around her.

Shela barked a command and six puddles of blood glowed an unhealthy green throughout the room, lighting the night in a sick radiance. Outside a horse neighed and, by one crate, a rat scurried out of the packing and across the floor towards the door.

Shela stopped as abruptly as she began, and looked at me with tear-filled eyes. I didn't know if she had any relationship with Drekk other than passing, yet I had seen them speak and I knew they shared confidences. She would have to tell me in private how she felt about our assassin.

Four Wolf Soldiers, of her personal guard, carried her litter. Without her telling them they carried her to the four corners of the room, and stopped by Drekk's dead body. It had been necessary for us to leave him in his own blood, spilled out on the dirt floor. His vacant eyes looked up at the ceiling, the bloody dirk still in his grasp. Whoever had killed him had disturbed him, yet still left his testament to the battle he had fought and lost.

"It is as Lanette says," she said softly, her voice cracking. "But what she could not know is that the men came only to kill her and Drekk. The sacking of the warehouse is a sham and nothing was taken. They would have put the whole place to the torch if they had the time."

"If *who* had time?" Nantar pressed her. I don't think the idea of someone going out of his or her way to kill his wife sat well with him.

"I see a talisman of great power, used to speak with Drekk after his death," she continued. "I see the signature that it has left here and, through that, I see *it*. I see Uman warriors placing this on Drekk's dead breast."

"Mercenaries," I said, after a moment's thought. "Uman killers."

"I see the talisman being placed in their leader's hands by a Man Wizard," Shela said. "I hear his words."

"*Dorkans*?" Glennen said, incredulous. "This isn't like what Dorkans do." He looked at me. "A plague in your house, your water running dry, your crops dying, some subtle magical thing – that is what Dorkan wizards – "

"There is no arguing, though," Nantar said. "My people have few Wizards."

Glennen looked pissed-off. I went to the litter and took Shela's tiny hand in mine, looked up into her brown eyes. "Are you sure about that last part?" I asked.

She shook her head. "There can be no doubt," she said. "The amulet they placed on Drekk's dead body absorbed most of the secrets from his head. That left a powerful signature behind – I can see that amulet as if it were right in this room. It is for that reason I know so much of what has transpired here this night."

She spoke that way when she used her magic – she became this other, mystical person. She *knew* things.

Drekk had designed the security at the estate in Thera. Why else take him out first?

"The estate," I said. I caught Glennen's eyes, held them with my own. "That's why they killed Drekk. He designed the security at the estate."

***

Wolf Soldiers guarded the periphery of the Casa de Mordetur. I left a good quarter mile of open space between the walls and the nearest stand of trees or building, and they had created no secret ways in or out. All of my security hadn't stood up for a second against twenty Uman mercenaries with knowledge of the best ways to gain entry.

Lanette had survived again, but Alekanna and the house staff had not. This time the evidence of torture was plain for anyone to see. The merc's had wanted the rest of us, and badly.

"She screamed and screamed," Lanette sobbed into Nantar's shoulder. She had hidden herself under Shela's and my bed and had still been there when we had burst in looking for her. I felt suspicious that they had missed her, but then they may have already thought her dead. Shela's truth telling showed that she hadn't conspired with the enemy.

"They wanted to know where Glennen and Lupus were," she continued, sobbing and perhaps going into shock. "Alekanna told them, but they didn't believe her."

"Twenty Uman mercenaries," Nantar said. "You're sure?"

"A Man leading them," she said. "I couldn't see them, but I could hear them. Some had Volkhydran accents."

"So the Wizard *was* a Volkhydran," I said.

She shook her head. "I don't think so," she said. "The one leading them had that thick, Dorkan voice."

"So all of the mercenaries weren't Uman," Glennen said.

I was thinking on this now. Something made deadly sense. I looked at Nantar.

"Volkhydrans, Dorkans and Uman working together?" I asked him.

His brown eyes met mine. "I noticed that, too," he said.

The king looked up at me from the floor, where he held the bloody remains of the mother of his children. Her eyes were still open, the look of horror on her face showed that she had died from unbelievable pain. As a well-born lady who had lived her life with noble people, Alekanna could never have imagined that sort of treatment.

Glennen looked into my eyes and I looked into his. Glennen had been a warrior before he became a king. I knew what he wanted without him saying it.

The Volkhydran government, or at least a part of that government, had organized this. They had worked with Dorkans and with Uman mercenaries.

Which meant that the Trenboni had provided them, or the Sentalans, or perhaps Eldadorian rebels. Men would have used Man mercenaries unless they had a reason not to. Getting them from another nation would be such a reason.

If the King of Eldador squashed rebels, that was his business and no one would interfere. If he pursued revenge against an outside force that sponsored them then that might be questionable. If three or more other nations acted in concert and the King of Eldador retaliated against them then Eldador would be declaring war, no question about it. Especially if the Trenboni had involved themselves.

Under Fovean Law an act of aggression between sovereign governments demanded action by the Fovean High Council. Eldadorian Councilmen would then argue his case, present evidence, seek allies in the Council and call a vote. If successful, they would demand sanctions, levy fines, raise tariffs and embarrass those nations before the local communities.

And that didn't mean *jack* when your wife lay dead in your arms. Even less when you told her kids about it.

So he couldn't do it himself, and he really couldn't go looking for anyone else. This was the sort of thing you hired a bounty hunter for – to get revenge for you and keep it quiet, because you couldn't get involved. Glennen knew I wasn't a bounty hunter, but I don't think it bothered him.

"Every last one of them, Lupus," he said simply. His eyes were like stone, his jaw set, his wife's blood on his face and hands. "Whatever you need, you have it."

"I have no problem with that," I answered him.

***

I went to sleep that night after Shela personally warded every entry into and out of the estate, and 5,000 Wolf Soldier guards split responsibilities for a five-section, twenty-four hour watch, meaning that at any one time there were 333 of them patrolling the property or the surrounding area while 333 slept and 333 performed maintenance duties or thought up better ways to protect us. Glennen traveled under my personal escort back to Eldador the Port, a Wizard with him in constant contact with a counterpart here.

I dreamed of an innocent woman with a look of horror on her face, trying to convince a group of mercenaries that she didn't know anything while they tortured her.

I woke up in a cold sweat, Shela watching me with her knowing eyes. She sat in a rocking chair to my right, nursing Lee. I had finally started to get my mind around this plan I'd been involved in.

"They have come," she told me.

The room stood in shadow, with only the light from a waning moon through its one window to see by.

A bounty hunter sat in my bedroom. A real one.

He'd picked a chair in the moonlight to my left, light from the room's window to his right side casting a shadow across his face. He could be out and on the run in a moment. His features were dim and indistinguishable to me. He had walked past all of Shela's wards and my guards to get here. He wouldn't have done that alone.

"You are not our favorite person," he told me simply. I sat up in my bed, dressed in leggings and bare-chested. The Sword of War hung on the wall above me.

"If not for that one," he continued, indicating Shela, "you would be dead now."

"If not for that one," Shela said, indicating me, "*you* would be dead now."

"And so," he said, inclining his head in the gloom. "You put out the call for us, and I am here. Know that any ill will you may have for us, or us for you, is suspended for this negotiation. Know as well that you have offended us, and we *will* eradicate you, be you The Conqueror, The Just or Duke of Thera."

"And is that what you are trying to do now?" I asked.

He laughed, low in his throat. "Were we the ones behind these attacks, we would not have killed an innocent. The bounty on your Free Legion is temptingly high but, in fact, our interests lie in the chaos and animosity you spread, not in your demise."

"He speaks the truth as he sees it," Shela added. I would have guessed as much.

"What will it take to end your interest in me?" I asked, from the top of my head.

"Your death, and no less," he told me. Shela didn't need to tell me that he spoke the truth as he saw it.

"And yet you come here," I said.

"I was curious about your defenses, and I wanted you to be able to tell your allies that we were not involved in this," he told me. I didn't doubt that he possessed a wealth of knowledge about this situation. There would have to be a level of intelligence gathering involved in what they did. It would be good to have them as allies if I could pull that off.

That wouldn't happen tonight.

"The Trenboni, the Dorkans, and the Volkhydrans did this?" I said. I guessed about the Trenboni, but who else had more practice in uniting other nations against each other than the ones who housed the Fovean High Council?

"I have no reason to tell you that," he said, simply.

"Make him tell me, Shela," I said in his same, bland voice.

He lunged for the window and then slammed back into his seat just as quickly, his hands welded to the arms of his chair by Power. Even in the dark I could sense his hateful look.

"Aggressions were suspended," he said.

"Information was promised."

"*We* decide what information."

"Doesn't look that way to me."

He sat quiet, fuming. If he worked with another bounty hunter, then he or she should have attacked by now. My ears strained for any reason to rip the Sword of War off the wall. I didn't kid myself that I would be a match in regular combat for a bounty hunter, but the Sword of War gave a hell of an advantage, and Shela provided another.

I didn't come here to die fighting fairly.

"It was those you mentioned, with the Sentalans," the bounty hunter said. "I am surprised you knew of the Uman-Chi."

"I am not without resources," I said. I had guessed right then that the Uman were Sentalans, not Trenboni. That made more sense in afterthought. Eldadorians rebels weren't really a possibility. Eldadorians were too busy being happy to rebel.

"You would have been wise to use them, instead of invoking the Guild in Outpost IX," he said. "You would have been wiser still to use them rather than to hold me here now."

"What are you going to do, kill me for it?" I asked. "When you take away your enemy's recourse, you take away any motivation for him to fight fair."

"Your recourse is a fatal one," he said calmly.

You had to admire the confidence. To threaten me in my own home, in front of a woman whom he had to know could kill him with a glance.

"A lot of people have told me that," I said. "And they're all dead, and I'm not.

"I believe you that you're not involved. Get out."

He stood and leapt out the window, Shela having released him. I didn't normally leave it open – he must have done that on his way in. If he got caught on his way out, then that was on him.

"Do you sense anyone else in the room?" I asked Shela.

She thought for a moment. "No," she said, finally. "There was one other, and she is gone. I am surprised that they wanted so badly to tell us that they are not involved."

"I am surprised that the other didn't attack," I said.

"The Free Legion is becoming a force to be reckoned with. If it survives this then these bounty hunters probably don't want that force turned on them."

"They must know that is going to happen anyway," I said. "The Free Legion won't tolerate continued threats against its members."

"Nor will I," Shela said, darkly. Sitting in her rocking chair, nursing her new baby, she looked to me like some dark demon mother. Shela had many facets to her and some of them weren't that pretty.

"Tomorrow is another day," I said. "We'll be focused on Drekk's death, now."

Shela stiffened. "And Alekki's," she added.

I nodded, got up out of bed, took her hand in mine. "That is my worry," I said. "And it is yours. Not the Free Legion's."

She looked into my eyes through the night gloom and nodded. We just stood there, listening to Lee nurse, for a very long time.

***

"There is a saying where I come from," I said, sitting in my War room, in the Casa de Mordetur, with Shela and the rest of the Free Legion. "'If you mess with the bull, you get the horns.'"

I'd built my War Room with chalkboard walls, a long table, chairs and no windows. The walls behind the chalkboards were lined with cork to prevent anyone from listening in on us.

"These are very strange people who birthed you, Lupus," D'gattis said.

"Don't I know it?"

A week had passed since the attack on Drekk and the Eldadorian queen, the first of the cold month of Power. Glennen had returned safe to his palace. Wolf Soldiers, Free Legion Soldiers and Sarandi had marshaled. The word had gone out and 1,000 loyal Aschire had already begun the march from their woods. They would be here in a few days.

Drekk had run a network of spies in every nation, dipping into our gold to pay them. These men and women were from our own troops, returned to their homelands and established as guards, journeymen, craftsmen and hand servants. Drekk had seen to it that, at different times, their pay came either from Outpost X, myself, Ancenon, D'gattis, Arath or Dilvesh. Thorn or Nantar had trained or recruited them, or I had. Drekk had spies who watched the spies, and had documented it all in a series of encrypted, leather bound journals entrusted to his unofficial second in command.

That second stood before us now, the journals on the table. Even I couldn't read them.

"So you are Karel of Stone," I said to him.

I had heard of him in Outpost IX, and from time to time in foreign courts. Where Drekk had been a mystery, a shadow in the shadows, keeping his appearance and his reputation quiet, Karel made of himself an extravagant, actually infamous thief who like Drekk claimed to be able to take anything from anyone and not be caught. A Scitai, the Uman-Chi maintained an alarmingly large bounty on his head, as the man who had robbed the Trenboni royal treasury not once but twice.

"If not then my mother has some explaining to do," he answered me. Like me, he had blue eyes and was tall for his people, a remarkable three feet and one inch in height. He had brown hair and wore armor made of bearskins, turned inside out. He wore a rapier over his shoulder much as I wore the Sword of War.

I already didn't like him.

"I can vouchsafe Karel of Stone," D'gattis told me. "I have known him for many years."

"A friendship whose logic eludes me," Ancenon commented. He wore no politic smile now – Ancenon wanted to arrest Karel on site and D'gattis had actually stood against him to prevent it. In this I tended to agree. We needed Drekk's second to run things, at least until a replacement for Drekk could be found.

"Oh, I have friends that I can't be seen with in public," Nantar said, wearing his usual smile. "One of them used to be Thorn here."

Thorn glanced sideways at him. He had taken the news of Drekk's death personally and seemed more sour than usual. Probably why Nantar kept at him like that.

"You are able to read those journals," Dilvesh said. Dilvesh had been the first to come when he heard of the attack. He had reaffirmed everything that Shela had told us, not that he needed to.

"I helped Drekk work out the encryption," the little thief said.

"And the spy network?" Arath asked.

"In place," Karel said. "They will need to be paid as usual or they will dissolve, I'm sure. Like cats, keep feeding them and they will keep coming around."

"Cats aren't notoriously loyal," Ancenon remarked.

"Don't underestimate cats," Karel said. "They don't wag their tails like dogs but they know what to do to get their dish refilled."

I had to smile at that. Personally I hated the little fuzz balls but I could see the truth in what Karel said.

"And what do we know from this expensive network of Drekk's?" Ancenon asked. Ancenon didn't strike me as real happy right now. I doubt that he liked what he was about to find out any more than he liked the one who told him.

"Drekk's and my contacts in Outpost IX are extensive," Karel said. "Nowhere else is there such a preponderance of unneeded servants, so it is very easy to sneak more in to watch things."

Arath barked a laugh. Shela smiled as well. She had been busy replacing the house staff and cleaning the manor herself during the process, including cooking our meals and feeding her horses. It made for a mountain of work for a new mother, but I knew she loved it. Nothing seemed as clean to Shela as when she did the work herself.

"There is no doubt but that Angron Aurelias himself knew of the attacks and actually cooperated," Karel continued, condemning the King of Trenbon.

"Lies!" Ancenon shouted, slamming the long table with his fist.

"That information does support what we know already," Nantar said. He and I had discussed how Ancenon would react to the news of his King's involvement. Neither of us had guessed that he would embrace the idea.

"The bounty hunter also confirmed that Uman-Chi had been involved," Shela said softly.

"Why?" D'gattis said. "Shela, Karel, all of you, I know my people. Do not think we don't know how the world sees us. We are a people motivated first by our own self-interests. How would those interests be served by eliminating the Free Legion?"

"D'gattis, do you know what your Free Legion stands for to a nation like Trenbon?" Karel asked.

"Of course he does," Ancenon snarled. He still stood, glowering at Karel from across the table. "Our shipping brings more wealth to the market place in Outpost IX – "

"And our armies offer more threat to that market place, Ancenon," Arath said.

"No one would dare attack Outpost IX," Ancenon said. "Everyone knows that."

"Everyone knows a lot of things," Thorn said. "I don't think the Uman-Chi spent centuries talking about 'invincible Outpost IX' because they wanted to prove it."

"Better to use their power to prevent any other nation from growing strong enough to try," Dilvesh said softly.

"Which is what provoked this action against us," said Nantar.

Everyone nodded.

Ancenon and D'gattis were visibly mortified. If their own nation wanted to eradicate the Free Legion, that meant them as well. Life takes on a different tone when your own people want to kill you. I had learned that in a jail cell.

The Prince sat back down.

"Eldador poses an even worse threat than the Free Legion," Karel continued. "Every court in the land is under siege as word spreads of peasants paying less than one silver in five to their liege lords. No one understands this uck-nomuks that Lupus invented. Volkhydrans especially are convinced that this is a new way to wage war."

"What?" I said. I sat stunned.

"*That* makes sense," Dilvesh said.

I looked at him.

"War is fought by one nation to eliminate another," Dilvesh said. "What better way to defeat your enemy than to impoverish his nation by denying them their just gold. One could fight a bloodless war more effectively with gold than with soldiers."

"But cutting taxes increases gold revenues," I argued.

"Tell that to the Volkhydrans," Karel said. "Personally, I don't believe it, either. Families are trying to emigrate to Eldador from all over Fovea. Even Dwarves are coming here. Tell a baron that he is going to have fewer peasants, and that the ones who stay want to pay less than half their tithe, and you have some very unhappy and vocal barons."

I looked at Shela, she looked at me.

This whole thing was my fault. I had thought that I lived in a void. I wanted my changes to affect every nation on Fovea and never thought twice what the Fovean nations would think of that.

"World shaking changes shake the world," I said, more to myself than to the rest of them.

"What?" Karel's blue eyes peered into mine.

"Nothing."

"The question that remains is what to do about this?" Arath said.

"Before we answer that, we must first know who is involved," Dilvesh warned.

"I think we know that already," said Thorn.

"Do we?" asked Dilvesh, looking at Karel.

Karel went to the chalkboard and, with a piece of chalk, sketched a rough drawing of the Fovean region. I had been to every part that he had sketched except for Toor, and still I had a hard time imagining it the way he drew it.

"The Free Legion's enemies are the ones most directly affected by its success," Karel said. "Dorkan, who has lost sea power because of the intervention at Katarran. Sental, whose farmers are coming to Eldador in droves. Volkhydro, who feels threatened by the expansion of Free Legion power in what they consider to be an Uman nation, and Trenbon, who is most directly threatened by a wealthy neighbor to the south, where you seem to like to spend your gold.

"Even now, Eldador could afford to put enough ships on Tren Bay to neutralize every Tech Ship that Trenbon has. Trenbon believes that you are to blame for this."

"Then perhaps it is time for this experiment with mercenaries to end," Ancenon said, looking the rest of us in our faces.

I hadn't even considered that idea and felt glad to see that no one else had, either. Even Karel of Stone looked skeptical. D'gattis seemed pensive, arguing the idea in his head perhaps. Thorn was more emphatic.

"I will be damned before I let some greedy Trenboni tell me how to live my life," he said.

"I don't see any other alternative," Ancenon said.

"I do," Arath said. He stood, Thorn and Nantar with him.

"We have armies, we have warriors, we have lancers and squads and Wolf Soldiers and Sarandi, Ancenon," he said, looking right into the Prince's silver-on-silver eyes.

"None of which will stand against Trenbon's might," D'gattis said.

"I am not so sure of that," Dilvesh said.

"I am," I said softly.

They all looked at me. I had made it clear that there would be retaliation, whether they joined me or not. They likely didn't expect that I would come in on this side.

I looked up from where I sat. "If we have spies, then they do," I said. "If we know something, then they will know it soon. I don't expect the Uman-Chi, the best Wizards on the planet, to just sit there and let us come to their island with superior forces and superior tactics."

"They would call the High Council to defend them," Ancenon agreed with me.

"We can't defeat the united Fovean armies," D'gattis said. "Even with Eldador standing with us, we would not prevail."

"So your bull and you horns are nothing?" Arath asked me. I had stolen his thunder and he didn't like it.

But his plan wouldn't work. Go right for Trenbon and we would fail. I knew it.

"Do you know how to eat a bull?" I asked him in return.

"With a fork and knife?" he said.

"You cut its throat and bleed it," said Thorn.

"Spit it," said Karel.

I shook my head. Shela laughed, sitting next to me.

At the end of the day, Shela was at least as smart as I was. In fact, I tended to see her as smarter. Certainly not very much got past her.

"One bite at a time," she said.

***

I stood with D'gattis, Arath and Ancenon on my marshalling field, which had once been the coliseum of Thera. It was too small now for the Theatre au Thera but it made a good place to speak to my Wolf Soldiers all at the same time.

Two Spears did that now. He excelled at these rallying speeches. He could make men so eager to fight and die that you had to worry about them killing each other right there in their anger.

"You are committed to this scheme," Ancenon asked me.

"I am," I said.

Nantar's Sarandi were marching to Andurin as we spoke, Thorn and Nantar riding to meet them. Dilvesh had commissioned a ship to sail for Eldador the Port. Karel had set himself up a base here, in the War Room. We'd need him, at least for a while.

Two Spears told the Wolf Soldiers that, if the enemy had their way, Lee would be raised as a whore in the streets of Outpost IX. In a few moments his sister would walk out into the marshalling ground to stand next to him. Those men loved that little girl, their little Princess, in the odd way that fighting men have of forming an emotional bond with the families that ruled them. Like the Kennedy's and their Camelot and little JFK Jr., saluting his father's funeral procession.

You might love your nation but you fight and die for your family.

"If you take the Free Legion against Outpost IX, then you will not prevail," Ancenon warned me.

"I have no plans for the Free Legion to attack Outpost IX," I said.

Ancenon lead the Free Legion, not me. He must be pretty nervous to be having this conversation with me.

"But your Wolf Soldiers are not of the Free Legion," D'gattis said.

"No, I wouldn't imagine that they are."

They stood quiet. Shela walked out to stand next to her brother. An angry roar rose from my Wolf Soldiers, almost palpable hatred for those who would *dare* to threaten Lee, their collective child. Lee screamed in shock and surprise, and they roared louder.

If they noticed Ancenon and D'gattis standing up here, there would likely be a riot. Hate made as powerful a tool as love. Certainly you could get people to kill for either reason if you motivated them properly.

"I would have to stand against you, if you marched on Outpost IX," Ancenon said.

"As would I," said D'gattis.

"That might not sit well with Adriam," I said.

They didn't respond. Two Spears asked who here would lay down their life for Lee.

Every sword left its scabbard.

"Why would we sit with Adriam?" D'gattis asked.

"Well, I think we all do, eventually," Ancenon said.

Slang, slang. It always betrayed me.

"I think that he means that Adriam won't allow it," Arath said. Finally someone understood me.

"The fire bond," D'gattis said.

"Move against Trenbon and you betray it," Ancenon said.

"I think not," I said, smiling slightly because I couldn't help it.

"Are you willing to risk that?" D'gattis asked me.

I thought of Alekki, who bounced my baby in her arms and smiled at my wife, her friend, and never treated anyone other than decently.

Would I risk the wrath of a god to avenge the death of my queen, if I admitted that I had one? Would I burn in a fire for my king, who had made me a noble from a common not just from needing me but also in his respect for me?

That was a question of faith. I had no faith. I *knew* what my god expected of me, because he told me. I had *proof.*

"If you betray me to your people," I said to them, "then it is you who risk the fire.

"Keep that in mind when you wonder if you owe more loyalty to your god and to the ones who got you in and out of Outpost X alive, than you do to the king who ordered your assassination."

I turned and looked him in the eyes; saw those dim cornea that no one practically ever sees in their silver-on-silver visage.

"And both of you think long and hard on what it means to come after me," I informed them.

Below us, Shela held Lee up, screaming in fear and anger as the Wolf Soldiers bellowed out their rage and swore to give their lives to protect her.

Arath looked at the two Uman-Chi, as they stood dumbfounded, watching my men swear to kill their kind.

"Irritating, isn't it?" he asked them.

***

That night Karel of Stone burst into the anteroom to my bedchambers and demanded to see Shela and me.

"Demanded?" Shela asked my Wolf Soldier guard.

"Yes, my Lady," the guard said. He stood at stiff attention. On this world, sometimes they *did* kill the messenger.

She looked at me and held her hand up. I shook my head. There were things we could do to Karel of Stone if we had to that were less permanent than killing him. Being killed is hard to learn from.

I sat on the edge of my bed, Shela in her rocker, Lee in her bassinet. I wore my house clothes, the leather pants that I had grown to love and a white blouse. Most nobles wore slippers but most nobles weren't affected with a memory of Fred McMurray.

Karel entered in boots, his bearskins and a silver question mark, turned upside down, on his breast.

"You remove that now, Karel," I said, standing. That was going too far.

"I would if I could," he told me. "I thought you or Ancenon had-"

"Shela," I said, interrupting him.

She closed her eyes, then opened them and shook her head. "Your Free Legion members have an aura about you that is this fire bond," she said. "He has the same aura."

"Well, that is kind of convenient," I said.

An hour later Ancenon, D'gattis and Arath were in my chambers with the Free Legion's newest member and my immediately family and I got my answer.

"Not really," Ancenon told me.

"How so?" asked Arath.

Ancenon stood and paced for a moment, framing the answer to the question in his mind.

"I believe that it was no accident that we found Outpost X where others failed," he said finally. He looked at each of us with his silver-on-silver eyes. "I believe that we are moving toward something, and that Outpost X provided nothing more than an excuse to bring us all together."

"It is the nature of prophecy that a moment should bring together a band to fulfill a purpose," said D'gattis.

"And that these things should appear as happenstance to the participants," said Ancenon. "Such is what it appears to be now."

"So why add Karel, then?" I asked. "Or Dilvesh, for that matter. Why force them into the fire bond, especially Karel who is with us already."

"Dilvesh brings into the group the Natural Trinity," Ancenon said. "With Drekk came Eveave, the Taker and the Giver. When he left us, Eveave was not represented and became jealous, and so another of her ilk, a similar man as well, replaced him."

"I do worship Eveave," Karel conceded.

"And so do about a million other people," I said.

"But none of them so much like our Drekk," said Ancenon.

"But Karel is nothing like Drekk," I said.

"Thank you," Karel said, dryly. "Not to disrespect the dead, but the man was a stone."

"And you are *of* Stone," D'gattis pointed out. "I think that to the Taker and the Giver, you and he might be indistinguishable."

"Drekk *could* take anything he wanted from anyone who had it," Arath admitted.

Karel sighed. "He was quite talented that way," he said. "Although I usually managed to do it more and to keep more of it."

"A fit replacement for Drekk," Ancenon said.

"And if I don't find the replacement to be a good fit?" Karel asked.

"I think there is a slight chance you might," Arath said, a smile on his lips.

"And you can always take it up with Adriam."

We brought Karel through a portal at the estate to the tower at Chatoos. From there we were transported once again to Outpost X.

The place never changed. Maybe there were more or fewer rats. Maybe we had a few less bars of gold. In the beginning we had all withdrawn heavily from here. Even Dilvesh had relented and taken several bars to further some pursuit of the Druids'. Now the footprints through the throne room were blown over with dust. I came here when I wanted to be alone, not to withdraw wealth.

"So much," Karel gasped, looking at the gold. "Enough to buy an empire."

"Depending on the empire," Arath said. "Some aren't for sale."

Karel grinned up at him.

I wondered if this was a dream or a nightmare for a professional thief. More gold than he could imagine, and he couldn't steal it because it already belonged to him.

Karel looked up at me with a look in his eyes that might have held the same question.

"Did you build Thera on this?" he asked me seriously.

I smiled down at him. "I started Thera with this," I admitted to him. "Now Thera keeps me from here, except when I want to think and watch the rats."

"I wondered if all of those emulating you were doomed," Karel said.

"Some are," Arath said.

"Some are not," D'gattis warned him.

Karel grinned up at me.

Wow, did I not like him.

Chapter Two

Payback

"You don't seem to want me around," Karel told me.

I was losing favor with the Free Legion. I spent too much time not being a part of what they did. They had important conversations without me – things happening which I didn't know about. The Fire Bond didn't provide enough reason anymore to tell me everything. Karel's addition and my position on Trenbon, as well as the Uman-Chi's, restated that. We all had our own lives going on and I had been the start of it.

I had caused the trouble we found ourselves in. I felt that to the center of my soul. Every day I thought I knew what War wanted from me now, and every day I thought that I might have learned more. I served as the catalyst to a disaster that would be huge.

"No," I agreed. We were by the corral, where Blizzard and Shela's horses ran. There had been a few acquisitions, including a feisty pony that I planned to give to the little thief.

"Why?" he pressed me.

Direct for a thief. Drekk would have just found out the information on his own and then swallowed it for his own security purposes. Karel of Stone seemed more likely to attack the issue so that he could overcome it.

I looked down to my right at him. We were leaning against the fence, him against the lower rail and I against the upper. "I don't know you, and I don't trust you," I said. "Even in the fire bond, I think that if there is a way around it, then you will find it."

"Already have," he told me, looking at the pony. I raised an eyebrow. "Hire some friend of one of the many enemies you've made and tell him about why Outpost IX survived the Blast like Outpost VII. Let him put the parts together and within a year Conflu will be in Outpost X, the gold will be gone and the fire bond dissolved."

I thought about that. "Not bad," I told him.

"If you want to survive in this life you have to think about escape routes before you go in anywhere," he told me.

"Kind of surprised you would be friends with D'gattis," I said, seeming to change the subject.

Karel sighed. "D'gattis and I go back pretty far," he told me. "I could have killed him the first time I sacked the treasury of Outpost IX. He could have done the same to me the second time. No idea why he didn't, but we like each other's company. I steal for him from time to time and he made these leathers for me."

"Magic of some sort?" I asked him.

He nodded. "Soft as a baby's butt, but stronger than steel."

I turned from the corral and he followed me back to the estate. I needed to see if any of the Free Legion remained to say good-bye to. Ancenon and D'gattis had stayed in Chatoos, and Arath had said that he planned to go soon.

"Have you ever been to the Scitai-occupied portion of the Silent Isle?" Karel asked me.

I told him I hadn't.

"Funny thing about that," he told me. "The Uman-Chi recently conceded that it constituted an act of aggression for them to maintain Tech-Ships off of our coast."

I looked down at him as we approached the estate. He didn't look up, but kept his blue eyes focused straight ahead.

"Really?" I asked him.

Karel left Thera soon after, Arath with him. Since Drekk and Alekki's death I had seen in the eyes of every one of my allies that they were guarded with me now. I had been the first to pick his own nation over the Free Legion, regardless of the reason. Ancenon and D'gattis were always loyal to Trenbon, but until now they had never stepped in front of one of us to defend it. I acted specifically against their homeland now, and the fact that their own king wanted them dead didn't make them any happier about it. I am sure they reasoned that the proper discussion with their patriarch would smooth over everything, so long as I didn't make it all impossible by acting directly against their nation.

Picking sides is a deliberate thing. There is no easy way to break the decision to the loser, and it can be hard to recover from.

***

The wind whistled cold down the Llorando in the middle of Power. The mountain air poured south like the breath of the merciless god for whom the month is named. With the fall harvest in and no one really doing much more than battening down for the winter, the ships and barges that plied up and down her banks expected and saw little in the scope of activity.

Imagine, then, the combined surprise of the Volkhydrans and Sentalans when a thousand armed warriors, Nantar's Sarandi, landed across the river from Hydro, south of the Sentalan village called, simply, Sental One, and burned the southern-most Volkhydran/ Sentalan bridge to the ground. They tumbled its stone ramparts and cracked its base. What few guards were there to defend this link between two nations died in the first assault. The Sarandi stayed one day, then marched up the river from there on the Sentalan side.

No one thought it uncommon for an Eldadorian merchant ship to ply the Straights of Deception in Power with a load of goods. It had become much more difficult for Dorkan to stop Eldador from moving through the Straights, but not impossible. The Eldadorian garrison in Katarran had left and, although the city itself was a ruin, the port could be used as an anchorage with some difficulty. A band of Dorkans made a temporary camp south of Way Point and a Dorkan Wizard could report back with intelligence to a counterpart on one of those ships.

The Dorkans could patrol the reef or moor in Katarran and, working in teams, strangle the connection between most of Fovea and the outer islands.

When three Eldadorian merchant class vessels began to pick their way through the Straights, five Dorkan warships debarked their anchorage off of the Straights and made way to intercept. Following protocol, they would either ram the Eldadorians or sink them with catapult shot once they were clear of the Straights.

But it hadn't been so easy this time – the very planks onboard their own warships resisted the Dorkans and began to twist and leak as soon as they neared the Eldadorians. Taking water, these ships tried to make for land and were soon sinking too rapidly to save themselves. All hands abandoned ship and all were lost in the icy-cold sea, their land-bound compatriots left powerless to help them.

Two weeks later the incident repeated itself, and again a week after that. By the first day of Desire the Dorkans had lost eleven vessels and were weakened in their effort at sea.

By that time a second and a third bridge had been burned between Volkhydro and Sental. The Sentalans who had sought to stop the Sarandi had been slaughtered to a man. Fighting in squads like Wolf Soldiers, the Sarandi defeated two and three times their numbers in foreign warriors on foreign soil. Their losses were minimal.

***

I suspected that D'gattis and Ancenon would wait in Outpost IX to see what I would do. With Shela at my side, that could be anything. Without exception all ships entering the port at Outpost IX were searched, but now merchants complained that those searches were more vigorous than usual. They grumbled in the marketplaces about additional security and the impossibility of doing profitable business with these paranoid Uman-Chi.

The Trenboni government had obviously been tipped off. An Uman-Chi had come to my estate and begged permission to see me on the offer of a ducal position in Outpost VII. I had ordered him stripped and flogged and sent out to the street. There was formal protest. His magic had flared and been neutralized by Shela's. The 'desires of men' were pretty obvious.

I did the same for the Volkhydran, Sentalan and Dorkan ambassadors. In Uman City and as well in the port of Eldador those same nations' ships were burned in port with all of their wares onboard.

It wasn't enough.

***

Many believed that the Scitai on the Silent Island had evolved from holes in the ground. Others said that the Cheyak kept them as pets, like trained monkeys, or that they *had been* monkeys themselves.

When I landed five thousand Wolf Soldiers on their beaches in the middle of the night, using fishing vessels from Thera, I had the opportunity to look at their villages. They carved their homes in still-living trees and were expert botanists, keeping these same trees alive. They trained almost from birth with bows and arrows, slings and crossbows and a type of collapsible bow unique to their own people. They lived in communities of twenty to fifty and had been here for over a thousand years.

When the blast had come it had avoided them. They didn't know why. When the Uman-Chi had come, they had done the same for as long as possible, and then decided, much as had the Eldadorians with the Aschire, that there were no Scitai cities, therefore no Scitai nation, and that these were a subject people.

Like the Aschire, the Scitai didn't think a lot of the idea.

There were one hundred of them helping us to debark. We couldn't have done it without them. They knew the beach and the hazards of the shoals. Our ships had made a natural landing with no breakwater, which meant that we beached our ships and dropped brows to unload men and horses. Karel guaranteed that, for every man we saw, there were ten more in the trees providing cover.

I don't know how he pulled this off; Karel of Stone was not popular with his people. His father, Therok of the Plains, had appeared with a frown on his face when the first of my ships landed. They argued bitterly. Karel obviously hated the Uman-Chi and thought that any action against them strengthened the Scitai. Therok believed that there would be reprisals and, if Karel pushed too hard, then the Uman-Chi Wizards would arrive and solve the problem with the Scitai once and for all.

"The Uman-Chi need targets," Karel informed them. "When they come here they will find none."

"A fire through the woods will find you wherever you hide, son," Therok told him. "And burn hotter than vengeance with Uman-Chi Wizards behind it."

We were standing on the beach in the middle of the night. The moon cast a bluish tint on all of us. Two Spears marshaled the men and then drove them into the woods. Each sergeant had orders to keep contact with his lieutenant, each lieutenant with orders to keep contact with his captain and the captains, each with a map of the Silent Isle, were keeping us spread out over miles.

Even if we were discovered, we were just a band of ten Wolf Soldiers here for no apparent reason.

Shela approached us, riding her gelding. Lee remained in Thera with a wet nurse, guarded by a thousand Wolf Soldiers who knew that their lives were forfeit if anything befell her, not that they needed a threat. Two Spears had done his job and done it well. These men would lay down their lives for that little girl and sneer while they did it.

Shela looked down at all of us. The two Scitai looked up at her, towering from over three times their height on horseback. I stood with my arms crossed over my breastplate, waiting to hear what she had to say.

"No Uman-Chi draws breath within ten miles of this place, Therok of the Plains," she said, her voice mystical as it always sounded when she used her power. "None will while I walk this Isle."

Therok clicked his tongue and Karel smiled his mischievous smile. "And how are you so sure, girl?" the older Scitai asked her.

Karel answered for her. "That is the Lady Shela," he said, loud enough not just for his father but also for the Scitai who were working with us to hear, "whom you know better as the *Bitch of Eldador*. Do you question her power?"

Therok's eyes widened. So did Shela's. I had never heard that nickname before but they clearly had, because Therok stammered out an apology and excused himself.

She dismounted and towered over Karel, what I could only call a snarl on her lips. The look she wore in the moonlight reminded me of that time she was nearly raped in Steel City. I wondered if Karel's death would be as painful.

I didn't care. I didn't like him.

"The *Bitch of Eldador*?" she repeated.

Karel's eyes widened innocently. I didn't think that would help him. "I didn't make it up," he told her.

That didn't mollify her – I would have been surprised if it had. "How long have *I* been the *Bitch of Eldador*?" she asked.

Karel spread his hands. "You killed a man in Glennen's own court," he said. "The Bounty Hunter's Guild has called you by that name since. Surely you must have known…"

Shela remounted her horse. She had been moody since Lee's birth and worse since the attack. This news didn't make her any happier. This was a bad day to be a Bounty Hunter. That's ok – I didn't like them, either.

Karel looked up into my eyes. I had noticed that about him – another difference between Karel and Drekk. Karel looked right at you when he spoke, like he *really* wanted to know what you had to say.

"Surely she knew," he said.

I laughed. "I wouldn't have been the one to tell her," I said. "Actually, I'm surprised you're still alive."

Karel pulled his head back like I had tried to slap him.

"You're serious?" he asked me.

I laughed again. "My friend," I told him, "the last person who pissed her off that badly got cleaned up with a broom and a dust pan."

I turned and went looking for Two Spears. Over my shoulder, I added, "Why do you think they call her the Bitch of Eldador?"

Let the little man chew on *that* for a while.

***

The Fovean High Council met on the fifteenth day of Desire to discuss "these outlandish goings on." By then every bridge between Sental and Volkhydro had been destroyed. Hundreds of warriors on both sides of the Llorando had died trying to defend them, but the Sarandi were veterans with Wolf Soldier training. Many worried in both nations that the bridges would not be rebuilt when the fall harvest came next year and that there would be no portage between Sental and Volkhydro. This meant higher costs for Sentalan goods that would now have to be shipped instead of carried by wagon to market. With the grain on ships already, why bother moving it through Volkhydro? That meant economic depression for that nation.

Dorkan, on the other hand, couldn't ship to anyone because Koran pirates had grown bold and raided their merchant ships. They did this because there were so few Dorkan warships, due to heavy losses by them at the Straights of Deception. Again, hard times for a Fovean nation while Kor could expect to grow stronger.

Angry debate shook the Council and many pointed fingers. The cold stone benches at their outdoor coliseum were heated with words, most of these pointed at the Eldadorian delegates, with suspicious glances for the unscathed Toorians, Confluni and Andarons. Dorkans still complained of an entirely unjustified action against them sparked by Eldadorian opportunists and Trenboni with no proof.

The Eldadorians were hearing none of this, however. They claimed to be able to deliver incontrovertible evidence of an international plot to kill the Queen of Eldador. That plot extended to the Free Legion, no member of which had been seen in over a month, save for rumors of Nantar in Sental. The Free Legion was becoming a force to be reckoned with - a force to be *answered*.

Supposedly you could hear them arguing from a mile away – which explains why they didn't hear *me* coming through their main gate.

I had learned a lot since coming here. I had learned to fight, and to kill. I had learned what it meant to be loved and hated. I had seen that luck is an essential part of life, but taking advantage of it is still a skill. I had learned that most of what had happened to me, for good or ill, had been my fault and my responsibility.

When you learn that sort of lesson you don't change – you realize how much the same you are. When other people think that you've changed, they're seeing that you've realized that. I had heard before that change is the only constant. Now I understood what that meant.

Another thing that I had learned is that if you are going to hit someone, then *hit* them. Hit them hard and make them think twice before hitting you back. There is no glory in being hit back, it just hurts and leaves you weaker. When your enemy exposes his jugular then you cut it while you have the chance before it is *your* blood on *his* shoes.

Because the Trenboni didn't see the Scitai as a threat to them, they didn't guard themselves against the Scitai-occupied forests of Trenbon. Scitai scouts led five thousand of us past the few Trenboni patrols or, as we got closer to Outpost IX, through them. Within two miles of Outpost IX I ordered forced march while my lancers under Two Spears slaughtered Uman warriors with impunity.

I approached the main gate at the head of a vanguard of those thousand heavy lancers. Four thousand Wolf Soldiers marched double-time behind us in squads of ten. They marched with their swords out and their shields down, the sun glinting from naked steel. We broke out of the forest onto the hard-packed plain that surrounded the city, heading straight for the merchants' plaza and the city's huge main gate. A bell from one of Outpost IX's many towers announced us and warned the city guard of our coming.

Even though they were on high alert, warned of a pending attack, a mere hundred Trenboni mounted warriors greeted me no more than two hundred feet from the Outpost IX murder hole.

Civilians looked at us in disbelief. Who would bother to visit Outpost IX with so many, or dare to march on the Trenboni capitol with so few?

The Uman-Chi Captain of the Guard wore a gold breastplate and the image of a falcon on his breast. His mount pranced up to

Blizzard's side and he demanded to know where I had received permission to land armed troops on the sovereign nation of Trenbon.

I killed him myself. My blood brother, Two Spears, took command of my lancers and led the follow-up attack. A thousand heavily armored horsemen crashed into the Trenboni mounted warriors with lances down, pushing them right through the city gates. Five hundred Scitai and five hundred Aschire archers cleared the walls and towers that defended the murder hole and protected the entrance to the city. Where the Aschire archers were incredible, the Scitai made them look like amateurs, shooting through tiny arrow slits in the city's stone walls to kill the Uman archers who guarded the main gate.

I took Outpost IX's invincible gate before the screaming from the marketplace could alert the city watch. Her portcullis, unused for years, dropped haltingly, a screech of metal protesting against rust and dirt. One of my squad sergeants pegged it open by breaking the head of a pike off in the mechanism as we took a tower. Scitai and Aschire archers swarmed into it, assaulting the tower on the other side of the gate with five squads and a barrage of arrows.

When I held the gates I entered the city with a steady stream of soldiers in squad formation. My lancers went first, slaughtering the final remains of the mounted guard. By the time the first handful of Uman warriors scrambled to the defense of Outpost IX my Wolf Soldiers held the open center just inside of the main gate. The Trenboni home guard advanced as a mob onto the white cobblestones and met squads that hit them from the front and both sides before they could even get organized.

Meanwhile Shela and five of her acolytes held back Trenbon's growing magical defense. They fought that battle from every rooftop and tower in the city. I saw sheets of flame fly down the main street of Outpost IX and dissipate before our marshalling army, lightning fell like rain and sputtered over our head. I received little shocks from the Sword of War as we assembled behind the gate, readying our push down Outpost IX's main street.

It didn't take long. Captains coordinated lieutenants, who barked orders at sergeants, who assembled their men. We had been doing it for a year. Smart squads fell into a patchwork of men and steel, centered around my heavy horse.

"They're ready," Two Spears told me. "Are you?"

I nodded. He grinned like a kid with candy. Death didn't mean a lot to Two Spears.

I knew the feeling.

The heavy horse went first, slow from the start but then gathering momentum as a surge of flame and lightening cleared out magic resistance to their movement. Outpost IX's main street formed a long, straight path to the royal palace, and iron hooves made sparks on cobblestones as their momentum grew, pennons snapping from their upraised lances.

I stayed with the infantry. We marched double-time behind the horse. The key here was not to let a gap form between the main army and the van. If they were smart, they were assembling far down the road, before the palace, and would try to get Two Spears to engage them while they cut in behind with their own horse to challenge my squads.

The heavy horse would have a hard time getting turned around on the main street, and by the time they did my foot would be entangled with their defenses, which assuredly outnumbered me.

The resistance didn't wait around for me to ponder any more. The horse met their first armed brigades, another mass of soldiers, before we went four blocks. Two Spears stayed at a trot and casually ran them down, to his credit. Behind them, three times their number in bowmen rained arrows down on my horse as they emerged through the foot soldiers. Had they been in full gallop they would have been unable to slow down in time to drop behind my infantry, who were better able to handle the barrage.

My squads of ten marched forward with their shields high, our pikemen and our swordsmen crouching close behind the shield men. They pressed forward with minimal losses until they were too close for arrow fire. Now from behind the archers, the Trenboni foot that had been assembling while we fought swarmed forward, trying to catch my men encumbered and out of formation. Two squads went down and two more were retreating, my center giving way, as wild-eyed Uman in heavy armor and with long swords threw themselves against our shields, our pikemen in no position to repel them.

Forward came the heavy horse again, hooves clattering on cobblestones in a short sprint to meet the new threat. Their lances lowered like a wave as my squads broke to left and right to open a channel for them to pour through, into the charging Uman warriors, skewering them on their lances as some tried to press forward and others to retreat.

When the horse engaged, fire and lightening rolled out of every open window and down from every flying bridge on the street, straight toward them. I winced, thinking they were lost now. Not even Shela could repel all of that so quickly.

And she couldn't, so instead she and her acolytes attacked the buildings and the bridges themselves. Stones exploded out of ancient buildings and bridges crumbled under Wizards who had prepared themselves for her assault but not the stone around them. Outpost IX was the objective; Outpost IX was the focus of Power. Outpost IX, then, became her weapon against them.

The energy dissipated, crisping but not burning my heavy horse. Men swore and horses screamed, and then suddenly Two Spears found his troops in a dead run down the street, toward the palace, my infantry behind him in full charge.

Both horse and footmen annihilated double and triple their number in city watch and Trenboni regular army, fighting heroes' style, trying to defend the palace. The heavy lancers rumbled down the main street like thunder, leaving dead and dying in their wake. Archers from the rear of our army, Scitai and Aschire, answered the Trenboni with deadly accuracy, clearing towers, rooftops and flying bridges. I marched past shattered lances covered in blood and dead Trenboni in rent armor. Here and there a widow wept alongside a fallen warrior, or a family gathered together to watch in shock as we marched past, our steel cleats clinking on the cobblestones.

No one believed that they would ever see foreign warriors advance in triumph through the streets of Outpost IX. No one who lived here thought that anything would disrupt his or her way of life. Blood flowed red through the gutters like a river into the sewers beneath the city, in what had once been thought the safest place in Fovea.

We marched down the main street where I had once ridden Blizzard. Again and again, the enemy massed and charged in a mob. My shieldmen held them, my pikemen stabbed them, my swordsmen slashed at them if they found their way around our edges. If they pushed a squad back or overwhelmed them then a portion of the horse wheeled back and overran the defenders. We'd driven deeper into the city now, and we could use their side streets to move our horse back and forth past our lines. We proved once again that organized warfare would prevail against an armed mob.

Swarms of arrows buzzed through the air, met by the crackle of energy from spell casting or finding marks among the Uman warriors of Trenbon. Aschire would send their arrows arcing high, over our men, and the Trenboni would have to raise their shields. Scitai would pepper them from between our troops, finding marks I would have thought impossibly difficult. Then they'd switch and kill even more.

Finally we were there, approaching the royal palace at Outpost IX ahead of a bloody swath through the city. Here thousands of fresh Uman royal guard had massed, men who spent more time standing motionless at doors than swinging swords on a battlefield. The interior gates were closed, the merlons on the palace walls manned with archers, with catapults, with steaming buckets of oil. Surely, they were thinking, these troops were worthless against that fortress, especially considering that we had come so quickly, and left so many possible enemies behind us.

Which is why we peeled off to the right and proceeded directly to the coliseum of the Fovean High Council.

We met almost nothing to stop us. It seemed like an entire lifetime since I had been here. A perfunctory guard of fifty Uman warriors in the royal crest of Trenbon crumbled before a single sweep of my heavy lancers. What few archers they maintained on the walls fell pin-cushioned by my Aschire and Scitai bowmen. Even that same, greasy Uman from so long ago, whose breath I thought I might still smell hanging on the air, lay bleeding on the cobblestones.

I stepped up to the dais before the assembled Fovean High Council. No one in history had attempted such a thing before, and the delegates screamed in outrage.

Uman-Chi arrogance had made it possible. The proper training and planning, the proper patience, had made it happen. I heard my steel heels clang on the stone steps as I walked. I had known that Ancenon or D'gattis would betray me; I had counted on them to focus all of the city's attention on an attack coming in by the Bay, stripping the city garrison to man their navy. Xinto had taught me that the Uman-Chi barely considered the Scitai at all when they thought of their Silent Isle. Now Karel of Stone, much as I didn't like him, had helped to make this happen.

My men ringed the coliseum and my archers had taken up positions along its walls. Two Spears had engaged the Trenboni Royal Mounted Guard. A thousand Trenboni horsemen with swords tried to match an almost equal number of armored knights with lances. I had confidence in my blood brother and most trusted Captain.

"Silence!" I ordered the collected delegates. They shouted their outrage at me and to each other. Why should they listen to me? They were the sacrosanct ambassadors to the Fovean High Council.

I drew the Sword of War and, stepping down from the podium, plunged it into the chest of a Dorkan Councilman. One of his peers stood for a moment and started to speak, sparks dripping from his right hand as he raised it. A moment later blood flowed from his ears and eyes as he fell back dead in his chair. Shela just crossed her arms beneath her breasts.

Two Uman-Chi delegates took their chance and stood with power dripping red gobbets from their outstretched hands. Before they could complete their casting, Scitai archers pin-cushioned them. Surviving delegates cast nervous glances one to the other. Many had magical skill but we had the drop on them. Between Shela and the archers they couldn't be sure of their lives.

I stepped back up to the dais. They were quiet now. I could just barely hear the creaking of Aschire and Scitai bows as they sighted delegates and guardsmen or supported my lancers.

I had played this moment over in my mind. What could I say that would keep them from attacking me again? I could slaughter them as an example, but that wouldn't change anything. Their nations would just send more and paint me a massacring maniac with goat horns. I could tell them what I knew but why waste time making accusations if the law wouldn't punish the accused? Why point blame if the guilty didn't care who caught them?

Sometimes the world needs to not feel good about what it is doing. Sometimes the pain of a woman who didn't do anything but love her husband and her kids needs to be felt by all.

Sometimes it's just personal. Alekki had been a sweet soul, and Drekk a good friend. I looked out at these delegates, these collected ambassadors.

"You came for me and mine," I said to them. "Your own assassins tried to kill me, my wife, my friends, and my king in my home. You failed.

"An innocent women, the Queen of Eldador, paid the price. Tortured to death by your orders.

"Now I'm the one with all of you at my mercy."

I looked at them, let that all sink in.

"Now you fear for your lives, as she did," I told them. I let them see the two things that might give them pause: my utter contempt for this High Council and my ability to step outside of their rules and strike them where they felt the safest.

How many had sputtered in surprise at the thought of anyone attacking Outpost IX when I first came here?

"When you make an enemy and give him nowhere else to go, you may think you'll break him, but you run the risk instead of making him stronger than ever he could know," I told them.

"You've done that with me," I said. "Now you've reaped what you've sewn. I don't recommend another harvest."

I turned on my heel and I left. I mounted Blizzard beside my wife and her gelding and I lead my Wolf Soldiers from Outpost IX. My lancers cleared the streets before us and my soldiers set fire to everything that they could burn, hurling torches through open doors and broken windows. Archers shot flaming arrows into buildings and rooms. Their Wizards now had to choose between fighting us and saving what remained of their city.

The main gate had been closed and spelled before we could return to it. *The Bitch of Eldador* raised one hand in defiance to the Uman-Chi spell casters while her acolytes held off the magical barrage that built up against us. In moments the gate exploded from its mountings to fly almost a mile into the harbor.

No sooner did it happen than one of our Wizards fell from his horse, a green slime where his eyes used to be. I saw Shela waver and then rematerialize, her gelding neighing nervously as this happened.

"Be quick, White Wolf," she told me. "We don't have much longer before we meet their best and most dangerous."

So much for the moral dilemma over "save the city or kill the invaders."

I nodded and called for double-time march out through the main gates. Two Spears torched the remains of the market outside of the city gates while my archers kept theirs pinned down, covering their withdrawal from the towers.

We'd gotten out of the city alive, but we hadn't won yet.

Chapter Three

Exit, Stage Left

An important part of any invasion is having a plan for what to do if you actually survive it.

I couldn't keep the city, so I really, really needed to leave it. More importantly, I needed to leave it alive – preferably with those members of my entourage whom I hadn't gotten killed already.

I didn't want to march back across the Silent Isle to the Scitai-occupied portion with every Trenboni warrior they could muster on my tail and their Wizards turning my soldiers into frogs, neither did I really believe that the Trenboni Navy would sit idly by while I boarded my Theran fishing vessels with my remaining warriors.

We double-time marched it to the wharves, now almost four thousand strong. There we found the merchant ships from the Free Legion Shipping company which Ancenon ran, but which we were all welcome to use any time we wanted to. While I'd been making bloody war on the Trenboni and killing delegates to the Fovean High Council, Dilvesh, who bore the green symbol of the Free Legion, the question-mark turned upside-down, as our only Druid, had been commandeering Ancenon's ships and ordering them to dump their cargo. The ships had come here on legitimate business from the day before, and the Trenboni fleet had focused on keeping ships out, not in. I'd arranged to have all manner of products shipped from Thera into Outpost IX, either directly or through other ports. Ships come here on legitimate and actually pretty normal business brought no attention to themselves, and now it was just a matter of using them.

Each ship had orders to leave when her capacity in horse and warriors were onboard. From there we made a mad dash to Thera and the safety of Eldador.

"Think that they'll call for an embargo against us at the next council meeting?" Dilvesh asked me. He, Shela and I took the same ship and had pulled away from port. All around us our vessels were peeling away from the wharf as soon as they were loaded.

"I think we may see them before that," I said.

Dilvesh had his own reasons for doing this. I knew them from what I had experienced with the Druid in Conflu. Dilvesh' purposes might be his own, but they served mine here and now.

I spat into the ocean in the wake of my lead ship. They'd come after Alekanna and the Free Legion because they thought there'd be no consequences for their actions. Let them see the high price for guessing wrong.

Karel of Stone, the newest member of the Free Legion and the one whose mark was silver, had decided to stay on the Silent Isle. His people would be recognized as a part of the raid and might feel retribution. Shela had promised to make an appearance on their portion of the Silent Isle if she had to.

"Sail, ho! Trenboni Tech Ship!" I heard from the crow's nest.

"Where away?" our captain called. I didn't know the man. The sailors in Free Legion Shipping were Ancenon's, not mine.

"To stern and closing, five sails!"

I turned and crossed the wheel deck, putting my hands on the well-worn railing to stern, where I could see five ships pursued us, running against the wind. A mystical breeze that would affect no other ship propelled Trenboni ships. I had marveled at them before but not now.

"We might have to put a few ships in their way to hold them while the rest escape," Dilvesh told me.

I would do it if I had to but I didn't like it. I also didn't think that our merchant ships were going to hold off the Trenboni for very long. If they could overrun us then they would, and had plenty of time for it during the long voyage to Eldador from Trenbon.

"Shela?" I asked my wife. She focused her eyes past the horizon, then closed them and turned back to me, shaking her head.

"Water is not my god," she said. "And Power isn't in play here, not like he'd been in Outpost IX. Those ships are the combined effort of powerful Wizards, White Wolf. I am no match for them."

I nodded. Shela wasn't invincible; she'd just been smart about picking her battles.

I turned to the Druid standing to my left, dressed in his usual white robe and brown cowl, his curling green hair peeking out from underneath it. His brown eyes searched to stern as mine had.

"The trick with the boards?" I asked him.

"I can," he said, "but not before we're in range of her weapons. If I'm swimming for my life or on fire, I won't be able to cast spells."

And people thought I had a strange sense of humor.

I turned back to Shela standing to my right in her Andaron raider outfit – the black leather halter and skirt slit up the side, dressed in thigh-high boots with flat heels for riding and a black leather overcoat with narrow lapels and wide sleeves which would not inhibit an archer; the cut of its back down to just above her knees.

"Is one of our other Wizards available?" I asked her.

She closed her eyes and then opened them immediately. "I have Devinor," she said. "He is solid."

"Have him attack us," I said.

"What?"

"Shela, do it!" I told her. "Set our sails on fire. Dilvesh, make us take water – not a lot and nothing you can't fix. Remember we have horses."

The Druid looked at Shela, Shela looked at me. She shrugged and did what she'd been told. He closed his eyes and followed suit.

A sailor screamed in our rigging when our sails exploded in a sheet of flame. The ship lurched to one side a moment later, our sailors screaming "fire" and "breach" at the same time.

We were dead in the water; the Tech Ships would overtake us in a moment.

"They will sink us as they pass," Dilvesh said.

"Prepare to repel boarders!" our captain cried.

"Belay that!" I barked. The captain turned on his heel on the open poop deck and turned his face up to the wheel house to see who'd countermanded him.

"Fight your fire, save your ship," I commanded him. "Leave boarders if there are any to us."

He nodded and redirected the crew.

We waited breathless as the Tech Ships fanned out. Magic eyes scanned us; my skin crawled at the thought of it.

"What are we doing?" Dilvesh asked me.

"There is a place where I am from where men go through the snow on sleds pulled by dogs," I said. "Sometimes there are wolves in these places. When the wolves are starving, they will attack the men on their sleds, and outrun the dogs."

"And?" Shela asked, irritated. She'd almost exhausted herself, her will the only thing keeping her on her feet, and she likely wanted to see her daughter again.

"And sometimes, when you can't fight the wolves, you push one man off of the back of the sled. He dies, but the rest live."

"I don't want to be thrown to these wolves," Dilvesh said.

"If the wolves are smart, then they keep after the sled," I said. "More meat there, and you wouldn't throw one to these wolves if you didn't know you were no match for them."

"You think they will bypass us and go after the fleet," Shela said.

"I think they won't waste their energy on a sinking ship," I said. "I think they'll let Water have us and go after the rest."

They closed on us. We could see their sails, then we could see their sailors.

"We're within their range," the captain called to us from the poop deck. His crew had confined the fire and but they'd done it with water. The ship leaned badly, the man-powered pumps unable to keep up with the flow. The horses screamed in the hold, Blizzard among them.

"Dilvesh?" I asked him.

"Still too far."

They kept coming, fanning out, ready to pass us, or getting out of the way for one to take the shot.

"Dilvesh?"

"Soon."

"She is powering her weapons," Shela said. "I can feel it."

"Don't do anything," I said. "They might just be checking to see if there is a Wizard here."

"I won't be able to protect us -" she said.

"You wouldn't be able to anyway," I interrupted her. "Not against five ships and their Wizards onboard."

She bit her lip.

We waited. The shot didn't come.

"By the power of Earth and Water," Dilvesh shouted, reaching out a pale hand like a claw toward the Trenboni ships. "I command thee, part!"

The nearest Tech Ship pitched forward as if it had hit a shoal. Next the one beside it did the same, and then the other three.

Fire lanced out of the sky at us. Shela lowered her head and held up her hand to protect the ship, her long black hair falling to cover her face. The crow's nest caught on fire. Another sheet of flame came at us from another of the ships and again she held up her hand in defiance.

"Fix us, get us out of here, Dilvesh," I said.

He intoned, and the fire on the ship blinked out. I didn't see the hull fix itself, but I had to assume it had.

"Captain, how long to rig sails?" I called.

"As fast as we bloody well can!" he told me. He had better things to do than answer my questions.

Another wave of fire rippled across the ocean, followed by another effort by Shela to defend us. This time they scorched the hull.

"I can help you," Dilvesh said to Shela.

"A few more attacks like that and you will have to do it all," she told him, her long, black hair already wet with her sweat. "Such power!"

They'd already rigged the jib and unpacked the mainsail on deck. The ship inched forward on that one small sail's effort.

A bolt of lightning flew toward it. Those Uman-Chi were no fools! This time one of our own sailors stood up and took the blast, falling dead in the water that the rest of us might live.

"Such courage," Dilvesh muttered.

"Dilvesh, fight their fire," Shela said. "I will take their energy attacks. Can you give us rougher seas?"

"I might," he said.

The sailors were hauling the mainsail. The Tech Ships ported badly, one of them down to the water line. Even if the Uman-Chi could repair their hulls they would have to pump out the water.

Another lightning bolt. Shela fell to her knees. It skipped across the deck and scored the rails.

The sailors kept hauling. Dilvesh took up the fight for Shela.

"Sails up!" the captain called. Dilvesh waved his hand in a circle over his head and then pointed at the mainsail. It filled with wind and the ship lurched forward.

A sheet of flame overran the stern. A blast of lightening blew out the side of the wheel deck.

Shela stood and held out her hand. Another lightning bolt – she moaned as she diverted it. Dilvesh squelched the fire.

The next sheet of flame didn't make it to the ship. A bolt of lightning seared the water of Tren Bay but didn't touch us.

Shela passed out unconscious. Dilvesh sat down next to her.

"Let's not do any sledding," he said to me.

I smiled.

***

The ships returned us to Thera, where the Wolf Soldiers debarked and were greeted both by the thousand I'd left as home guard, and a cheering throng of Eldadorians who considered this victory their own. The Uman-Chi weren't a people whom most loved, and Queen Alekanna had been popular. Glennen had made no secret of whom he blamed for the attack on the manor that had cost the Queen her life, and neither had I.

I took a day to rest and then started down the long road to Eldador the Port from Thera, one hundred Wolf Soldier guards in tow. People along the way, in little towns and hamlets that had been springing up like daisies across the countryside, would step out and wave to us as we passed. When we camped, they came to beg us to tell our stories, to meet the infamous Wolf Soldiers and, if they could, perhaps The Conqueror himself.

Of course, that was me, and I really didn't feel much like The Conqueror, more like the guy who took a cheap shot at the Trenboni and got away with it. We told our own stories and we heard theirs, about the coming shortages of food from Sental, the worry that maybe this would all backfire, and of course the love for the Heir Apparent, which also happened to be me.

I'd been brought here from Earth by a god named War, as his instrument. I'd been told to lead a successful life. Some might think that rising from common peasant to Duke and generally the most feared military man alive right now would qualify, but War didn't feel that way. He wanted more.

He'd informed me recently that he wanted me to take over the monarchy of Eldador, and to do that meant to get Glennen out of the way. The problem was that I really liked Glennen. Glennen had shown faith in me when I had just been a mercenary with this idea of an army like the French Foreign Legion. Glennen had been a friend to me just because he liked my character, and I kind of didn't want to assassinate him.

War had this bad habit of torturing me when I didn't do things his way, and I *really* didn't want to go through that again. If I had to go through that or kill Glennen, then I'd kill Glennen.

If I had to go through that or kill me, well – there ya go.

So now I had to do this balancing act that involved pleasing a god that could torture me, a King that could ruin me and a *whole* lot of people who now really, really wanted to kill me, and who'd probably like to do that in the messiest way possible.

So when common farmers came up to me with this look of worship in their eyes and said things to me like, "Oh, wow, you're The Conqueror!" and "We love you, Duke Rancor the Just," it made me feel like a real scumbag sometimes.

Because I was on my way to be *named* the Heir and then put the process for Glennen to be something other than my King in motion, this made for one of those times.

When you get right down to it – I'm really not that nice of a guy.

Chapter Four

The Sled Dogs

I sat with Glennen and his kids in Eldador the Port, in the royal palace. I told them all of the attack on Outpost IX, the sack of the invincible city, the warning. He felt satisfied with what I had done. That's a good thing because I don't know what more I could do.

The kids all cried, even his oldest son, Tartan, almost a man. I could see that the boy hated showing his weakness but I couldn't blame him myself. They had all loved Alekanna. They all knew what had happened. They'd been told what had been done to avenge her, and they knew that, unless we had to defend against some retaliation, than there would be no more. They understood that they should be keeping their guards up for a while.

"She still isn't here," Glennen said to me once the kids filed out. He had been drinking. He had always drunk, but in the days that I had been here he hadn't stopped once.

"The kids saw that more clearly than the rest of us," he drawled. "They are the ones who have to get over this."

"Don't underestimate your own need," I said. "You're drinking a lot."

He shook his head. "N'more than usual," he said. "You don't know me like you think you do."

"I guess not," I said. No point in arguing with him.

"Yer goin' back to Thera?"

I nodded. "The Free Legion is meeting there," I said.

"Betch'er Uman-Chi are kinda upset, what with you blowing gates off their city like that," he chuckled, more to himself than me.

Then he looked me in the face. "Wuzzit with you and gates, anyway? You know how expensive those things are?"

Yep, he was drunk all right.

Glennen called court and named me Heir to the Throne of Eldador later that day. His Oligarchs nodded sagely and the royal court as well. They'd had to deal with him more than I had. One of the Oligarchs informed me that he felt especially loyal to me now.

We both gave Glennen a year before he drank so heavily that I had to step in and run the whole shooting match.

From there I returned to Thera. On Blizzard's back I did it in four days – the Wolf Soldier Lieutenant whose command they were had a fit but it wasn't like he could do anything about it – they made it to the city three days after I did. The cold weather made the road hard and encouraged Blizzard to his greatest efforts. He had gotten his belly wet on the ship and the run did him good. At some points I could barely contain him. I arrived at the Casa de Mordetur to find the rest of the Free Legion already there.

We met in my War Room on All Gods' Day. We planned to celebrate in the city afterwards. Ancenon and D'gattis were livid, Karel of Stone amused. Dilvesh and Nantar and Thorn were ready to write the whole thing off and Arath had already been in contact with the Toorians to negotiate shipping their summer wheat and natural fruits and vegetables in preparation for the Sentalan shortages predicted next years. I had already decided to invest heavily in Toorian futures and had quietly bought into a shipyard in Andurin, where I could start building ships to move south.

It surprised me how much I missed Drekk. His quiet contempt for everything material, so unusual in a thief, had been a stabilizing factor. I still anticipated his next raw comment. Funny that I should miss the Uman who barely spoke to me, except to tell me that I'd done something wrong. It is strange how you can come to count on that sort of thing.

Perhaps it really *is* your critics that make you.

Karel of Stone could replace him in his own way. He reported from the same network. He told us that there were thoughts of retaliation, but that they were few and not serious. If we could sack Outpost IX and walk away from it, then we could go anywhere.

I don't know what had inspired the thief to help me. He knew I didn't like him.

"The damage will take years to repair, if it can ever be repaired," D'gattis told me directly. "Some of what is lost is Cheyak architecture which can never be replaced. The rest is extremely expensive –"

"No," Arath said. He was emphatic, half-standing. "Not a chance."

"Of what?" D'gattis answered him. His ambiguous eyes flashed angrily.

"Of using gold from Outpost X to rebuild Outpost IX," Thorn said.

"I don't believe a vote has been called," Ancenon interjected.

"I would vote, `No`," Nantar said, flatly.

"As would I," Karel said.

"And I," Dilvesh joined them.

D'gattis regarded me with even more hatred. I just shrugged. This wasn't my doing.

"I'm told that Trenbon just made a great deal of wealth on some sold property," I said off-handedly.

Ancenon slammed his fist down on the table, fuming. Karel of Stone laughed outright.

"Do you *know* how many were made to suffer in this raid of yours, Lupus?" D'gattis demanded.

I nodded. "Four children, a husband," I said. "A woman whose last moments of life were humiliation and pain."

"The children and wives of two *thousand* Trenboni Royal Guard," Ancenon added. "Merchants and tradesmen facing the rest of the winter with *nothing*."

"This might be said of the Sentalans, and of the Volkhydrans, as well, Ancenon," Nantar said, softly. "And yet, you don't seem to want to spend gold to help them."

D'gattis sniffed. "*We* cannot be held accountable for the people of every nation in the world, Nantar," he informed us.

Thorn stuck his nose in the air and did his best to imitate him. "Neither," he said, "can *we*."

It ended that simply. If the Uman-Chi called for a vote to rebuild Outpost IX, then it would go against them. The Fire-Bond prevented them from taking the gold to do it themselves. I firmly believed that they only wanted the credit and the glory of donating to the rebuild, without having to actually extend themselves.

None of the Free Legion stayed for the All God's Day celebration in Thera, which marked the end of the old year and the start of the new. Shela and I ended up staying in and having the house musicians play for us. She'd been trying to teach Lee to smile and I lay back in the luxury of a break from wondering who would be the next person trying to kill me, or who I would need to kill.

It wouldn't last.

***

I awoke in the morning with my wife in my arms, my daughter already up and watching us from her bassinette, the sun shining through an open window and a message delivered to me from a liveried Uman.

The new staff still needed to learn the rules like, "If it is one of those very rare times when I decided to sleep in, let me."

"Shall I return after you dress, your Grace?" he asked me.

I nodded. This was one of those mornings when I could have really used a cup of coffee.

He excused himself, the head butler, an older Uman, closing the doors to the bedroom behind him.

"The whole staff needs work," Shela said, stretching.

"How did our beloved daughter let you sleep in late?" I asked her.

"She didn't you oaf of a man," she said. "You slept through three feedings and three changings as well. Your ability to tune out the sounds you don't want to hear is making you a poor father."

"But a better husband," I added. She didn't get it.

I pulled on my leather pants, a loose fitting shirt and house slippers. Some nobles would have added robes and ascots and all sorts of other things, but I didn't go in for that.

Some of the same nobles would have met a messenger like this in the throne room or someplace similar, but that also wasn't in me.

I left the bedroom with Shela unbuttoning her blouse for another feeding; I passed the head butler and biffed him on the back of the head.

"Send someone into the bedroom when I am asleep again, and you will be cleaning stalls in the stable," I told him.

He nodded.

That was me.

I found the Uman in the big circular anteroom just inside of the main door. The room had been tiled in black and white like a checkerboard and a wooden stair with a bronze frame descended counter-clockwise along the wall from a second floor landing. The landing opened up to a roof garden that Shela loved, and could be lined with archers if we were defending the house from attack.

That was me, too.

"Your Grace," the Uman greeted me.

I nodded.

"The Heir is summoned back to Eldador, the City," he said, "by order of your liege lord, the King, Glennen Stowe."

How could I be so not surprised?

"How soon does he want me?" I asked.

"I am to escort you on horseback," he said. "So as soon as you may."

I shook my head. "Is there trouble, or don't you know?" I asked.

"I would be a poor source of information to you," he said, spreading his hands, palms up. "However, I can tell you that it is the royal Oligarchs who summon you in the King's name."

Crap.

"Rest after your journey," I told him. The head butler appeared from behind me. "Afeer, here, will provide for you. If you would like to sleep, we will provide for you."

"Thank you, your Grace," he said.

"It will take me a day to get my affairs in order. Afeer will assign 500 Wolf Soldiers to escort you back to Eldador the Port."

"You, then, decline the invitation, your Grace?" he asked me. You could read the worry on his face.

I shook my head. "I will leave tomorrow and catch up with you the next day," I told him. "We will arrive in Eldador together."

He nodded. I turned. Normally, I would have talked to him more, but you don't do that when you're a Duke and the Heir. Kind of a pain in my ass, but there you go.

Back in our room, Shela sat in her rocker, our daughter to her breast. Shela practically glowed. For just a moment, I wondered if I could get out of going to Eldador.

No way. I stood and watched her, my shoulder on the doorjamb. She sat and let me, waiting for me to speak.

"The Oligarchs are summoning me to Eldador."

She looked up. "That didn't take long."

"I would be more surprised if they *didn't* call, I think."

"So would I," she agreed, then looked back down at Lee's face.

"So you want me to stay here when you go?" she added.

"Am I that predictable?"

She smiled. "You are so predictable, I can use you to tell what time of day it is."

"Cannot."

She kept smiling, then after a moment said, "You would have said, 'us' if you wanted me to go with you."

I hadn't even recognized that.

"How long will you be gone?"

"I don't know. Depends on the situation."

"How many Wolf Soldiers are you taking?"

"Five hundred."

She nodded.

"You know I want to go," she said.

"I know. If it's more than a week, I will send for you."

"Thank you."

I bathed, dressed, and assembled my own Oligarchs. I gave them the information they needed to run the place. Who could do what, what they shouldn't decide on, and some more instruction on the security of Thera.

"I am not declaring martial law," I said, "but if you think that a ship pulling into port is suspicious, or if you see a band of more than three men come in, or if small bands *keep* coming in, use the Wolf Soldiers to arrest them or, if they resist, kill them."

That made all three frown. "We have a tourism trade..." Thebinaar began.

"We won't if we're overrun," Ann told him.

"Who would try to sack Thera?" Def snorted.

"Who would try to sack Outpost IX?" I asked him.

"Still," Ann continued, as if none of us had spoken, "three is too low. If someone is trying to sneak in an invasion force, they need no less than 10,000. That means you have to move in groups of twenty or more, or your outlying army will be detected before you have in half your numbers.

I shook my head, thinking of how few men had supposedly been inside the Trojan horse. "Just a few men inside to start killing guards, then your army strikes before you know you're unprepared."

"But that argues to increase our outlying patrols," Def said. "More of them searching deeper. More thorough."

"Are we trusting other Eldadorian cities?" Ann asked me.

I thought about that. I'm the Heir, I knew that Rennin approved of my appointment, but I also knew that Groff of Andurin didn't share his opinion. He didn't want it; he just didn't want me to have it.

"I am going to say that any party of armed troops has to say why they're here," I said, finally. "Eldadorian cities have sacked each other before. And increase the patrols. That's a good idea."

"How many troops are we keeping here?" Thebinaar asked.

"I am only taking 500 as a personal guard."

"Horse?" Ann asked.

"Mounted infantry. I need to move fast," I said.

She nodded. "Then we have seven hundred heavy horse in the city, and another five hundred in training," she said. "Two thousand, three hundred Wolf Soldiers in the city, and another thousand in training."

"A thousand?" I asked. We had never had a thousand in training.

"Sack the un-sackable city and you would be surprised how many want to cast their lot in with you," Def said. "I turned away two thousand more, and put them on the trail to Angador."

I smirked to myself. "That should come as a nice surprise to Arath," I said.

"We will be back up to pre-invasion strength before the War months," Thebinaar said. "Depending on our losses in the summer campaigns, we could be twice this size next year."

"Until then, we are vulnerable," Ann said.

"Well, not vulnerable, so much as affected," Def said. "There isn't anyone who is going to come here to this city with 10,000 troops. Even the Trenboni can't muster so many to that end. And until they do, we won't lose the city."

"Which means we will continue to grow," Thebinaar said.

If it could only be that simple. In my own mind, I knew exactly what I would do now to draw us out and weaken us. I could only hope that my enemies weren't thinking of it.

There were plenty of those now.

I marched through the gates of Eldador the Port at the head of 500 Wolf Soldiers, Blizzard in his full barding raising and lowering his head as Eldadorians and tourists stood aside for us. The wolf's head banner snapped under the flag of Eldador on my lance and on my standard bearer's pole.

I arrived on the 21st day of the month of Adriam, in the eighty-second year of the reign of the Fovean High Council. The wind blew cold, the horses loving it. At a time when most market places had shut down, the one in Eldador thrived.

I'd been told that the one in Outpost IX had yet to be rebuilt.

We marched to the palace gates, near the center of the city. The streets bustled with people in their furs or heavy cloth overcoats. Some stopped to look at us, some didn't care.

We weren't in the city twenty minutes before a rider met us from the palace.

"Your Grace, Mordetur of Thera?" he asked.

"And you are?" I responded.

"The squire of the Oligarchs, your Grace," he said. "I am here to ask you to proceed to the palace with haste."

"We are going there right now," I told him.

"With greater haste," he said. I'd seen that look in the Navy. Something very bad had happened.

I kicked Blizzard into a canter, the Wolf Soldiers behind me doing the same. One blew a single note on a bugle to clear the crowd, which came as a real surprise to me because I didn't know I had buglers.

We got some good speed down the main way. The thunder of two thousand hooves gives you plenty of warning to get out of the way, especially on cobblestones. We were at the palace in less than half an hour.

A huge fountain had been built outside of the gates to the palace. A statue of the goddess, Life, here depicted as a beautiful girl in a short skirt and large bare breasts, spewed water from her hand in many high, arcing streams. The breasts, of course, nursed the world.

They had probably not been intended for Glennen to cop a feel, but then, I don't think he asked the sculpture. By even casual observation, he was propositioning her, dressed in a breach clout that accentuated the extreme size of his hairy belly.

"Oh, crap," I said.

"Oh, I hope he doesn't," the squire said. "Although he does pee in the fountain when the mood strikes him."

As we got nearer, we could hear his slurred speech as he argued with the statue.

"C'mon, gurlie, you can give us a little taste, eh?" he told her. "Maybe jess a li'l dribble? I could do with jess a dribble."

I rode Blizzard right to the fountain's edge. "Your Majesty," I said.

He turned, trying to adjust his bleary eyes. "Who? Lupus, you bastard, issay you?"

I smiled. "It is," I said. "Can I bring you back to the palace?"

"Not till this bitch here gives me some rec'nition," he said, scowling. "I'm a bachelor, now, yanno."

How did I know this would be at the root of it? "Your Majesty, I can get you a woman who would appreciate you, if you want one," I told him.

He looked at me owlishly. "Not that child you married?" he asked.

Yes, it had been a good idea that not to bring Shela.

"No, some other."

He squinted his eyes at me. "Not her sister?"

"No," I said. I held out my hand to him. "Please, your Majesty. Come inside. You must be freezing."

He looked down at himself. "Yanno, I don't feel it. But yeah, maybe I will put some pants on."

He stepped onto the wall of the fountain, put his weight on its slippery surface, and of course did a back flip right into the pool. I saw his head smack the statue.

I don't think Life had appreciated his offers. Five of my men were off their horses, me with them, as we leaped to his aid.

I knew enough to be careful as we moved him. "Watch his head and neck," I told them. One man pulled his sword and we tied his head to it with a few rags, then secured the sword's blade to his back, immobilizing him as best we could. Meanwhile four Eldadorian regular army brought a litter from the palace and we rolled him into it, to bring him back inside and to his rooms.

Hundreds of people saw the debacle. I would have worried about the scandal, except that it had probably been going on since I left. We'd gone *way* past scandal.

***

Glennen lay on his bed, sodden and freezing. The room had been built to be lavish, with gigantic bay windows and real glass to look through. The hard wood floor had been polished to a shine, except where our steel-shod boots had marred it. His four-poster bed came with a canopy, piled high with quilts. A table stood by the door and couches by the window, the bed and the far wall, where a gigantic mirror hung.

He hadn't shaved in several days, but he had been drinking regularly. His son, Tartan, stood to one side of his father as two royal healers tended him. His Oligarchs and I spoke quietly at his tables.

"How long has this been going on?" I asked. I had just dispatched the captain of my guard to bed down the men and stable the horses.

"Since All Gods' Day," one of them said – the one I had met first, who had come to Shela and me in our hotel room. It occurred to me that I either didn't know or didn't remember any of their names.

"He began drinking early, he drank all day and into the night. Then he started to break things, until he passed out. Two days later he started again."

"This is what he does now," another said. They were all male, all Men, and all old. "He drinks, he attacks, and he tells us things that are on his mind."

"Sometimes they are terrible things," the third said. Of the four of them, he was the only one with short hair. Like the others, his was white, his robes were white, and he wore sandals. They all carried a twisted oak staff as a sign of office. I didn't know why.

"He cannot cope with the loss of the Queen," the first said. "And of course, we can hardly hold him responsible for his actions."

"Except that we must," the fourth Oligarch said.

Couldn't argue with that. I knew alcoholism when I saw it. He wouldn't stop if he didn't have to, and he didn't have to unless his kingdom revolted or someone assassinated him.

This could play right into War's hands, I thought. No point in taking the King out if he was going to do it for us.

I had seen some sailors go pretty far down this road. Drinking yourself to death is real.

"There is no way to get Tartan to take over in his place?" I asked. Tartan, hearing his name, looked up at us. "Even just as reagent or something, for the duration of his treatment?"

All four shook their heads as one. "Eldadorian law in unique, in that the monarch has all power to rule. Glennen always feared that somehow his Dukes would rise up against him."

"Can he proclaim a new law?" I asked

They nodded. "You are wise, your Grace," the second said. "When he is sober, or just a little drunk, we must get him to proclaim that the Heir can assume power in a crisis of health."

"I will commence the document," the fourth said.

"No, I am the Heir," I said. "It should be Tartan – "

"Tartan has no standing to rule," the third said. "If he were to suddenly take power, it would look like a coupe."

"And it will look exactly like that if I take over," I said. "And do you really want *me* to be in control of Eldador right now?"

"Your recent attack on Outpost IX," the fourth said.

"You fear that it will be a direct affront to the Trenboni," said the first.

"I fear that they could use it as justification to retaliate against anything Eldadorian that they want, and legitimize it before the Fovean High Council, which I just royally pissed off," I said.

They all nodded, and then I realized that my use of slang has been interpreted as I intended. Had they adapted or had I? Tartan approached us with a healer.

"He will live," the healer, a white-hair Uman in a yellow robe, said. "You were wise to bind his head – his neck had snapped. We have repaired it."

"I owe you another debt, your Grace," Tartan said.

"I am at your service," I said, inclining my head to him, "and to your family's service, your Highness."

"Actually, it is you who are 'Highness,' your Grace," Tartan said. "If I am correct on the rules of etiquette, then highness falls below majesty, and you are the heir."

"Correct as ever, Prince Tartan," the third Oligarch said. "You are my brightest pupil."

He nodded.

I squared off on Tartan, so I could gage him. "We need to get your father well," I said to him. "Do you agree?"

He didn't look into my eyes, which I didn't like. He looked at his father, then the Oligarch's past me, then at me, but at my face, not my eyes. "I do."

"And if we can get him to give you the power to rule in his place, until he is well, would you work with us, and be guided by us?" I asked

He looked in my eyes for a moment, and then looked away. "Would I do as you say, and would I give power back to my father when he felt well?" he asked.

I nodded.

He thought about it.

That answered it for me right there. He would agree, but he didn't know for sure that he meant it.

I'd have to get myself out of this one. I smiled to Tartan and I took his shoulder in my hand for a second, but I excused myself and found where my Wolf Soldiers were bedded down, and joined them.

It had been a hell of a day.

***

Later in the royal Eldadorian court, I sat alone on the throne atop the dais, at the end of the long, royal gallery.

One day it would be imperial, I knew. Royal was good enough for now.

"And you can see, your Grace," the Earl informed me, "the implicit growth of the project affects not only my own earldom, but the Eldadorian nation."

Blah, blah, blah – the man had been droning on for thirty minutes. The Rule of Fifteens came to mind again, as it often did in such circumstances.

Any meeting that took more than fifteen minutes had a second agenda. Anything that took longer than fifteen seconds to say was probably a lie.

"I humbly add that this nation's prosperity has astounded the world under your sage leadership..."

Damn, I thought to myself. *He is sucking up to me. That is another ten minutes at least.*

Eventually they would learn that I didn't respond well to it, and they wouldn't do it anymore. The political animal is still an animal. It hunts to survive. It learns its prey's strengths and weaknesses, or it dies.

I had been in Eldador the port for two days. Glennen had roused this morning for a while, then gone back to sleep. His neck throbbed, and the first thing that he wanted was mead. I had talked him into breakfast tea, but I could smell that they had put something in it when it came. He had ordered me to sit for him at court, then rolled over and gone back to sleep.

I think the Earl wanted to build a granary or something. I missed that part of the dissertation. Really didn't matter because I planned on telling him, "No," regardless.

I wished I were with Shela. It looked like I would be sending for her.

"You munificent opulence has changed Fovea for all time..."

I wondered what 'munificent' meant.

Having or showing great generosity.

I started on the throne. The Earl either didn't notice or didn't care.

You need to know these 'three dollar words' *if you want to rule these people.*

I had a feeling that War hadn't asserted Himself to correct my grammar.

You think you do great things?

"I hope to," I thought in my mind, knowing that He would hear it.

***

And I stood in a field, feeling the hot sun on me, my calloused hands on the plow before me, the smell of my own sweat mingled with the hearty funk off the horse before me, of the newly turned earth beneath my feet.

I wiped the sweat from my forehead, and looked toward the great city, Eldador, where I had never been. Even now more masons were hauling more stones to her, as if more stones would make her greater, as if the sun could not set on enough of it.

"I paid for those stones," I thought to myself, bitterly. "A share in 6 of everything I own, to the drunken king for his wine and his stones and his better life, while I live in a stick house with a roof that might leak."

And I stood on the solid, wood decks of the newest of the war ships pulling from Eldador the port, and I wore the uniform of a boatswain and looked up in pride at the Eldadorian flag, flying from the single mast.

The first mate had told me that most sailors die at sea, the rest are lucky if the scurvy and the whores don't leave them too twisted to lead a normal life. I didn't care; my father and his before me had been sailors and I would be one as well.

"Mount the main and hard aport," the first bellowed. The quartermaster spun the wheel and we picked up the breeze. The mains'l snapped and billowed out in all of her glory, the spray from the prow of *White Stallion* splashed on my face and filled my nostrils with her salty spray.

To one side of the quarterdeck stood a squad of Wolf Soldiers. Haughty bastards who had never smiled in their whole lives, who never drank with the crew, who never did anything but kill or plan to kill – they are a plague on Eldador in my opinion. The Heir put them everywhere to remind the rest of us how things would be when the King's health finally failed him.

Gendine, my best friend, clapped me on the shoulder, seeing my glare. "Be still, Vark, they are blooded veterans, and you are still a 'wog.'"

That they were. I ran to the rigging, my bare feet gripping the planks beneath me as the ship topped a swell.

That didn't make me like them.

And my woman screamed, from our one room home in Thera. I paced outside the door, on the street, passersby nodding their respect to me or, if they knew her, giving me their good wishes.

The midwife tended her, I assured myself. The midwife knew what to do.

I couldn't even afford to replace the bedding after her labors. At best I might replace the straw ticking and turn the mattress. The bed covers lay on the dirt floor.

This great land of prosperity called Eldador; it had not been so great for me. I had come to here a Volkhydran, my Lord's gristmill empty and his water wheel spinning free. There was nothing there anymore. There would be nothing for a long time.

In Eldador they took almost no tax, and so all of the mills were hiring. That didn't mean that they had room for a Man. Men were lords in Eldador, Uman worked the mills and the fields and the armories. Uman would hire 1,000 more Uman before they gave a wage to a Man.

My woman screamed again, bringing forth a new voice to this world, a new mouth to feed. Whether it would be my son or daughter anyone might guess. My woman is a whore, bringing wage to the table while I go from mill to farm to factory, begging for the chance to earn a wage.

She screamed and I could imagine that she blamed me, for my mistake to come here.

***

"*Enough!*" I shouted. The whole court jumped before me. The Earl became quiet, looking bewildered at my rage.

I had misspoken myself. I stood, and I glared at the Earl.

"You think that I am a child, that you can massage my ego and impress me?" I demanded of him.

He blanched. Lupus the Conqueror was a killer. They all knew what I had done to Sammin.

"Leave me," I demanded. "Court for the day is adjourned."

One of the Oligarchs approached me but I glared him away. A mural of Alekanna to the left behind the throne worked as a door and I used it. Let the masons make a new secret entrance for the security of the Heir. I wasn't in the mood to be protected.

This is beneath you.

"Apparently it is not," I snarled, knowing that the one I snarled at had *the pain*. That if He invoked the pain, then I would be helpless and do anything He wanted.

You are the instrument of War, he informed me. *You do what you must, and what no one else can.*

"Whatever that is."

I took long strides down the back halls, to the King's quarters, from where I could get to my own. I could hear the steps of the squires who attended me – no less than three for the Heir, no less than five for the King.

The Fovean Kings underestimate your ambitions. They still believe that they can control Eldador politically.

"I am sure that Constantine XI thought the ambitions of a twenty-one-year-old Sultan could be solved politically until Mehmed II overran Constantinople in 1453."

As you have demonstrated with Outpost IX.

"I didn't think it would be lost on You," I said. "I thought the world should see what I would do to anyone who came after me."

Which is not the only reason that I did it, and which He surely knew. People *love* to follow men who are 'fearless', because they can lose themselves in their maniac ambition. It is a lie to say that if you have nothing then you have nothing to lose. If you have nothing then you have everything to gain with the right person leading you.

My whole life demonstrated that.

You near your purpose, then, instrument.

Would I make the world better if I controlled it all? I would certainly make it better for me. History showed that kind of thing wouldn't benefit too many more people.

The Egyptians had enslaved entire races at the height of their power. They had buried their wealth in giant pyramids just to prove that they could do it.

The Eldadorians held apartheid-style dominance over their subjected Uman people. They enjoyed a better lifestyle now, but if this capitalist experiment were to fail, would it be Man or Uman whose children did without? Would I have or want Uman nobles in my realm? Would Sammin be dead now if he were a Man?

As for me…

I pushed open another concealed door and I entered the King's apartments. Glennen wasn't here – there were too many drinking hours left in the day for that. His squires would drag his drunken body in here, shave him and bathe him and put him to bed, when the booze had overwhelmed him.

I was kidding myself thinking that I could have plied him off with some tea.

"There is a price for everything, my love," Shela had told me.

When I had prayed to War, he had warned, "You have barely begun to do as I desire. *"*

Now I thought I knew what he wanted.

"The gifts of War are not without price," I quoted my wife.

Nor should they be.

"I was a loser about to die, and you made Lupus the Conqueror, the White Wolf, Scourge of Trenbon, blooded bounty hunter, the Killer of Conflu."

I made nothing. That is not the way it works.

"But there is also Rancor the Just, the liberator, the avenger. The one who humbled Outpost IX – the only one."

That is as much you as the other, but this is made of your own choosing, your own free will. That is how it works, instrument. It is all free will.

"And now it is before me to take the next step, open the doors and fulfill the mission of my god."

This is what you are brought here for.

"Just because it looks like I can do this thing, does that mean I should?" I asked quietly.

You are the servant to a god. You must learn to separate yourself from what you, as His instrument, may or may not do. You must have faith.

"Faith, or pain, you mean."

If that is how you must understand it.

"That doesn't sound very much like free will."

If a god could be frustrated, as I am sure a god could, then I could sense it in War. He was not used to having His will questioned.

You are already aware that you cannot trust Tartan Stowe, he told me.

"Yes," I said.

And that only you can be trusted for that seat and that power.

He didn't need me to answer, so I didn't. I had already decided on it, but the idea that War had made the effort to tell me...

Yes, he added. *Finally, you have come to a glimpse of what I have in store for you.*

Chapter Five

Consequences

The second day of the month Eveave began cold, dry and bright. Our beloved monarch marked that morning with another drunken display, and that evening my slave girl and my daughter entered the city.

Glennen got liquored up and decided that he needed more children, so he went hunting for women through the palace. He actually had a troupe of them running for their safety and their own lives through the halls and back rooms of the palace before I could be notified.

I didn't have to hit him to subdue him, but I came close. I stood in his way and told him that he would have to go through me to get to them.

He swung, but he couldn't focus so he couldn't hit. I pushed his hand aside a first, a second and a third time. He called me a treasonous bastard and said he would have me hung.

"Who are you going to give the order to?" I asked him. "Who is carrying out your orders for you now?"

That made him pause.

"I'll tell you, I am," I said. "And I do everything for you, including wiping your ass when I have to. And I have to do it, because you've chased everyone else away."

He looked right at me, right into my eyes, and had one of those moments of lucidity that drunks sometimes have.

"They have all abandoned me?" he asked. "They all left me, like Alekanna did?"

I stared into his eyes, made him look back at me and said, "She didn't leave you, our enemies killed her. And your friends didn't leave you, you chased them away."

He collapsed against me, sweating and stinking and, after a few moments, sobbing. He knotted his fists in the material of my shirt, at my shoulders, and leaned his weight on me. He swore that he didn't like what he had become and would change.

He went to sleep and, the next morning, started drinking again. We moved all of the female staff where he couldn't get at them.

I had a better time with Shela's arrival. She acted happier to see me, and no one got hurt.

I had her consult with the royal healers, hoping that she could repeat her success with Genna on the king.

"You don't understand these things, White Wolf," she told me, "so you won't understand why we can't help him."

"Try me," I said.

We were in my Spartan room, already in the process of being made less Spartan by her addition of a bassinet, more furniture, some tapestries and a different bed. We were sitting on a pile of quilts at the foot of our bed because Shela hadn't decided on chairs for us.

She sighed, taking Lee to her breast and doing this jiggle with her that she did when she was thinking. She didn't rock my daughter as much as bounced her, but I think it comforted both of them.

"I was able to cure Genna," she said, more to the air than to me, "because Genna was afflicted. A physical ill had been forced on her body, which I could find and attack.

"Glennen brings this on himself from grief and loss. I could heal the damage done to his body from the strong drink, but it would just make him better able to harm himself. It's a thing in his mind that is broken, an idea that he can't rid himself of, that in the drink he can find a clarity or an ease from the grief and pain, or at least a way to step away from it."

I nodded. That sounded like a good summation of alcoholism to me. And they had to decide to get better on their own, or they had to give in to it, one or the other. Until then, you could dry them out a thousand times and they would just go right back to what they were doing, because they didn't see anything wrong with it.

"But we still have to deal with the drunken monarch," she concluded. Lee finished and Shela shifted her to her shoulder for burping. If I behaved myself then sometimes I got to do it – Shela knew no Master when it came to her child.

"Maybe not," I said. "If you have known a real alcoholic, then you know the problem has a way of fixing itself."

"You mean the yellow sickness, which takes their insides and destroys them, colors their eyes and breaks the veins in their nose, until they die."

I nodded.

"Do you really want to let your liege lord die?" she asked me.

I thought about it. I owed my title to Glennen. He had fostered me in Eldador and named me 'Heir.' His faith in me had made me strong. I had killed for this man, and risked everything, for his wife, his friendship, and his faith in me.

My god wanted him dead. He wanted me to replace him.

I couldn't just let him die.

I couldn't stop him, either. I tried watering his drink, but he simply drank more.

I dutifully sat in court as Heir and spoke frequently with those Oligarchs here as well as mine in Thera. The month of Eveave progressed on, as time will.

"We are the emissary of Trenbon," the Uman said, one of a party of five who had petitioned to plead their case before the Eldadorian court.

This should be interesting.

I allowed them to approach the throne, dressed in the royal livery of the House Aurelias, of the Silent Isle. Each wore an eagle on his breast.

"We petition for reparations, for the actions of your subject, Duke Rancor Mordetur, against Trenbon, for his illegal invasion of the Silent Isle, his violation of the moratorium on violence against the persons of the Fovean High Council, and for the damages done to Outpost IX, both in loss of property and in loss of life."

Neither the Uman language nor that of Man had a word for 'cajones,' but if they had, I would have used it.

"We see no justification for reparations," I said, instead, "on the grounds of self-defense."

"Self defense?" the Uman seemed incredulous.

"Thera was attacked first," I stated.

"You have presented no proof of this," the Uman insisted.

"Of an attack on Thera?" I said. "I have the body of a dead queen, the word of the Duchess of Thera, numerous Wolf Soldiers and testimony from members of the Free Legion."

"Irrelevant," he sniffed. "And, as you must know, un-presented to the Fovean High Council."

I looked at the Oligarchs. The one I had come to know as 'One' nodded.

"Under the Fovean High Council's charter," he informed me, "evidence wasn't evidence until proxy delivered it, as you once did for the Great Dwarven Nation, and debated by the members."

I had emissaries to the Fovean High Council, but only the monarch, not the heir, could command them. I could not send my own proxy for the same reason.

I hadn't seen it necessary to shove something in front of Glennen to sign, and that had been a tactical mistake. I should have covered that base and hadn't.

"And what evidence do you have, then, that the Duke of Thera had any involvement in your alleged attack on Outpost IX?"

The gallery enjoyed a moderate amount of laughter as the Uman sputtered.

"The city was sacked," he said.

"We have no proof of this," I said.

"No proof?" he repeated. "There are thousands of dead."

"I have seen none of these," I said.

"Your Highness, you were there," the Uman said.

"And I saw none of this, prove otherwise," I said.

They were dumbfounded. However, the same rules applied. They would have to present that evidence from Angron or one of the other Fovean monarchs, and then the Eldadorians would have to debate it with the rest of the Fovean nations. We would have to be given the opportunity to speak through proxy, and clearly we hadn't.

They must have been thinking I had a guilty conscience or something. They didn't know me.

"Your Highness, is it your position that Outpost IX was not attacked?"

"It is our position," I said, "that you have no proof that it was attacked by *me*. Not proof that has been presented before the Fovean High Council."

"No less than 1,000 nobles –" the Uman began.

I shook my head. "I'm sure they saw a man in a war helmet and armor," I said. "Prove it was *me*."

"You spoke before the Fovean High Council," the Uman argued. He became more and more flustered.

"And who will present that evidence?" I asked him. "Which of the delegates to the Fovean High Council, and from which nation, has decided to antagonize – um, implicate – me?"

I felt reasonably sure that none of them right now were lining up to alienate me directly.

And I could be called as the accused, but only my monarch could force me to attend, and that wouldn't happen any time soon.

The nobles who had written the charter had not wanted to be subject to the High Council over their own leaders. That had probably seemed like a clever way to avoid certain responsibilities at the time.

"This leaves us in a difficult position," the Uman said, finally.

"No," I said. "Your position is to leave, mine is to let you. What could be simpler than that?"

Indignant, that is what they did. My Eldadorian delegates would be shamed before the High Council now, for my playing so underhanded a trick.

I didn't care. I hadn't invaded to make them like me.

***

The delegates left the city that day, according to my Eldadorian sentries. I would need more efficient spies.

At the end of the day at court, the Oligarchs anticipated me.

"We have taken the liberty of calling Glennen's council," the second told me, as we walked through the palace to the dining room.

"We shall dine, and speak with them," said the first. "The lady Shela has been informed and will attend."

"There are missives from your Free Legion associates, as well," the fourth said. "You are informed that they would like 3,000 Wolf Soldiers for the summer campaigns, in Volkhydro and in Sental."

I nodded. No chance of that happening. I knew it already.

If I were a gambling man, I would bet that Volkhydro wanted to take part of the harvest, and that Sental wanted to weaken Volkhydro to prevent just that.

"And how is our beloved monarch?" I asked.

They looked at each other, then at me. "We are informed that it took ten of your Wolf Soldiers to keep him from charging out of the palace gates," said the third. "He wanted to go out into the streets and spread the wealth of Eldador with the common folk."

I could only imagine what he thought that might be.

"I want Wolf Soldiers in all of the key guard positions throughout the palace," I informed him.

They exchanged glances. "The house compliment of 1,000 can be sent to the royal foot," three said. "Your five hundred and Lady Shela's thousand could replaced them here."

We were outside of the dining room now. As heir, they expected me to fill Glennen's place at the head of the table, if he didn't make an appearance. That had happened one time, and he had puked into his salad and passed out at the beginning of the meal. I still preferred that to having to nod and smile at his drunken rambling through a meal.

"However," the second among them said, "the House Guard are chosen for their loyalty to the monarch. They take their positions seriously, not just for the advantage of such duty, but for their love of the Stowes. There are four children whom they protect, not just the King."

"They will not simple depart," the third said.

"Not peacefully," the first agreed. "And open combat with them-"

"Will make me look like an usurper," I said.

I'd had this conversation before, but not with them.

"There's a Wolf Soldier named, 'J'her,'" I informed them. I'd noted his service. He'd been with me at Tamaran Glen, and at the Sack of Outpost IX, as it was being called.

"Have him sent to me."

All four nodded. Every night we waited respectfully outside of the doors for Glennen to arrive. Guests would be seated before him, so that they could stand in attendance when he entered. However I would be expected to enter right behind, to learn from him how to conduct myself at the meal.

"One of your advisors is a bounty hunter," the third Oligarch warned me. "And we are informed already that they do not see service to you as an obligation of theirs."

"So why is he here?" I asked.

"He is Tom Kelgan, and he is an essential part of the intelligence here," the fourth said. "Even if he must be replaced, then we must speak with him and learn what he knows."

I nodded. If he did the job of our Drekk, then we couldn't just boot him out the back door and be rid of him – not if we wanted the intelligence of the nation to keep running. I would need my own people, however. Whether Glennen got better or not, we were going to have to run things.

"I think that propriety has been served," the third Oligarch told me.

I nodded again. They threw open the doors and the court stood.

There were dozens. Glennen had supposedly hated to eat alone. Hectar, the Duke of Eldador, sat to my right with his wife whose name I always got wrong. They had a son, Hectaro, seven years old and already being aimed at Lee.

The Oligarchs sat at the four corners of the long table, to disperse their wisdom. There were a few court barons – landless men with titles who hung about the palace looking for ways to further their positions or their wealth, and to be pains in my ass. They all knew that the duchy of Thera went up for grabs when Glennen couldn't rule any more.

Daharef, the general who had replaced Sammin, and his latest honey, an Uman this time, sat next to a man who wore a breastplate and had daggers crossed behind his shoulders. He stood with the table between us, his back to the wall, away from the one great window that faced the bay, and he looked me right in the eye.

He had red hair brushed out and hanging over one shoulder, a moustache that drooped past his mouth, and green eyes that bore right into me. No need to guess who he might be.

There were other people I hadn't seen before. I hadn't been outgoing enough as the Heir. I didn't consider them beneath me; I just didn't have a lot of time.

I walked to the head of the table. Shela stood in front of the seat beside mine, beaming at me because she still hadn't gotten used to this. The Oligarchs took their places; I took mine, nodded regally, and sat. They all sat as soon I settled in. Shela touched my hand and, when I turned to her, shot me a smile.

I broke protocol and kissed the end of her nose. That earned a polite titter at the table, and the Duchess of Eldador looked sideways at her husband.

"We are pleased that all of you could attend," I said. "I – um – We are informed that We are to mix business with pleasure, and discuss affairs of state."

"Mix business with pleasure?" Hectar asked me.

Uman servants entered with platters. Just as in the Fovean eateries, we didn't order food and it didn't come in courses. The table would be piled high and then we would take what we wanted.

Shela took my plate and filled it, so that the other guests could eat. No one would take a bite before I did.

"We mix the business of the day with the pleasure of your company," I explained.

Several nodded. "What a bright way to look at things," the Duchess commented.

Slang breaking in my favor? That was promising.

"Our first issue," said Oligarch two, leaping into business, "is the state of our relations with other nations."

"No," the red-haired man said. "The first issue is your state of relations with *me*."

Even the servants paused over that. Calling me out at dinner probably made for an even larger breach of protocol than the kiss.

"It is, is it?" I said, looking at him directly.

"This is our bounty hunter advisor, Tom Kelgan," the third Oligarch said. "He is in charge of –"

"He is a representative of the bounty hunters' guild," one of the barons said. He was a slight man in elegant clothes, sitting next to Kelgan. He was either really brave or really naïve. "He has sworn to bring you to the justice of the guild."

"What makes him think he will survive this meal?" I asked, as Shela laid my plate down before me. I picked up a fork and took a bite so that the others could eat. Most looked nervous as they reached for food.

"I thought the safety of a dinner guest ensured," the bounty hunter said, reaching for a stack of cut meat with a two-pronged fork. He did it with his left hand, so that his weapon hand would be free.

Suddenly he dropped the fork, which a moment later glowed red, singeing the dinner table. He held his hand and looked at Shela and me.

"I don't like the nick name you gave me," Shela said. "And I am aware of no custom that says I can't make you a pile of ashes, any time I want."

"Your Highness," Oligarch one said. "Shall I call the guard?"

"We don't need them," I said, making a dismissive gesture. A servant came to my left and offered me mead from a pitcher. I held up my bowl for her. I didn't want it, but if I didn't take it, none of them could have any.

"You seem to crave the wrath of the guild," Tom Kelgan accused me. "I assure your Highness, if I am harmed – "

"The guild that wants me dead at all costs will want me dead at costs that they had never before imagined?"

He looked at me, I looked at him, and he couldn't help but crack a smile.

"You do not let yourself be intimidated, then, I see," he said, picking up a different fork to get himself more meat. He winced as he piled his plate, his left hand still sore from the burn.

"We have noticed this of his Highness," Hectar commented.

"Many have," one of the barons commented drolly.

Again, a small laugh.

"Shall you be keeping me on," he continued, "or is this my last meal?"

"Will you be bound by a fealty?" I asked.

He considered this. Clearly he expected it.

"There are more ways out of a fealty than out of a room full of doors," the baron next to him commented. That drew some looks. Had to be pretty bold to essentially say, "Stupid" to the new boss.

I noted the baron. Maybe a military commission for him. The army needed risk takers.

"Yet there is honor in taking an oath, regardless," Tom said. He looked at me, considering.

"I would ask you to be bound to my protection," he said. "But I don't think you're likely to do it, and I see what it means to offend you.

"Yes," he said, finally. "You are well aware that I am a spy for the guild."

"How would I think otherwise," I said.

"They *will* take you, your Highness," he warned me.

"Heard that before," I said. "But, you know, all of the people who've said it are dead, and I'm not."

He controlled himself better than I did. He made me wish I *was* a bounty hunter right then. You just had to like the way he handled himself so easily.

"Our second point of affairs, then," the fourth Oligarch said, "would be affairs with other states."

Several nodded. A lot of them had questions about how we handled the delegates from Trenbon. Was this wise? Well, we weren't paying reparations.

"They demanded reparations, your Highness," said Hectar, "because they want to sack our ships."

Many at the table nodded. I grinned and turned to my new general. "How goes our Theran project?"

He smiled, looked at the bounty hunter, then at me.

"If he is worth his salt, he already knows of it," I said.

"My salt?" he asked, and looked at a bowl with a small spoon in it. "Am I to be charged to spice my meal?"

I grinned. "In ancient times," I said. "There were nations who had no gold to pay their troops, and paid them instead in rare salt spices. Hence, worth their salt."

"I have never heard of this," commented one of the Oligarchs.

"It isn't a well-known fact," I said.

"But a considerable option, if the men would sustain it," the Duke said. "It would be much simpler to dole out spice than silver and certainly more economical to the kingdom."

"Something to consider," a baron said.

"Regardless," Tom said, "I am well aware that you are building your own ships in Thera. I am aware as well that you seek to enhance them magically, as has Trenbon.

"Trenbon has three hundred years more experience than you do," he added, then took a bite and chewed, adding, "and the best wizards on Fovea," through his food.

I grinned. "A surprise for them, no less," I said.

He shrugged.

"The status of our armed forces," the third Oligarch continued.

"We have the maximum compliment of twenty thousand," Daharef said, "and your Wolf Soldiers, whom I am told could take them without a sweat."

"Conflu had one army of thirty thousand," I said, stabbing at a piece of meat. "The limit of twenty is meaningless if all nations don't abide by it."

"That is surely why they are so secretive," the baron who would soon be in my military added. I looked directly at him.

"This is the Baron Jaheff of Andurin," Oligarch two said. "He was elevated a year ago, when his Majesty…"

"Got drunk and generous," Jaheff said. Hectaro barked a laugh, drawing a stern glance from his father.

"Glennen made me an Earl the same way," I said, nodding to him. "And for my skill at making money. What is your skill, Lord Jaheff?"

"Being in the right place at the right time, it seems," he said. "My father is Duke Groff of Andurin's brother, a common merchant. I have no skill at trading this for that, and an older brother who does. I am as like to hurt myself as another with a sword, and no shoulders to bear armor, I am afraid."

So much for the military aspect, though I couldn't help feeling that I should find a use for this man.

Dinner continued for a while, with more talk like this. One of the barons, Tenlen, had responsibility for the treasury, and reported that we wouldn't starve, but we didn't see much profit, either. We had barely a city and certainly no village up to date on its taxes.

"In honesty, your highness," he told the room, "the more the cities make, the less they seem to want to pay."

"They are conserving their strength, it seems," Tom said. "Especially Yerel of Uman City. He didn't send a payment at all last month.

"What's the law on that?" I asked Oligarch one, who sat to my left.

He considered. "I can say that he has breached the law," he said, finally, "but I cannot say that there is a penalty for it."

"His Majesty would usually appear in person and collect," Oligarch two said.

"I would not advise that," said Oligarch three. "However the heir actually has no power to demand taxes."

I looked at Tom directly.

"How big is his private army?" I asked.

No hesitation. "Three thousand men."

I looked at Daharef. "Does that seem large to you?" I asked.

He nodded. "Eldador the port has only four thousand."

"The heir has no power to invade a city within Eldador," Oligarch four said.

I nodded. "He does have the power to hire outside aid, however," I said.

"All business transactions of the state are within your domain," Oligarch two said.

I smiled and took a big bite of beef. It tasted really, really good.

Chapter Six

Under New Management

One great thing about a palace is that it's made to have too many rooms, so that it takes up a lot of space and looks grand. The downside is that it employs too many people, making it expensive as hell to run.

The royal family lived in the 'family tower,' which made up one of the four towers that took up the outer corners of the palace. The family tower consisted of a big room where Glennen slept, then stairs and a room above it for Tartan, then more stairs, a few guard rooms, and then rooms for the other kids. At the top a big, empty room took up a whole floor and had nothing in it. From there you could get to the upper, open air floor where you could station archers behind a parapet with merlons.

No one ever went to this big room, and you could get to it without going through any of the other rooms. No one but the royal family and their guards were allowed in the family tower – and me, of course, not because I had any sort of right to be here, but because they were all afraid of me.

J'her had been a farmer once – an Uman from outside of Steel City. He'd had a few bad years and he'd lost his farm to creditors, and the local Earl had taken it. J'her's wife had bailed on him with his kids. That had pissed him off, and he'd gotten into the habit of massacring anyone who took up residence on his old farm, until he got caught and was sentenced to death.

This was the sort of person whom Ancenon didn't want in the Free Legion.

This was *exactly* who I wanted in the Wolf Soldiers.

"J'her," I said to him, when he entered the room at my summons. Part of the test had been for him to get himself up here. Apparently he'd passed that.

"Lupus," he returned. My Wolf Soldiers called me by my first name, every one of them. It wasn't familiarity; it was a different type of respect. In my world, God had no name, because no name could contain Him. I had no title for the Wolf Soldiers, because no title could measure their adoration of me. I'd made that up, but a few successful battles down the line and they believed it.

I gave them a second chance, in a land where *no one* gave someone like them a second chance.

"I remember you from the Battle of Tamaran Glen," I informed him. "I noted you at Outpost IX. You're a Captain in the Pack now, aren't you?"

A sergeant in the Wolf Soldier Pack commanded ten men. A lieutenant commanded five sergeants. A Captain commanded as many as ten sergeants, or a total of five hundred warriors.

I was thinking of reducing that to five lieutenants, and then a major who would control four lieutenants, or an even thousand.

"I was promoted after Outpost IX," he informed me. He looked me right in the eye. His face was cut by a hawk-nose, his eyebrows thick, green and stern. He kept his hair short where most preferred long, like mine.

I told him of my plan to restructure the Wolf Soldiers, adding, "I need names of warriors who are ready to be lieutenants."

He nodded, saying nothing.

This guy was perfect.

"While we're doing this," I said, "I have a real need to get the Eldadorian Regulars out of the palace, and to replace them with my Wolf Soldiers."

J'her looked deep into my eyes, as if the thoughts in my brain were accessible to him, if he looked deep enough. Who knows – maybe they were? Uman are a strange people.

"They won't like that," he informed me.

"I'd be surprised if they did," I answered.

He nodded. "When?"

"I've got something to do," I informed him. "While I'm gone, find a reason and make it happen. You're a Major now – the first one. When you take over the barracks, make sure you have an office and your own room."

He took the promotion without comment. This sort of thing was normally done in ceremony; however I had means to send the word out when I wanted to. I'd do that as soon as I left here.

"I'd like to see Wolf Soldiers, not Eldadorian Regulars, guarding doors when I get back," I said. "It won't be more than a few weeks."

J'her nodded.

"And don't make it something I'm going to hear spoken about," I informed him. "It would be bad if a lot of loyal Eldadorian Regulars went missing, or if the rest of them were scared and wondering if they were next."

"I agree," he said.

I pointed at the door with my chin. He came to attention, made a fist over his heart by way of saluting me, and then dropped the salute, turned on his heel and opened the door for me. I walked out and he followed me out of the family tower.

It was nice to have one thing go my way.

***

The month Eveave ended as cold as its beginning. My Wolf Soldiers marched in perfect formation down the long road from Thera to Uman City, their cleats digging into the soil, in the frigid months when no one ever made war.

It made sense not to. Men exerting themselves in the cold would sweat and get sick. The frozen ground made marching easier, however food became scarce and we could find no forage, so we had to either move supply wagons, which cost a mint, or carry our supplies with us, which slowed our army to a crawl. I'd chosen the latter.

Snow would make the roads impassable, when the snow melted, the mud made them worse. Blizzard stomped the hard ground, bobbed his head and snorted, loving it. He thrived at the head of 1,000 heavy lancers, a fog exploding from his nose.

Two Spears, beside me, held the van. Behind the horse were 3,000 Wolf Soldiers, a third of them un-blooded recruits. I mixed them in with my veterans, who in the first two days of our march spent most of their time getting them to march in order and to focus. There were more than a few out-right beatings. At night we made our small city, which took twice as long in the cold, and then still found the time to run close order drills at night.

There were fifty attempted desertions in the first night. The horse ran them down the moment we learned of them. I lined them up, walked down their row, and beheaded one in ten, in the tradition of 'decimation,' used by the Roman army as punishment for retreat.

The Roman Legions didn't retreat. Mine didn't desert. A few asked if they could leave, but I didn't say, "Yes" and they didn't push it."

In the second week of the march, they were showing me something. You could hear the telltale stomp of an army that moved in unison. The whiners were few and far between, and the men wouldn't tolerate them. When we stopped for the day, they fell apart like the pieces of a puzzle, each to his or her own designation without needing to be told. I'd looked for this in my army – they thought and they fought in unison like the machine I'd made of them.

There were women in my Wolf Soldiers, who held their own right next to the men. If they wanted to screw on their own time, that was their business. If they wanted to rape, then we settled that in-house, and it wasn't pretty. Women had their place in the Pack – they made better archers, for example. They could be good shieldmen and pikemen but, more importantly, they had good ears and some instincts that men just lacked. A squad of men all hell-bent for leather to go sprinting into trouble could get some 'wait-and-see' advice they needed from the women among them, just as a squad of women could be more brave if they had faith that the men among them had faith in them.

The weather still held. Half of our supplies were gone, meaning that if we kept the pace, we would have a week outside of Uman City before food became an issue. I owed that to the women, too – they stretched the supplies better, and they wouldn't just eat anything. I could have Free Legion Shipping move us purchased goods if I had to, but I would have already with only men.

"How are the horse coming?" I asked Two Spears, as we rode.

He shook his head. "I had them just like I wanted them," he said, "and then you give me these green troops, on horses they don't know the tail from the mane of, and you think I can just make them an army for you?"

I laughed.

"I have a good core – the core will fight," he said. "They are the veterans from Outpost IX. They know combat.

"But half – they are the ones who trip over the others. One stuck his lance into the ground and almost speared himself last night.

Two practiced against each other and knocked each other from their horses, then their horses, they crashed into each other."

"I think I saw that," I said.

"And how are you, fighting without my sister at your side?"

I still expected her to show up. She wouldn't this time, though. We needed her in Thera, to hold the Duchy in place in case anyone took this opportunity to attack us. In Eldador the port, the Oligarchs would have to hold power as best they could, and control our beloved monarch. J'her was doing what he was doing, sort of as my unofficial regent – vague enough so that no one knew what power he had.

We were approaching Uman City. Surely they knew we were coming by now. In a few hours we would be able to see the city walls. We would press on until we were a mile away, and then camp outside like a siege army. I would enter with four wizards, two from Dorkan, one an Eldadorian and one an Uman-Chi.

I had personally disgraced him. Outpost IX had been carved into sections with different families responsible for them, and his family had run the gate and towers. They had been relieved. He had been out to sea and been duped by our 'throw one to the wolves' trick, and managed with his officers to make it back to Outpost IX.

Uman-Chi live a long time, Uman and Men less so. He would see many generations of us come and go, and they wouldn't remember his shame for so long as his own people would.

There are a lot of ways to birth a Wolf Soldier.

A fast rider came back to us, up the road from Uman City. We rode out to meet him, not because we couldn't wait, but to make sure bad news didn't make it to the men.

I'd chosen Andarons for all of my fast riders. He came from the Red Tail tribe, a clan that had some kinship with the Long Manes. Two Spears knew him and liked him.

"Report," I barked at him.

"Their gates are closed, the Eldadorian flag flies from the walls. Peasants are shuttered in their houses, and their herds are in, not roving."

That is what you did to make ready for a conquering army. They knew why we were here.

"Are we the first here?" I asked.

He nodded. "We have seen no sign of the Free Legion," he told me. "I spoke with other outriders. In the winter, though, there would be no dust from their army. We would have to be right on top of them to see them."

It was true. The hard packed ground, cold with frost, wouldn't kick up any dust.

I dismissed him and looked at Two Spears. "Pick a squad of heavy horse," I ordered him, "send them in the direction of the Plains of Angador. They can go today, and all tomorrow, then they come back if they haven't found the army."

We had asked for Ancenon's help, but had left before he could have contacted us. They were under no obligation to come if they didn't want to – the Fire Bond didn't cover this.

With this few, I could siege Uman City, but I couldn't overrun it. Not when they were ready for us and hiding behind the city's walls.

Two Spears dispatched the men. We would have to see what a few days brought.

***

I rode up to the gates with my wizards. Two Spears had the army in construction of the small city. Tomorrow we would train on the field. Compared to the last three weeks, it would be an easy day, just to sprint and charge and parry.

We had about five days of food left. We couldn't mess around. Even if I sent a fast rider for aid, the men would be hungry for two days unless I could get food from Uman City.

My herald approached the gate, the Wolf's Head banner of the Wolf Soldiers snapping from his standard.

"Make way for Lupus the Conqueror," he said.

That got a curious reaction at the gate. They'd been expecting the Heir, no doubt.

"The gates are closed," the gate guard shouted back.

Uman City had a single gate, pointed out to the plains. It opened to the left on a series of pulleys. A portcullis stood before the wooden doors, which could be dropped at any time. On the Bay side they'd built long, fortified wharves, slick with ice and inaccessible to us. They didn't do much trade at this time of year, the fleets had been called in and the sailors manned the gates. The city wall had no gate on the Bay side, and the port seemed more like its own city.

Beside the portcullis and the gate, on the right, stood a tower that reached fifteen feet higher than the city's 25-foot wall. The towers had been built fifty feet across, and showed arrow slots on every level, to the outside and within the gate.

Walk your army in there, and you would lose ten men or more a minute. If you were smart, you put your shields up against the arrow slots and hoped you could destroy the main gate before they could pour hot oil down on you.

You could send a squad in with a battering ram, but the first few waves were going to die.

I sat my horse outside where the guard could see me. The Uman-Chi had a spell that protected us from arrows in case someone got brave.

"We would speak with Duke Yerel, or his proxy," the herald pressed him.

More talk behind the gates. Why didn't I proclaim myself the heir, or the Duke of Thera?

Those were Wolf Soldiers on their front lawn. But they were on the wrong side of the wall to do much.

"May we treat with him alone?" the guard called down, finally.

The herald looked back at me, and I nodded. He withdrew, and I trotted Blizzard up to the gate.

The gate groaned open about a quarter of the way, and an older man in chainmail armor trotted a dappled gray warhorse out to meet me. His hair shown as gray as the horse, cut close to his scalp, and his face clean-shaven. He was an Uman, but as big as a Man. He nodded and I nodded back.

"Your highness," he said, "I am Jak, Captain of the Guard."

"Well met, Jak," I said.

"I must ask your intention," he said.

He looked me right in the eyes, but you could tell he didn't want to. A soldier followed orders, like them or not, and closing the gates to the Heir wasn't an order that he liked following.

"I am here to speak with his grace, Duke Yerel," I said, "under treatise of the King of Eldador."

He looked at me more directly. "The King hired you?" he asked. "Why would he hire the Heir to do the duties of the Heir?"

"He hired the Free Legion," I said, "of which I am a member."

He opened his mouth, and then closed it. He opened it and closed it again.

"His Majesty has sent mercenaries to the city?" he asked.

"He has sent tax collectors," I said, "under hire."

"This has never been done before," he commented, as if he could argue us away.

"Times change," I said, simply.

He thought about that. "I can tell you," the captain said, finally, "that Yerel will not open his gates to invaders."

I nodded. "You know of course," I said, "that the Heir has no power to order him to open his gates, or to collect taxes."

"Yerel has made this point many times in the last few days," he said.

"And the Heir cannot order the army into an Eldadorian city," I added.

"Again, the Duke made this clear to me."

I looked back at the Wolf Soldiers, then back at the Captain.

"We aren't here as Eldadorians," I said. "We are here *for* Eldadorians. If Yerel doesn't see me today, he will have this army and even more Free Legion warriors on his doorstep, and we won't be here to talk."

"That sounds like a threat, your Highness," he warned me.

"A threat is something that someone might not do," I corrected him. "This is a promise – as soon as the Free Legion reinforcements arrive, I will destroy your gates, purge your walls, take the coin owed the state, and bring Yerel to Eldador the Port in chains."

The Captain nodded. I dismissed him, and he rode back in through the gate. I got Blizzard out of the murder hole before they realized that they would be the first group to die if I invaded.

Uman City had been laid out much the same as Outpost IX was: outer wall, inner wall, cobblestone streets and a central palace with its own wall. They had no coliseum for the Fovean High Council, no flying bridges soared above us, however I saw where flying bridges might be, if they'd wanted them.

They had only one gate, but the walls had the same kind of towers, only shorter. Someone had probably seen Outpost IX before they made this city, and then came as close to it as their budget would allow.

I walked in with my wizards and a 50 Wolf Soldier retinue, more to show off five squads than because I thought I needed them. Five squads wouldn't hold off the whole city guard, no matter who they were.

We marched down the central way to the palace. Wolf Soldiers who were veterans of the sack of Outpost IX looked on in wonder and recognition, just as I did. I hadn't been here before, but it felt like I had.

The palace gates were open. I doubted those would close until we actually attacked. The streets were crowded with civilian onlookers, some watching quiet and dour, others waving scraps of cloth with my Wolf's Head insignia drawn on them and shouting, "The Conqueror!" News of a military victory travels fast, and no one loves the Uman-Chi. Still, I think that most of them didn't like that army outside of the gate.

We entered the palace, and here my expertise ended because I hadn't been in the palace at Outpost IX. I saw a similarity to the palace at Steel City, where the inner gates were a straight shot from the outer gates. The palace exterior included towers and tiers and a grand marble stair leading up to its double doors. We marched past liveried Uman warriors and in to a main hall that mirrored Outpost X, right down to the gallery on the right hand side.

Cheyak tradition ran deep.

Yerel sat on a raised dais, on a throne carved of stone. He had no one there to advise him like Glennen and I did. He looked the same as when I had seen him in my home in Thera, except that he looked angrier now than then.

"Your Highness," he greeted me.

"Your Grace," I returned.

"I am told that you are here to collect taxes," he said. He came straight to the point. I didn't feel like sparring with him, anyway.

Well, the conversation wasn't over, either.

"You are delinquent," I said. "Are you able to deliver?"

"I can deliver," he said, "but I see no reason to do so for the Heir. You have no authority to collect tax or tithe."

"You will note," I said, politely, my helmet under my arm, "that I am not here as an Eldadorian, but as a member of the Free Legion."

"And I find that strange," he said, leaning forward, "because the Free Legion are under my employ."

Didn't see that one coming.

"They are?" I asked him. I felt my scar twitch. "That would not explain the troops on your gate."

"Oh, I assure you, I hired the Free Legion last month, to clean out Aschire raiders near my city," he said, half of a smile on his face. "They have been busy for me."

Now, *that* would suck, I thought. We had an agreement with the Aschire, an agreement through me, and that I depended on, that said that there would be no combat between the Aschire and the Free Legion.

I knew for a fact that every member of the Free Legion knew of that agreement. If they broke it we would never be able to incorporate the Aschire into our larger plans.

My first instinct right then was to bail from here, hunt down Ancenon and smack him down for screwing this up. I actually put weight on my left heel for a quick turn when it occurred to me.

Ancenon did a better job planning than that. He'd lived much longer and learned much more than I had. Ancenon Aurelias would not screw himself in the long term for some short-term gain, because Uman-Chi live for centuries, and they just don't think in the short term.

Yerel had tried to play me, and he knew just how to do it. That was pretty smart. I couldn't help myself from smiling.

"You are amused, your Highness," Yerel said.

I looked him in the eye. "No member of the Free Legion," I said, "would harm a purple hair on the head of an Aschire, for any amount of gold or silver."

He sat up straight, probably because I called him a liar in his own court, rather than because I had caught him in a lie.

"I take offense," he said.

"As well you may," I pressed him. I knew I had him. He was bluffing, and no one bluffed who held a good hand.

"And I will demand satisfaction," he said.

I smiled. I could take Yerel. He might have been a warrior, but that had been years ago.

"You shall have it," I said. They don't throw down gauntlets here. I had mentioned it once, and been told quite plainly that it was a stupid waste of an expensive piece of armor.

"Shall we use seconds, your Highness?" he asked me, "or will you be fighting yourself."

"I fight my own battles," I said.

I had been so pleased with myself that I didn't think before the words came out of my mouth. Why the hell would he want to ask about seconds?

Unless…

The man who stepped out from behind the stone throne could have been Nantar's bigger, meaner brother. He was armored from head to toe in thick plate, carrying a sword with a blade four feet long over one shoulder and a mace on his hip.

"Well, I am an old man," Yerel said, "and I shall choose a second. May I introduce you to Varoth, of the Bounty Hunter's Guild?"

Crap.

You had to admire the planning. You really did.

The Bounty Hunters approached Yerel and got him on their side, probably with some dispersion against me. Then they betrayed him to me, through their emissary to Eldador, to encourage me to come after Yeral. Now, of course, they supported Yerel with this warrior so he stayed on their side. This got me to do the one thing that they couldn't arrange on their own: open up direct combat between them and myself.

I could see where they had cut Shela out of the picture as well. If she were here, Varoth would already be dead. They knew I wouldn't bring the whole family to a siege, and Alekanna's assassination was still too recent even to consider leaving the baby alone. I am sure that, if we had, then Lee would be in the possession of the Bounty Hunter's Guild anyway right now, and Varoth would be delivering the message, "Give us yourself, or we will settle for your daughter."

That tended to say that they already had someone in the palace at Eldador, but I couldn't focus on that now.

On the first day of the month of Weather I stood on the square, just within the main gate of Uman City. Two hundred of my Wolf Soldiers stood as my witnesses. Whether I won or lost, they would wait until combat finished, then take the gate and the tower.

Two Spears sat outside the gate with 1,000 heavy horse. When the gate opened, they would charge directly to the palace and slaughter anyone who resisted. The foot would be right behind them. On this side of the gate, I could take the city with what I had.

I wore my armor tight. My wizards had already thwarted three attempts to cast spells on me. I let them respond in kind. The Uman-Chi felt certain that he had blinded at least one of their wizards.

Varoth stepped into the square. He held his sword in both hands. It looked similar to the Scottish claymore, long handle, over-stated cross guard, a foot of steel with no edge at the base, then sharp to a point on both edges. He didn't swing it in any fancy way, just held it before him, point down, waiting for battle to begin.

His mace hung from his hip. Seemed to me that the mace would be a better weapon to start out with. My armor would be a hell of an obstacle to his sword.

Yerel stepped out onto the square. "For the honor of Uman City," he said, and stepped back.

Varoth advanced. I pulled the Sword of War from over my shoulder and held it up between us.

He pointed his sword's point directly at my eyes, using a hand-over-hand grip. This would keep me from judging the distance from the end of the point to me, then he could stab at my face or he could swing from either side, changing his grip as he swung the sword over his head.

I stood my ground. I'd chosen a spot too near the crowd behind me. If he lunged, I would be unable to retreat without crashing into the spectators. As well, I'd taken a purely defensive posture. I had no assault from this position; I could only defend against his attacks. I would have to change my stance and my grip to fight, while he could keep swinging.

I knew I'd be facing the best swordsman they could throw at me. They wanted me bad, and this whole situation smacked of expense. They wouldn't skimp at the end of the game.

He came right in for the kill. Ten feet from me, then eight, then five. I couldn't tell the exact distance to the point of his sword. He held it perfectly in line with my eyes, creating an illusion of it being shorter than I knew it had to be.

I stood still as stone, barely even breathing. A good swordsman would think me scared of him, and finish me.

I didn't face a good swordsman, I faced a great swordsman. He thought five steps ahead where most couldn't manage one. I had a reputation for being devious and he knew that nothing ever appeared the way it seemed with me.

He stopped, and he took a good hard look at me, trying to tell what game I might be playing.

And the point of his sword wavered, and I knew the exact location of the end of that sword.

And I made a move that Saa Saraan from Outpost IX would have beaten me for, had he seen it. I hopped forward like a kangaroo, his blade scraping the armor on my shoulder and laying right next to my neck, and jammed the Sword of War into his breast plate like a spear.

Whatever the breastplate consisted of, the Sword of War didn't go through it like it usually did every other thing created by living hands. I actually expected that. The blow knocked him back, putting his sword right at the level of my face, and I immediately brought my own sword up within his guard, turned sideways so that I looked at the edge of his blade, and wrapped his arms up with my own.

He pulled back but couldn't disentangle himself. Our swords pointed out at crazy angles from our bodies and I'd put him totally off his guard.

He stepped in to disengage, and I stomped the instep of his left foot with my right cleat. He grunted in pain and I took a one-handed grip of my sword, using my left hand to push him away.

The blade of his sword scraped down my arm, but my armor took it. I went back to my two-handed grip in time to block a chop he sent to my knee, another to my head, and another back to that same knee.

I hopped back, and he limped forward, favoring his left foot. I immediately circled to his left, forcing him to pivot on his right to keep facing me. When he tried to advance on his right instead, I hammered at his defense, my sword spinning over my head to rain blows on his head, his legs and into his torso. He blocked them all, but he couldn't do that and advance, and he had a hard time retreating, having led on his right foot.

His sword finally met mine in the air, and he caught my cross guard with his. Leaning his weight on me, he took a step back and tried to pull me off balance as he retreated.

I leapt forward again and landed on his left foot with my right. He grunted again and I pushed him as hard as I could, jumping back from him.

His sword dinged the front of my armor. I left a trail of his blood from my foot.

I didn't offer quarter. I needed to finish this.

I kept circling to his left. He left a red smear on the cobblestones as he pivoted to face me. He worked it out now, trying to come up with a better strategy to come at me. I knew that, given time, he would probably do so.

And I couldn't just rain blows on him. He could probably fight me off and strategize at the same time. I had to go in for the kill while I had the advantage.

I faked for his head, faked for his right foot, faked for his head again and chopped down on the handle of his mace. He returned with a direct stab at my midsection, hoping either to pierce my armor or to force the point of his sword into a seam. I let him push me back with his sword, not knowing if his weapon could do what mine could not. The mace's handle clattered to one side.

I kept out of his reach, and the head of his mace pitched forward, no longer having the weight of its handle to counter-balance it. He stepped to his left and stumbled, his balance thrown off, and I darted in for the kill.

Right for the head – and he blocked me. Then for the leg, and he blocked me. I crossed the guards of our swords and then pushed at him with all of my strength, and he stumbled backwards, his left foot slipping on his own blood. I pulled my sword free and then swung right for his center, raining blows with all of my strength, taking shots that he could block easily.

After the seventh blow, I changed my grip just slightly and brought the sword down right on his hands. Defending your hands is the first thing you learn when you fight. Now I had him off balance and wondering what the hell I might be trying to do. Three fingers flew off and the sword slipped in his grasp.

I knocked the sword aside with a left-handed sweep, then punched him in the face with my right. He staggered, and I punched him again, holding his sword to the side with my sword in my left hand, and again.

Teeth dropped to the ground. I stepped forward, planted my cleat on his right foot, and pushed him.

And immediately slipped on his trail of blood. I fell on my back with a *whack* to my head, seeing stars.

I felt my armor ring as his sword crashed down on it. I felt the Sword of War in my left hand, but I couldn't bring it up to protect myself. My lungs ached from the fall and my sight became a confused blur.

I heard a shout from the crowd. He must be bringing up his sword for the kill.

I brought my left knee up and kicked straight out in what I hoped to be his direction. My cleat connected, with all of the force I could muster behind it.

The crowd moaned. I had a pretty good idea where I caught him. I brought the sword up and, as my vision cleared, saw him stepping back from me in a crouch.

The handle to his mace lay beside me. I threw it at his injured feet to slow him down, then took the chance and rolled to my right, to try to stand, knowing that I left myself totally open to him as I did so.

I heard him fall before I could get back on my feet. He had to have slipped on the handle. When I stood, shaky and my sword still in my left hand, I could see him on his butt, with his left elbow supporting him, and his right hand pointing his sword at me.

You had to admire his skill. Still not beaten, still a threat. I stood outside of the range of his sword and, with two blows, cut his feet off.

Which is what he should have done to me, but he wanted that glorious, killing blow.

He would be every bit as dead as I wanted him in a few minutes.

The crowd moaned again. I'd provided an inglorious end to a defining battle. As I had been taught, you could beat a better swordsman if you kept your wits about you and didn't give up.

I turned to the captain of my Wolf Soldier guard and with a whistle they stormed the gate and took the gate guard. We saw a little resistance, but the city's Duke had just lost by proxy. Technically speaking, they didn't serve him anymore.

The gate flew open and my heavy horse thundered in, trampling the bounty hunter where he lay dying. Yerel stood stunned to one side, his wife and a few kids around him. His eldest boy, probably thirteen by the look of him, looked up at me with hate in his eyes.

I'd gotten awfully used to that look.

***

Duke Jaheff of Uman City sat his throne uncomfortably. I stood beside him, this time as Heir, with the Eldadorian standard to one side of us.

All persons in the gallery bowed low to their liege lord.

"I am going to be really bad at this job," he told me.

"Nah," I said. "Those who can't, teach. Those who are really lost, lead."

He smiled up at me. "You lead a whole nation," he noted.

I looked down at him. "Those who don't watch their tongue, often get to see that organ right in front of them, where it's easier to watch."

He grinned up at me. "Good point, your Highness," he said.

I thought so.

We held court. Some people wanted compensation for the damage they'd suffered during the invasion. We decreed that taxes be lowered to fifteen percent now. That went over big; Yerel had been a hold out to the old ways.

He had a *lot* of soldiers here. He'd been waiting for us; he'd likely just hoped that it would take longer.

The treasury held a bunch of gold, too, although not nearly enough to pay the city's tax burden. I arranged to take a portion now and a portion later. I allowed Yerel to keep a son here for Jaheff to foster, and a daughter here for him to marry. Hopefully he'd learned enough as a court baron to at least tread water until he got the hang of things.

Yerel came with me with his wife, his eldest son, and two more daughters. I couldn't judge him as Heir, but I could take him prisoner as Lupus the Conqueror. It wouldn't be hard to get Glennen liquored up and decree him to be a common, and then I could do with him what I wanted.

I had already promised to foster his son. Yerel didn't seem as concerned about the daughters, and he knew his own fate.

So, after court, I poked around thinking these thoughts and wondering if I would be seeing the Free Legion coming late over the horizon when I found myself back outside of the throne room.

So, for a lark, I walked down a hallway that led from there. It had windows on one side and rooms on the other.

It ended in an octagonal room, with doors leading to different places. One hallway stood to my left.

I followed that one, which had dust on the floor and a groove down the center, leading upward at a slight incline.

This hallway led to a blank wall. Above it, up against the top of the wall, I saw what probably looked to any passerby as nothing more than an interesting design.

But I could read Cheyak, and to me it said, "Outpost V". I knew right then what probably lay on the other side of that blank wall.

And suddenly, it felt really, really good to have an Uman-Chi who had bound himself to my future.

His name was Avek Noir, of the House Noir, in disgrace in Outpost X.

He had been a Viscount. I had no idea what that title meant. I really, really didn't care. All Uman-Chi had titles.

He stood a little over five feet tall – right around Shela's height. His hair hung long down his back and around his shoulders, green in color and wavy. His face seemed more pinched than most Uman-Chi, who had longer faces. His nose pointed more like a beak, his chin was wide and flat and, like all Uman-Chi, his eyes were silver-on-silver. He had sworn on his honor, on his faith in Adriam, the All Father, and on the blood of his sons and daughters for all time, that he would be bound to me and be in my service, were I to give him the opportunity to prove himself again.

When he saw the inscription, he about fainted. It took him a while just to stop sputtering.

"You cannot know –" he began.

"I know exactly what is behind that wall, or should be," I said. "I know that it will be warded with a trap that shoots poison darts that will slowly kill whomever they hit.

"And I know that this city is built on the ruins of Outpost V."

"How is this possible?" he asked me. I knew I couldn't tell him the theory of how some Outposts had been covered in The Blast. I could, however, explain to him how it happened in my world.

"Over centuries, dirt tends to collect in something as convenient as a city," I said. "Especially an abandoned one. You can bet that, when the first Uman settlers came here, they found the palace and half of the wall, and built their city on top of landmarks that looked like stone floors but where in fact stone ceilings."

"But the walls of Outpost IX are twice this high," he said.

"I am sure that, were we to dig deep enough, we would find that there is more to those walls than meets the eye, and that this palace had, at one time, stood on a hill."

He nodded. "We theorize that the royal palace at Outpost IX had been built on a hill, but that the Uman-Chi had slowly converted the hill as they needed more space."

"Ready to look behind that wall?" I asked him.

He nodded.

First, he looked for the Cheyak wards, which we knew were there. That turned out to our benefit, because they were clever and, on first pass, appeared to be gone. Had we believed that, then we would have had the bones in our bodies liquefied over the next month. It took until his third attempt to find the wards that he discovered and to destroy them.

Then came the effort of taking down the wall. That was a big deal, because a palace runs on intrigue, and the moment we sent a building crew in here, there would be a bevy of people wondering why. Instead he spent three days devising a spell that would dismantle the wall and block the noise when it crumbled.

In that time my riders returned, and with no sign of the Free Legion. I sent a fast rider to our camp on the Plains of Angador to find out what had happened to my allies.

On the fifth day of the occupation of Uman City, Avek and I watched the wall deteriorate and two gigantic metal doors revealed.

"They probably covered them because of the ward," Avek told me. "The stones themselves were harmless, but touching the doors is lethal."

I bravely allowed him to push one open. He did so, and revealed a room stacked with moldering tapestries, rusted armor, and pitted swords. There were old, ruined paintings and a smell that said that a millennium had passed with no fresh air coming in here.

I saw a healthy stack of gold bars, of course. Not Outpost X healthy, but good enough to make paupers into princes.

Or disgraced Uman-Chi into favorites again. And that favorite would owe me everything, and be honor bound to remember it for as long as an Uman-Chi lives, which is a mighty long time.

I looked at Avek, he looked at me. He smiled, his silver-on-silver eyes flashing.

"I think things just got brighter for the folks at Outpost IX," I said.

Ancenon would regret blowing me off.

Chapter Seven

Flips and Flops

We saw the air temperature rise a bit during the month of Weather. We marched long days. I felt certain it would rain, and I didn't want the whole army catching pneumonia and being useless to me for two weeks.

Avek had left. He had taken a boat from the frozen wharves of Uman City to the Silent Isle, with 200 mercenary soldiers who had sworn him fealty, and 30 bars of gold.

There would be no fire bond between him and I. I already had his fealty, and I had faith he wouldn't break it. Not that I thought that he held me in any high regard or felt an extraordinary sense of loyalty, but that he had sworn it to his god, and I'd shown a real propensity for making his life better.

At the very least he would wait the relatively short period of time that is a Man's life before he decided that his debt had been paid and forget the Conqueror in favor of the glory of revealing Outpost V.

I wondered now how many cities on Fovea were Outposts. Not Steel City, I had been all through there, and it didn't come close. Not Eldador the Port. Waypoint had me thinking, and I hadn't seen enough of any other cities to say.

What if every Outpost held a treasure trove? There could be thousands of gold bars for me to find, if I could just locate them.

And who even said that all of them were occupied?

"You think too much," Two Spears informed me.

I smiled, lowering my head, seeing Blizzard's mane. I rode without thinking about it anymore. I moved with Blizzard and thought my thoughts, and planned my plans, and missed my girls more than I would have guessed possible.

Lee's smile filled my thoughts, even while I plotted out the Outposts, my enemies and my next move.

"Planning something terrible to do to my poor sister?" he taunted me, reading my mind.

"Been over a month, my friend," I told him. "I'm more worried about what she will do to me."

"We raise our women hungry," he said, and punched my armor. "If you fail to feed them, then they will bite."

"Tell me about it," I commented. Bite, scratch, all manner of horrible things.

"I did just tell you about it," he said. "You want to hear more?"

I laughed. Two Spears brooked no melancholy. He went through life as a force of nature.

"No," I told him. "You should be thinking of the girls in your harem, and which one of them you are going make your woman."

Two Spears laughed. "I think not, White Wolf," he said. "I will have an Andaron when I marry, or I will marry not at all."

"That's going to make some girls cry," I said. I wanted to say 'break some hearts,' but caught myself. It would take too long to explain.

"Women cry," he said. "What can a man do?"

Thinking of it, he could do a lot.

The rain started when we were ready to make camp outside of Thera. We were in the outlying villages that surrounded the main city, where men and women who could not afford to live in the city made small farms and scratched out a living, in hope of being able to trade their produce at the prices that the larger city brought.

I made the decision that we would march for four more hours in the dark, and be inside the city exhausted, rather than make a wet camp and wake up stiff.

I didn't get so much as a flicker from the men. I don't think that anyone liked a wet camp. If you weren't going to be able to sleep, you might as well be walking.

While we traveled, I thought, "A year ago, I would have put it to a vote." I knew now that they would have no respect for that. A vote in an army guaranteed that you had two sides angry at each other. It would breed dissention and it would have been my fault, and every last one of them would have known it.

I fought alongside my men, and they loved me for it. I paid them generously, and they loved me for that, too. I knew when to push them and when to be hard on them.

I didn't ask their opinion, because I ran an army, not a proletariat. If they didn't like it, they could do their time with me and bail.

The rain kept coming, and it slowed us. The sun rose just as we dragged ourselves into the coliseum, now the Wolf Soldiers' barracks. Men fell into their lean-tos and tents, whatever homes they made for themselves here, leaving watch to the reserves that I had left in Thera.

I wanted nothing more than to join them, but I didn't have it that easy. I had a nation to put out of my mind, and a duchy, before I got to sleep.

Shela met me in the stables as I brushed down an exhausted and wet Blizzard. I had the stable boy mixing some hot mash for a feed bag, to open up his sinuses and prevent him from catching a worse cold, if he had one already. Teams of stable hands were rubbing down horses with linens and stoking coal fires.

She flew across the dirt and hay into my arms, her lips all over my face. "I missed you, I missed you," she told me. "I cried myself to sleep every night."

"You did?" I said. "Were there ticks in the bed?"

She punched my armor and then kicked me. "I am told there was a bounty hunter," she said.

I nodded. "He wasn't much," I said.

She grabbed the top ridge of my breastplate and pulled my lips down to hers. After a she gave my face a good covering, she smacked me, hard.

"Do you see why you need me?" she demanded, her eyes burning into mine. "Do you see why you can't go out alone?"

I straightened up. There were tears in her eyes. I remembered the time in Conflu, where Ancenon had watched Thorn, Nantar and I in our mad dash through the forest.

It hadn't even occurred to me until know. She had seen the whole thing, without knowing my strategy.

She had seen me fall in battle.

I stroked her hair, and held her cheek, and let a few tears fall into my palm.

"You know you can't bring Lee into a battle," I said. "And you know that you can't leave her alone."

"I don't want to hear your *logic*, White Wolf," she said through gritted teeth. "I want to hear you telling me you love me and that I'll be by your side where I belong."

"I love you, Shela," I said. "And you know already that you belong at my side."

She hugged me through my armor. "It doesn't mean I don't still need to hear it."

I held her, exhausted on my feet, and let her have my love and my energy until she took her fill and released me.

"You're up early," she commented, taking the brush from me. She started working on Blizzard's mane. He would tolerate her now, barely. The groom was terrified of him. The blacksmith seemed ambivalent, but never even cleaned his hooves without chaining him. He had kicked his way out of a stall, slaughtered a gelding, bitten every single member of the stable staff, and crushed one. I put him up and brushed him as a kindness to them. The stable boy shouldn't earn combat pay.

"Actually, I'm up late," I told her. "It started to rain, so I marched them through the night."

She nodded. "You must be tired. Shall I bathe you?"

I shook my head. "You'll put me to sleep," I said. "What is urgent and what can wait?"

She thought for a moment. "The Oligarchs of Thera have handled everything here, and are in constant contact with the Oligarchs of Eldador. Glennen killed a butler who asked him if he had had enough mead."

I winced. Glennen was getting worse fast.

"We stopped an attempt to break into the palace," she continued. "They got as far as our room. I think they were looking for me."

I grinned. "That would have been unfortunate for them."

She smiled. "I don't kill *everyone* I meet, you know," she said.

"Do, too."

"Do *not*!"

"Did they catch the invader?"

"No," she sighed. "You have a warrior there named 'J'her', who's taken charge of the palace security, and he's supposed to be attending to it."

I nodded. She put the brush up and looked into my face, deep into my eyes.

"I think you can meet with your own Oligarchs and sleep," she said. "You are of no use to anyone exhausted. I know that Ann has questions for you, so probably the others do, as well."

"Go summon them to our chamber," I said. "And call for a hot meal. I'm starved. Something heavy so I'll sleep."

She kissed me and left. I had one thing to do for her before I went to the meeting, but it wouldn't take long.

***

I'd had this place built for me, and I'd done it with a few things in mind. One of them was that it would house a portal to Outpost X.

While I'd been in Eldador the Port, D'gattis was supposed to come here, find a room I'd set aside, and create that portal. The room was a little utility place made of stone, adjacent both to the main house and the stables. You could walk through it and not think twice.

You could be running away from someone and just disappear, if you knew how to kick the ward off.

I closed Blizzard up in his stall and I dragged myself to the little stone room. A few bridles hung on the walls; there were cobwebs in the corners at the ceiling. Feed stands with metal linings stood to one side. The linings made them rat-proof.

I pushed aside the bridles and found a drawing in the wall six inches wide. To anyone else it would look like a doodle by a bored child.

I smiled to myself. D'gattis might not like me anymore, but he was a man of his word.

A full stomach always made me sleepy. Eggs, oatcakes, strips of meat with heavy syrup and strong ale for breakfast had me yawning and belching at the same time. Shela had embarked on a mission.

Ann, Def and Thebinaar sat with Shela, Lee and I around the table in my room. Def had insisted on two tellings of the battle with the bounty hunter, getting angrier and angrier in the process.

"You should be dead, your Grace," he told me. "Dead, like an apple with a knife –"

"Def!" Ann snarled at him. Her eyes shifted between him and Shela. "I think the point is that he is *not* dead."

"I am glad he isn't dead," Thebinaar said, in his flat, accountant way. "I had a hard enough time training him right."

It came as close to humor as I'd ever heard from him.

"You didn't spend hours sparring with him," Def said. He looked at me in disgust. "I would ask what you were thinking, but I know what you were thinking. Don't think that way anymore."

"He would have beaten me in a fair fight," I said.

"You underrate yourself," Def spat. "A warrior green enough to fall for *that*, you could have beaten him."

"Let's just be thankful that we still have him," Shela said.

Def finally got the idea and contented himself with fuming. I had something else to grab his attention.

I went to my pack, which I had brought to my room, hanging with my armor and my sword. I pulled a package wrapped in oilcloth from it, not that it needed to be. I laid it on the table and sat back down.

"A present?" Ann asked.

"Open it," I said.

She did. She saw a bar of gold, with an insignia stamped into it.

"Impressive," Thebinaar said. "That looks like the seal of the Angron Aurelias, but it's different. Where did you get this?"

"Outpost V," I said.

"There is no Outpost V," Ann told me frankly.

"That's what I thought, until I took that from its unlooted treasury."

Shela reached out and gripped my arm. I knew that no one could listen in on us here. Shela had warded the bedroom even more heavily than the war room.

"White Wolf," she said. "Outpost V?"

I nodded. She knew we couldn't talk about Outpost X, but this was another issue."

"The myth of Outpost X," said Def, "is that it is packed with Cheyak gold and is hidden in Conflu. Are you telling me that the lost Outpost is V, not X, and that it is not in Conflu at all?"

"I cannot speak to Outpost X," I said, truthfully. I would explode or catch on fire or something. "But Outpost V is in Eldador, and it is called Uman City by you and me."

They were all quiet.

"That is impossible," Ann said, ever the pragmatist.

Def reached out and hefted the gold bar. "I think that it is not," he said.

Thebinaar nodded. "I know that everything makes sense after it happens," he said. "But this makes sense to me."

"It does?" Shela asked him.

He nodded. We were all looking at him. "There would have to be more Outposts, because there is VII and IX. Most people think that they are underneath Tren Bay, but that makes no sense.

"In fact, this makes me think that Outpost VII is *not* an Outpost at all, and a lot of other people think that, too."

"They do?" I said. I didn't. Ancenon had never said anything about it.

"It is too close to Outpost IX," he said. "I think the survivors of the Blast erected Outpost VII because they feared Outpost IX."

That made sense on every level.

"I have to see it," Ann said.

"We all do," Thebinaar said.

"Not me," Def said, shaking his head. "I have to totally repeat his swordsmanship training."

I groaned.

"Can you wait here while we go?" Ann asked.

"No," I said. "You remember, drunken king, enemies everywhere, assassination attempt on *me*? Not a good time for a vacation."

"It is a fact finding mission," Ann said.

"I am so sorry I taught you that term," I said.

"Too late to undo it," Thebinaar said. "You have to let us go, your Grace."

"I will let you go," I said. "But I cannot let you go for at least a month."

"I can wait a month," said Thebinaar.

"Good," Ann said. "While you wait, I will go."

"You will *not*," I said. I was getting frustrated. They sensed it, and were quiet for a moment.

"I will go in a month, and stay a week, and then Thebinaar will go, and then Def," Ann said finally.

I nodded. My eyes were full of sand and they knew it. I took the easy way out

"Anything else?" I asked.

They shook their heads. I didn't even wait for them to leave before I crawled into my bed between the thick, cool quilts. They filed out, Shela thanking them, as I closed my eyes and descended blissfully into dark rest.

It felt like a second later that I awoke to Shela stroking my hair, but now the room had gone dark. A candle flickered in a corner.

"White Wolf?" she said.

"Mmmmmmmph," I answered her, rolling stiff onto my back, my head like a brick. I must have caught something in the rain.

"You are called to Eldador," she said.

"There's a surprise," I said, leaving my eyes closed. "Did Glennen kill someone?"

She held my chin; her fingers cool on my skin. I felt her lips on my forehead, my cheek, and on my lips.

"No, my husband, my master," she said. "The Free Legion has laid siege to the city, under the employ of Trenbon."

Ancenon had *really* pissed me off.

According to fast riders from the outlying cities, there were eight thousand infantry and another two thousand horse on the battlefield outside of Eldador the port, and ten Trenboni Tech Ships at anchor outside the city to prevent relief. The entire Free Legion had come, with the exception of me.

I should have known better than to ignore the juggernaut of our mercenary army once I'd set it in motion. It had always been a matter of time before I took or lost control of it, and it looked like the latter.

Had I been the monarch of Eldador, then I doubt they would have moved against me. However, I was the Heir. That made Eldador fair game.

"We know that Rennin and Groff will stand with you, if you march," Ann told me. "I can have their armies in motion in a month's time."

"They will have the city in a month's time," I said. "They won't be content to siege for long. D'gattis isn't that patient, neither is Ancenon, and I doubt that Outpost IX has paid enough for an extended stay. They will first try to provoke the gate guard, then they'll try to call out Glennen personally, and odds are he'll put on armor and lead his forces out of the gate."

"The Free Legion has two hundred squads with Wolf Soldier Training," Ann said. "And their horses are heavy lancers like our own."

"Wolf Soldiers man the palace guard, and Wolf Soldiers will have to come to lift the siege," I said. Shela gripped my upper arm. "They are counting on the promise that I made, that I wouldn't do just that."

"Arath would love to show that he is superior to you in battle," Shela said. "He never really accepted your victory at Katarran, or the credit you received in the Battle of Tamaran Glen."

Another thing I would have been wise to consider.

"We would have to empty the reserves," Ann said. Def nodded, adding, "We have two thousand Uman militia here whom we can conscript to man the walls of Thera. We wouldn't be able to invade anyone, but it would take a sizeable force to be a threat to us. Even if you were engaged, we could hold the city for a week."

"Leaving Thera wide open like that would hurt everything," I said.

"As would losing the capital," Thebinaar said, as matter of fact as he could be. "Sack Eldador and kill the King while we do nothing and no one will have faith in Lupus the Conqueror."

That was an indisputable fact.

And it left only one thing to do.

With Shela beside me, I peered into an orb, similar to a 'crystal ball,' and saw Two Speers at the head of 1,500 heavy horse and 5,000 warriors in Wolf Soldier uniforms, marching in smart order in my squads of ten.

I couldn't attack the Free Legion. My men had made no such agreement.

Beside Two Spears, a big man in my armor rode an even bigger, white horse. He wore an amulet to protect him from magic attack, and this would shield him from magical seeing as well. No one knew my real name, and that meant no magic could find me.

A black-haired girl rode near the center of army in a wagon, an Andaron plains witch – wife to an Andaron Wolf Soldier. She was no Shela, she didn't come close, but she *looked* enough like Shela to convince anyone who couldn't actually put their hands on her.

The army marched onto the plains outside of Outpost IX, where the Free Legion had been lobbing rocks over the walls in an effort to draw the army out. Ancenon and D'gattis had managed to neutralize any magical attack from the city, and the gates stayed shut.

Yesterday King Angron Aurelias had announced the adoption of Avek as his favorite son, and the rejuvenation project of Outpost IX at his expense. The Noir's were back in favor at Trenbon.

Ancenon attempted to balance the scales now. Raining vengeance on Eldador would earn him quite a coupe among his people. He would be welcomed back as a hero.

By now, he knew that 2,000 from Steel City blocked his path back to the Plains of Angador, and another 2,000 from Andurin would be in place in another week to support my Wolf Soldiers. Outnumbered or not, when my Wolf Soldiers engaged him, and the city garrison swarmed out in support, that didn't leave a lot of room for Ancenon to move.

If he didn't see that, then Arath would. As soon as they caught site of the Free Legion, the heavy horse lowered their lances and charged, not at the Free Legion, but at the gates. The man on the white stallion led them. The infantry marched double-time behind the van, spreading in a wide arc out of range of the Free Legion's archers, to take up position with the horse. If the Free Legion tried to take the horse, they would double back to the infantry and play cat and mouse around their shields and pikes, preventing a straight charge and tiring out the mounts and the men.

Heavy lancers were good for long, sweeping charges, but not wheeling back and forth around pikemen and archers.

The Free Legion mobilized, but didn't charge. Their troops trained as squads marshaled up as a first wave, with the rest of the warriors forming up behind them as reserves. The horse stood stock-still on the right side, lances up, ready to attack or repel.

My horse took up their positions outside of the gates. To their left, my infantry formed up in a checkerboard of squads, ready to fight. On the wall, archers and ballistae made ready to support our side if we should either charge or repel.

The Free Legion, having done what they were there to do, picked up, turned tail, and ran. They would have no fear of Rennin's two thousand, and Groff would never catch them.

Ann burst into my war room, her face red from running. Her age and weight didn't make sprinting through the halls very easy.

"We're under attack!" she screamed.

***

I stood at the walls of Thera. There were already outlying farms burning on the horizon. An army of Confluni, 30,000 strong, marched in five columns toward me.

They weren't emulating Wolf Soldier training, which is what I had feared. They always marched this way. At some point in their history they had decided that this was the best way to move a large army and it is what they did.

They wore leather armor and leather caps. They carried long, curved swords or triple-curved bows. They wore round, wooden shields, barely more than a target but less cumbersome than ours, over their backs.

We had beaten them before, but under different circumstances.

"If we wait behind the gates, they'll ravage the peasants and kill thousands," Def said, "and then we'll have to come out and fight them anyway.

"Better to do it now."

I agreed.

Four thousand men in the uniform of the Theran militia double-time marched out through the city gates. Our walls weren't much anyway, our gate little more than a framed double-door. Thera hadn't ever been intended to be a hard point for an invasion.

Men and women stood in a mass. They had the large shields, the swords, the pikes of Wolf Soldiers, but they did what militia did – showed up when they had to, to die on their feet rather than in their beds.

"Those are some terrible odds," Ann said.

I nodded. She would have the reserves: 1,000 warriors inside of the city. We'd sent riders to call for another thousand Aschire archers to support the city, but the ride alone could take more than a week.

I took her forearm in mine, and then turned to Shela. She would stay right here, in the one, flat-topped tower on our wall. She and her acolytes would be our magic. The Confluni weren't great Wizards. Ours were.

"You stay alive," I said to her. "We are expendable, you are not."

She looked into my eyes. I saw no point arguing with her. She had said it before: I could beat her to death for disobeying me, so long as I lived to do it. An Andaron woman, Shela's first concern remained for her man.

She kissed me, and touched my chest. We would fight together again, she and I. We had done it before.

I still had some surprises.

The Confluni saw our army pouring out through the city gates and stopped wasting time burning huts and villages. They had something to hold their attention now.

They marched smartly from the outlying fields to outside of the walls, then five columns lined up as five rows to face us. The front would charge with short spears. The three rows after that had shields and swords. The last row had their archers ready. I frowned and nodded appreciatively – they would probably lose the first wave, but we would be in a tangle by the time they were through with us and the archers would pin cushion us before and after, keeping us from reforming before the next wave engaged.

No wonder the Confluni had such a reputation. A strategy like this would even give my Wolf Soldiers pause.

I imagined they felt very confident against the militia.

Commanders customarily make a speech to their men before they fought. I didn't do it much with the Wolf Soldiers. They didn't need any inspiration to kill. Militia would be quaking in their boots and need some bracing words. I kicked Blizzard's ribs and directed him between their approaching army and ours, huddled against the city walls.

"Today," I bellowed to them, as many looked up in surprise, "you fight for your homes. You fight for your wives, your husbands, your sons, and your daughters. You fight for the Lady Shela and Princess Lee. You fight for me, and my person, and the honor of the city of Thera, where you live.

"The Confluni come here, because they think that no one can stop them. They see militia, and think you are nothing. They come to spill your guts, to rape your wives, and to take your daughters away in chains.

"As you love them, as you love me, as you love Thera, take a firm grip on your swords and prove them wrong."

The troops answered me with a 'Rah'. Another answered us from across the battlefield, where loose earth from a fallow field separated us from our enemy. It had been raining, the ground turned muddy and it pulled at our feet.

I preferred this for training my Wolf Soldiers. The solider that could trot across this could sprint across the hard-packed soil of an actual battlefield.

I dismounted and gave Blizzard's reins to my groom. The stallion reared in anger. He knew the smell of a battle, he knew where he belonged when I waded into one, but he made too big a target for the archers and a charge of one wouldn't change anything, much as it had in the past. I took my place with the men and women of the militia, among the mob, an unfamiliar shield on my arm.

"Their archers are pulling back," one of my captains said.

"Shields!" I roared.

My order echoed up and down the line. Those who had them raised their great shields and the rest crouched beside those men and women. As luck would have it, we formed a ragged line that gave protection to all of us. I heard a few groans, but as the arrows fell deadly amongst us, they found the wall, and the ground, and then shields, but not very many of the troops.

A quick peek showed their spearmen had begun their charge beneath another flight of arrows. They had less than three hundred yards to go – quite a task for men in armor. But then, they were just going to drive us back against the wall, to be slaughtered by more arrows and their first wave of swordsmen.

"Hold formations!" I shouted. My captains echoed me, and others echoed them. The troops crouched tighter behind the shields. When the next flight of arrows fell I heard fewer cries of pain, over a sound like hail falling on roofs in a small town.

I would have expected another flight, but they probably didn't see the point in wasting the arrows. Let the spearmen throw us into a mess, then make better use of their archers as the second wave came.

The spearmen were less than thirty feet away.

It was time.

"Formations!" I bellowed, my captains repeating my words. "Repel invaders!"

With the precision of a machine, my 'militia' fell into squads of ten, four shields in front, three swordsmen behind them, and three pikemen behind them. A wall of shields, five feet high and 900 hardened warriors across snapped into place in front of the faces of 6,000 unsuspecting spearmen.

They crashed against our wall, held by our shield men, and skewered by our pikes. As they fell back, our swordsmen ripped into them as our front line advanced.

Some threw aside the coverings of militia to reveal the infamous wolves' head tabard and heavy armor of the Wolf Soldier pack. As a man, with no prompting from me, they shouted, "Vivat Mordetur!" in the old language of Men.

This wasn't rocket science. Ancenon wasn't stupid. He knew he couldn't attack me, and he knew I wouldn't attack him. We both knew that if he marched to Eldador, I would do just what I did: put my body between him and his goal. He would have to break away before my allies ripped him apart.

Anyone who hired him had to know that he and I wouldn't fight, and if they didn't then Ancenon would certainly tell them.

So the goal couldn't be Eldador the Port. The goal had to be whatever they wanted me to march from and leave unprotected. The goal had to be Thera.

So I dressed the militia and as many civilians as wanted money in a lighter rendition of the Wolf Soldier armor, and sent the lancers to protect them on the trip to and from Eldador. Then I dressed my Wolf Soldiers as militia here. No one knew how successful a call to the militia would be, so a full strength of Wolf Soldiers could be disguised.

"Forward!" I shouted. My captains echoed me. From behind me, Aschire archers rose up on our walls and shot arrows over our heads into the ranks of our confused enemies. I'd called for them the morning after I heard of the attack on the capitol, asking them to move at night with no cook fires, practically invisible to those watching the city.

Just another surprise for the Confluni on their new bad day.

With a ragged shout their second wave advanced, 5,000 strong, and took the teeth of our archers' assault. They fell in droves and we picked up the speed of our advance. We engaged them less than 100 feet from their reserves, rendering their archers useless. Their swordsmen ripped ineffectively into our shields and then felt our swords and pikes. Like a wisp of smoke laced with red blood, they evaporated before our advance, leaving us less than 60% of their army to face with almost no losses of our own.

The next wave advanced through a hailstorm of arrows, most of them not making it to our front line. We stomped through them and advanced on what remained of their army.

At that point their confidence started to waver under the barrage of arrows and the impending doom of our advance. If I had kept my heavy horse, I would have taken them from behind by now. Instead Shela finally decided that there would be no magic to counter and whipped a storm of fireballs into their midst. They scattered as their commanders swore at them and tried to whip them back into the fight, some with actual whips. My troops in advance engaged the clusters that remained, breaking into squads to chase down the scattered pockets of resistance.

I and my personal guard of fifty broke off from the main force in search of some of their commanders. At this point in the battle the captains would communicate back to me with runners, mostly kids who followed the army for food. Some of the captains were already emerging as being the ones who knew my mind and who could be relied upon for advice if they were closer, or whom I would tell to coordinate a force of other captains.

These would be my majors in the next evolution, J'her among them.

I homed in on ten men each with a single lock of hair, dressed in robes rather than armor, standing back from the rest. They realized that I had singled them out as I realized the same thing myself.

One raised his hand, energy dripping from it, and immediately fell flat on his back, thanks to Shela or one of her apprentices. The others knelt with their hands behind their heads. With their surrender most of the survivors of the battle on their side followed suit.

They'd been surprised by my Wolf Soldiers, now I found myself in control of thousands of prisoners. We took the men into custody, the leaders coming with me, the rest being stripped naked in the cold air of the early month of Earth. Some were bound with chain, some with rope, and some with their own clothes. I assigned six captains and their squads to take the prisoners, another five to put down the wounded on their side, and another five to collect our own wounded and see to their treatment. The rest went to guard duty, either into the outlying farms to check on peasants and look for deserters, or to man the wall in case their reserves were more extensive than we had seen.

We had gotten off lucky. I had guessed at a plot within a plot. I still had Ancenon to deal with – but he had probably realized by now that he had mortgaged his future in Trenbon for his position in the Free Legion. It would have gained him nothing to attack the 'Wolf Soldiers' even if he knew of my deception, but someone had been hard at work to remove me from the equation, and I needed to know whom.

***

There were prisons in my mansion in Thera, but not enough for thousands. My prisoners were now bound shivering in the center of the coliseum where the Wolf Soldiers billeted. They in turn had moved their residences back closer to its walls. Their leaders sat with me in my War Room, where they looked with interest at the table, the walls and the twenty Wolf Soldiers assigned to make sure they were cooperative. The Confluni here, as outside, were naked, more to intimidate them than because I feared hidden weapons.

It didn't seem to inspire much fear.

"There are rules for treating prisoners of war," one said to me. They had refused to give their names or any information.

"I know," I said. "The Confluni are notorious for breaking them."

He smirked, probably believing that I wouldn't do what his nation had become notorious for.

"I need your names," I said, "your cities, and to know who sent you."

"We demand to see a representative of the Fovean High Council," the same one said. He seemed an older man, by the wrinkles in his face, the grey in his one long lock of hair. The others clearly deferred to him.

"Let's be clear," I said. "I am Lupus the Conqueror, Duke of Thera and Heir to the Eldadorian throne. This is Shela, my woman, who is called the Bitch of Eldador."

Shela shot me a look, but she knew my mind.

"You are my prisoners after you invaded my home," I continued, looking him in the eye. "You aren't going to be alive for much longer."

I let that sink in. The other men looked sideways at each other, trying to keep their composure.

"How you die depends on what you can tell me, but rest assured, you *will* tell me what I want to know from you."

Chapter Eight

Aristocracy

We lost less than 100 men in the defense of Thera. It didn't surprise me. In his conquest of Gaul, Julius Caesar attacked as many as 300,000 with 35,000 and routed his enemies. In his worst defeats, taken totally unawares, he lost less than 1,000. Training in warfare is everything.

In the United States, it took tens of thousands of dollars to train one of me. Reactor Operators who controlled the multi-hundred-mega-watt nuclear reactors and maintained the systems could cost over one hundred thousand dollars to train individually. They took two years to educate and another six months in the fleet to qualify. Those men could step in and run the whole engine room if they had to.

The value in the training of a warrior is seen when you put him or her against someone who isn't trained.

Here they handed out swords and shields, pointed warriors in the right direction (or close to it) and hoped for the best.

The Confluni had done that, and now paid the price for it.

Five were still alive. One's skin smoldered. I hadn't taken out the leader, but removing him in order to see if that made the others bolder looked like my best bet.

"You will get nothing from us," he warned me.

"Not from you," I told him. "With that I agree. That makes you useless to me."

Shela raised her hand to him. His long lock of hair fell onto the table before him with a good chunk of the skin from his scalp.

He gripped his head, looked into my eyes.

"This is forbidden," he told me.

I held up my hand to stop Shela. "You would like an alternative?"

He lowered his hands to the table, brushed the lock from in front of him. Clearly he felt braver with other lives than with his own.

"I want my body sent back to Conflu," he said, "and you will offer my men the option to join you before you execute them."

"I think not," Def said. Ann and Thebinaar hadn't bothered to stay. Someone had to run the city. "How could we trust them?"

"How can you trust anyone who joins your number?" he asked. "Make them swear it, or kill them if they refuse. You have Confluni in your ranks. Our honor is no different than anyone else's."

"And what can you tell me?"

His compatriots stayed quiet, looking down. Other than to scream in pain, they hadn't reacted to me at all. This one did the talking. It made me curious to see what they did when I'd removed him.

"I can tell you that you are the most hated man on Fovea right now," he said. "And that my emperor, as well as the king of Trenbon, is terrified that you are going to take control of Eldador. They sent me here to disgrace you, and to get you to initiate a war with Conflu."

"What?" I said. I hadn't considered that at all. I had assumed they wanted Lee, the second part of the plan I had guessed at with the Bounty Hunter.

"It makes sense," Def said. "You were attacked by Trenbon, and you attacked Outpost IX. You are attacked by Conflu; they assume that you will attack Conflu in return."

"Only you would be ready with everything you had," I said. "You would catch me in a trap and crush me."

He nodded. "I think you will still attack," he said. "You are arrogant, so I think that you will try to take us on and beat us."

I had to smile. That sounded like what I would do. It made more sense than sitting here and waiting for the next attack, anyway.

"Who is your inside man?" I asked him.

"My what?"

Def looked nervous. I had the Sword of War over my shoulder. I moved as nonchalantly as I could to put him on my left, so that when I drew I could stab without risking him pinning down my sword arm. If I didn't get him, I could hold him until the Wolf Soldier guards could.

"Who do you have working for you, who is working for me?" I asked.

"Ah," he said. "You think we have a spy."

"If you didn't," I said, "how would you know which of your cities I would attack."

He smirked to himself, looked at his men, then at me.

"You will ship my remains back to Conflu?" he said.

"If you tell me," I said. "If you lie, she will know."

"On your honor?" he asked me, looking into his eyes.

"On my honor," I said.

"I know of one only, a Wolf Soldier called 'Klem.' But I am sure there are more."

I looked at Shela, she looked at me. We recognized the former Earl of Thera's name, and he had disappeared when I took his Earldom.

It wasn't an uncommon name, but I had met all of the Wolf Soldiers, and I hadn't let in that Klem. However, families here tended to keep reusing names, and I hadn't met his family.

Shela nodded – he didn't lie. I could find Klem.

I drew my sword, took a two-handed grip on the hilt, and lopped his head off. It bounced across the table onto the floor. His body slumped into the chair, then down under the table, pumping blood into a puddle around the chair.

His men looked nervous, my Wolf Soldiers didn't flicker. It might as well not have happened.

"Who is next in command?" I asked them.

***

By the morning, they were all dead. I didn't learn much, other than how much a mess like that pissed off the house staff.

I had the Dorkan Wizards looking for this Klem. I'd instructed them to be discreet. Once I found him, I might need to watch him and see what he did.

I met with the Confluni individually. They were pragmatic, if nothing else. Of just under 2,000 survivors, 1,600 were ready to join the team, and only 300 of them were lying about it. That added 700 bodies to Tren Bay and a healthy 1,300 to my Wolf Soldiers.

It took another day for fast riders to let me know that the army approached from the capitol. Two days after that, Rennin informed me that he planned to let the Free Legion go back to the Plains of Angador. In that time, I assembled the Wolf Soldier infantry, now over 6,000 strong in addition to what I'd left at the capitol, and promoted six captains to the rank of Major. Each captain had, plus or minus, a 'millennium.' A millennium included a thousand warriors under the Major, controlled by four captains, 20 lieutenants and 100 sergeants who fought as a member of their group of ten.

This took some rearranging of the command structure, but it would pay off. I could now, through six Wolf Soldiers, coordinate my army down to the last man. As we trained on the field, marching on the battleground where the birds still fed on the remains of Confluni soldiers, we could switch the positions of any two squads, any two millennia, or change their marching orders. The Confluni were easily adaptable to our marching style and adopted our structure quickly. Those I spoke with noted that their own people had nothing like this, and were nowhere near it.

A week later our militia returned to their burned homes and their buried and unburied dead. I had taken care of my own casualties and the populace had robbed the bodies of the Confluni on the first day. Most of the Confluni dead found their way into the bay, and some were buried for convenience or for their value in fertilizer. I broke down the heavy horse into a full millennium and a half, which would grow as we got more horses and more men. The Confluni were not equestrians and ninety percent of our horse, both mounts and riders, were Andaron. Two Spears, of course, had the full millennium.

He sat with Shela, Anne, Thebinaar and Def and I as we planned out our next move.

"Next week, I want to go to Uman City," Ann said. I nodded.

"I got a look at Glennen, your King," Two Spears said. "And he is a drunk and a fool. I smelled the urine on him as he thanked me for relieving the siege. One of the old men who tend him told me to tell you that he tried to order the army to attack the Free Legion soldiers, and was barely restrained."

"How did they stop him?" Def asked. Glennen, drunk or sober, was King. If he wanted to attack, the army attacked.

"Your man, an Uman named, J'her, said they plied him with strong drink until he passed out," Two Spears said. "Then when he awoke they plied him again."

What an ending for so vital a man.

Two Spears looked me right in the eye. "If you plan to replace him, White Wolf, then you need to be there now. If I were my father, then the Long Manes would sack Eldador the Port tomorrow, and expect to succeed."

I agreed. Ancenon probably could have had the city any time he wanted it. I wanted to go to the Plains of Angador and talk to the members of the Free Legion, but I had no time, and the next month belonged to War. They would be on their campaigns soon.

The time had come to bring the Free Legion to me.

***

I appointed Two Spears the Regent for Lee in Thera, giving him the ability to run the city in my absence. Five of my majors were left in the city under his command. Two more, the one in charge of the smaller millennium of horse and an infantry division, came with Shela and me to Eldador. This time we couldn't spare the horses, and took ten days in quick march to get there. It rained almost every day and it made the journey miserable.

Before I left I dispatched riders to the Plains of Angador under the flag of Eldador, commanding the Free Legion to present themselves, by order of the Heir, to the palace in Eldador, or to vacate the plains of Angador forthwith. In case Ancenon decided to call my bluff, I left instruction with Rennin to mobilize. He wouldn't take on the Free Legion – they would destroy him. He would instead establish an Eldadorian duchy on the plains of Angador when they left and people it.

I arrived in Eldador on the third day of War, to the news that the city of Outpost IX had begun full reconstruction, including new gates even more grand than the originals.

Glennen greeted us as we marched into the palace courtyard, unshaved and stinking of pee and vomit and stale booze. Just to be in his presence, even in the open air, had become an act of will, to which he seemed oblivious. He spent his days bleary-eyed, drunk and unable to focus.

His kids were in hell. I met with them and Shela as we set up in our rooms in the palace.

"He kissed me on the mouth," Alekennen complained, and justifiably so. I had heard that there could be no trusting Glennen around any female now. His oldest daughter was 13 and a woman by the standards of Men. "And he keeps telling me the things I have to do with men. I can't hear that from my father."

"Nor I," Tartan, his oldest son said. He was a copy of his mother, with the glowing features, slim bone structure and soft eyes. He stood tall like his father, a gentle giant, but one who had been slapped on the back too many times.

"If he isn't calling me a coward for not dueling him, he is telling others I'm a hero and challenging them for me."

I shook my head. "Guys, you have to know that it isn't your father, it's the drink that is doing these things."

Terran, his youngest and a boy, who should be thinking of his father as a god at his age, said, "You mean he has a haint?"

"No, Terran," Shela said. "No demon possesses him. He has the yellow sickness that those who drink sometimes have. He cannot help himself or what he does."

"Why doesn't he just stop drinking?" Alekennen asked. "I mean, he has to know it's ruining everything."

"No," I told her. "He doesn't know. The drink ruins his thinking, and the drink tells him that his thinking is clear. You can reason with him, but it is pointless. If he doesn't decide on his own to stop doing it, he won't stop."

"Will my daddy die?" Averee, his final daughter, asked me, looking up at me with Glennen's eyes in Alekanna's face.

I could lie, and easily, to one so young, but I think it is the greater cruelty. Better that they live in the real world, if they have questions like these.

"I have to tell you all, the odds are that the drink will kill him," I said, watching their eyes tear. "I have seen this before, and it is sad, and they become terrible people when it happens. I will do everything I can to keep you from him, if that's what you want. And if he *does* try to quit, we will do everything we can to help him.

"But you must be ready for the fact that, most likely, he is too far gone, and he will die."

Averee burst into tears and ran into Shela's arms. Terran took his lead from Tartan, who just stood straighter and nodded. Glennen pounded, "Be tough" into a kid who had very little toughness in him, and Tartan did his best to rise to it.

He probably realized better than anyone that he had not been named heir and, when his father passed, he lived at my mercy, Glennen having no family and Alekanna being of a house that had been wiped out in one of Eldador's many internal skirmishes.

When the time came, I wanted to give him a city, but I wanted him to show me first that he could be a Duke, without being told he already had the job.

Alekennen seemed the most pragmatic of the four. She never lived a day thinking that she would rule Eldador. She'd been born a girl, and she knew what nobles used their daughters for.

"You'll get me a husband if you're right?" she asked me.

I looked her in the eye, thirteen and a woman. Her time approached quickly. There were unmarried sons out there.

"I can probably get you a better one if it is before he dies," I said.

She nodded, turned on her heel and walked away. Averee clung to Shela for as long as she could, then broke away to be with her sister. Family was family, after all.

I tried to tell myself that this was what War wanted. He'd given me His command, He'd told me to replace Glennen. Now Glennen was doing all the leg work, and I only had to sit back and do nothing.

So why did I feel like I was holding a bloody knife, and the whole world was looking at me?

***

J'her met me in the Heir's chambers. Shela was complaining that dust had collected everywhere in the month we'd been gone, when he rapped on the polished double-doors and begged permission to come in.

I welcomed him and introduced him to Shela and Lee. Something came into his eyes as he looked down at the gurgling girl in her bassinet. He didn't offer and I didn't push it – in the Pack, you came in with what you had, and it was yours, no matter what.

"Where do we stand?" I asked him.

He looked down at the floor, around him, and back at me like I'd said something crazy.

"Who controls the palace?" I asked him again.

He raised his chin and eyebrows without saying, "Ahhh." He considered himself a comic in his own way, I assumed.

"I've been hearing reports that tell me you're in charge here, as much as you can be," I added.

"I run it all now," J'her informed me, simply. "The Eldadorian Regulars aren't even allowed inside the palace without our permission."

'Our,' not 'his,' I noted. Well played, J'her – make sure I'm in on it, and you're just running it for me.

"Did they make much of a fuss?" I asked him.

"Do you remember Daharef?" J'her asked me.

"The general who replaced Sammin," I answered him.

J'her nodded. "He's pretty dead."

Wow – I hadn't seen that coming. "That must have pissed – that must have made a lot of their commanding officers upset."

J'her shrugged. "I put him in a position where he was insulting me, and I called him on it. It was to first blood, but he didn't survive it. That sort of thing happens."

"So you gave them a way out from having to come after you," I noted.

He sat down on the one hard-backed chair in the room. Couches had been added, and a table, but the chairs were either not ready or not ordered, and for whatever reason we only had one.

Pretty ballsy of him to sit in it while I still stood.

Shela caught my eye and arched an eyebrow. Subordinates could get too familiar.

"I have to ask you something, Lupus," he said to me, looking me in the eye. "And I have to ask that you be very honest with me."

I parked my hip on the table and kept looking in his eye. His were brown, very steady. He'd faced death about as much as I had.

"Always," I informed him.

"You're not going to – what's the expression you use? – start 'knocking off' Eldadorians, are you?"

I wanted to laugh but just smiled. "No," I informed him. "I didn't even want you to take out Daharef."

"But you realize that some of them had to die," he said.

I didn't, but there was no point in fighting it. He was worried that he'd signed up with a bad guy. He was going to try to get permission to leave me if he didn't hear what he wanted to.

I'd have to back-pedal pretty fast if that happened. A lot of Wolf Soldiers liked J'her.

"I need my own people in charge here," I informed him, "because Eldadorian Regulars can't handle the King, and because we've put a lot of effort into making the rest of Fovea afraid of us. You know what Two Spears said, when he came back from here?"

J'her shook his head.

Shela chimed in, "He said that, if he were still with my people, then he'd come sack this city, because it would be so easy."

J'her nodded again. "If not for the Wolf Soldiers, it would be," he said.

"If not for the Wolf Soldiers," I agreed.

"But the Eldadorians could never admit that," he continued.

"Shame on them if they did," I said.

"Yes, a lot of it," he agreed. "But when they lose a fight to one of us, and then I use that as an excuse to start changing out their warriors with ours – "

"People are afraid of us for a reason," I finished for him. "No shame in that."

"And you're the Heir, after all."

We both nodded. We talked for a while. I let him know there was another promotion in his future. He didn't ask about it.

But I was happy with him.

Over the next three days we spoke more, and I tried to catch Glennen in some period of lucidity, so that he could at least have a chance to give the kids something decent to remember him by, but Glennen was a committed drunk now, and there would be no respite for him. His Oligarchs were clearly feeding him as much as he wanted in order to keep him manageable. I didn't know whether or not they knew that this would hasten his death.

One thing I'd noted was that, to sober him up, they'd toss him in a big, marble bath tub that sat in a room adjoining his room. Getting hot water into it involved a bucket brigade from the kitchens, and getting the water out involved another. The whole thing created a mess and it happened three times a week (and had been daily when Alekanna had been alive). These people had no concept of indoor plumbing or water heaters, so I spent an entire day with two of the Uman, Dwarf-trained engineers whom I'd brought with me from Thera and enlightened them to a world of running water.

On the third day, sitting in court, the Free Legion petitioned for my audience. I granted it to them and summoned Shela.

They were the same as last I had seen them. A year hadn't changed much. Thorn scowled to break glass, and D'gattis with him. I could see Karel grinning ear-to-ear, and Arath looked shrewd and pensive. Nantar clearly wanted to grab me in a bear hug, and Ancenon just as clearly didn't like being summoned.

Dilvesh just nodded to me, as if to say, "I know you, and you know me – and we have that no matter what else happens."

"We come at your request, Rancor Mordetur, as citizens of Eldador," said Ancenon, speaking for the group.

"I made no *request*, Ancenon Aurelias," I said. "We are most concerned over the siege of Eldador the Port."

"We were within our rights as mercenaries," Thorn scowled.

"But not," I said, "as Eldadorian citizens, which you are."

"I am actually a Trenboni," Ancenon said, "and a visiting representative of King Angron."

"Angron has declared for Avek Noir," I corrected him, looking him right in the eyes. "We are informed that it is *he* who represents the future of Trenbon."

D'gattis and Ancenon looked at me with silver-on-silver eyes, which made it difficult to tell if they were looking straight ahead or at each other. Their eyebrows, however, were telling.

"We were in fact under that nation's employ," Ancenon said.

"Which you took instead of that offered you by Eldador," I said.

"We received your offer too late to act," D'gattis said.

"And yet, you found time to answer Trenbon's offer," I countered.

I could tell he wanted to say that he got Trenbon's offer first, but Shela stood right there to detect the lie. At least I knew, right then, that the bounty hunters weren't working with Conflu and the Trenboni, unless they simply knew of the plot and acted on it.

"You will note," Ancenon said, "that when your personage presented itself, even in clear effigy, we retreated before you."

"You're saying you knew it wasn't me?" I pressed him.

"That horse was *not* Blizzard," Thorn scoffed.

I should have known better, but there isn't a horse like Blizzard.

"We stood away from Eldador and collaborated in the ruse against our client, because we are Eldadorian citizens," Ancenon said, looking right at me. A lie, but a good one, and one that everyone could live with. Even when it got back to the Trenboni, they would know the truth and not feel betrayed.

If I wanted to make things hard for Ancenon, I had my shot right now. But it gained me nothing and lost me what little I had left with him.

I nodded. "We will expect you at the royal table tonight," I said.

Ancenon looked irritated but nodded and thanked me. Throwing capes up over their shoulders with a flourish, they turned and exited, dismissed.

Well, that was new.

Waiting for the King when you knew that he'd passed out in a puddle might be a persistent pain in my ass, but protocol demanded it, and it *did* get me fifteen minutes every day with the Oligarchs.

"Your Free Legion is in attendance," three told me.

"And as you requested, it is they, and us, and none of the court barons, most of whom are chagrined and vexed with you," one added.

I smiled. "Chagrined *and* vexed? When does a revolution begin?"

"We need alliances for the upcoming change of crowns," four complained. "And a court baron is a powerful ally to a duke with a city's resources behind him."

"No one likes how you handled Yerel," three commented.

"Everyone expected you to raid his city, but not depose him," one said.

"And now they're wondering who's next?" I said.

All four nodded.

A part of me said, "Let them wonder," but that part needed to think about every single city in the nation trying to go its own way at the same time, which could happen.

"Invite them to meet me by twos and threes," I said. "We can't do anything official with the King here, but I can meet with anyone I want. Tell them I need their advice. People love to give people like me advice."

"I know I enjoy it," two said. The other three smiled.

"Protocol is satisfied, I think," three said.

We entered the royal dining room, the people at the table rising to meet us.

We dined on the usual stacks of meats and cheeses, with more fish than usual, because this late in the season fish became the most plentiful food. As the next harvest grew through the summer, we would eat more things like fish and grains, until the next harvest, when we would have more fruits and vegetables.

I got that hug from Nantar, a bone-crusher to be sure, and gripped the wrists of everyone but the Uman-Chi. They showed some hesitancy around the Oligarchs at first, but it didn't take long for them to open up.

"I was never fooled by the Theran militia, of course," D'gattis bragged. "Much less your impersonator."

"Those *were* my lancers," I said.

"Well, the lancers," D'gattis said, with a flick of his hand. "No match for ours, of course."

Arath just grinned to himself.

"And our Sarandi are no different from your Wolf Soldiers," Nantar commented.

"Except, as well, better trained," D'gattis added.

"And what are your plans for them?" I asked.

They looked to Ancenon, who looked at them, and then at me.

"You are certain of these advisors to the King?" he asked.

The first Oligarch said, "You might remember, your Highness, that we were the ones who first recruited you."

"They have my complete confidence," I said.

Ancenon nodded. "We are for Sental, to invade into Volkhydro."

"We nearly were for Volkhydro," Arath said. "They offered more money, but we would have had to pay to billet our men."

"So we are doing better this way," Thorn said. "And no one ever starved in Sental."

Shela chuckled. I didn't get the joke.

"We wanted to make you aware as well," Ancenon said, "that we were invited to Andurin, and to Vrek. Groff of Andurin is clearly wondering if he can break off the Andurin peninsula from your nation. Ceberro of Vrek wanted us to invade Kor on his behalf, but he wanted us to conquer it for him."

"I think he is going to do that anyway," Arath said.

"Kor isn't actually an Eldadorian city," I said. "Although I may someday change that. I am worried about Groff of Andurin, though."

"You should be," D'gattis said, delighting in my difficulty. "Andurin has 15,000 foot soldiers and could levy the coastal towns for 15,000 more if he had to."

"Not that they could stand against Wolf Soldiers," Nantar said. "He wanted us specifically to meet your troops with ours."

I frowned. I thought Groff, if not a supporter, didn't want the job of Heir for himself. His loyalty fell to Glennen, not to Eldador.

"I have a lot of contacts in that part of the world," Karel said.

I looked him in his blue eyes. "Aren't you going to Sental?" I asked him.

"I can't see why," Karel said. "There isn't anything for me to tell them that they don't already know. If something comes up, I could take a short boat trip there. Andurin is a port, after all."

"I agree," Arath said. "I don't think it does us any good for Andurin to become an independent nation."

"I would think otherwise," D'gattis said. "It would create a new nation to make war for, and against."

"I wouldn't allow it," I said, looking D'gattis in the eyes. "And I wouldn't have a lot of tolerance for anyone who helped them."

"And I don't see what you could do about it," D'gattis said, leaning back in his chair. "If it were me, and I were to –"

His chair exploded underneath him, and he crashed in a cloud of splinters to the ground. The look of rage that crossed his face changed to surprise as he tried to stand and flew like a doll against the wall.

"This is intolerable," Ancenon said, standing and throwing back his robes.

"I wouldn't do it if I were you," Dilvesh said, quietly.

Ancenon looked at him, his brows down in a scowl.

"I was even getting sick of listening to D'gattis bait him," Thorn said.

D'gattis stood slowly, expecting to be put back down. He faced off across the table, directly at Shela.

"I am a member of the Free Legion and a Trenboni – "

He flew back against the wall again. I saw Shela fuming. She took her position as my woman seriously in any regard, and far more seriously when she thought anything threatened me.

This time Ancenon stepped in to protect D'gattis, raising his hand in a white blaze of power. Shela raised hers up to meet his, and both surged with energy.

"Enough," I said.

Ancenon didn't back down, so Shela couldn't. D'gattis stood, and I didn't doubt that D'gattis would gang up on Shela if he thought he had a chance to put her down.

Then Dilvesh rose, and all he did was put his thumbs and index fingers on the table in front of him. He turned his head to his left and to his right, not really looking at anyone.

Ancenon's hand suddenly became visible through his spell. The blaze of white dwindled back to nothing, and he sat back down, exhausted.

He turned his head first to Dilvesh, and then to me.

"You helped to create the Free Legion, will you now tear it apart?" he asked me.

"Are you sure you're asking that of the right person?" I said, and looked at D'gattis.

"If you think that my rise to power in Eldador is a threat to you," I said, "then you are entitled to your opinion. If you think you can act against me within the Fire Bond, you do so at the peril of your god.

"But act directly against me and my interests in Eldador – try to get the Eldadorian Dukes to split off from me - and I will forget this Fire Bond and consider you my enemy. You Uman-Chi have seen before what happens to those who oppose me."

D'gattis straightened, then turned and left the room. At the door, he looked over at Ancenon, probably to see if they were leaving together, and then stormed out without him.

"That didn't go well," Nantar said.

Shela just sighed next to me.

"His family and mine have lost much favor for our association with you," Ancenon said. "When we wouldn't stand against you in your invasion of Outpost IX, we were forced to explain the Fire Bond to Angron, and then could not explain the reason why we had stepped into it with lesser – "

He caught himself before he said, "Races," but you would have to know nothing about the Uman-Chi not to know that they felt that way.

"Meanwhile the Hunters have made me almost a favorite son," Thorn said.

"My people tell a story where it was me who invaded in your armor," Nantar said, grinning through his beard.

"I wonder where they got that idea?" Karel said to him.

"Who knows how these things spread?" Nantar said, grinning wider.

"Among the Druids, we see the balance that our Lupus brings," Dilvesh, said. "Some power some day would oppose

Trenbon's supremacy on Tren Bay. Be glad that it was not the Confluni."

"We would have ripped the Confluni apart," Ancenon said, a smile on his face.

"And their answer would have been to throw more bodies at you," Dilvesh said, then looked at me. "How many did you kill in Thera?"

Why lie? "Almost 29,000."

"And the bodies?" he asked.

"Feeding fish in the bay," Shela said. "Maybe 500 were buried. We sent one of their commanders' bodies back to Conflu."

"Multiply that by a thousand," Dilvesh said. "That is how many you would send to Water in your battle with them. Believe me when I tell you that you cannot know how you would change Fovea and the disaster it would be."

"The Fovean High Council would not allow it," Ancenon said, indignantly.

"We've all seen how effective they are," Thorn said. "Are the Dorkans even sending emissaries anymore?"

Ancenon fell quiet. I hadn't known that Dorkan had pulled out from the High Council, but it didn't surprise me, either.

"So I'm going to Andurin?" Karel said, probably hoping to save the conversation.

"I would like that if you can spare him," I said.

"He is right in that there would be little for him to do," Ancenon said. "His people won't fight for us as they will for you."

I smiled about that. I don't think I would make him love me more by telling him whose gold now rebuilt the damage I did.

The meal broke up after that. Ancenon had to find D'gattis. Thorn actually wanted to speak with Shela about some Andaron something. I ended up going out to the stables with Nantar, Arath and Dilvesh. Karel went somewhere on his own, but he didn't say where.

"I heard about the battle for Thera," Nantar said to me. "Arath, of course, speaks of nothing else."

"Even with all of us in Conflu, they were not so easily bested," the woodsman said.

"How long do you think it will be before they adopt Wolf Soldier training?" I asked them, seriously.

"Years," Dilvesh said. "Maybe never. You've beaten them twice. The Andarons have defeated them more than that and they don't ride horses."

"Horses aren't suited to their Andaron border," I said.

"Your method isn't suited to their idea that we are all inferior to them," Arath said.

"That isn't just the Uman-Chi, then?" I asked

The others laughed. "I think you will find that every race on Fovea is convinced they hold that position," Dilvesh said.

"When in fact it is clearly the Volkhydrans who are superior," Nantar added.

Arath shoved him, widening his grin.

I felt the smile come off of my lips. "I think I might be in too deep with this whole issue," I said.

"This business of you being the Heir to Eldador?" Nantar asked.

I nodded.

"Well, I know I wouldn't want it," Arath said. "Better a general than a King. The nations line up to kill a general one at a time."

Nantar barked a laugh. Dilvesh took my shoulder. "I don't think that anyone who ever stood at the threshold of where you are ever thought any differently. It is a daunting thing, to be responsible for so many lives."

"I know," I said. "The Wolf Soldiers want what I do. The Eldadorians just want to be alive tomorrow. I don't know if I can bring them that."

"Not the way you live," Nantar agreed. Arath nudged him again.

They had clearly spent the last year together, getting to know each other, supporting each other. I seemed an outsider now.

"I didn't want to discuss this with D'gattis in the room," I said, finally.

"The Trenboni are trying to kill you?" Arath said.

"And the Confluni are working with them?" Nantar added.

"And the Bounty Hunter's guild?" said Dilvesh.

"Well, yeah."

"He knows," Arath said.

"He probably likes the idea now," Nantar said.

"Well, he won't stop it, anyway," Arath said.

"D'gattis is a loyal Uman-Chi," Dilvesh said. "He wants what is best for his nation, and he sees his future there. Ancenon is more of a pragmatist. He has a belief that there will be a new Uman-Chi nation called Angador, and that he will father it."

"He might change his mind about that, when I tell him something I learned lately," I said.

They waited. I chewed it over in my mind. I needed something to bring them back in the fold, and to get them to think I had some more to offer to the group.

"Let's get everyone back together again," I said, finally. "No Oligarchs, no titles, just Free Legion."

"Very well, for breakfast in the morning then?" Dilvesh asked.

"I don't think D'gattis is too far away yet," Nantar said.

I nodded. "Yes, breakfast in my personal chambers. I think that Shela has the wards up there to give us privacy."

"This is big, guys," I said, looking at each of them. "This changes everything."

Chapter Nine

Archeology

Shela warded the bedroom as I thought she had. She embraced the idea to have the meeting of just Free Legion, until she found out that she wasn't included.

"He will threaten you," she warned me, her arms wrapped around me and her head pressed against my chest as we stood in the middle of the Heir's chambers. She'd taken to wearing palace dresses with long, blue and white skirts that ballooned out around her hips, and plunging necklines. The whole thing rustled like fall leaves against me.

"I'll have Adriam looking out for my safety," I said. "No need to blow up his chair or kill him."

"There are other ways that he can get at you," she told me, pushing away and looking up into my eyes. "You cannot think that any Fire Bond means anything to D'gattis. He won't kill you, but he will help anyone who wants to and think himself innocent, and if Adriam disagrees after the fact, you will be just as dead, or worse."

I ran a hand through her long, black hair. It was morning and my fellow Legionnaires would be coming soon. I had already sent for them in their chambers. "You and I know that, when it comes to magical might, D'gattis is no match for you, and we both know that, when it comes to guile and deception, we are no match for an Uman-Chi.

"Our best chance," I said, looking into her beautiful brown eyes, "is to give him such a stake in us, that he doesn't want us dead."

"And you think you can do that?" she said.

"If not," I told her, "you can always sink the ship he's on when they pull out of port."

She grinned and kissed me. I had been kidding, but I felt just as sure that she hadn't been, and that it would bother her no more to eliminate D'gattis than it would him to kill her.

She left with Lee and I watched her, the wiggle beneath her formal palace dress still more than enough to drive me wild.

I didn't wait long for Nantar, Thorn and Arath to arrive together. I greeted them at the door to my chamber, and turned to see Karel sitting on the corner of my bed. He grinned at the idea that he could indeed get past me. I would have to ask him how he did it.

Dilvesh came alone. When he arrived, we sat at the table, and Uman servants in green Eldadorian livery piled it with breakfast foods: oatcakes and fried meats and eggs and fresh milk. The five of them, male or female, had their long hair pulled back into a pony tail. I liked strong tea in the morning and one of the females poured it for me, bending at the waist and smiling into my eyes, but no one else took any. We sat and commenced to eat as the Uman-Chi entered.

I think they expected us to rise, but we didn't. We'd left two seats at the table open to them, but the table itself was overcrowded and they pulled the seats away, to watch us eat from the other side of the room as the Uman filed out. They sat saying nothing, waiting for me to make my move.

As I had with my advisors, I rose and crossed the room to where my pack lay by the bed and withdrew a bar of gold, wrapped in oilcloth. Rather than place it on the table, I handed it to D'gattis. He almost dropped it for the unexpected weight.

He unwrapped it in his lap and studied it, then handed it to Ancenon.

"We have seen this before," he said, looking at me.

"Have you?"

They turned toward each other, then to me. "This is the Cheyak seal," D'gattis said.

"It is," I agreed.

Dilvesh stood and walked over to them, his heavy riding boots clunking on the polished wood floor. He took one look at the bar and his jaw dropped. He turned to me, looked into my eyes, then grinned and sat back down.

"What?" Thorn insisted.

"Does that resonate like Outpost X?" I asked the Uman-Chi.

Ancenon focused on it, then looked several times between the bar and D'gattis. D'gattis did the same thing, and then they began to mutter to each other, then looked up at me.

"Where did you get this?" D'gattis asked me.

"Where do you think I got it?" I asked them.

D'gattis sighed, exasperated, and brought the gold bar back to the breakfast table. The other members of the Free Legion studied it with interest, picking it up and handing it to each other, except for Dilvesh who kept watching me.

"You found another Outpost?" Ancenon asked me. "Or you just found this evidence of one?"

"I found this evidence of one, in Outpost V," I said.

There it was, cat out of the bag. Everything hinged on this now. This could make me, or this could burn me down.

"And I know the truth of Outpost VII," I added.

The Uman-Chi straightened in their chairs, their faces pointed at me. Even they couldn't hide their excitement.

"You know that the Cheyak did not make Outpost VII," Dilvesh said.

Arath, Nantar and Thorn regarded him, then the Uman-Chi. Karel of Stone just laughed.

"There is the best-guarded non-secret in Fovean history," the Scitai said.

"I do not agree," D'gattis said.

"Oh, come on," Karel said. "You have been to Outpost IX, and to Outpost X. Are they anything like Outpost VII?"

"There is nothing to say that all Outposts are built the same," D'gattis said.

"Outpost V is a mirror of Outpost IX and Outpost X," I said.

"And you have been there?" Ancenon insisted.

"Yes," I said, "and odds are that you have, too."

"You mean walked over it, like Outpost X," Thorn said.

Dilvesh shook his head. "He has walked its halls," he said. "Look in his eyes. He went right to the vaults from the throne room, like he did in Outpost X, but this time he knew to avoid the wards."

I nodded.

"Where?" Ancenon asked me again.

"I need a guarantee first," I said. "I know that Outpost V is covered by no Fire Bond."

"And your guarantee?" Ancenon asked.

I looked right at D'gattis. "I am tired of your alluding to your willingness to work with my enemies against me."

"I have no idea what you mean," D'gattis said. Thorn clicked his tongue, and even Ancenon looked away from him.

"Then you are too stupid to be trusted with the secret," I said. "I think I will keep it with me."

"We will rip Eldador apart," D'gattis warned.

"I have a lot of soldiers who think you won't," I told him. "And like I said, you've probably already been there. I could take you right to the city, and you wouldn't know it if I didn't tell you."

They were all quiet.

"You said that this would change everything," Arath said. "I think I just figured out how."

"You think that the lost Outposts aren't lost," Nantar said. "You think they are just not realized."

"Not all of them," I said. "But I think most of them are where we can find them."

Ancenon slammed his hand down on the arm of his chair. "Where is Outpost V?" he demanded.

"Your cousin won't let me tell you," I said.

D'gattis sighed. "You may have inferred that I would be amused or furthered by your downfall," he said. "And if that is so, I apologize to your frail ego –"

"Not even close, D'gattis," I said. "I want your word, on your name, on the lives of your children future and past, on your honor, and in the name of Adriam, that you will help no one who would act against me, directly or otherwise, and warn me if you become aware of any enemy of mine."

"That is a serious oath," Dilvesh said.

"And made in the Uman-Chi tradition," Ancenon noted. "Which I was not aware you knew."

"I knew Cheyak, didn't I?"

They had never had an answer for that, although I think they suspected.

"And you think you can find more Outposts," D'gattis said.

"I know I have a theory," I said. "Which is more than you have."

"Then I swear," D'gattis said, standing, just as Avek had stood, "on my family's honor, and my own, on the lives of my children future and past, and in the name of Adriam, the All Father, that I will never act against you, or aid anyone who would act against you, directly or otherwise, and that as I learn of your enemies, I will report them to you."

I nodded, and I thanked him. He sat back down and waited.

I looked Ancenon straight in the eye.

"Uman City," Dilvesh said.

"I could have told you that," added Arath.

***

Every time I think I am being clever, it turns out that I'm not. Every time I think I have it all figured out, it turns out that I am a step behind the rest of the room.

This turned out no different.

"Of course it's Uman City," Nantar said, exasperated. "Where did he just come from?"

"Thera," D'gattis said.

"Do you think that Outpost V is Thera?"

"Well, I have been there," Ancenon said.

"And to Uman City, as well," said D'gattis. "And its walls are too small to be the walls of an Outpost."

"It is half covered," I said. "Its palace, which I believe once sat on a hill, now sits at the level of the ground."

"Like Outpost IX," Ancenon said, looking at D'gattis.

"And Outpost IX itself once sat on top of a mountain," Arath said. That's why Trenbon is an island now.

"So Outpost V sat at the top of a valley, which had been the plains of Tren before the Blast," Thorn said.

"That makes a lot of sense," Karel said. "A lot more sense when you know where Outpost X is."

"And they never found the treasury?" D'gattis said.

I shook my head. "They built a wall over the door to it. Anyone touching that door would be crippled. It probably scared the hell out of the first people to move back into the city. As far as the people who lived there knew, it was a blank wall at the end of a useless hallway."

"And what did you find in it?" Ancenon asked.

"Less gold than in Outpost X," I said. "A lot of ruined art and useless swords and armor. I have someone there cataloging it now."

"Who?" D'gattis asked me, leaning forward.

"Ann," I said, smiling. "She is my Oligarch – and –"

"A priestess of War, or so you think," D'gattis told me. Ancenon shook his head.

Oh, crap.

"You filthy-" I began.

"For the love of Adriam," Thorn said.

It was true. "How many of you knew this?"

"I would have told you," Nantar said. "I think I speak for Arath and Thorn as well."

They nodded. I looked at Karel. No need to ask about Dilvesh.

"I suspected, but I saw no need to do anything until I knew," D'gattis said. "You would have asked her, and you probably already did, and she already fooled you once."

"Not everyone is susceptible to a truth saying," Dilvesh said.

"Not the priests of Eveave, anyway," Karel said. "There is another surprise for you."

Oh, this just kept getting better.

"Ann is an agent of the Dorkans," D'gattis said. "A wizard, to be sure, sent originally to recruit the other Dorkan wizards in your employ."

"When he couldn't do that," Ancenon said, "you recruited him as your advisor, thinking him Ann, a priestess of War, whom he killed."

"A glamour is an easy thing, especially for a Priest of Eveave," Dilvesh noted.

"And he is in Uman City right now," Ancenon noted.

"Probably not," Karel said. "I would be long gone by now."

I whistled for the servants, waiting outside for the end of the meal. I sent one of them for Shela, who returned quickly. It didn't take long to get her up to speed, but as soon as she saw the direction of the conversation, she drew her own conclusions.

Her eyes unfocused then refocused a moment later. Even with the glamour, she knew the essence of the one we thought of as Ann.

She unpacked her crystal, and looked into its depths. The Uman-Chi looked in with her, leaving no room for the rest of us.

"He is on a fast ship," Shela said finally. "He has many crates, and is bound for the Straights of Deception."

Ancenon smiled, looking up.

"She is just now passing the Silent Isle."

D'gattis had already left.

***

Two Trenboni Tech Ships pulled into Eldador the Port a week later. Glennen himself greeted them, wheeling drunkenly down the wooden dock with twenty Wolf Soldiers around him. More than once they kept him from walking right into the water. D'gattis and two Trenboni captains, both Uman-Chi, stood patiently while Glennen slurred his way through a greeting where he gave us his insight on Trenboni and Eldadorian friendship.

One of these very ships had joined in the blockade here the month before. I couldn't tell if Glennen even remembered it. He offered each of the Uman-Chi a barrel of mead, then asked them if they were here to discuss the death of Alekanna.

"We come to speak with the Heir, your Majesty," D'gattis told him. "If you recall, I helped him to exact vengeance in your lady's honor."

It had probably been the wrong thing to remind him of, because Glennen took a swipe at D'gattis right there. To their credit, the Wolf Soldier squad around him had him separated from the Uman-Chi and moving back to the palace before D'gattis really had the time to appreciate what had just happened.

Fortunately, all Uman-Chi saw Men this way, so it came as more of a disappointment to them than a surprise. I'd come with another 40 Wolf Soldiers, and D'gattis stepped over to me and nodded.

"Your monarch is a disturbed man," he said.

"I know."

"You should strive to do better," he said.

"I will do my best."

D'gattis nodded.

"Did you get the wizard?" I asked.

D'gattis' eyebrows dropped like two anvils over his eyes. "Of course we obtained him."

"I had hoped you would," I said. "Can he be transported, or do you need to contain him some how?"

"Contain him?" D'gattis asked.

"Keep wards on him to contain his magic."

"There are no such wards."

"So, how are you keeping him from making himself look like one of our sailors and just walking off of the ship?"

The other two Uman-Chi looked at each other with alarm. D'gattis looked down for a moment, then at the two Uman-Chi, then down the dock.

"You will excuse us," he said. "There are things to unload, if you would."

They left down the dock. I sent the Wolf Soldiers into the ship to unload it. There were some neatly stacked crates that rattled when they were moved, and these were loaded into a cart to be relocated to the palace. By the time we had the cart back into the royal courtyard, D'gattis and a guard of Uman dressed in the red Trenboni livery were manhandling a Man in a torn purple robe through the palace gates.

A person with no cornea has a tough time shooting a dark look, but D'gattis managed it. Seeing as I had pointed out the mistake, it had become my fault, and of course had I forgotten then D'gattis would remind me of it.

"Glad you got him back," I said.

"Thank you."

"Who knows how much damage he would have done?"

"Yes."

"Do you need me to take him?" I asked, looking as sincerely as I could into his eyes.

"No."

"It might be a good idea. I have resources here -"

"I can manage him."

"You're sure?"

"Quite sure."

"Because –"

He looked me right in the face. You could see that he had been exerting himself.

"I am over two centuries old, Lupus," he said. "I know what you're doing, and it isn't funny."

"Is, too."

He sighed. "You have somewhere to bring him?"

"Follow the Wolf Soldiers," I said. "Is it safe to have him in the same room as this stuff?"

"It is," D'gattis said. "There are things I want to ask him about."

"You haven't interrogated him?"

"Not successfully," he said, directing his men to follow him, who were unpacking crates. "I know your woman has some talent in that regard."

I nodded. "She does," I said. "But it is more of a last resort with me."

"Between the two of you, then," he said.

I sent two more Wolf Soldier guards to summon the rest of the Free Legion and the Lady Shela.

As we quick-stepped after the Trenboni Uman and their prisoner, D'gattis asked me, "Why do you insist on calling her that?"

We passed through the palace gates to an outer entrance to its lower floors, where we had cells with bars and more experienced jailers. Glennen had captured Dorkan wizards before.

"What should I call her?"

"She is your *slave*, Lupus," he said. "If I know Andaron culture, you can't marry her, so she is neither Duchess, Lady nor anything else."

I hadn't thought of that and Shela hadn't brought it up. I think that she liked the idea of being noble, after Alekanna had her influence with her.

This would require some investigating.

We arrived in a torch lit room within the bowels of the palace. There were thick, iron bars set in the ceiling and the floor, with manacles on the walls and rings in the floor and ceiling. We pulled open a gate and shoved the wizard inside, the Uman already pulling off the prisoner's clothes.

His build looked the same as Ann's. Hair covered his paunchy belly, hanging over his genitals. He had very little hair on his head, saggy jowls, and angry brown eyes. His teeth were yellow, but he had them all.

We chained him by the wrists to rings in the ceiling, and by his ankles to rings in the floor. Then the Uman guards slammed the iron door to his cell and a blue light flashed through the bars all around him.

According to the local Oligarchs he could cast any spell he wanted to (we had no way to prevent it without robbing him of his ability to speak) but the magic in the bars would reflect his magic back at him. I told this to him as he hung there.

"So when you test it, use a glamour, not a fireball, because I'm not ready to kill you yet," I said.

"Although I assume that day is coming," he said. His voice sounded effeminate like Ann's, although it had sounded masculine coming from a woman.

"I wouldn't make any long term plans, no," I said.

"You don't plan to torture him to death?" Ancenon said, entering behind us.

"Got a religious problem with that?" I asked him.

"Yes."

"You might want to leave, then," I said.

"Surely there are other ways," Ancenon said. "I know he can evade the truth-saying, but perhaps we could pay him off."

"Well, offers are going to be very attractive to him soon," I promised. That drew a scowl from the Uman-Chi.

"Got any problem with not feeding him?" Nantar said, coming in with Arath and Thorn.

"How long?" Ancenon asked.

"Until he dies or tells us what we want to know," Thorn said.

"No good," I said. "If he makes it through the first couple days, his systems start to shut down and he doesn't feel pain anymore."

"Really?" Arath said. I nodded.

"Perhaps a spell that just makes him feel that hunger?" Nantar said.

"Someone would have to create it," Dilvesh said, entering. "And that is more difficult than you would think."

"Not more than I think," I said. "I know nothing about it."

"Clearly," D'gattis said.

"Perhaps I could tell you what you want to know," the wizard said. We all looked at him. "I am not averse to trading information for my freedom."

"The problem is that I wouldn't believe you," I told him frankly. "And I know that a truth saying won't work on you."

"Only if I seek to protect myself," he said.

"And how will we know if you are not?" D'gattis said. "The spell prevents detection. It cannot itself *be* detected."

"I will agree to a binding," he said. I hadn't thought of that. "I will swear to Eveave not to take action against you, or to lie to you."

D'gattis smiled. "And you would, then, have the same guarantee from me."

I hadn't thought of that, either. A binding became mutual.

"The least you can do is not to harm me, were I to capitulate to you," the wizard said.

D'gattis looked at me, then Ancenon, then back at me. "I think that I will take my cousin back to Trenbon," he said, "while you and your woman discuss this situation with our guest."

The wizard's eyes widened. He had been with me for a long time. He knew full well what Shela would do to him, and how little it would bother her to do it.

The Andarons, I learned over and over, were not particularly empathetic.

"I appeal to the god Adriam," the wizard said, looking right at Ancenon. "And I ask for His protection."

"You are not of His children," Nantar said.

"We are all the children of the All-Father," Ancenon said.

Politics was bad enough without throwing in religion.

I didn't need to ask to know that Ancenon wouldn't just scurry off oblivious, and I sure as hell couldn't make him. The wizard knew all about the Fire Bond.

So we can't hurt him, we can't force him – it came to me so quickly and so suddenly that I actually laughed out loud, drawing a stern look from Ancenon and surprise from the rest.

"You would not mock -," Ancenon began, but I interrupted him.

"I can get the information from him, and I won't do so much as scratch him," I said.

***

Fertilizer isn't hard to get in an agrarian society. Fertilizer with a good amount of ammonium nitrate is, unless you know where there are sheep, which I did.

Put that in a copper pot with a lid, and boil it with some water. Move it through a 'clapper' or one-way valve, so that as pressure changes in the pot, it doesn't suck the fumes backwards through the system.

Move the fumes through a second pot of cool water, and contain the fumes into a long metal vial, which you want to keep cold, so that it keeps a negative pressure.

It didn't work the first few times, so I had to make a little foot pump with a bellows. Then it worked really well. The stink of the water in the second pot told me that I had probably done it right. The contents of the vial were at high pressure, but I had anticipated that and made a butterfly valve so that I could seal it and release its gas when I wanted to.

"You are going to disgust him into telling you what you want to know?" D'gattis asked me, making a face next to the second pot.

"I am going to make him happy," I said. Ancenon and he had watched the four-day procedure with interest. Arath, Thorn, Nantar and Dilvesh had taken the Free Legion soldiers, the Legionnaires, to Sental. Karel of Stone had left for Andurin.

"Happy?" Ancenon asked.

"Happy," I said. "So happy that he doesn't care about anything."

"And then he will tell you what you want to know?" D'gattis said.

"That is the theory, yes," I said.

D'gattis looked at Ancenon, who looked at D'gattis. "You can't say that Adriam doesn't want him happy," D'gattis said.

"I would think just the opposite," Ancenon said.

"And if it doesn't work," Shela said, sniffing at the middle container as I disconnected it, "Do we pour this vial brew on him?"

"That vial brew," I said, "is probably one of the most effective cleaners you will ever find."

She raised an eyebrow. "Is it?" she asked.

"Don't breathe it," I said. "But if you use it in an open space, it will clean anything. You will want to wear something to protect your hands."

She regarded the container skeptically.

Meanwhile, we took the vile and returned to the wizard.

We found him in the cell where we left him, the worse for wear. Apparently he hadn't taken our advice about the bars. His face had been burned and cracked, his naked body singed, and he'd lost some hair. The chains that held him to the floor and ceiling where scorched but intact.

"Perhaps we should just leave him to his own devices," D'gattis said. "He can torture himself until he is ready to reveal his secrets."

The wizard grimaced at him. Ancenon placed a holding on the door to the cell, so that two Wolf Soldiers could open it and not be attacked by him.

"How do I do this?" D'gattis asked.

Entering the cell with the wizard had become too dangerous. He had taken to attacking his jailers and seriously hurt one of them. As a result, no one fed him and the floor around him lay slick with his waste.

I had a copper tube that led from the vial to a cup. The tube stretched long enough to be flexible but strong enough not to leak. The bindings were wrapped in cloth and hog fat, but I barely trusted them.

"Put this cup over his mouth and I will open this valve," I said. "Make him breathe it, and try not to do so yourself."

"It will harm me?" he asked, concerned.

I shook my head. "I just don't want to deal with you happy," I said. I met his eye as best I could. "Actually, maybe that would hurt you."

He shook his head, took the cup, and walked into the cell.

The wizard attacked him, but D'gattis stood on his guard, and the wizard had been sorely weakened. The floor bothered the Uman-Chi more than the occupant.

He forced the cup over the wizard's mouth and then held the back of his head so he couldn't pull away. I waited for the wizard to turn red before I cut the gas on. I knew he would hold his breath, so why waste it?

He finally exhaled, then inhaled. The gas carried no odor, so he knew nothing but the breeze he felt on his face. I watched him as he breathed, thinking it nothing more than air.

Spells either work or they don't. Nitrous oxide takes its time to do what it has to.

In three minutes, perhaps less, he relaxed visibly in his chains and grinned to himself. I cut the gas off, and indicated to D'gattis that he could lower the cup.

"How are you, my friend?" D'gattis asked him.

He lowered his head, and then looked up drunkenly at the Uman-Chi. "Oh, I'm fine," he said.

"And what is your name?" he asked. "You never told me."

"Shhhhh!" he said, and grinned. "A wizard must not tell his name!"

"You may whisper it, if you like," D'gattis said. "I won't tell anyone."

"Mmmmmm, I don't think I should."

D'gattis held the cup up to his mouth, and I gassed him a little more. His knees bent a little and he hung more in his chains.

Nitrous oxide isn't any type of truth serum, if there is such a thing. It's an anesthetic. I'd had it when my wisdom teeth were removed years ago.

After the fact I told my doctor all sorts of things about me that he thought were very funny, but didn't actually believe. They were all true. Just like a drunk will confess things he doesn't really want to, the nitrous will lessen inhibitions. That gave us the best shot we had to interrogate him.

Thank all of those sailors in the automotive hobby shop at 7th street base in San Diego. They had told me how to make nitrous for when they went street dragging in Tijuana. The shop kept the ammonia that we created as a by-product for cleaning.

It can blow up in your face if you do it wrong, so I didn't do it wrong.

I cut the gas off, and D'gattis took the cup away from his mouth. He had a grin on his pudgy face now, blinking rapidly to keep his eyes open. "Whuh wuz you askin' me?" he slurred.

"You're name," he said. "You can tell me your name, certainly."

"Makall ak Damaharr," the Dorkan said. "Of the Black Fist."

I turned to Ancenon, crossing my arms in front of me. "The Black Fist?" I asked.

He nodded, still watching the interrogation. "They are wizards who specialize in espionage," he said. "It makes sense. We have caught them before in Outpost IX."

"Wow," I said. "How do you detect them?"

He turned his head toward me. I looked right into his silver-on-silver eyes, long enough to see the faint cornea. Then he turned back to D'gattis.

Ancenon had no reason to give me state secrets.

"Do you want us to help you get to Dorkan?" D'gattis asked.

"Yes," he said. "Haff to – um, haff to get to Dorkan City. Haff to report on Outpost V."

"Outpost V?" D'gattis asked. "You said you wanted to tell me about Outpost V."

"I di'?" he looked blearily at D'gattis.

"You were afraid you might be captured," D'gattis said. "And you wanted me to also have the information."

"Capt', capt'," he mumbled. "There was a ship from Trenbon."

"Yes," D'gattis said. "You don't have much time."

I looked at Ancenon. "He is really good," I said.

"He has done this many times," Ancenon said.

"You can tell," Shela commented, standing behind us. I felt her lay her hand on my shoulder.

"Outpost V – it is Uman City!"

He reached for D'gattis, and his chains held him. His face turned up toward the ceiling, then back to D'gattis, confused.

"They have us," he said. "We don't have much time!"

Makall seemed hesitant. We gave him more gas.

"What izzat?" he asked.

"It makes you stronger," D'gattis lied. "You might be tortured, you will need your strength."

Makall looked worried, then stared blearily around the cell. He turned his face back to D'gattis.

"I tried to get a message to them," he said. "Through Klem."

Shela gripped my shoulder.

"Klem, the former Earl?" D'gattis asked.

Makall shook his head. "He is dead. His son, who took on his name."

I had suspected this much.

"Shall I get him to safety?" D'gattis asked.

Makall shook his head. "He is guarding the Duke. He is just biding his time."

"To kill him?"

"To take his daughter."

Shela bolted out of the room before I could turn around. I yearned to join her, but I had to hear this, and no matter what they promised, I no longer trusted the Uman-Chi.

"The Dorkans want this?"

He shook his head. "The bunny hunters!" he said, and giggled to himself.

"They are working with the Dorkans?"

"They haff to. They haff to know about the Outposts."

"What about them?" D'gattis pressed him.

Makall leaned closer in his chains, and whispered something. I couldn't hear it, but D'gattis' face reacted to it, and I'd never known a man more stoic.

D'gattis nodded, and taking back the cup with him, he returned to the doorway, stepping around the mess on the floor.

He left the cell, and he cleared the tube from the door. The two Wolf Solider guards closed and locked it, and Ancenon released his spell.

He looked right into Ancenon's eyes, and something passed between them. Ancenon looked thoughtful, frowning, and then nodded. D'gattis looked at me.

"Those swords and tapestries and things you thought were useless," he said. "They are in the crates we brought back to you. They are priceless relics of the Cheyak nation.

"They are probably more than that," I said, "or you wouldn't be looking at me like you are."

He frowned, then turned his face away, back to the wizard. He probably wondered if I would be able to get the same information out of Makall that he had.

If Shela had a say in it, I would probably get that and more. He would know that, too.

"Those relics include art that verify that you are right, that there are more Outposts, and that Outpost VII is not on the Silent Island, but beneath the waves of the Bay. From them, we can find the other Outposts."

He turned toward Ancenon again, who nodded. He sighed. Clearly he didn't think he needed to tell me this.

"One of the Outposts is Alun, in Volkhydro," he said. "Another is in Toor, and there are two more in Conflu."

"And?" I asked. This information wouldn't have gotten the reaction I saw out of D'gattis. For an Uman-Chi who already knew about Outpost X and V, this might seem mildly interesting.

He sighed. "The shocking thing is not that the information is there," he said. "The shocking thing, which you disregarded, was that the armor and the swords you found were not a thousand years old, but closer to four hundred."

"So someone figured all of this out four hundred years ago?" I asked. "That is probably how the rumor of Outpost X got started."

Ancenon shook his head. "We have known of Outpost X for more than four hundred years, your Highness," he said. "The fact is, the wall that you thought had been raised to protect Men from the vault door hidden there, originated instead to hide it from any Uman-Chi who might wander down there.

"No Uman-Chi would build that wall," he said, and looked me in the eyes. Again, I could see the silver cornea on the silver iris.

I thought of Avek. He'd had reason enough to keep this secret. Or did he?

"Someone entered that room, and then sealed it with a Cheyak ward," Ancenon concluded, although I had already figured out what he would tell me. "Four hundred years ago, no Uman-Chi could have done that, even if they wanted to. Four hundred years ago, the Uman-Chi were trying to find a homeland, and were searching for any place that had a Cheyak identity. Someone who knew the truth about Outpost V had helped to disguise it, to keep it from them."

"Clearly, some Cheyak have survived the Blast."

Chapter Ten

Families

I'd heard what I needed to from Ancenon and D'gattis. I could dispose of this Dorkan wizard later. I was worried about my daughter now.

I marched straight back to my quarters. Ten Wolf Soldiers sent by Shela met me half way. Their sergeant saluted me, making a fist over his heart.

"Lupus," he said, "the Lady sends us for you."

"My daughter?"

"She is well, Sir," he said. Shela knew better than to send half of a message. "But there was an attempt on your apartments."

I nodded. "Assemble the Pack," I ordered him. "Asleep or awake, on duty or off, 100% of them, no excuses. If they don't or won't show, execute them."

He saluted, turned on his heel and left.

I had a traitor to find.

Shela sat in the rocking chair in our apartments, nursing Lee. She bolted from her seat when she saw me.

"Look at it," she demanded, pointing to the door. "Look at it and tell me what you see."

I squatted down and studied the doorjamb, expecting to see evidence of prying, but saw nothing.

"Not there," she said, her voice filled with fear and anger. "The hinges, look there!"

I leaned closer. They were shiny brass, letting the door open in, so that it could be kicked in, but not have its hinge pins removed and slid open. At first I saw nothing, and then on the lowest of the three I saw a tiny scratch, shiny and new.

I tapped it and the top of the pin jiggled. I put my fingernail under the brass top, and it lifted away easily, revealing an iron pin, its top merely dipped in brass.

"You could-" I began.

"Pop it with a magnet," Shela finished for me. "That isn't the work of any soldier, any spy. That is the planning of a bounty hunter who knows what he is about and is setting up his attack."

"Klem may be a bounty hunter, then," I said.

"Or be working with one, or have their training," Shela said. Lee fussed at her nipple, and Shela moved her to her shoulder. Patting her back nervously, I could see how this rattled her to her heart.

"White Wolf," she said, "we cannot allow –"

"I have the Pack assembling," I said. "You will come with me, and I will ask each one them where their loyalty lies, if they would ever betray me, and if they know or are Klem. That should catch our spy."

She nodded. "And if that doesn't reveal him?"

I looked her in the eye. "I can get more of that gas, if I have to," I said. "But understand that this is going to hurt morale, and hurt it badly. After this, we will have to do something to show that we have faith in the rest, and don't blame them for this happening."

"What will you do?" she asked.

I smiled. I already knew.

***

The Wolf Soldiers, 'the Pack,' stood at attention in the palace courtyard, a wide open space paved with grey flagstones, between the palace gates and the granite stairs leading up thirty feet to two giant red, wooden double doors. Discipline was their bread, duty their water. They were on their second chance, and they knew they were more feared and better respected than any troops who marched on Fovea. They defeated ten times their number if they had to, and took it in stride.

This would slap them right in the face, I knew, but it had to be done.

"There is a traitor among you," I said.

The comment ripped an audible gasp from them, not as one would hear in a court, but as one would hear on the wind.

"One, named Klem, infiltrated the ranks, got past me, got past the Lady, and stands with you now. He has already prepared an attempt on Lee, my daughter."

Shock turned to rage. Lee had become as much the daughter of every one of them as mine.

"I will have him," I said. "If he steps forward now, he will merely die. If not, he will wish he died."

No one moved. I gave them a slow count of thirty. Nothing.

"Very well," I said.

They were in thirty rows of fifty. I went to the first man on my left on the first row, and looked him right in the eye. He was a Volkhydran. I remembered that he had been a farmer who killed his tax collector for suggesting that his taxes would be forgiven for a roll with his daughter.

"Where does your loyalty lie?" I asked him.

"With the Wolf Soldiers."

"Would you ever betray me?"

"I would rather die."

"Do you know or are you Klem, or have you worked with or heard rumor of him?"

"I have not."

I stepped to my right, and looked the next one in the eye. She was an Uman, a whore from Sental, where whoring was illegal. I asked her the same questions, and got the same answers.

And the next, and the one after that. For an hour, I asked them the same question, and Shela verified them. I'd gone one thousand deep into them and she stood dead on her feet from the effort, but she would let no other take her place. She would know for herself.

Just as I wouldn't have given this job to one of my majors. This matter involved the Pack, and myself as Pack leader.

"Are you –" I began.

His dagger flashed toward my stomach, catching me unaware. The side of my hand blocked the blow before I even thought of it, and my other hand had him by the neck.

His knee came up to my crotch, and every soldier on every side of him had a hand on him.

"Hold your ranks!" I ordered. "Hold your ranks."

This would be just the way a Bounty Hunter would work. Have one betray himself somehow, so that another could sneak through.

The men and women closest held him as, from the corner of my eye, I saw another man cross from the ranks in front of me to the ranks behind. Those nearest him had been distracted by my actions and thought nothing of it.

"In ranks, *now*," I ordered them, and walked right to the man.

The women next to him found herself the fifty-first in her row, trying to line up. Before I even got to her, she stepped back into the row, into a vacancy left from those who had taken the prisoner.

I walked directly past her, to the man who had moved. He stood stock still at attention, like a Wolf Soldier.

"Where does your loyalty lie?" I asked him.

"Sir, I have already –"

"Where does your loyalty lie?" I asked him, again, looking him right in the eye.

"With you, Lupus," he said.

"He lies," Shela hissed.

He had no time to draw his knife – the men and women around him had him. The rest held ranks this time.

Now I had two.

I went back to where I left off, and asked my questions again. The answers were more emphatic now. They had their justification; this was no paranoia on my part.

This time I got to the last man. Shela simply left with two female Wolf Soldiers to help her. She would probably sleep all day, but there would be a wet nurse to watch our daughter, and we had already verified her loyalty.

"Your honor has been tarnished by these two," I said. "Normally, I would take them, question them, and find out what they know. However, in this case, I already know what I need to.

"You enter the Wolf Soldiers, and we ask no questions of your past. I won't change that now.

I looked for and found J'her, his hands on the first man I'd caught.

"They are traitors," I said, looking him in the eyes.

"When I see them again, I want them to be alive, but make sure they *look* like traitors."

He smiled. This man had killed three families who had tried to settle on his farm, until Rennin caught him.

He knew what to do.

When I came back to the courtyard an hour later, Glennen sat on the ground by the palace entrance at the top of the stairs with a bowl of mead. As much of it had soaked into his shirt as remained in the bowl. He hadn't shaved, and he smelled like piss.

"I look a mess, dun I?" he slurred, looking up at me.

"You have looked much better, your Majesty," I said.

"Still look better than those two," he said, pointing into the courtyard.

"I would hope you do, your Majesty," I agreed. I couldn't see the men, for the Wolf Soldiers around them.

He sighed, and I looked back down at him. He squinted up at me, the light obviously hurting his eyes. We stared, then he looked away, and back at me.

"I am a mess," he repeated.

"Yes, you are, your Majesty," I said. "Are you telling me you don't want to be?"

"No one wants to be like this," he said. "You don't know the pressures of running a kingdom."

I could have argued that, but why?

"When I drink, I can focus on my work, and not think about *her* all the time," he said.

"She was a great lady," I said to him, because I meant it, and because I hoped he would find his way back. There would be consequences for that. So be it.

I admit I'm afraid of War, but he doesn't own my soul yet. Glennen is a good man, albeit a lost one.

I acted no different without Shela.

I looked down and he had the bowl to his mouth, the alcohol seeping into his beard. At first I thought that he had splashed some on his face, and then I realized that those were his tears.

It was hard, this whole husband and father thing.

I went on to see the high price of treason among my Wolf Soldiers.

They parted for me, standing at attention. Both men were lying on the stone courtyard in their own blood. Both were breathing. One had a foot missing, the other's hands were crushed. Their hair lay in two piles, and their faces were bloody and bruised, their eyes swollen shut.

There were teeth on the ground near them, as well. The men and women nearest them had bloody knuckles. One woman squatted down between then, a curved skinning knife in her hands. I recognized her as one of my captains. Each of the spies showed marks on his back from her efforts.

J'her stepped up next to me and looked me in the eyes.

"Two traitors, presented to you, Lupus," he said.

I nodded. "They look like traitors," I said.

"Would you rather they look like whores?" the woman squatting between them asked. "Because that can be arranged, too."

I grinned. "Maybe later," I said. "Stand them up.

They were pulled to their feet. They couldn't have stood otherwise. One I recognized, the other looked totally different. I opened my mouth to ask if they were sure this second one hadn't somehow managed to trade places with a loyal man, when I saw how much he looked like Earl Klem.

"He had a glamour," I noted.

J'her nodded. "A glamour usually fails if you pull out their hair," he said. "The magic bleeds away."

I didn't know that, but I nodded. I stepped up in front of Klem's son, first.

"Thought to get some retribution for your father?" I asked.

"Thought to do to you what you did to me," he said.

"So you steal Lee?" I asked.

"The Bounty Hunters want her."

I looked at the other one. "Why?" I asked.

Blood flowed over his lips from his missing teeth. "I'll nebber tell you, you scum," he said, spraying a mist of blood in front of him.

One of the men holding him punched him in the stomach, the other kneed him in the groin. His knees buckled and he had to be dragged back up to his feet.

"Fetch a wizard," I said.

J'her sent one of the men off. The Bounty Hunter smiled. "A truth telling will do you no good," he said.

"I don't need a truth telling," I said. "All I need to know is the nearest member of your family. I don't care if it's a second cousin, male or female – you think you were treated badly? Wait until I'm done with him or her."

His bruised lips curled.

"If you haven't satisfied my curiosity before the wizard arrives," I said, "then no matter what you tell me, that relative will be tortured to death, and you won't get this offer again until the *next* member of your family is sought. If there isn't one, then I will settle for people you knew in your childhood. You have met a lot of people in your life – you are willing to tell me what I want to know for one of them."

"You are lep den a demon," he told me, looking in my eyes.

"You are wasting time," I told him.

He didn't look away, neither did I.

"I need water," he said finally. I looked away as if to order it, then turned and punched him square in the nose, breaking it. His blood covered my steel gauntlet.

"Drink that."

He licked his bloody lips, smiled, and spoke.

The lack of teeth slurred his teeth. A man needs his teeth to speak, and the bruised and swollen lips made it no easier.

He confessed that he'd come here to get near enough to me get Lee – that I already knew. The Guild planned to make me trade myself for her – that I had guessed at.

The Bounty Hunters had informed the Dorkans not only of my role in the Battle of Two Mountains, but of my statement to Aniquen outside of the gates of Outpost IX, and how that had led to the sack of Katarran, and how I had profited from that sack.

That came as a real surprise to me, but only one man could have put all of that together.

"There is a Bounty Hunter named Xinto, who is a Scitai," I said to the other captive, the *real* bounty hunter. "Do you know him?"

"Do you?" he asked me, looking in my eyes, which got him a smack in the gut.

"Answer."

"Everyone knows Xinto," he said. "Xinto brings one gold coin in ten to our coffers."

Xinto knew of the plan to go to Outpost X, and Xinto knew that we were still alive and suddenly very, very wealthy after.

So Xinto knew that we had *found* Outpost X, and Xinto came from Conflu.

The wizard entered the courtyard with the Wolf Soldier guard. I turned back to the Bounty Hunter.

"You have satisfied my curiosity," I said. Then I looked to the Wolf Soldier to his left.

"Cut off his head, his legs, and his arms, and then send all six parts of him to Dorkan City, in the care of the Bounty Hunter's Guild."

I turned back to young Klem.

"You are a traitor to the Eldadorian state," I said. "You can rot in a cell for forty years. That should mellow you out."

"Aren't traitors hung?" he asked me.

"You want to die," I told him. "I want you to think on how you failed and what it cost."

I looked down to his missing foot, then back up at him, and grinned in his face, looking into his swollen eyes. "Don't worry, Klem, I will make sure that, if it gets too easy for you, it will become harder."

***

That night I lay in bed with Shela in my arms. Lee had herself a little nest in our bed, wrapped in blankets on her stomach, her head pillowed on her mother's breast. A squad of Wolf Soldiers guarded the door, and Wolf Soldiers stood every watch in the palace.

Glennen had tried to kiss the lips of one of the female captains, and had to be restrained from going further, but to her credit, she hadn't gutted him.

Shela's breath felt comforting on my arm, as I told her of what had transpired today.

"Do you think that Ancenon knew of Xinto as a Bounty Hunter?" she asked.

"It would be pretty sloppy of him," I said, "no matter how you looked at it. If he knew, then he had let Conflu and the Bounty Hunter's Guild know that we found Outpost X. If he didn't, then he seemed unaware of a secret that a lot of people knew."

"I think he is so used to ignoring Scitai," she said, "that he didn't even consider it."

"Sloppy," I repeated. She'd likely nailed it, and I would have to ask him when I saw him next.

"What do we do now, White Wolf," she asked. I could feel her warm hand on my stomach, moving down to my groin. "Do you hold this nation together until its monarch recovers or dies," she asked. "Or do we go forward in his name?"

I smiled. Shela didn't waste a lot of time.

"I spoke with Glennen today," I said.

"So did a Wolf Soldier, I am told," she said.

"Yes, that wasn't the disaster that it could have been," I said. "For which I am grateful. But he still thinks that he has to drink to do his job and not miss his wife."

"I haven't seen him do any job," Shela said.

"Drunks never realize that, unfortunately," I said. "In his mind, he probably thinks he's working harder than the rest of us."

"What is your plan for his children?"

I thought about that for a few minutes. I had put a lot of work into that and hadn't gotten far for my effort.

"Tartan, I think, should learn something of the military," I said. "I need to find an Eldadorian commander who can train him. Alekennen needs a husband, but I'm going to settle that tomorrow. There isn't a lot we can do with Averee and Terran. When they're older, we'll get the girl a husband. I don't know how Terran is going to turn out, but I would hope to get him at least a barony."

Shela nodded. "There is nothing wrong with being a common, you know," she said. "I'm informed repeatedly that, call me what you will, I am one."

I sighed. "I've been looking for a way to broach that with you," I said.

"You want so much for me to be your equal," she said. "That is neither my place nor my desire, and it never will be. I am a slave, White Wolf. I am *your* slave. I would cry it from the tops of every tower in the city if you let me, but only if you let me, because I am yours.

"I have no desire to be anything more."

I gave her a squeeze and she kissed the skin on my arm. "I think 'mother of my children' is a pretty important role for you," I said.

"As do I," she said. "And I know that my children are free to choose a life in this city as prince and princess, or free on the plains of Andoron. Just marry Lee well and teach our sons to be men."

"Maybe not so cruel as I am," I said.

She lay quiet, and then she said, more softly, "So it did bother you, what you did today," she said.

I sighed again. "I would be a monster if it didn't," I said. "But the traitors had to be purged, and the purging had to strike fear into the heart of anyone who would follow them."

"I think that it will be a brave Bounty Hunter indeed who crosses The Conqueror next."

"They do tend to end up dead," I said.

"And not nobly," she added.

We were quiet for a moment, and then she said, "The palace is in fear of you because of what you did."

"Just for that reason?"

"The palace cook calls you, 'The Demon with Angel Eyes.' The former Eldadorian Captain of the Guard used to call you, 'His Excellency, Death.' Right now, the house staff won't invoke your name, for fear you will appear."

"Wow," I said.

"It seems to me a trend is forming, White Wolf."

"Hard to argue with that," I said.

She settled in next to me, moving Lee to a pillow at our heads. We had a lot to do the next day, after all.

Listening to my girls breathe, I thought that this might be one of those rare, best portions of my life. I had wealth, power, security – not bad for a guy who'd been looking at twenty-five to life for manslaughter if lucky. War's price might be high, but worth paying.

No, he didn't own my soul yet, but he'd put a down payment on it. The man named 'Randy' who'd come here couldn't have done what I had done today. He wouldn't have even considered going after someone's family. If he'd thought to threaten it, he'd have never actually *done* it.

Lupus the Conqueror formed his morality from a certain knowledge of what his god wanted of him. He could do these terrible things because he knew that there would be no punishment for it.

The cost of proof, instead of faith.

***

I sat at court in Eldador the Port, the gallery thick with courtiers. I had personally made sure that they had all of the blood and teeth and whatnot cleaned off the flag stones in the palace courtyard. This meeting meant a lot.

"His Grace," the herald said, "Duke Groff, of Andurin."

Groff entered with a purple cape flowing from his narrow shoulders down to his heels. I remembered him as a tall, thin man, with gray hair flowing straight back from his forehead down his back. He had an angular, severe nose and pointed chin, with dark brown eyes set back in his head. He took long, purposeful strides down the carpet to the dais. Behind him, obviously hurrying to keep up, were a dozen guards, their swords clanking at their sides.

I didn't think people could bring swords before me, but I had worn mine to meet King Glennen, and been made quickly glad of it.

I'd stationed one hundred Wolf Soldier guards within charging distance of the throne. They served the dual purpose of guarding me and keeping Glennen from stumbling in here, but they were armed.

He stopped at the stone circle before the dais, where Shela had once killed a Bounty Hunter, but didn't enter it.

"I came to speak to his Majesty, the King," he said.

Well, the gauntlet lay down before me. The question being would I pick it up or let it lie there.

I doubted very much that he would stop if I didn't react to him, so I took the bait.

"I sit for the King," I said, looking directly at him. "Glennen has a schedule, you don't merit changing it."

Gauntlet back to you, you muther.

He looked stunned. Clearly he knew I needed his support and thought he would get some sort of explanation or apology. If I did that, then I would be at a disadvantage to him.

"I can return when he is less busy," he said, his words clipped in anger.

"You will find you have apartments ready for yourself and your family," I said. "Your men can be billeted in the house of the Eldadorian guard, outside the palace. We had sought to thank you for your excellent support of the Eldadorian state against the Free Legion, but if you would rather have that from the King, I can ask him for his time on your behalf."

"I thank you," he said, "but I can have my own conversations with the King."

I nodded. "As you will. You are dismissed."

That earned another look, but he turned on his heel and left.

At least *that* went as planned.

Groff, of course, rated an invitation to dinner that night. We sat him at the King's left hand, where an Oligarch usually sat, and scooted the Oligarch down three seats to be next to his eldest son. Groff attended with his wife, and had tried to bring his own guard in as well.

"Your man J'her is an excellent officer," Oligarch two commented to me. "He had Duke Groff believing he'd be safer without them."

I nodded. "Thank you," I said. I needed to learn his name some day. "It was a pleasure to elevate him, and I see great things for his future."

"Has he been with you long?"

I opened my mouth to answer, to be interrupted with, "I know where it is, damn your ass," from down the hall.

"Of course, your Majesty," Oligarch one told him.

"But perhaps you would like to go this way first?" Oligarch four added.

A moment later, Glennen rounded the corner to the main hall and saw Oligarch two and me waiting for him at the door. He had on clean clothes and someone had shaved him and combed his hair, at least, but a yellow stain of mead had already marked the front of his blouse, and I could still smell the pee on him as he approached.

"Your Majesty," I said, lowering my head to him. He barked a laugh and slapped my shoulder.

"Where are th' kids?" he demanded, looking past me to the door.

"Within, awaiting you, per your custom, your Majesty," Oligarch three said.

"Well, are we going in, or what?" he asked.

Oligarch two rapped the door, and two Wolf Soldiers within opened it. They stood at attention and announced, "His Majesty, King Glennen Stowe, of Eldador!"

Glennen staggered in, bumped into a Wolf Soldier, then into the back of one of the barons' chairs, pushing him into it. The embarrassed baron scrambled to stand back up as Glennen used the backs of the chairs from there to his seat at the head of the table to support himself as he took his place.

He sat before I and the Oligarchs could find our positions, so we scrambled into them as the rest of the guests sat. Groff raised an eyebrow but said nothing.

"Mead!" Glennen demanded. A porter brought him a bowl immediately. I refused any and took water instead. Shela had a small glass.

Glennen drank from his bowl, then held it out to be refilled. He looked owlishly around the table, then his eyes landed on Shela, or rather her chest.

"How have you been, lil' girl?" he asked, a grin on his face.

"I have been well, your Majesty," she said, looking down demurely.

"Still with this great oaf of a man?"

She smiled. "I prefer him," she said.

Glennen looked at me. "I need to send you as my emissary to Andoron to get me one of these," he told me. His breath reeked from rotting teeth and booze.

"Perhaps if we let it be known that you prefer Andaron females," I said to him, "then they will come to you as is befitting a King."

He grinned to himself. "Yes, that is good," he said, and took a long drink of his mead, spilling a portion of it down his shirt.

The servants brought the platters, and everyone adjusted himself or herself to let them pass. There were two females, but both stayed at the far end of the table.

"You, girl, come here," the King called. Groff, I believe, caught the look of dread on her Uman face. She curtsied and brought her platter to the King, for him to choose from.

She unwisely held it at the level of her stomach, which of course let him get a clear shot as her breasts. He reached out with a hand greasy from the meat he handled and gave the left one a good squeeze.

"Ah, there you go, girlie," Glennen rasped. She blushed crimson and made another mistake and turned instead of backing away. He took a handful of her backside through her skirt, making her squeal, as she tried to escape and clobbered the back of Groff's head with the tray.

"Your Grace, I am so sorry," she said.

"You are pardoned, of course, my dear," Groff said, placing a hand on her waist to guide her to his other side, where Glennen couldn't get a shot at her. "Please, if you would set your platter down here."

"Oh, you don't have to take that from these Uman," Glennen snarled. "Girl, you apologize to Duke Groff."

"I apologize most humbly, your Grace," she said.

"From your knees, girl," Glennen demanded.

"Your Majesty, that is *not* necessary," Groff said, shocked at the idea.

"Oh, ho! Yer telling me now," Glennen said, slamming down his bowl of mead. The spray from it showered Groff and his wife. "I s'pose you think yer King now?"

"Your Majesty," Groff said, "you know that my loyalty is –"

"Your loyalty," Glennen interrupted him, "is and has always been to what suits Groff. Do you think I forgot about when you left me in the Aschire forest? Turned tail? Ran away?"

"Your Majesty, I did *not*," Groff began.

"And now you call me liar?" Glennen demanded. The rest of the table sat quiet now. Glennen normally had a temper, but Glennen drunk and challenged might do anything.

Glennen's eyes found the girl, already on her knees, and he pointed his finger at her. "What are you doing?" he demanded. "Don't do that here!"

She arose, held her hands in front of her, and looked down as demurely as possible.

"Lupus!" Glennen roared. "Where is he, damn him!"

"Right here, your Majesty," I said, from the first chair to his left.

He turned as if I had popped out of the air. "Lupus, Rancor, whatever yer calling yerself," he said. "I want you to take this liar out and cut his head off."

"Cut his head off, your Majesty?"

"You heard me," he said. "You torture people around here all th' time. You think I don't know it? If I tell you to cut someone's head off, you cut it right off, damn you!"

I nodded. "Shall I do it now, or after dinner?" I asked him.

"Well, are you hungry now?" he asked.

"I could eat," I said.

"Damn you, Lupus, I have to do all of the thinking here. What use is having you as Heir?

"Eat, let him have his last meal, then take him out and kill him."

I nodded. "Very well, your Majesty."

Groff looked at me, alarmed. I met his eyes, then shook my head slightly, and went back to my meal.

His wife had been so flustered she could barely keep her seat. I hoped it didn't occur to Glennen that she would soon be a widow.

Dinner went no differently from its beginning. The food came slowly because the female servants weren't helping. Glennen grumbled about that, how slow the mead flowed, and how hard his life had become. Tartan tried to ignore him and talk to Groff's son. The court barons avoided conversation of any kind, and Hectar, who had been warned and not brought his family, only leaned over and talked to Groff once.

Dinner ended with a final round of drinks for all of us. Glennen wanted to tell some story that seemed to be about four Aschire and a whore, but he kept losing his place in it. After ten minutes he took a long swig from his bowl, fell out of his chair and puked all over Groff's boots.

Six Wolf Soldier guards and an Oligarch removed him from the hall while the Court Barons beat a hasty retreat and the rest of us pretended nothing was wrong.

"Your Grace," I said to Groff, finally, "would you be so kind as to accompany my wife, Duke Hectar and I to another room?"

"I would be honored, your Highness," he said. He patted his wife's hand and motioned for his son to follow. An exiting court baron, seeing that I clearly didn't intend to kill Groff, took the opportunity to offer to escort Groff's wife back to her apartments.

We walked quietly back to the throne room and from there to an anteroom where guards often waited in attendance. Shela lit its one torch, hanging in a wall sconce, and I leaned against the back of one of its four chairs, while the other men sat at the table and Shela stood behind me. Oligarch one had joined us uninvited while the other three attended to the King.

"Your Highness, shall I fetch your sword?" Hectar asked me.

Groff looked sideways at him.

"He almost earned the pointy end of it this morning," I said. I met Groff's eyes directly. "What were you thinking at court?"

"I had come to see the King," he said, lamely.

"Do you think we have him at court in his condition?" Hectar asked.

"I am surprised you have him at table," Groff said.

"He's still the King," I said. "If he wants to eat at dinner, he eats at dinner."

"Mostly, he wants to drink until he pukes, rape servants and tell us how hard his life is," Hectar said. "You will make an enemy of me if you pursue your intentions with Lupus here. I do not want his job, and I think you don't, either."

"What intentions?" Groff said.

"Hiring the Free Legion to help you break off from Eldador?" Hectar said.

"You could not have believed that they would not report that to a fellow member," the Oligarch said.

"They approached –" Groff began, then looked at Shela, who smiled at him.

I wouldn't have needed her for that one.

"The Free Legion doesn't go out to sell their services," I said. "They receive requests for employ."

"Yerel was a friend," Groff said. He looked at Hectar, then at the Oligarch, then at me.

"Yerel, Hectar and I have been with Glennen since before Eldador was a wild land," he said. "I owe my life to him, and he to me, more times than I can count."

"Don't forget that Glennen ordered this newcomer to shorten you less than two hours ago," Hectar said.

"And Yerel wasn't paying his taxes," I said. "He used the money instead to grow his army."

"Clearly, the man was about to revolt," the Oligarch said. "I must be emphatic with you, your Grace, that the nation of Eldador can survive a drunken king, but not the loss of its major cities."

"Under Glennen, I was free to pay my taxes when I chose, if I chose, and to renegotiate them," Groff said. "Now comes this man, and I am supposed to pay on a new schedule, no talk about it, as some lackey."

"And under this man," Hectar said, "my duchy isn't supporting the entire Eldadorian nation, the troops are paid on time, we can cross the Straights of Deception as we chose, and can actually build a navy worth a damn."

"And let us not forget," the Oligarch added, "that the schedule that you desire, you would never consider for those in your fealty."

That quieted Groff down.

"What I propose is two-fold," I said. I turned slightly, so that they could all see my face.

"First, no more actions against the Eldadorian nation, and you pay your taxes on time, and in the amount agreed upon."

Groff looked at me directly, waiting for me to continue. When I didn't, he nodded his head slightly.

"Second, Alekennen is of a marriageable age, and I propose there is none better than your son."

"You wish to make my son the Heir?" Groff asked.

I shook my head. The Oligarch said, "The Heir is named, your Grace. Even were he not, it would fall to Tartan then Terran before Alekennen's husband."

"However, it ties your family to the name Stowe, and the name Stowe's prestige shall survive past this King, regardless of who succeeds him," I said.

"Your word on that?" Groff said. "Because it would be more expedient for you to succeed and then to name them all commons, and then there is my son in a useless marriage."

"My word," I said. "No less than a duchy for Tartan. I don't know about Terran, but some nobility."

"Hectar, you are well with this?" Groff asked him. "Your son is younger than mine, but not much."

"He has two daughters," Hectar said.

Groff smiled, and Hectar added, "And let us not forget Lee. Who knows where I will set the boy's ambitions?"

My stomach contracted when I thought of marrying Lee off, but I just laughed and put my hand on Hectar's shoulder.

Groff looked at his son. "You are well with this, lad?"

"I am, father," he said. "She is a comely girl, her name is good, her father is healthy, if unstable. When she gives me sons, I will teach them not to drink."

"Probably best," I said.

I wanted to discuss more about troop limits and to arrange for him to meet Duke Jaheff, when the door burst open behind us.

I recognized one of my captains, with ten Wolf Soldiers behind him. "Lupus," he said.

"This better be important," I said.

"Most urgent, if we may have your ear," he said.

I excused myself, and left the small room with the Wolf Soldiers, and shut the door behind me. "What?" I asked, looking him right in the eye.

He was an Uman, with severe features and hands like an artist. I'd made him a captain more because of his expert swordsmanship than his leadership skills. I thought to give him a training command eventually.

"Lupus," he said, "Karel of Stone has notified you by fast messenger that he has achieved his mission in Andurin, and proceeds now to Vrek."

"Vrek?" I asked him. Karel was supposed to get Groff to come here, which he did, and then set up a system of spies there, which he should be doing.

"He claims that the Duke of Vrek informed him that he would be moving onto the Plains of Angador, and establishing a colony there.

"Vrek is moving against the Free Legion."

Chapter Eleven

The Good Fight

It didn't take a genius to know what was going on.

Duke Ceberro of Vrek, according to the Oligarchs, had a reputation as an opportunist, and an opportunity like the Free Legion creating a sophisticated training compound and then abandoning it wouldn't be lost on him.

"If he has been fed information on your Fire Bond," Oligarch two said, "then he may believe that attacking an Eldadorian is like attacking you, and that he is actually safe from the Free Legion."

We sat together in a mirror of my war room from Thera. Four Oligarchs, J'her, Shela, Groff, Hectar and I sat around a round table, torches burning on the cork walls. I had been notified of Karel's actions less than an hour before.

Oligarch one shook his head. "The Free Legion laid siege to Eldador the Port," he said. "So Ceberro knows better."

"But if he knows of the Fire Bond," Oligarch three said, "then he will be calling for the Heir to stand with him in defense of his new lands."

Oligarch four nodded. "He would believe that the Free Legion can never attack you."

"Also disproved by the siege," Oligarch one said. "Wolf Soldiers lifted it."

"It is widely known that Lupus did not attend," Oligarch two said. "In fact, there is more talk about the Battle of Thera."

"That was a significant victory for the Wolf Soldiers," Oligarch three said.

"Perhaps you are looked at now as greater than the Free Legion?" Oligarch four said.

"Have no doubt of that," Groff said. We all turned to him. He'd been included because he had a view of this from the outside.

I'd never wanted my Fire Bond commitment to be known of by people outside of the Free Legion. It represented a liability to me that I didn't need, and this obvious weakness which I'd known would be easy to exploit. On the other hand, certain other people whom I trusted had to be made aware of it, otherwise my actions were going to look like those of an usurper. My grandfather had told me once that if you are the only one who knows something, it's a secret. Otherwise it's a story.

Grandpa had been a smart man.

"The longer we know you, your Highness," Groff said, pointing his sharpened features right at me, "the more we see you do the impossible. The Battle of Thera was an impossible victory. So few shouldn't stand against so many. The Confluni legions are infamous."

"Ceberro is a fighting man," Hectar said. "He picked a city in the wild because he wanted to carve out civilization from nothing. He sees himself pushing into Toor, so it is no surprise that he has pushed into the Plains."

"We'll need to know how far he has gone already," I said. "I want fifty riders sent to the plains immediately, forty to remain watching, and ten to relay reports to and from there as things change."

Oligarch one nodded.

"We can't send Wolf Soldiers to rout them," Shela said.

"We should not rout them at all," Groff said. He stood, his hands on the table. "The Free Legion pays no tax, and in fact have acted against Eldador. I cannot think that you would side with them against one of our own Dukes."

"Ceberro should have consulted with me –" I began.

"With Glennen, you mean," Hectar said. "Which I know he didn't do. The Heir doesn't really decide these things the way our laws are written."

I raised an eyebrow. "Shall we turn this over to Glennen, then?" I asked him.

Groff and Hectar scowled. "Our point," said Groff, "is that you are Heir to the Eldadorian throne, your Highness. If you wish to take that throne and keep it, as indeed you clearly seek to do, you need to do more than to hold the capital. You need to hold the country, and you cannot do that without support from your Dukes."

"He is right," Oligarch three said. "Your Highness, if the city of Vrek wishes to push its ambitions onto the Plains of Angador, where there is no Eldadorian city, then you cannot directly oppose them."

I turned to Shela, who looked into my eyes. She didn't have to say that she agreed for me to know that she did. The Free Legion would have to lose this fight.

I sighed. "Send the riders, watch them," I said. "I want to be kept apprised of the situation."

I turned to Oligarch three. "Extend to Duke Ceberro my most polite invitation to meet with him and to learn from him," I said. "Clearly, this is a military man."

All four Oligarchs nodded as one. Groff and Hectar exchanged glances, then turned to me.

"I will put Eldador before the Free Legion," I promised them. "I know where my future lies."

"If I can speak frankly, your Highness?" Groff said.

"Please," I said.

He took a moment and chose his words. He looked around the table once, the severe features sweeping us rather than identifying us. I thought to myself, "That is something a leader learns – make the room hang on your words, when you have something important to say." He did that now.

"You know that all of Glennen's Dukes, and most of his Earls, were his chosen men when he founded this nation," he said.

Hectar nodded. I hadn't spoken to Hectar as much as I should have. Here was an untapped resource that I should have exploited. There seemed to just not be enough hours in the day.

"Rennin, Hectar, Yerel, Glennen, Ceberro and I, we were the closest," he said. "Men like Klem, Devarre, Endjen – they were there, and they were helpful, but they didn't pick up a sword and stand toe to toe with Swamp Devils or Shree or Taranji. When it came time for killing, the six of us did it.

"You are come new to this land," he said. "Your ways are strange. They work – for now – but they are strange. You give horsemen sticks and teach your men more about marching than about fighting with swords – and they beat their enemies, as if war were walking. You take less from the peasants and have more to show for it, as if peasants managed their money like kings.

"And then, suddenly, you are not just among us, but above us. You are the one who Glennen turns to when his wife is killed, and you avenge him by sacking the invincible city. Yet there are those of us who know that, had he never met you, then Alekanna would still be alive."

My hand dropped to the Sword of War, and Hectar held up his own and said, "Your Highness, do not think for a moment that this is said in disloyalty or challenge. Glennen made the same point to me. He never blamed you, but had he never met you, then Eldador would not be the growing threat to Fovea that it is now, and no one would care enough about her to assassinate her Queen."

I squeezed the pommel of the sword but didn't draw it. "To be honest with you," I said, "you're repeating what's been going through my head since the assassination happened. I have to admit that one of the reasons I felt like I had to crush Outpost IX was to get over the guilt from that good woman's death."

"If you can admit that," Hectar said, "then I can admit to you that, given a choice, I will be a part of Eldador the threat, rather than Eldador that is no threat at all."

"And I," said Groff. "I can accept you, Rancor Mordetur, as Heir and, when the time comes, King.

"I can accept Wolf Soldier guards in the palace, and I can accept Wolf Soldiers sacking the cities of those who would raise a hand against Eldador, if there is no other way."

He looked me in the eye, his severe brows down, and added, "Wolf Soldiers, your Highness. *Not* Legionnaires."

Hectar nodded, and the Oligarchs with him.

So be it.

***

My daughter had her first birthday in the month of Life. I gave her a doll with a ceramic face, and eyes that closed when she laid it down. She cherished it and kissed it over and over, calling it her 'bebe'. Its hair came from my own head.

My hair had grown down to between my shoulders now. I wore it back over my head, with a gold circlet to keep it in place. I still dressed in leather pants and a plain white shirt, but my boots were always shined, and my face never showed stubble.

On that birthday, Duke Ceberro arrived to attend the royal court, as did Ancenon, D'gattis and Karel of Stone. I doubted very much that the timing was a coincidence.

Karel's spies were everywhere, including here. Drekk had been no different.

"His Grace, the Duke Ceberro of Vrek, and the Lady Jameen of Angador," the herald announced.

Ceberro moved like a mountain of muscle and steel. Heavier than Rennin, taller than Glennen, the ground shook when he walked, and the gigantic mace at his side thumped with every step.

His hair had gone gray and hung from his tonsured scalp to his armpits. He had one eyebrow, still black, across both green eyes. He had a hawk-like nose and his mouth formed a thin, pink line. His armor mirrored mine.

He stopped right in the center of the circle, and he looked me right in the eye.

"Your Highness," he said, bowing. His Lady curtsied politely.

"Your Grace," I said, inclining my head in respect.

"Vrek was summoned to your presence, to speak of military matters," he stated.

"We appreciate your efforts," I said. "How goes the conquest of the plains?"

"We shall make a city named Angador where the rogues once held their training," he said. "I am already raising walls."

I nodded, impressed. "And this Lady, she shall be its first Duchess?" I asked.

She smiled and looked away. Ceberro turned his head to her, and then back at me, and said, "She was born a common, but now she is with me. She is my Lady, my consort and, Adriam willing, the mother of my children, when they should arrive."

"I wish you well in that battlefield as well," I said. "I've ridden those plains myself. In fact, if you would indulge me, it is my daughter's first birthday, and I would have you to the royal table for a feast."

He lowered his head. "We are honored, your Highness."

I dismissed him, and went on with court. Seemed that the war raged between Sental and Volkhydro, and Free Legion shipping did very well moving goods from Sental 1 to the rest of Fovea. This increased the demand for ships, and increased the flow of Volkhydran immigrants to Eldador. Sental paid the Free Legion in grain and barley, and of course they now had nowhere to send it, which created an influx in the Eldadorian markets, depressing the price for our own farmers.

The farmers wanted protection from the flood of grain, and the merchants wanted land grants to find new ways to exploit it.

Others wanted to be able to cull the Aschire for its wood, which of course I couldn't allow. That meant I had to dispatch Eldadorian Regulars to protect it, so that these others didn't do it anyway and touch off a war.

And the Trenboni were back, as delegates for the Fovean High Council.

"Is there still a Fovean High Council?" I asked Oligarch two. "I thought perhaps they had run away."

"Still very much present," one of the three Uman-Chi said. I looked closer and saw that they had sent, in fact, Aniquen, whom I had bested on the plain outside of Outpost IX. He looked to see that I recognized him, and then added. "Which is, of course, not how Lupus the Conqueror prefers to leave his foes."

"You were my foe once," I said. "Do you claim that we have unfinished business?"

"Not at all, your Highness," he said, with that snotty smile that Uman-Chi have. "In fact, I come seeking peace, not war."

"Peace?" I said. "Whom would you have me at peace with?"

"Well, Eldador is in fact the victim of Confluni aggressors," Aniquen said. "So you might, then, seek the help of the Fovean High Council toward that end."

"You might note that, as you made clear, those enemies were not left alive."

"Well then," Aniquen said, without missing a step, "there is this devastating war between Sental and Volkhydro."

"Eldador is not involved in that affair," I said. "And Eldador shall not be drawn into that affair."

"And if the call is made for the Fovean armies to intervene?" Aniquen asked.

"That shall be taken on its merits," I said. "I cannot say that the armies of Eldador will stay home if called upon, neither can I say that they are at the beck and call of the Fovean High Council."

Aniquen nodded. "I should like to speak, then, to King Glennen on this matter."

"I am sure you would," I said. "However, he is indisposed. I am at your disposal, and you have heard me."

"This is not in keeping with –" he began.

"Is there anything else?" I asked, interrupting him rudely. I knew the Uman-Chi. That was an unforgivable slight.

I think he leveled a glare at me – it's hard to tell with those ambiguous eyes – so I met it. I disliked him, and I saw no benefit in acting otherwise.

He turned to one of the Uman who'd come with him, and took a package from his hands. He opened it and held the contents up for me to see, a marble carving of a rearing stallion, in white.

"In celebration of your daughter's birth," he said. One of the Oligarchs was already descending the throne steps to retrieve it.

I couldn't suppress a smile. "I didn't expect this," I told him, frankly.

"A child is a cause for celebration," Aniquen informed me. "We see them rarely among our people. Every child is a chance for change, for improvement, for new insights into the world. A child is a precious thing, your Highness, no matter whom the father."

He could have left that last part off, but I thanked him. The Oligarch couldn't lift the statue so a couple Wolf Soldiers helped him with it.

"Eldador withdrawn from the Fovean High Council is Eldador with no friends in Fovea," the Uman-Chi warned me. "Such an Eldador would have a difficult time on Tren Bay."

"Fortunate for Eldador, then, that this is not your decision to make," I said. I agreed with him that I couldn't withdraw from the Fovean High Council. But I could be the France of the EEC and get away with it.

"You are dismissed," I said, and brushed him off with a wave of my hand, looking away. He turned on his heel, passed giggling courtiers in the gallery, and out the throne room door.

"Perhaps poorly advised, your Highness," Oligarch two whispered to me, ascending the steps again.

"Probably," I said, loud enough for the court to hear me. "But the emissary they sent tried to kill me once. A statue doesn't forgive him that. I'll be more civil to one who didn't."

He smiled and nodded. I ordered a division of Eldadorian foot from Steel City to patrol the Aschire border and protect it from woodsmen. Rennin wouldn't want or need wood from there, and he would best be able to spare the men. I ordered Oligarch three to write him a letter of explanation and to have it to me before I went to bed, then called court over for the day.

Hectar and J'her were waiting for me with, of all people, Tom Kelgan. By rights the man should have been in shackles in the dungeon with the wizard that I still hadn't decided on. In fact, he stood not three feet from me, a sword over his shoulder, looking me right in the eye with an irritating smile on his lips.

So I punched them. Four Oligarchs, a major and a Duke stood stunned as the Bounty Hunter's blood sprayed them down.

The next took him in the nose. He went for his sword and I pinned him by the neck to the wall with my left hand, then caught his left wrist in my right hand, twisting it so that the knife he held didn't find my stomach as he had intended.

I slammed his head against the stones as all four Oligarchs protested as one and Hectar's hand found my shoulder. J'her already had a dirk out and in position to be driven into the side of Tom Kelgan's head.

"Met your friend, Varoth," I said, looking into his seething green eyes. "I didn't like him real well."

"I am told he didn't live to regret it," Tom Kelgan said. His eyes stayed fixed on mine, but he released the dagger. Blood already seeped into the red hair on his head and moustache. Hectar pulled the sword from his shoulder sheath without removing his hand from my shoulder.

"You weren't smart to set me up," I said, and released him. "But you were plain stupid to stay here after."

"I gave you my word I wouldn't act against you, and you knew I was a spy," he said. "I stayed because you still bear watching. Don't blame me if the Guild hasn't found a way to you yet."

"This is more insolence than the Heir should hear," Hectar said. J'her nodded. "Certainly, you have killed bounty hunters before, your Highness."

I looked in his eyes, not really knowing what I would see. If I had been him, I would have stayed, too. I would have wanted to see how the target handled it. But I knew Tom Kelgan to be smoother than I, better at this sort of thing, more mature. He had played me better than I would have thought possible, making him not just smarter than I, but smarter and wiser.

A threat to me – but keep your friends close and your enemies closer. If I knew whom I dealt with, and I knew that person's advantages, then I knew more about him than I would about his replacement, who would surely follow if I dispatched this one.

"From this point on," I said, "you lose a finger for every weapon you bring into my presence. After you run out of fingers, I start on toes. After toes – well, by then you deserve what happens to you."

He nodded, and I released him. He rubbed his neck. "The Guild is still pursuing allies against me?" I asked him.

"I never agreed to inform on the Guild-"

The back of his head made a hollow 'thunk' when it hit the stone wall, my fist in his eye.

He might be smarter but I didn't have to like it.

"Your temper is going to be your undoing, your Highness," Kelgan told me.

"It will undo you in less than a minute," I said. "But then you will look a lot worse and have a *lot* less blood in you."

He sighed, threw a futile glance to the others there, and sighed again.

"The Dorkans know what you know of them," he said. "The Guild used the knowledge they were receiving from Klem to support what they were finding out through your Oligarch. Klem's family is in Conflu."

"And Duke Ceberro?" I asked him.

He hesitated, and I looked at J'her.

"I am tired of this," I said. "Take him to Shela. Tell her I want him sore, but not dead."

"We approached him, and we explained your Fire Bond and how to exploit it," he said. "He wasn't interested. We offered him gold, he still didn't seem interested."

"How do you know this?" Hectar asked him.

"I receive regular reports, so that I can tailor my advice back to the Guild," he said. "As a top operative, I can be trusted."

I looked back at J'her. "How many Wolf Soldiers are watching us now?"

"Twenty."

"Strip him, look in every crevice, get all of his weapons, take him to Shela."

"I told you the truth," Tom Kelgan complained.

I looked him in the eye. "You hesitated," I said. The Wolf Soldiers were already forming up next to J'her.

"And you pissed me off. Bet you don't do either again," I said, leaving with the Duke and the Oligarchs. I heard steel clatter as it hit the ground.

When we were out of earshot, I looked at Hectar and, as we walked, asked him, "What were you thinking?"

"When?"

"When you brought him armed into my presence?"

"J'her turned him up among the courtiers today," the Duke said. "He knew who Kelgan was, and he knew that you hadn't had him to dinner since returning from Uman City. He told me that we should bring him to you, and I agreed."

"That was a lot of initiative," I said.

The Duke looked at the side of my face. "You don't allow that among your soldiers?"

I smiled without looking at him. "I let them be their own men and women," I said. "J'her had been a farmer once. He is a lot more than that now. I am impressed with him."

Hectar just nodded. I liked the fact that J'her thought to build a bond with the Duke. I still planned to have Shela verify his loyalty again. Trust is a luxury that had burned me before.

"Where are we going, your Highness?" Oligarch two asked me.

"The stables," I said.

"Shall we ride, then?" Hectar asked me. I had it on good authority from a stable hand that he had gotten close enough to Blizzard to be bitten.

"I hope so," I said. The stallion had been cooped up too long. "But I have another meeting to attend, and that is as good a place as any, and better than the throne room."

The royal stables were out behind the palace building, within its walls, and accessible by a back exit that went near my own quarters. As we approached them, I could see Karel of Stone riding his pony within its grazing fence, and D'gattis and Ancenon watching him from the fence itself.

Both of the Uman-Chi were dressed in their usual robes. Karel wore his bear skins, even mounted. He seemed to be trying to show the pony how to take direction from his knees, while he shot arrows at a target I could barely see.

The Uman-Chi watched me with their ambiguous eyes as I approached with Duke Hectar and my Oligarchs. They barely acknowledged me, which told me more than if they had.

"Welcome," I said.

They nodded.

"You were taken care of with rooms and all?"

"All fit for a visitor," D'gattis said.

"You handle your anger well," I said. Why game around?

"We have had a lot of practice with you," Ancenon said.

Hectar chuckled.

"I remember a rough warrior on a rogue stallion," Ancenon said, "and he could be relied upon for great secrets and trusts."

He wanted me to justify myself. As with anything the Uman-Chi did, there would be nuance within nuance, and, of course, if I played their game, I would look stupid and end up apologizing like a good Man.

"Was he the one whom you led the Legionnaires against?" I asked him, frankly. "Or was this the one whom you warned the Trenboni about?"

"These are issues which we have thoroughly explained," D'gattis said.

"And yet, there it remains," I said. "You're upset that the compound on the Plains of Angador is invaded, and you think I allowed it."

"You didn't prevent it," Ancenon said.

"I cannot within the laws of Eldador," I said. "And I'm bound by them. I will never attack you, I will never allow your persons to be attacked, but I cannot prevent a Duke whose support I need from overrunning the compound that you didn't think to defend and, unlike you, I didn't give him the information that he needed to do it."

"We didn't think we had to defend it within your borders," D'gattis said.

"You wouldn't have if you had told me what you were doing," I said. "You are hundreds of years old. I overrated your intelligence, for which I accept blame. But had you simply said, 'Declare our estates off limits,' I could have made it an Earldom or something and you would be protected for a minimum amount of taxes."

They looked at each other, then at me. I knew I wouldn't outfox them, so I just told the truth. The blatant truth is nice in a pinch.

"Rest assured that our intelligence –" D'gattis began.

"Cousin," Ancenon said. D'gattis looked like he had been stung, much as Aniquen had looked a short time before.

Karel rode up on the pony, no hands on the reins. It didn't stop where he seemed to want it to, but it did stop pretty close to us.

"I love this animal," Karel told me.

"You've made good use of it," I said.

It was a pinto, distinctive like Karel. It suited him, I thought.

"I'm taking over your duties as recruiter for the Free Legion," he told me.

"That makes good sense," I said.

"You will continue to recruit your own Wolf Soldiers?"

"I think that's best, especially now that you have Sarandi," I said.

"I suggested that we winter in Sental, then look for another base in Eldador," he continued. "They think you should build it, or provide us room on your estates in Thera. I told them you would never go for it, and suggested the Andurin peninsula, right in the center."

I nodded. The peninsula offered a vast plain, relatively open, and could bear a city.

"How about I make Arath an Earl and then you raise a city?"

"Can you do that?" D'gattis asked me.

"I can get Glennen to do that," I said.

"He is in the barn, after all," D'gattis said.

Oh, crap.

"Alone?" I asked.

"Your Wolf Soldiers are watching him," Karel said. "If he's still awake, I'll be surprised."

I sent Oligarch one and three after him. They were used to it.

"Is the Dorkan wizard still alive?" Ancenon asked me.

"Yes," I said.

"No," Hectar said. I looked at him.

"Another matter of which I didn't get to tell you," he said. "He died today trying to escape. Blew most of his skin off."

Crap again.

"The palace wizards disposed of the body," he continued. "I think they were afraid you were going to carve him up and send him to Dorkan."

"That wasn't well received," Karel said. "I am informed that they considered destroying the whole city to get to you."

"That would have been an interesting way for them to meet Shela," I said.

D'gattis actually smiled. "You have a skill for spreading anger," he noted.

My Wolf Soldiers and both Oligarchs were directing Glennen from the barn. Straw covered his clothes and hair, his eyes looked bleary. He wore a stained grey tunic and dark brown trousers, but you could still see the dark stain on the inside of his left leg.

I made eye contact with one of the Oligarchs. He shook his head and looked away.

It was a real shame with him.

***

Dinner saw my daughter as the guest of honor at the royal table. She got to sit with the big people, her 'bebe' in a seat next to her. In my own tradition she'd been provided with a frosted cake in her honor, most of which ended up in her thick, black hair. Sycophants and friends showered her with gifts in order to remain in my favor and off of Shela's possible hit list. I looked on with pride when none of them had the prestige of her dolly.

"Have the marriage offers begun yet?" Ceberro asked me. He sat next to me. His woman cozied up to mine. I found it somehow amusing that now he was me, and I had become Glennen, from two years before.

"Hectar has his hopes," I said. "I've arranged for Groff's son and Glennen's daughter."

"He told me," Ceberro told me. "I'm also informed that I am well advised to accept fate and declare for you as Heir."

I looked at him seriously. Lee had decided that the more cake she wore, the more smiles she got, and the race began between the cake, her efforts and her mother's.

"How do you feel about that?" I asked him.

He looked me straight in the eye. "In honesty?"

"Always."

"I am a better man for the job," he said.

"You think so?"

"I am sure of it."

"You would match me?" I asked him. "Stand against Glennen's chosen Heir?"

"I would."

"Fists or swords?"

He grinned, took a look around the room, and then back at me.

"Fists," he said. "And I trust your wife isn't invited."

"She isn't my wife," I said. "And even if she were, she wouldn't be involved. In fact, rest assured that she will be there."

"You know I will thrash you," he said.

"I know you will try."

He grinned even wider. "In the morning?"

I nodded, and gave my attention back to my daughter's celebration.

All in all, it hadn't been a bad day.

That night I held Shela in my arms. Lee lay in her crib, her dolly wrapped up in both arms as if she thought someone would take it. Shela watched her through the crib's bars.

"A bit of cloth and pottery and hair," she said, her voice sounded distracted, "and I think she loves it more than she does me."

I chuckled. "You never had a doll?"

"Never," she admitted. "I almost want one now."

It occurred to me that I had never seen another child with a doll here, either. When I had described it to the seamstress who had made it, she had seemed to know just what I meant. She'd gone to the potter on her own, and had suggested using my hair for its.

"I think it is in a girl's nature to want a baby," I said.

"Surely," Shela agreed. "Just as it is in a man's nature to fight and make war."

I lay quiet for a moment. "I meant to ask you –" I began.

She turned and looked at me. "I didn't want to do what I did to Kelgan," she said. "But you commanded it, on my daughter's birthday. I stopped arranging her hair, I took him to the dungeon, I made him scream in pain, and then I went back to arranging her hair.

"If this is what you want of me, then I will become it, but White Wolf, please do not make of me your vile torturer."

She slid into my arms and I held her. It hadn't occurred to me that it would bother her. She could be a cruel bitch when she had to be. Lately I had been trying to define her, and getting it all wrong.

Maybe I would never get my mind around my slave girl. It might even be a good thing.

I fell asleep before I knew it - another dreamless night to commence the start of the second year of my daughter's life.

Chapter Twelve

A New Beginning

Duke Ceberro of Vrek stood taller than Two Spears. He couldn't make claim to my height, but he might be in better shape. He had ridden here; he had been in the campaign for the Plains of Angador. I had campaigned, and I knew what kind of great shape you got into when you did it.

I practiced in the swordsman's gym, with my Wolf Soldiers and Eldadorian trainers, but it felt to me like they held back. Saa Saraan had kicked my ass all over his gymnasium, and no one did that here.

Ceberro and I both dressed in leather leggings. New leather pants felt tight and binding. Worn leather pants felt like your own skin, and you moved in them like you were naked.

His pectoral muscles bulged like Nantar's. His upper and lower arms showed blue veins. I had more meat on me.

"I want you to know that I am undefeated," he told me, stepping into the sand circle. We were in the swordsman's gym within the palace. A few of the barons, Hectar and his family, Shela and Lee, the Oligarchs, Glennen and his family, and Ceberro's entourage were there. Wolf Soldier guards stood at the door.

The sweat running off of Glennen smelled like pure alcohol. His kids stood next to Shela. He stepped into the ring between us, looked at Ceberro, then at me.

"I am told by Duke Ceberro that he should be Heir, and that you've accepted his challenge?" Glennen slurred. He hadn't gotten drunk yet, but he'd managed hung over. One of his attendant Wolf Soldiers held a cup in his hands – no point in guessing what I'd find in it.

I grinned. Ceberro fought his battles on all of the fronts. I hadn't even known that he and Glennen had been talking. "My pardon, your Majesty, but I would not presume to enter into such an agreement without consulting you."

He barked a laugh. "You enter into a lot without discussing it with me," he said. "Like marrying off my daughter. I wouldn't have allowed this otherwise."

I raised an eyebrow. He played dirty. Ceberro must feel pretty sure he'd beat me. He better hope he did.

I stepped into the ring. "If that's what the Duke wants to tell you," I said, "then I am more than willing to kick his ass for it."

Ceberro raised his eyebrow. "You kick?" he said. "Only women kick."

Glennen laughed and raised his hand. He looked at Ceberro, then at me.

"I expect you to show me why I trust you so much," he told me.

I nodded. He lowered his hand and stepped out of the ring.

Ceberro charged me like a bull, head down, fists pumping. He'd clearly gotten used to being the biggest guy in the ring, and sought to use his superior size to overwhelm me.

I was bigger. I side stepped him and punched him with my left fist in the kidneys. The crowd let out a sympathy groan. He grit his teeth and turned, and I pasted him in the nose twice and then stepped back out of his reach, leading with my left.

He turned his shoulders to put his back to my left, trying to make me focus on his back or his head, where he could hold his arm up and defend from me. Then I would be open to his right.

He closed. I turned on my right foot and suddenly stood a foot closer to him, leading with my right. I punched him twice in the face and once in the throat with my right, then caught his right cross with my left and hit him in the left eye directly. He swung wildly with his left; I ducked and then had both of his hands on his right side. Now I had him in a classic position and I took advantage of it, grabbing both hands with mine, turning and flipping him. He hit the sand hard, and I followed up with two to the stomach before he could move, then stepped away from him.

"Wow," Glennen said. "I believe that is the expression you taught me?"

I grinned at him for a second, bouncing on the balls of my feet, then stayed focused on Ceberro.

He clearly didn't know what had hit him. I hadn't gone berserk but I felt the blood pumping, the excitement, the good pain in my fists from hitting him. I considered helping Ceberro back to his feet, but this type of guy would punch you on the way up, so I waited.

He rolled onto his hands and knees, took a breath, then got to his feet. He faced me with his fists up, a cut over his left eye, his nose bleeding and his lips smashed. He looked pissed and didn't try to hide it. He hadn't laid a hand on me the whole time. He spat a gob of blood on the floor, looked at me, and then at Glennen.

"It is his wife, your Majesty," he said. "Clearly, I am beset."

Glennen laughed. "I think you are a bad loser, Ceberro," he said. "I have seen his wife's work. You are still alive, so she has done nothing to you."

"You have seen me fight," he said. "I am not so easily bested."

"I've watched the battle," Glennen said. "And I know what I've seen. If you want me to have her leave, I will."

"It would make no difference now," Ceberro complained. "Look at what his wife's spell has let him do to me."

I stepped up, because this really started to piss me off. "First," I said, "she is my slave, not my wife.

"Second," I said, and waited for him to meet my eyes. "Accuse me of cheating again, and I will call for swords, not fists, and I will wait for you to heal, and I will carve you to pieces with Shela a mile away just to prove to you what a woman you are. I don't need anyone's help to beat a rank amateur like you."

That got him. He swung and caught me right on the jaw. I stepped back and he caught me in the stomach, and again, and again. As I had with Two Spears, I held my fists in front of my face and let him work the stomach, taking what he had, until I felt his blows begin to weaken.

Then I treated him to a one-two combination to the jaw, leading with the right this time, leaving him staggering and his mouth open. I closed it with my right, hit him in the stomach with my left, feeling it sink into his unready muscles, then grabbed his shoulder with my right. I pulled him past me, kicked the back of his knee with my heel, and folded him over backwards onto the sand.

I stood over him. When he tried to rise I punched him right in the nose. He tried to rise again, and I hit him again.

"I can do this all day," I said.

"You won't let me rise?" he asked.

"Apologize for accusing me of cheating," I said.

He tried to rise, I hit him again.

"Like I said, I can do this all day."

He turned to Glennen, then back to me. I had hoped that this would be an amicable fight. He had fooled me. I wouldn't let that happen again. I knew he'd say that I didn't beat him fairly. I wanted to be able to counter later with his admission now. I didn't care how I got it.

"You didn't cheat," he said. "May I rise now?"

I held out my left hand, he took it with his. As I predicted, once I'd pulled him three quarters of the way up, he swung on me, looking for another shot to the jaw. He misjudged the distance, however, and missed my face by half an inch.

I yanked him to his feet and knocked him back on his ass. This time he just sat there.

"I can't beat him," he said, looking at Glennen.

"It appears you can't," the king said.

"I concede, then," he said. He looked at me. "I am defeated by you. You've beaten me. You are the Heir."

I nodded and stepped out of the ring. Shela ran to me and gave me a warm hug and a hero's kiss. Hectar pounded my back. I looked past them and saw that the Uman-Chi were in attendance, watching us with ambiguous eyes. They were against the far wall, by the single entrance to the gym. Ancenon nodded to me, and I nodded back to him.

Shela wouldn't have helped me. D'gattis wouldn't have thought twice about it. They had a debt to pay to Ceberro.

I felt Glennen's heavy hand on my shoulder, and turned to see him smiling. Two Wolf Soldiers were helping the Duke up off of the ground. He looked at me, spat blood, and looked at me again. I made an enemy here today, another one I didn't need.

"Let's all drink to this," Glennen said. "Invite your Uman-Chi, Rancor. Let us celebrate a new beginning."

I thought, "You've got that right."

***

We sat at the royal dining table. Glennen had the mead flowing. Ceberro tried to match Glennen bowl for bowl. I decided to watch myself. The Uman-Chi and Hectar drank wine.

J'her had the security of the palace if I had too much. Jameen had left with one of the court barons and, as far as I knew, hadn't sought out Shela. She'd taken the baby to the stables.

Glennen recanted some escapade he and Ceberro had gone on into the Aschire. Ceberro laughed along, wincing at the pain in his smashed lips. The Uman-Chi listened politely and I could tell that Hectar had heard the story before.

"You know," Ceberro interrupted, "your own Eldadorian warriors are defending the Aschire right now from your own merchants."

Glennen slammed down his bowl. He looked once around the room, then at me. The liquor hadn't incapacitated him yet, but it had impaired him.

"And who ordered that?" he demanded.

"I did, your Majesty," I said. "He wouldn't be trying to use it to anger you if it had been anyone else's edict."

Ceberro raised his eyebrows in surprise. D'gattis actually chuckled, and Ancenon looked sideways at him. Hectar opened his mouth to speak, but Glennen interrupted him.

"So you admit that you are supporting the squirrels," he said.

"They are Eldadorians," I said. "If I let our merchants chop down their trees, they'll retaliate against the merchants and we'll have civil war. An internal war will see Dorkan soldiers on the Andurin peninsula in a month, rest assured. They're still angry about our actions in Katarran."

"Merchants are chopping their trees down?" our monarch had been given too much information.

"They want the wood to house Sentalan grain," Hectar said. "The Heir has seen to it that we profited mightily from the war between Volkhydro and Sental."

"Us or the Aschire?" Ceberro challenged him.

Glennen waved him off. "The Aschire don't care about grain or gold," he said. "Why was I not informed of this war?"

"You were," I told Glennen. "We discussed it at length a week ago. You told me that you wouldn't mind leading a few thousand Eldadorians in among the Uman and having at them."

Glennen grinned at that. Ceberro took a drink and scowled.

"Trenbon shall be sending peace keepers," Ancenon offered. "That is, if the hostilities continue."

Glennen laughed. "Uman against Uman. The Volkhydrans will carve you to bits. It takes Men to fight Men."

Hectar grinned to himself on that point. D'gattis took a sip of wine to hide a smug look.

"Clearly, the most effective fighters on Fovea are Wolf Soldiers," Ancenon said. "And they are from all races."

"That *is* true," Hectar said. "You can't talk to a military man right now about anything but the invasion of Thera by the Confluni."

Glennen slammed his hand down on the table. "Conflu invaded Thera?" he demanded.

"Months ago," Ceberro said. "I believe it was 30,000 defeated by half their number?"

That was a mistake, I thought. It made Glennen seem stupid to the person who mattered most to him: Glennen.

"I believe that Thera at the time had 4,000 foot," Ancenon said, his eyes not clearly focused on anyone. "And their lancers were relieving the siege of Eldador the Port."

"From you," Ceberro added.

"And, so," Ancenon said. "We were under the hire of the Trenboni at the time. When the Wolf Soldier horse intervened, we quit the field."

Glennen put his bowl down and considered all of this, as if hearing it for the first time.

Ceberro scoffed. "No four thousand could defeat thirty," he said. "Even from the walls of Thera."

"We defeated them on the field," I said. "And if you would like to enter war games with the Wolf Soldiers, you are welcome to try your luck. I can assure you, the numbers are correct."

Ceberro had likely seen the war games in Thera when the Wolf Soldiers defeated the Legionnaires. Everyone knew of the battle of Tamaran Glen. Wolf Soldiers were reportedly invincible.

Ceberro just looked down into his bowl.

The future with him would suck, I knew. He would pull this crap and make as much trouble for me with Glennen as he could. His Eldadorian troops would pull stunts in the battlefield if I needed them, and he definitely planned to withhold taxes, so that I had to either treat him like Uman City or give him a free pass and piss off every other city in Eldador.

Glennen said, "Why am I hearing all of this for the first time?"

I looked him in the eye. "You aren't, your Majesty," I said. "I have kept you up to date with everything."

"Am I getting old?" he asked. "Am I senile, that I don't remember?"

"If I may speak plainly," I said, "your Majesty, I think it is the drink."

"You think I drink too much, do you?" Glennen said, looking me in the eye.

"You know you do," Hectar said. "Glennen, you are drunk almost all of the time. I have personally peeled the piss-soaked pants from you, as have Rancor's Wolf Soldiers, the Oligarchs, and your personal assistants, until we couldn't trust you around them."

Glennen slammed his hand down on the table again. "What do you mean?" he demanded. "Why couldn't you trust me with my own staff?"

"You have tried to rape most of the women," I said, coming to Hectar's defense. "As for the men, you stabbed two of them. The Wolf Soldiers are the only ones who can handle you when you're really drunk."

Glennen stood in fury, slamming his hand down once again. Ceberro seemed caught between satisfaction and fear. It depended on whom Glennen decided to vent on.

"I have never raped," he roared.

"I can summon the servants," Hectar said. "And you can choose the wizard for the truth saying. At one point you were going to go into town –"

"Enough!" he bellowed. His face turned beet red now. I could see the look in his eyes, not just the anger from being accused but, behind that, the realization, the shame, that he knew that he couldn't be sure of his innocence.

His honor had been his life. People had followed him, made a king of him, for his character. Who was Glennen the drunkard?"

"Bring Shela here," he said suddenly. "Bring her, bring her right now."

I looked at a Wolf Soldier guard and nodded. He bolted out the door in a moment. Glennen sat back down, his face still red, his hand on his shoulder, rubbing it.

He turned in his seat to face Ceberro. "Did you know of this?" he asked.

"I have been absent, Glennen," he said. Not 'your Majesty,' I noted. There was a time to play politics and there was a time to put it aside. I think Ceberro wanted to take advantage of an opportunity if it presented itself, but it would be suicide to blame me for this now, especially if he had just called for my woman.

Glennen looked at Hectar. "You?"

Hectar looked away, and then looked back at him.

"I know you miss her," he said. He put his hand on the table, as if on his friend's arm. "I know what she meant to you.

"I know you can't stand to think of her, so you drink instead. But I have watched you chase your children away, and you have done things you would have killed another man for. Rancor holds the kingdom together, but he isn't the king and he hasn't the power to do it forever. Did you know Yerel from Uman City tried to revolt?"

"Yerel?" Glennen blinked in surprise. He reached for his bowl of mead, then looked at it and pushed it away.

"Is he dead?"

"I'm holding him in Thera," I said. "I deposed him. He's a common, and I had you name another Duke of Uman City."

Glennen shook his head. "I don't remember," he said.

"It happened on the day we pulled you naked out of the fountain," Hectar said. "I had to sign your name at your order, because you were too drunk to do it."

Glennen reached out his left hand, open and closed his fist, looked at it like it didn't belong to him. "This makes the world close in on me," he said.

Sweat poured off of his forehead and down his face. His breath sounded shallow. I looked into his eyes. He stared at his hand as if he could see nothing else.

Oh, crap!

"Your Majesty," I said. "Is there a pain in your chest?"

"I," he said, and wet his lips. "I – can't breathe."

"Does your chest hurt?" I asked, more forcefully.

He looked at me with his mouth open, a ragged hole in the center of his face. The color drained from his cheeks, from red to pale. He didn't seem to recognize me.

"I, who?" he said.

I leapt to my feet and ran to him. "Hectar," I said. "Get Shela here, and get her here now. Send Wolf Soldiers for royal healers."

"Your Highness," he said.

"*Go!*" I ordered him.

Ceberro stood, looking like he wanted to get between Glennen and me.

"What are you doing?" he demanded.

I knocked him out of the way. Ceberro flew backwards over his chair, crashing to the floor and breaking one of its legs. I hadn't meant to hit him that hard. I put a hand on Glennen's arm, and it felt clammy. I turned to the two Uman-Chi, watching all of this as they might a play.

"Do you know what a heart attack is?" I demanded.

They turned to each other, then back to me.

"His heart is damaged from the strain of his drinking, and his weight," I said. "It is about to stop. If it does, he'll die. Can you do something for him?"

"We cannot subvert Adriam's will, if this is when He will take him," Ancenon said.

"Can you heal his heart?" I demanded.

Ancenon looked at me with ambiguous eyes, saying nothing. Uman-Chi knew that Men had short lives, so another one dying, even a king, didn't surprise them.

Shela burst in the door, Lee in her arms. Lee's eyes were full of tears and she clutched her doll.

Glennen's eyes rolled back in his head and his breath had become raspy.

"Shela, can you heal him?" I demanded.

"What?" she said. She hurried down the dining room, past the chairs, moving as fast as the bulky skirt to her dress would allow her. "White Wolf, what is happening?"

"He thinks that Glennen's heart is under attack," D'gattis said. "I can detect no magic."

"It is the yellow sickness," I said. That had been her term for it. "His heart is about to stop."

"Oh," she said. She stopped dead in her tracks, as if afraid to approach him.

"White Wolf, there is no cure for that," she said. She looked into my eyes, I could see her sadness.

"I have told you, the yellow sickness kills."

"No!" I demanded. I turned him over backwards in his chair, laying him gently as I could on the floor. The table stood in my way, and without thinking I threw my shoulder against it, knocking it back four feet to clear room for him.

Wine and mead flew everywhere. The Uman-Chi leapt gracefully back. Hectar stood behind me, trying to help me, and Ceberro stood behind him, watching from where he'd picked himself up off of the floor.

"What can I do?" Hectar asked.

"Nothing," Ancenon said. "Lupus, I will prepare him for the next world, if you will let me. I know he is a child of the All Father. But I know the yellow sickness, and your slave is right. It kills."

I took Glennen's hand in mind. His breathing made a horrible sound, his eyes coming in and out of focus, as if he were already looking into the next world.

"Glennen, listen to me," I said. He didn't look my way. "Glennen, don't give into this. Be strong. You can fight it. Stay awake, stay with me."

War wanted this, and I was supposed to want it, too. I didn't care. My cheeks were wet with my tears, sprung out of nowhere. My nose clogged with an itching mass. Here it was – this was the event I had been anticipating and dreading.

No! Not only no but *hell no*! War could turn me inside out while I was still alive – I didn't want this.

His head turned away from me, I took his jaw in my hand and turned it back. "Glennen, no! Don't give up! Fight it!"

It sounded weak and stupid to me, but I didn't care. I didn't think I could do CPR on him if his heart stopped. I doubted very much that anyone here did heart surgery.

"She is here," he whispered. He opened his eyes and looked at me.

"Rancor, she is here," he told me.

"No, Glennen, don't go to her," I said. He wanted to give up. Now I realized that he'd been trying to kill himself all along. If he thought he could get to Alekanna this way, I would lose him.

"Alekki," he said, turning from me. "Alekki, I am so sorry. I let you die, my love, my queen."

"Glennen!" I cried. I saw my own tears fall on his face, and I didn't care. "Glennen, look at me!"

"I missed you so much," he said.

"Lupus."

I turned to see Ancenon. I felt his thin-fingered hand on my shoulder. With a strength that surprised me, he pulled me up and away from Glennen. I reached for him, but Ancenon turned me away.

"Lupus, let him go," he said. "His time is done. He goes to his reward, from the All Father."

"He can't –" I began.

"That is not for you to say," Ancenon told me.

I looked into his ambiguous eyes, the silver cornea barely distinguishable from the silver iris. He gently moved me aside, took my place, kneeling, and took Glennen's hand.

He began to pray for the King's soul.

"No!" I raged. My fist fell like a hammer on the corner of the table, denting its surface. It burned like fire.

Ceberro, Hectar and, from somewhere, J'her were on me like coyotes. They pulled me back from Glennen and Ancenon, to a corner of the room, pinning me to the wall. Hectar said something, but I couldn't make it out.

The berserker rage came over me. I welcomed the violence.

And then Shela put herself right in front of me with Lee in her arms. My dark-haired daughter, her 'bebe' bent over her arm, looking soulfully into my eyes. She reached out and touched the skin on my face, leaning out of her mother's arms.

"Dada," she said. Her first words. I focused on her, my girl. Felt her cool fingers on my burning skin.

"Dada," she said again.

She dropped me right to my knees. I wept openly, five feet from Glennen, the energy from the rage dispersing from me. My hand and shoulder throbbed. I held my head down, saw the tears puddle on the floor.

I had thought so many times how much easier my life would be if Glennen would conveniently die. I could have accepted finding him in a puddle of his own puke in the barn. This ripped me apart – to have to sit with him, helpless, as he gave up.

He had pushed the bowl away. I saw it. He'd taken an interest. He was about to turn the corner.

We'd come so close to getting him back!

***

I don't know how long I knelt there. I didn't know that Men traditionally expressed their grief here. I didn't know that they would have left me there for a week if I wanted to, and said nothing about it to me afterwards.

I didn't know that the behavior I saw as normal from Glennen, to just get back to work after Alekanna died, had seemed strange to other Foveans, and that my behavior, to fall apart, had been normal to them.

I didn't know and I didn't care. The sun had risen out of the windows and the shadows were short when I finally looked at them. Shela waited there with Lee, leaning on the long table, watching me. I didn't see Glennen. His blood and puke and urine stained the floor five feet from me. The table had been pushed up against the far wall.

I placed the same hand I had used to hit the table on the floor, and used the same shoulder I had used as a battering ram to brace myself as I tried to rise. The pain in both made me gasp. I grit my teeth, tried again, and finally got to my feet.

Shela came to me slowly, as if afraid that I would explode or hit her. I watched her, saying nothing.

"Your grief was great," she said.

"The man was great," I said.

She nodded. She regarded Lee, who sat quiet, just watching me. "You know that this daughter of yours stood your vigilance. She wouldn't be removed from the room, or nurse, or even soil her diaper, waiting for you."

I grinned. I reached out and stroked her cheek. She bit my finger, a needle-sharp baby tooth piercing me.

"He died," Shela said finally.

"I know."

"His Oligarchs are preparing him," she said. "The bells from Adriam's temple have been ringing. J'her doubled the Wolf Soldier guard and sent for another thousand from Thera."

"Probably a good idea," I said.

She took my hand and looked at it. It throbbed. She turned it over, and I could see the meaty side swelling.

"Not broken," she said. "I have never seen bones so thick as yours. No wonder no man can beat you."

"Well," I said, grinning, "I am a tough guy, you know."

"Not so tough," she said, and she kissed my lips gently. "Not so tough that you don't mourn his dying."

I felt a tear roll down my cheek.

"You know, I feared you would react like you always do," she said.

I felt my eyebrows drop.

"Oh, you know what I mean," she said. "You would work it into your plans, your schemes, and you would build on it. When I walked in, I wondered if you would use this to convince the other Dukes to turn on Ceberro, or to justify an invasion of Conflu."

"Ceberro," I said. "So you know –"

She kissed me. "I am not stupid, White Wolf," she said. "I saw him in the ring. You beat him so that he could beat you through me. How better to overturn The Conqueror than to repaint him as The Coward. I have rescued you before – people would believe I did it again."

"He must be enjoying himself now, then," I said. "Lupus the Weeper."

She shook her head. "Before he left, he said to me, 'Protect him well, that is my King now.'"

"Ceberro?"

"No man can doubt how much you loved him," she said. "And many did, White Wolf. Many thought that you were an opportunist carving your ambition from a keg of mead. Devarre even thought you might be feeding him liquor."

"Who?"

"Devarre?" she said. She punched me. "One of the Oligarchs? I wondered if you knew their names."

I smiled. "Was it that obvious?"

"You called him 'Two' once," she said. "I don't think you were aware of it, but the rest of us enjoyed a laugh after."

I just shook my head. She released my hand. The swelling had gone down now.

"Plains magic?" I asked her.

"The benefits of owning a witch," she said.

I kissed her, let her tongue into my mouth, tasted this girl who loved me. It went on long enough were Lee started to bat our faces and to giggle.

We broke the kiss and looked at her. Her own face turned red, and Shela immediately held her away.

"How long did she work on *that*?" I asked.

Shela just snorted and beat a path to our chambers.

I sat there, rubbing my hand, looking at the dent in the table. I sort of remembered putting it there, but not really. I saw another next to it, on the side, where I had shouldered it into the wall. The table had been made of some hard wood; it was a miracle that I hadn't broken something. It sure felt like I had.

Another thing that had played out well for me. Even my weakness made me stronger. King of Eldador, and the Ceberro problem taken care of, unless of course he'd just scammed Shela. Ceberro the opportunist - and what an opportunity for him now. If he wanted to take advantage of me, he would have already.

Might as well go see, I sighed. If he quit the palace, then I'd know that he'd left to marshal his troops in Angador and Vrek.

I left the table, the chairs and the mess for the servants, walked to the door, and pulled it open. I planned to go to find Hectar, to get his opinions, then to meet with the Oligarchs.

Instead the nobility crowded the hall. Ceberro and his family, Hectar and his, the Oligarchs, the court barons, J'her and forty Wolf Soldier guards, standing at attention.

"His Majesty Declared, King Rancor Mordetur of Eldador!" my major announced. They all went down on two knees. We had no tradition here – I would be the second king of Eldador. Apparently the resident Dukes had worked it out with the Oligarchs. I stood there, stunned, not knowing what to do. I searched for and found J'her's eyes. He grinned at me, and then saluted, his hand over his heart. I saluted back.

"Stand," I said. "All of you, get up."

They stood, hesitant, waiting to see what I would do. This was critical, I thought. Screw this up and it will haunt your reign.

"I thank you all," I said, simply. "This is a difficult time, for Eldador and for me, and for each of you, I am sure. We have lost the father of our nation, a great man, and a uniter.

"Let us take a week to heal," I said. "For a week, if any man or woman comes to the capital who is hungry, let him be fed. If any comes who is poor, let him have shelter. If any come who is full of fear, let us protect him.

"We are an Eldadorian family," I said. "Let us look after our brothers, our sisters and our cousins."

They applauded. Hectar and Ceberro looked at each other, then at me. That had to sound pretty radical to them. So be it.

We could find worse things in life than being good to each other.

Chapter Thirteen

Bells and Whistles

"When Glennen took the throne of Eldador," the priest of Adriam said, "he stood in his armor, on a pile of stones, and he said to the rest of us, 'I am your King.'"

We stood on the steps of the royal palace. A Man named Dred Barr, the high priest of Adriam for the Eldadorian city, and whom I had never met, officiated from the highest step, right before the gigantic wooden doors to the palace. Every baron, every earl, every Duke of Eldador, and every wealthy commoner who could get a place, had come to this event. Avek Noir had come to represent the Trenboni with Ancenon. Four Uman delegates of Sental, the bearded and furred representatives of the cities of Volkhydro, the lithe horsemen of the major clans of Andoron, including my father-in-law, Kills with a Glance; even a delegation of black-haired, yellow-skinned Confluni had come.

There were black men in white robes called, 'Toorians,' who had sailed in from the Silent Isle. Eldador had been a good trade partner with them, bringing their native fruits and pelts to the north and reselling their wood-crafted furniture.

For a week we had given away bread and housed the homeless. The ranks of the Wolf Soldiers had doubled. J'her complained along with Two Spears that we would never train them all.

We had all agreed that we would have the ceremony, then the funeral, and that this would be our tradition. Never let Eldador be without a monarch.

So we all crowded the stone courtyard between the gates to the palace walls and the steps to the palace doors. Shela had dressed in a beautiful red gown that showed off her cleavage. Lee wore another gown to match, cut more for a baby. Glennen's kids were in black, of course. Alekennen already cozied up to Groff's son – she would leave with them to start her new life as his prospective bride.

"So let the new King, Rancor Mordetur, who is already known to us as the Just, the Conqueror, and the Wise, come before the All Father now."

I stood up next to the priest, and faced the crowd of thousands. I looked up and saw the Aschire bowmen on the walls. Grim-faced Wolf Soldier guards in pristine gray and black tabards stood posts everywhere. If the city turned out now, it could probably turn back the combined Fovean armies.

Which is what I wanted, because if anyone ever wanted to move against Eldador, the time had come.

"Rancor Mordetur, do you take on the legacy of the Stowes, to rule this land with wisdom and with justice?" the priest asked me.

"I do," I said.

"To what god do you swear your oath?"

"To War," I said. Plenty of warriors worshipped war. I heard a murmur, however. Glennen had worshipped Adriam.

"Then be recognized by your people as his Majesty, Rancor the First, of House Mordetur, King of Eldador."

The crowd cheered. The monarchs here didn't wear crowns. I wore the circlet that I usually wore to hold my hair back, and my armor, because Glennen had worn his on his crowning.

This was as much tradition as Eldador had. This turned out to be a pretty good thing, too, because it stopped the crossbow bolt that took me right in the chest a moment later.

I remember thinking, "Wow, the sky is really blue today," before I even realized that I lay on my back.

"Alarm!" the cry rang out. The sky flashed yellow from the defensive spells that encircled the building. Close those doors, now that the horse had left the barn!

Shela kneeled at my side, her hand at my neck. Lee screamed herself red-faced. Rennin and Ceberro were on either side of me with their swords out, and no less than one hundred Wolf Soldiers circled all of us. The priest made a hasty retreat; I placed him as more of the church-going religious man than any type of hero.

"White Wolf?" Worry painted Shela's face.

"I don't think it did more than knock me down," I said. "Rennin, a hand!"

Rennin took me by the front of the breastplate and hauled me to my feet like a doll. My chest throbbed dully, but in that general 'someone just punched me' pain, not the 'Oh, look at the bolt sticking out of me,' pain. As if I needed more evidence, I actually stepped on the offending weapon.

Shela scooped it up before I could get to it, and it glowed red. I thought that she wanted to destroy it in her anger, then I realized that she was using it instead. Not hard to guess for what.

"Bounty Hunters," she announced. "He is a Dorkan, and he is within the walls of the palace still."

"Can you find him?" Ceberro demanded. He did it too forcefully for my tastes. I didn't trust him, no matter what he said to Shela.

Shela's brown eyes scanned the warriors around us and landed on the captain of my Wolf Soldier guard. She reached out with the left hand and touched his forehead. "Accept my power," she commanded him.

I knew this man as Tehern, a Volkhydran who had killed four men in a drunken brawl over a woman. I had purchased him from Ulep's headman for one hundred gold coins. He was a pile of muscle with hair, beetle-browed and with weathered skin. He looked like nothing more than a fighting man, but he possessed a sharp and cunning mind and he had done well with the Wolf Soldiers.

He took a step back, the fear obvious in his wide, staring eyes. He closed those eyes and opened them again, then shook his head.

"Do you see the face?" she asked him.

"I do," he said. "I – oh, War, I see the face!"

She nodded. "That is the man who would kill Lupus," she said. "Bring him."

He nodded and left with his guards without even looking at me. I shouted, "He'll be going for the dungeons," and a few of my Wolf Soldiers turned and nodded to me as they ran after him.

"Why the dungeons?" Ceberro asked.

"Either they found a way in through there," I said, "or he will hide there. They're extensive. Our trying to find him with magic isn't going to be a surprise to him, so he is going to want to be somewhere where he can hide from someone tracking him."

"But if he's a suicide attacker?" Ceberro argued.

I shook my head. "He would have done the job with a sword or dagger then," I said. "He thinks he is going to get away and brag of this."

Rennin looked me in the eye. "He won't," he informed me.

I nodded. The courtyard boiled in pandemonium. Nobles and commons looked for someplace to be other than wherever they found themselves, as people tend to do when you fence them in and don't tell them why. Wolf Soldier guards held their perimeter, many of them probably recognizing the men and women who had sentenced them for their previous crimes. That had to be sweet, I thought. Getting to jail your jailer. Even with my Wolf Soldiers' knowing that they couldn't exactly poke these nobles with a sword, just the position that both were in had to be rewarding.

It might have been years since that fat cop with bad breath had told me I would do time, but I'd still love to have him in my dungeon now.

I called for J'her. While I waited I tickled Lee's nose to quiet her. Her mother held her almost distractedly as her mind and Power sought out our new enemy.

A one-year-old, she looked right at me. I thought about how she had quelled my anger with a touch of her hand. Funny how your daughter has that power over you. She gurgled and cooed at me as I made faces at her.

J'her pounded up the stairs two at a time, in his usual Wolf Soldier uniform, alone.

"Your Majesty," J'her said, as he approached me.

I punched him in the face with my steel gauntlet. I held the Sword of War in my hand before I even thought of drawing it.

I would have let anyone else draw. J'her had served me well, however, and he deserved better.

He reached for his weapon and I marked him, parting his steel breastplate like silk. Rennin and Ceberro stood stunned behind me as I pressed him down the stairs, cutting his arms and his legs as he struggled to get his sword out. Wolf Soldiers were sprinting to my side already.

Faster than my Wolf Soldiers, Aschire archers pin-cushioned J'her with arrows. Some bounced from his armor, but the rest found his face, his elbows, the backs of his legs, anywhere where a chink showed in his armor.

He fell to his knees, and then to his face. He never got his sword out or a word of explanation. He had said enough.

"Your own man?" Ceberro asked, his voice hushed.

I flipped him on his back with my toe. His eyes were ruined with arrows.

"This isn't J'her," I said. "No Wolf Soldier would call me 'Your Majesty.' This is either our Bounty Hunter or another one."

"Another," Shela said. She laid her hand on his back, and his face changed. I recognized the Uman ears. A glamour had made him look like my Major.

J'her charged toward me with three squads behind him; through the crowd and up the steps. This time I simply looked at Shela, who concentrated for a moment and nodded. He stopped at the body, then looked at me.

"This is my fault," he said to me, absolute in his loyalty. "Lupus, I should have done better –"

"We are fighters, not guards," I said. "And he was disguised as you, with a glamour. I don't know how we would have done this differently. It isn't that they attacked us, J'her, it's that they failed twice that matters."

"We have nobles from every land complaining," J'her informed me. "We have sign of the Bounty Hunter trying to go over the wall, as well. The Aschire claim to have marked him. We found a fresh blood trail in the palace already, leading to the dungeons as you expected."

"Keep me up to date," I said, and caught myself. "Let me know what you are doing, as you do it."

He nodded and took off. Rennin had a squad removing this new bounty hunter.

"You know, most people whom they want to kill, oblige them with dying," Rennin informed me.

"You are making no friends among them," Ceberro agreed, trying to get in on the joke.

"Well, your Grace, I think I have already made sure they won't be sending me gifts on All Gods' Day. I want the two of you to help me now."

"I am at the service of the King of Eldador," Ceberro said, and lowered his head. Rennin looked at him, rolled his eyes and then looked at me.

"What do you need, your Majesty?" he asked.

"I want these nobles herded into the throne room," I said. "Wolf Soldiers will make them go, I want you to invite them instead, and tell them I want to address them and explain what's going on. People who think they are powerful love that."

Rennin frowned, and gave me a look. "He and I are people in power, you know," he said.

"Shall I tell you why I am doing this, then?" I asked, looking him right in the eye.

He opened his mouth, then closed it. "I never really know if I like you, Rancor Mordetur," he said.

"Of course you don't," I assured him. "I'm cruel and irritating. No one likes that."

He shook his head and left with Ceberro. I turned and left with Shela and the remaining thirty Wolf Soldiers. It occurred to me right then that I *really* needed a cape, for exits like this. Such a stupid thought made me smile to think it.

"You're in good spirits for a man attacked not once but twice," Shela said.

"It's a relief," I said.

"A relief?"

I nodded. "You knew as well as I did that they would try something today."

She said nothing. She had barely slept the night before, and I knew she didn't care about the king thing. She'd dreaded the whole event and she knew like I did that I was a sitting duck out there. She hadn't said a word, but she had suffered as if I were dying.

"It's over," I said. "And they didn't get us. You are alive, I am alive, and that little girl in your arms is alive.

"That and a fast horse, what else do we need?" I asked her.

She laughed at that. "You have barely ridden him," she said.

"Still faster than any horse you'll ever own," I told her.

"That sounds like a challenge," she informed me, tossing her black hair and smiling.

"Tonight at twilight," I said. "Once around the city. We'll wear him out well. Then when I beat you, I'll take you back to our new, royal rooms and I'll take you like a king takes a concubine."

"Oooo," she said. We were coming to the throne room now. "I have never been a concubine."

"A harem of one," I said. "How lonely for you."

"The children will keep me company."

"Children?"

"Well," she said, and shot me a sly look, "you should want a son, and then a son after him, because not all children live to man. And there is no guarantee that they will all be born boys."

I counted back from today to her last period, and couldn't be sure if it she had skipped it. But then, we had cooled off a lot since Lee and the trauma of Eldador the Port. Blizzard wasn't the only one who needed more exercise, I decided.

All four Oligarchs were in the throne room. I looked for any sign that they were being held against their will. The bounty hunter was out there – this would be a good place to lay in wait.

"They are who they are supposed to be," Shela whispered to me. The Wolf Soldiers took up positions throughout the throne room. More of them were filing in. Behind us, Krell came into the room with a troop of 10 Aschire.

"Well met, my Lord," I said to him. I wanted to extend my hand and then caught myself. They don't like to be touched. He approached me, and he lowered his head and raised it.

In Aschire, 'Yes, you are the boss, and I am not the boss.'

"I owe you my life," I said.

"You do not," he said. "You were killing him. However the Aschire owe you much, your Majesty, and the forest has a long memory."

"It will grow under my reign," I promised him. "I will assure you of that. Whenever I have needed them, the Aschire have been at my side."

"I have brought one whom you might remember," he said, and smiled. Nobles were filing into the throne room already. Ancenon, Avek and D'gattis were coming right for me.

Krell turned to his left, and a girl stepped out from behind him. She was gray-eyed; taller, and her purple hair had gotten even longer than I remembered, but I knew her from the way she looked me right in the eye.

"Nina," I said. She dressed in leather pants and a leather vest, with a quiver over her shoulder and a bow alongside it. She wore a leather headband, all in black.

"You look like a grown up girl," I said.

"Well, I am a woman now," she told me. "And that was one of my arrows in that man's eye."

I nodded, impressed. I wanted to squat down and look her in the eye, but she had declared herself a woman, not a child.

"You must remember Shela," I said, and she stepped up beside me. "This is my daughter, Lee."

She beamed. There is nothing a little girl loves like a baby. She waved at Lee, who treated her to a giant smile.

"We both have daughters now," Krell said. "Have you chosen a protector for her?"

I shook my head. "Shela is sufficient, although in fact we need someone to look out for her tonight," I said.

"My daughter has decided that she has learned what she can in the Aschire, as if there were such a thing."

"She's decided to pursue her talents?" I asked him.

He nodded. He was an Aschire – they are direct. In fact, they didn't get more politic than this.

"I will take her as my daughter's guardian, and my woman's apprentice," I said. "I think Karel of Stone would be amenable to giving her some instruction in other arts."

"He is well renowned," Krell said.

"I will replace my life with your daughter's," Nina vowed. She gave her father a glance, and immediately took up a position behind Shela. Somewhere between eleven and twelve, and ready to kill if she needed to.

Ready to kill *again*, I reminded myself.

"You will need to remain and be one of the last people to leave, Krell," I told him. "I have to make a change with the way things are, to ensure that the Aschire can't be invaded by other Eldadorians."

"We are *not* Eldadorians," he informed me, flatly.

I sighed. "If you are not Eldadorians, then attacking you is not an offense against Eldador. Do you want that?"

"No."

"Then *be* an Eldadorian, just for today, and help me to ensure that not even an Eldadorian can set foot in the Aschire without your permission."

He nodded, looked speculatively at me, and then walked away without a word to me or to his daughter.

Nobles piled into the gallery. The Uman-Chi were upon me a moment later. They nodded to Krell as they passed him, and he nodded back.

"You are well survived," D'gattis said. "I feared for a moment that your reign would be a record short one."

"You know me better," I said.

"Your Majesty," Avek said, "may I congratulate you on behalf of the Silent Isle?"

I nodded, and looked him in the eye. "I hope that this might improve relations between our two people."

"If that is your wish," Avek said. "I can assure you, King Angron Aurelias has no desire to quarrel with the Conqueror."

"Not with an entire nation's resources behind him," D'gattis said, dryly.

"Although the results of previous disagreements truly ended the Noir's," Ancenon commented.

"We have recovered," Avek responded.

"Please, gentlemen," I said. "The Silent Isle is well-served by all of you."

D'gattis clicked his tongue. "That doesn't work with you," he commented.

"No?"

"No," Karel of Stone said from behind me. "You aren't a courtier, your Majesty. You are a Conqueror. Be what serves you."

This surprised me. As he stepped around in front of me, I noted that I hadn't seen him enter and I hadn't seen him with the Uman-Chi. In fact, I hadn't invited him, not that it mattered. He seemed to go where he wanted.

"I went with J'her," he said. "He's a good man. He is pursuing your lost Bounty Hunter into the dungeons. That was a good instinct of yours – I thought only I knew of the passages below the city."

"Well, I sure wasn't one who knew," I said.

"You're a king now, Lupus," he said. "You aren't supposed to know anything. But if you know that, then that is something."

The other three nodded. Wow, it always surprised me how much I didn't like Karel of Stone.

"I don't suppose you could make yourself useful on my behalf?" I asked him.

He bowed. "I am ever at your royal service," he said.

D'gattis grinned and Ancenon rolled his eyes.

I shook my head. "I am going to speak to the Foveans, then to my own nobles," I said. "I will be speaking to all of them, then to my Dukes."

"You need to know what to say?" D'gattis asked – probably what passed for humor with him.

"I need intelligence on the lesser nobles," I said. "I want to know who talks to whom, when they know that it can't be me watching them."

He grinned, looked me in the eyes, and then spun on his heel. He left in a moment.

"Already not able to trust your own nobles?" Ancenon asked me. "You learn quickly, if nothing else."

"Not to change the subject," I said, because I really wanted to change the subject, "but how go our efforts?"

Ancenon sighed – he didn't like being diverted. "The war ended with Glennen's life," he said. "The Sentalans and the Volkhydrans found that they shared a common interest, in that they are too afraid of what you are planning to weaken each other in war. We've scouted out the Andurin peninsula for a place to winter."

"Are the Legionnaires back already?" I asked.

D'gattis shook his head. "In a month," Ancenon said. "Perhaps less. We are in no hurry, and we have safe passage in Sental. We engaged the Volkhydrans three times. They didn't do well."

"On the fourth they did better," D'gattis added. "Arath is a competent general but he has a Man's years. He'll be dead a century in the time it takes an Uman-Chi to command a battalion."

"The fourth?" I asked.

I couldn't tell if Ancenon looked sideways at D'gattis, because I couldn't tell *where* those ambiguous eyes pointed, however his posture marked him clearly unhappy. The gallery filled quickly – I would have to take the throne soon. I actually wanted them to see me speaking with the Free Legion's most important man, to reinforce who remained an ally to Eldador.

"It seems your scarred protégé Karl Henekhson took the field with a few thousand Volkhydrans dressed as peasant farmers. They showed up with poleaxes disguised as pitchforks and with their swords and armor hidden under their furs. We sent out six hundred to dispatch them and lost them all when they attacked us."

I smiled despite myself. Good for Karl, even against the Free Legion. "Arath must have been upset," I said.

"What vexed him is that, after, his Volkhydrans wouldn't engage us. They kept trying to draw us off of the fields we were protecting. It was an obvious ploy to get us to engage them while other troops came in behind us either to loot or flank us. Meanwhile we trampled half the crop that we were supposed to save from them."

I nodded. "That was his plan," I said. "He had no other forces."

Ancenon lowered his eyebrows, but then the Oligarchs were taking their places around my throne. I had to go, Shela with me, and leave the conversation for another time.

"You know, Nantar said the same thing," D'gattis said to Ancenon, forgetting or not caring that I would hear him.

Kills With a Glance and his swarthy Andarons had the part of the gallery closest to the throne. He nodded grimly as I passed. Beside him were the Dorkans, who looked stonily into the air above my head. Beside *them* were the Volkhydrans, then the Confluni, then the Sentalans, and finally farthest away were the Trenboni, Avek and Ancenon just seating themselves before I did. They were invited guests and as such didn't need to rise in my presence, especially considering that I stood on the open floor when they entered.

Aschire and Eldadorians, as hosts, stood by the entrance to the throne room. Krell held his bow in his hand.

Also left standing were the Toorians – the rest simply left no room in the gallery, and I had no way to accommodate them. To their credit, they sat down tailor-style on the floor before the gallery, their hands on their knees and their white robes spread out around them.

I climbed the steps to the throne. I would have sworn that there were suddenly more of them, that they were higher, that the climb had become a journey. The throne itself, made of stone, seemed impossibly large now that it was mine. I had bruised my ass on it for hours. Glennen had felt that a man who sat too comfortable on the throne would lose it. In fact, I had contemplated a pillow, except that I would look like a princess sitting on it.

I turned, the throne behind me. Shela took her place sitting on a step a level lower than me, our baby in her lap and Nina standing behind her, her eyes in the crowd of nobles. Wolf Soldiers held every door, one hundred strong that could be seen and another hundred that couldn't. J'her had the security now. This would be his place from this point on, with the house guard.

I sat. As a king I didn't stand to address people, they stood to receive me. The Oligarchs, I think, were happy just to see my butt hit the seat on the first try.

"I welcome you to Eldador," I said. "I thank you for your support, and assure you in the confusion of the coronation. Eldador the Port is secure. One of the assassins from the Bounty Hunter's guild is dead already, and if the other hasn't joined him, then he soon will."

I heard a murmur. I had expected it. You just didn't talk about killing Bounty Hunters. Maybe I deserved their heated vengeance.

"Eldador, on this day, begins anew," I said. "Under Glennen, we began a path to a newer Eldador, an Eldador that makes a better ally, a more valuable trade partner, and a better place for a man to live and raise his family. Our taxes remain the lowest in known Fovea, our goods the least expensive, and hopefully our justice the most even."

I looked straight down the throne room's center aisle and saw Rennin, Groff and Ceberro standing with Jaheff of Uman City, the newest of their peers. They all had their arms folded over their chests. They were ready for me to do this in my characteristic, "Bet you never thought that I would say that" style.

Krell stood apart from them and didn't look at them. His Aschire crowded around him. His people were still on my walls, my eye in the sky.

"We will continue on the path that Eldador has taken," I continued. "We will continue to support the Fovean High Council. We maintain our tax rate; we will maintain our economic and our military policies, however our relations with other nations *must* change.

"Eldador has, in the current year, been the target of most of you, either directly or through mercenaries. As well, as we saw today, the Bounty Hunters' guild has been insistent in pursuing their ambitions here.

"We will seek no retributions for past actions. But as we begin anew, we make clear, we shall tolerate no more attacks, and we shall not be satisfied with turning them. Invasions as were attempted in Thera this year will be met one hundred times, both within and without the charter of the Fovean High Council."

I smacked my hand down on the stone arm of the throne. The Oligarch's jumped. Even Glennen, I knew, had been more politic.

"Eldador shall pursue peace, but Eldador is not afraid to pursue it with a sword, Wolf Soldiers and Theran lancers. What happened in the city of Outpost IX we will export one hundred times to the next of our invaders."

Rennin broke from the other dukes and marched himself down the center aisle to the throne room. A moment later Ceberro followed him, then Groff, then Jaheff, then Hectar. They marched to the circle before the throne, then turned, then folded their arms, and they said nothing. Their actions spoke louder than their words as they threw in their lot with me.

After them came the Earls. Some of them I knew from court and from Thera. Some of them were strangers. I should have spent the last year getting to know them, but I'd made so much of my reign hands-on that I couldn't. They filed in behind the Dukes. After them were the court-barons and landed nobles, most of whom I knew better because they either lived here or they were here so frequently asking for favors.

And after them, entirely to my surprise, came Krell. He stood right next to Rennin, between him and Ceberro. Both of them looked at him, then straight forward again.

A united Eldador. Glennen hadn't delivered on it. I really hadn't, either. Anyone could bring them together in a moment of nationalism; especially if they were pissed off at the idea that the Bounty Hunters' Guild held them in such low regard that they would attempt an assassination in front of all of them.

Anyone could unite them here. Keeping them united, that would be the real accomplishment.

"Now that this is said," I said, and I stood as I said it, "let me again welcome you. There is food to eat and beer and wine and mead to be drunk. Enjoy yourselves and be recognized by the new Eldador. Let us spend the War months speaking of peace."

They didn't applaud because, again, they didn't do that here. The Uman-Chi stood together, they inclined their heads to me, and they left, led by Avek. Then the Dorkans did the same – that really surprised me. The Dorkans hated me more than anyone. Next came the Confluni and the Andarons at the same time, following the lead of the others. Kills threw me a wink and a smile as he left. Next the

Sentalans stood, looked at the group of us standing united, and nodded as one before leaving through the double doors.

Finally the Volkhydrans stood. Henekh Dragorson led them. He hadn't changed since last I saw him. He looked as rough and hairy as before, and the scowl told me how happy he wasn't.

I looked for Karl but didn't see him. Someone had to mind the store.

"I know you, Lupus the Conqueror," he said. "You are King of Eldador now, but I know you, and I have seen what you do to those who oppose you."

I nodded. I could respond but I didn't. The nobles were immobile, waiting to see what he had to say.

"My King is Gharf Bendenson of Volkha," he said. "And my King needs to know your ambitions."

"A stronger Eldador, more trade," I said. "Free trade within our borders."

He shook his head. "You aren't a merchant, you're a killer," he said. "Where are your ambitions?"

Now I got him. I almost told him, 'South,' but the Toorians were still here.

"I think you and I both know that someone is going to have to test what I said here today, Henekh Dragorson," I said.

"Yes," he agreed.

I waited a moment, lowered my voice and said, "Don't be that nation."

I frowned, he nodded, and he inclined his head. He led his delegation from the gallery.

"And Henekh," I said.

He turned.

"When you see Karl, tell him 'well done.' They never guessed what he was up to, even after he did it."

He grinned a yellow-toothed grin, inclined his head again, and left.

That left Toor. I had never in my life even met a Toorian. The only ones who had seen me had been delegates to the Fovean High Council. I traded with them but had never met them myself.

They stood, then inclined their heads, and they walked off without saying anything. That left me with the Eldadorians. Wolf Soldiers closed the throne room doors, and Rennin immediately turned on his heel.

"I really wish I had known you were going to do that," he said.

"I know," I said. Now I needed to be the peer, not the king. "I wanted to have this meeting first, fill you in and then meet with the Foveans, but the attack came and this had to happen."

"How much of that was true?" Groff asked me.

"All of it," I said. "The lowered taxes have brought a flood of people from all nations. We can offer them land and jobs and we can tax their earnings. I can increase the size of all of your holdings by more than one hundred percent if you let me, and I can make you wealthier than you are now."

They nodded. They had seen Thera – it had become an economic juggernaut. Those who had lowered their taxes had seen their revenues climb and their lands swell with immigrants hungry for land and jobs.

"And about your ambitions?" Ceberro asked. He looked me in the eye. "Henekh Dragorson wasn't wrong, your Majesty. You aren't a merchant."

I smiled – I couldn't help it. I was the avatar of the god War, not Eveave.

"Be ready for one of them to decide that we are going to grow too powerful, too fast," I said. "And be ready for one of your cities to be determined to be the perfect place for an example."

They looked at each other, then at me. They didn't want to be treated like pieces on a board. I had just informed them that there is a good chance that I would get some of them killed, and they had no reason to doubt me. Probably not what they expected on my first day.

"I am Genden," one of the Counts said. "I am of Tonkin, on the Andurin peninsula. I am probably the city you are talking about."

The port of Tonkin was similar to Thera, and yes, that made him a likely target.

"And when I am besieged, and when my fields are burning and my people are dying or coming to me and demanding I relieve them, what will I and my two hundred Eldadorian foot expect from Eldador the nation?"

"First, know that as soon as he is before me, I will be adding a Man, Arath, to the peerage and, as an earl, he shall be given land and title at the center of the Andurin peninsula."

"Arath, the leader of the Legionnaires," Rennin said.

I nodded. Rennin turned to Groff.

"How do you see that, your Grace?" he asked.

Groff's severe features drew in on themselves. He lowered his face, then looked up at me, into my eyes. The room had gone quiet.

"I think," he said, "that if the Free Legion is going to base itself in Eldador, then it should be taxed, and it should be encouraged to believe it has a stake in us. We have seen how beneficial Wolf Soldiers are to Eldador. Legionnaires and Sarandi shall further reinforce us."

"Except that they all leave in the War months," another Earl said. He didn't identify himself. Ceberro looked up at me.

"We will need to demand that they leave no less than one thousand reserves in the city," he said.

I nodded. "I will make it a condition of his elevation," I said. "I think you have schooled him in the folly of doing otherwise."

They all laughed at that.

"And I think we need an Earl for your holdings in the Plains of Angador," I said.

He considered. He had already started a city, I knew. He would want someone he could control.

"Tartan Stowe would be a good choice," Rennin said.

All eyes turned to Tartan, who normally sat quiet during such meetings. He was old enough, if he had a good advisor. Well, I only knew one Oligarch's name.

"Will you join the peerage, lad?" I asked him.

His eyes found mine. His slight build came from his mother, with brown hair, brown eyes, white skin and a dancer's frame. He looked nothing like Glennen. One too many slaps on the back, one too many accusations that he didn't rise to his father's high marks.

Too much time thinking that his dad was a drunken slob.

"I serve the kingdom," he said, simply. "If this is where I am needed, then this is where I will go."

"Ceberro can school you," I said. Ceberro nodded. "Devarre will go with you as your personal advisor. He has been a great aid to me."

The Oligarch nodded.

"And I will be elevating Two Spears of Thera to the rank of Duke, only because Thera is a duchy, and I will need to keep him there. Thera shall remain the home of the Wolf Soldier elite guard, but those troops are now at Eldador's disposal."

"Oh, good, another Duke," one of the court barons quipped.

"Plenty of fresh blood in the peerage," said another.

"The Uman-Chi already make fun of us," Genden added.

"Not so much since we sacked Outpost IX," Rennin said. Again, more laughter.

I knew Rennin would be the key to my realm. His support legitimized me. Now he wanted to recreate my victories as Eldadorian victories.

He had a son I knew. Like Hectar, he probably had his eyes set on Lee.

"And while I am expanding the peerage, I am going to make the Aschire a Duchy, and Krell of the Aschire its Duke," I said.

Krell regarded me evenly. Rennin threw him a disgusted look, but made sure that he had it out of his system before he looked back at me.

"Is that wise, your Majesty?" Oligarch one asked.

"It is the best possible solution," I said.

"Such title is meaningless," Krell said. "The Aschire is the Aschire. If you make me a Duke, as you call it, then every Aschire is a Duke, and every tree in the Aschire, and every squirrel, and every rock is a Duke."

There goes the peerage," that same voice quipped.

"He can't even understand what you are offering," Ceberro said. "If the Aschire is to be a Duchy, then let us build a city and pick a Man –"

"No!" Krell and I said together. The Aschire turned back to me, gaging me.

"It is we who do not understand the Aschire," I said. "Because we have made no effort to. However the Aschire is not a place for stone walls and roads and tilled farms. It is wild and untamed and free. It is a part of Eldador and we would protect it, and to protect it we must give it title and recognize it."

I turned back to Krell. "You don't want this, I know," I said. "And it will make a stir among your people, and you fear that our ways will corrupt you.

"But you must call yourself a Duke and you must call the Aschire a Duchy to the rest of Fovea, knowing that it is meaningless there, because 'Aschire' is meaningless to the rest of Fovea."

He nodded. I felt gratified that other nobles nodded as well. Rennin wouldn't shake his hand, but he wouldn't find it offensive enough to call me on it, either.

"If there is nothing else, I want you out among the Fovean nobles when we leave here," I said. "Let it be known that Arath, Two

Spears, Krell and Tartan are to be elevated. Devarre, I want you with Tartan, but not too close. Let's see who comes to him to test his loyalty."

Ceberro cleared his throat and looked at me then around the room.

"If I could speak with my Dukes, then – please would the rest of you depart, with my thanks and my appreciation, and my pledge that this new Eldador is your future, as well as mine?"

The lesser nobility filed out. Now three of the four Oligarchs, my Wolf Soldier guard, Shela and her new apprentice, and the Dukes, including Krell remained with me.

"That was ill advised, your Majesty," one of the Oligarchs said. "You cannot be sure that all of the nobility is behind you."

"I'm sure that they are not," I said. "I have no doubt that one of the court barons at least will go immediately to someone outside of Eldador and report that they had better stay away from Tartan."

"In fact, I am counting on it."

Chapter Fourteen

Faith and Love

On the third day of the month of Order, we dropped Glennen into the 'Tomb of Kings,' which our stonecutters had been madly creating since the King died.

Dred Barr gave a eulogy about what a great guy he had been. Rennin and Ceberro said their part as well. I tied the whole thing up with a statement about the New Eldador.

I hate wakes and funerals. They aren't for the dead because the dead don't care, and they aren't for the living because it is a misery for the living. Especially when you are committing *such* a great man like Glennen. People didn't know if they should cry for the passing monarch or feel good that his suffering had finally ended. Everyone knew that he died in drunken misery – and everyone could see what that had done to his children.

After they sealed the stone cover on the stone crypt, which Hectar had built on a promontory outside of the city that overlooked the Bay, I lead a procession of nobles and merchants from there to the city, with everyone filing out behind me in a daze.

Arath had arrived finally. He rode with Karel of Stone and Dilvesh beside him. He looked more weathered and wiser than I remembered him. I had discussed his elevation with him the night before, at dinner with court barons and with visiting nobles who were now his peers. He seemed amused that I thought this would be a good thing for Eldador.

"You just make it harder for the Free Legion to invade you, not impossible," he said.

"We can discuss that if it happens," I said. "It gives the Legionnaires a home, the Free Legion as well, and my enemies will think twice about invading me outside of the War months if you are right there."

"And you get to pay tax like the rest of us," Ceberro told him. It turned out that Arath and Ceberro were becoming great friends, now that Ceberro officially ranked him. The opportunist had finally found his next opportunity.

As I entered the gate on Blizzard's back, the gigantic wooden panels open and the Wolf Soldier and Aschire combined guard at the ready, I looked down at the people who didn't yell, "Boo," and didn't cheer, but who just recognized that a new era had started, and that it would affect them.

They couldn't do a thing to help it along, and they couldn't do a thing to stop it. They could live their lives and pay their way and hope to their particular gods that they were left out of it as much as possible.

I wouldn't have liked that, but of course I was the one making it happen.

I had spent this new part of my life here, the chosen of a god, and my god spoke to me directly. I knew what he wanted and I knew what to do, to a degree. I had to guess a lot, but I knew when I screwed up.

These people, they had *faith*. They prayed to their gods, who *never* answered. I had discussed this with Ann, and even if she had been a phony, I believe that she had answered me true when she informed me that the gods had been forbidden to speak to their subjects – that this involved some *rule* that they had to exist by.

I'd answered part of the reason why He had brought me here, but no matter how you spun it, I had no *faith*. I *knew* my god's will.

I thought these thoughts as we rode along the cobbled path from the outer to the inner gate. People did what people did in any city. Commerce continued because people still had to eat. Porters ported and merchants haggled, kids ran chasing dogs and their mothers called after them.

I had seen cities once as steps toward my destiny. Now I saw them as a place to live. I admit, I liked it the other way.

"You are pensive, your Majesty," Rennin said to me.

He had pulled his roan charger up along mine, and I hadn't even noticed. I took another look around. We had caught the second bounty hunter and my Wolf Soldiers had cut him down. I had ordered him stripped naked and thrown in Tren Bay. That didn't mean that there weren't a dozen of his friends still in the city.

"He was a great man," I said.

Rennin nodded.

"He meant a lot to me, Rennin," I said. "He started all of this. You might say that they were my ideas, but he let me implement them. Anyone can come up with an idea – not everyone can decide to act on it, or even know if it is a good one."

"He had great faith in you," the Duke informed me.

I turned to him. "Really?"

He nodded again. "That day I saw you in your Theran estate, I informed him of how I knew you and what you had done in my city, and that he should not trust you."

I raised an eyebrow.

"He laughed," Rennin said. "You didn't know him long, but I can tell you that he was a man who laughed. He put his hand on my shoulder and he pointed to you, and he said, 'That one – that mind boils like a cauldron, and even the spill can make you rich.' I knew I could never turn him against you."

I laughed. Shela rode up on my left a moment later, on her gelding.

"There is an unfamiliar sound," she said. "What makes a White Wolf howl, finally?"

"My failures, of course," Rennin said. "He doesn't have any, so he has to enjoy ours."

"It is more of a burden than most could bear," Shela said. "I raced him last night and he defeated me on his horse, which as you know is the best horse of any horse."

"He has to have the best horse," Rennin said. "What else to carry the best sword and the best armor?"

"Which we all can see, because he is the tallest," Shela added. They enjoyed this. They didn't leave a lot for me to say. I thought I always made mistakes and screwed up, but apparently they didn't see it that way.

"Are we talking about the new king?" D'gattis asked, riding up behind us. Avek and Ancenon were discussing affairs of Uman-Chi futures and D'gattis had found himself on the outside of that conversation, as he had with most conversations between the two. He had tried his hand as a hanger-on for a while, but I could see that he liked it so little, that he had lowered himself to talking to us.

"How could you have guessed?" Shela asked him.

"I heard best and tallest mentioned many times," he said. "That had to be your White Wolf or Adriam himself."

"Oh, come *on*," I said. "I am not a god."

"Of course not," Rennin said. "Because no god could say, 'I am not a god,' but you can, giving you a power that not even they have."

"He bears up to it well, though," D'gattis said.

"My point exactly," Shela said. "In fact, I think he bears up to it better than anyone else could."

We approached the gates to the palace finally. I had never been more grateful to see them. "I think I need to start a tradition where no one speaks to the monarch on the day of a funeral," I said, although I grinned as I said it.

"That would be the *best* tradition," Rennin began, but I gave him a look that quieted him.

"I have seen to the ceremonies," Shela said, relieving me from my attack. "Your new earls and duke are going to wait outside of the throne until you welcome everyone, and then be called to receive their titles."

"Call them as commons, remember," Rennin said. "They aren't dukes and earls until he says they are."

"How many of these have you been to, in other nations?" I asked Rennin.

"This doesn't happen in other nations," he said.

"No?"

"How could they? Sentalans are a collective and elect leaders by committees. Volkhydrans all are chiefs of their cities, and their sons replace them. They have a king but it is a simple ceremony to install him, and it involves a lot of drinking. The Hydrans have Dukes and Earls, but they are just chiefs of a different name. Dorkans are lead by the most powerful wizards."

"Andarons have nothing similar," Shela said. "The city tribes elect the best among them, the horse tribes are lead by the one who is best loved by the tribe."

"And Uman-Chi rarely die," D'gattis said, "although I am told that Angron came to his seat by the will of his father, who was appointed by the Cheyak."

"I will have to ask the Dwarven emissaries," I said. "I'm concerned that I'm naming so many nobles."

"Don't be," Rennin said. "Glennen named us all on his first day, and you are naming far fewer than he. No one is surprised you want to make changes and empower your own people."

"How is this done in your land?" D'gattis asked me.

"We vote," I said, without thinking.

Stupid, I cursed myself.

That got all of their attention. "You vote?" Shela asked me.

I nodded. Damage control time! The gates to the palace loomed up on either side of me as I said, "We have three groups who chose between two parties. The two parties hate each other and fight constantly about everything. They spend more and more money to convince the members of the third group to join one group or the other, and the third group demands more and more for its vote – so, of course, some travel out of the first two groups to join the third."

"That is…" Rennin said, trying to put a face on it.

"That is insane," D'gattis said. "And if I hadn't cast the truth saying myself, I would say you are lying. It is no wonder you don't think like Men think, Black Lupus. Your people are mad."

"We are a nation based on the idea of ideas," I said. "We hold free speech above all else, because we believe that there is nothing more powerful than a thought."

They were all quiet. D'gattis lowered his head and became pensive. Shela just looked at me, as did Rennin.

Before I knew it I'd arrived at the stables. That was a shame because I had led the whole procession there. I heard some chuckling and a few gold coins changed hands when we stopped – apparently they were betting on how far I would take them.

"Now that your tour of the royal stables is complete," I said, to a general chuckle, "those of you who would prefer to stable their own mounts, as I will be doing, may, and the rest will find that we have business in the throne room."

I also didn't realize that, if the King stabled his own horse, then that immediately became the thing to do, and they would all try it. The Free Legion had no problem, neither did the real equestrians like Rennin and Ceberro. Groff's son ended up in a pile of dung with his saddle on top of him, and the stable hands were run ragged answering questions. One stallion got loose and reared at Blizzard, and my stallion sent him packing with a bloody shoulder before I could get him under control.

From here I led the procession to the throne room. Shela and twenty Wolf Soldier guards went to the royal chambers to change Lee. I found myself surrounded by Uman-Chi before I realized it.

"Can you repeat what you said before?" D'gattis asked me, in broken Cheyak.

All languages sounded the same to me, if they were spoken properly. The same if I read them, once I could. If I heard someone who hadn't mastered a language, then I could hear the actual words, and I could recognize them for what they were. So when a Man spoke poor Uman, I heard Uman.

If D'gattis spoke in Cheyak to a Man, any Man, then this conversation needed to be kept so secret that no one could be trusted to hear it.

"There is nothing more powerful than a thought," I said. "Is that what you mean?"

The three Uman-Chi looked at each other, then at me.

"What?" I asked.

"Did you know that every Uman-Chi spell caster comes to that conclusion, on their own, to signal their readiness to cast spells?" Avek asked me.

"And that it can take centuries for them to come to it, if they ever do at all?" Ancenon added.

"If I knew that then I wouldn't run around shouting it," I said. "I would have some respect for your tradition."

"It isn't that," Avek said. "Those words were believed to be beyond the ken of Men and Uman. In fact, it was believed until moments ago that only Uman-Chi and the most solemn Dwarves might realize their truth."

"And you come from a nation – we assume of Men – that embraces it as a fundamental belief," D'gattis said.

"But – there are Men who are Wizards, who cast spells," I said. "Shela – "

D'gattis shook his head. "Let me speak in these allegories that you love," he said. "Imagine that you were born a swordsman, but had only ever learned the dagger."

Click – I got it. I nodded and held up my hand.

"You see?" Avek said to Ancenon, who nodded.

"What?" I demanded.

"Your reasoning," Ancenon said. "We have all remarked on it. Past the ken of simple Men."

We were nearing the back entrance to the palace. Rennin and Ceberro were walking together and watching us. Jaheff had run ahead – I didn't know for what reason.

"Well, it was obvious," I said. How could I explain a renaissance to them – a revolution that had totally changed human thinking?

"To you," Avek said. "Just as your prior statement was obvious – to *you*. Yet we speak of no simple truth, but of *the* truth, Your Majesty."

"We speak of certain aspects of our faith," D'gattis said. "We speak of the building blocks of what we believe."

Faith, I thought. I think a lot about faith.

"Do you know what faith really is?" I asked them.

They looked at each other, then at me.

I sighed. There were Wolf Soldiers running between the procession and the palace – my palace. That left me a lot to accept. My palace – I'd become the one responsible for this nation, for these lives. No more Heir, no more putting things off on Glennen's failings. The buck really *did* stop here now.

"Faith is the color gray," I told them.

They smirked as one. Simple Man thinking, yes?

"If evil is black, and good is white, then faith is that area of 'what if,'" I told them. "Faith is where you ask yourself, 'Am I allowed to do this?'

"Because if you knew – if you *knew* what your god wanted of you…" I left my voice trail off.

"You would be a monster," Ancenon said.

We all regarded him. I wanted to hear this, but I had lived in fear of it since the moment that my mind first went down this road.

"If I follow your new allegory," Ancenon said, "then evil is not the presence of opportunity, but the possibility of absolutes."

D'gattis nodded. "If I follow Adriam, then I will not kill the innocent," he said. "But who is innocent? If I know, for example, that the Dorkans are innocent of nothing, then I can kill Dorkans with impunity, and terribly."

"And if I know that all Andarons are innocent," Avek continued for him, "then I am helpless before them. No matter what they do, I cannot kill them."

"Such an existence would be hell," Ancenon said. "The one who lived without faith, with absolutes, would commit the most unspeakable evil, perhaps to lay down his head at the chopping block at the end of it all."

"My people believe in a savior," I told them. "He died for our sins. In a world of faith, then couldn't that mean that he died for those who killed the innocent for mistaken reasons of faith – for the sins a man couldn't know he committed, because he could not know the will of his god?"

They were all silent at that. Here, they called a demi-god called 'Steel,' the savior, but they didn't know why.

"Black Lupus," D'gattis said, "the Uman-Chi have watched you with wonder since we returned from Conflu, and you were reported to the King by Ancenon as a formidable Man. You improved on those feelings with your expertise as a military man. You turned that wonder to awe and anger when you sacked Outpost IX. You turned those feelings to a grudging respect by becoming the king of this nation and totally changing it in a short span of months."

"And I will confess to you now," Avek said, "that I am sent here by Angron himself to negotiate a peace with you at all costs, because there are Uman-Chi who believe that you will soon be unstoppable."

"After he did everything he could to kill me first, of course," I said. I looked from him, to Ancenon and to D'gattis. I knew they had to have some knowledge of the King's plans. Ancenon had once been his heir, after all. They must have danced on a fine edge between the oath and their loyalty.

Avek nodded. "Even when I entered the service of the Wolf Soldiers," he said, "I knew that Angron considered you a threat to the Silent Isle and, as someone who knows his people, I felt certain that he would try to dispose of you.

"And as someone who has known you, and has an understanding of you," Avek continued, coming dangerously close to confessing our agreement, "I am obliged to tell you that, if I or these two Uman-Chi repeated this conversation to the King's council, you would terrify a man with the wisdom of one thousand years, and that there are Uman-Chi who would stop at nothing to find this home you claim to come from."

"And that only because every attempt to eradicate you has failed," D'gattis said.

I walked past my old suite of rooms while we spoke in heated Cheyak. It would remain empty until I named another heir. I had a whole tower now. I let Glennen's kids keep their old rooms, only because I had no other use for them.

"There is nothing more powerful than a thought," I said. "And your fear is that I think the most powerful thoughts of all."

They nodded.

It hit me like a slap in the face.

I understood what War wanted from me, and why.

Karel let me know that Tartan had been approached by the Confluni *and* the Trenboni, but had turned both down flat.

"Whether this was because he knew he might be tested, or because he honestly holds his commitment to you close to his heart, is your guess," the Scitai said.

Karel, Shela and I were in my personal chambers with Lee, who seemed to be having a frank discussion with her 'bebe', wagging her finger at it and making nonsense sounds.

"And the rest of the peerage?" I asked him.

He smiled, leaning back on his pillow on our divan. "Dorkans are leaning pretty heavily on your Tren Bay coastal towns," he said. "They want to be able to build towers on your coast."

"And install teleportals," Shela scowled. "Who gave them permission?"

"The Baron of Britt," Karel said. Britt referred to the peninsula west of Eldador the Port. "His name is Jahon, and he complained non-stop that he can't make a living on his land."

"His land is a stretch of rock covered in salt spray – I would be surprised if things were otherwise with him," I said.

Karel frowned and nodded.

"The baron of Tonkin didn't give a firm, 'No,' either," Karel said. "I would give him a few days before confronting him – he might want to report this to you and see what you want done."

In fact, Genden had requested an audience with me for the next day. It was getting late, and court would be hard to make in the morning if I didn't get some sleep.

"I appreciate your doing this," I said to Karel. I still didn't like him, but I had plenty of use for him. That was good enough.

He nodded and left. Shela deposited Lee in her bassinet, quickly becoming too small for her. Now that we had Nina, we were preparing to transition Lee to her own room in order to get some privacy. Nina had wanted to join us here as well, and had reconciled herself to an adjoining room.

"Planning on conquering me tonight, your majesty?" Shela asked me, her eyebrow raised.

I laughed and took her in my arms. "I've conquered you a lot lately," I informed her. "Your territory must be getting sore."

She laid her head on my shoulder. She didn't want to admit to me how she had been affected by the attack at my inauguration, but I knew. She'd been hinting that she wanted another child – this might be coming to a head now that my life had been threatened.

"You live your life at such a pace," she told me, "no wonder Blizzard loves you – you travel faster than he does. I worry that if I blink too long or sleep too deeply, I will miss you."

I smelled her hair, all evergreen and straw. She was my dark spring, I thought to myself right then.

An Earth mother who could turn into a hurricane on a dime.

I spontaneously shoved her into our bed, flipped her onto her stomach and took a fist full of her hair. She whimpered as I bent her neck back, then threw the back of her dress up to expose her.

"Your *majesty*," she gasped, a smile on her lips.

I slapped her behind and drew another whimper.

The least I could do for such a woman was to conquer her occasionally.

Sleep that night was interrupted by a strange noise. It wasn't singing or wailing, but a mixture of both, like the old style of Spanish crooning I'd learned in grade school.

Shela lay snuggled down into the comforters, Lee held her bebe in her bassinet. I rose quietly and set my feet to the cold, wood floor. Some people preferred carpet, but I'd rather that the cold hurt my feet and wake me up.

I padded out of the royal bedroom into a parlor we kept, which led to it. Here we had a table, couches, chairs and book cases with nothing in them. Glennen hadn't been an avid reader but had loved hunting, so there were all manner of mounted animal heads which I personally found repulsive.

The parlor had an exit to the outer hall where a squad of Wolf Soldiers would be standing guard, as well as a break off to an informal dining room I didn't even know existed before today, and a couple other rooms which were likely for servants or such. One of these we'd outfitted for Nina, and the wailing came from there.

My first thought: if the Bounty Hunters came at me through that sweet girl, I didn't care what it took, they were over.

I opened the door and found the purple-haired girl in the center of the room, on a thick-pile carpet, her knees tucked up under her chin and tears streaming from her eyes, looking up at me like the loneliest and most lost soul in the world.

"I – I'm sorry," she informed me, in Aschire. "I tried to be brave, but the walls are stone."

She'd lived every day of her life in the Aschire forest. She'd slept in the boughs of trees surrounded by her tribe, by animals that she considered a part of her, all these living things.

And here she sat in what she must have considered a tomb. My heart melted. I sat down next to the poor girl, and she immediately found her way into my lap.

Her head tucked under my chin, her fingers interlaced mine. The girl couldn't have weighed as much as my saddle. She pressed her ear to my chest, her tears soaking into the cotton shirt I wore, and she sighed.

"I'm sorry," she told me.

I hugged her with my free arm. "Don't be sorry for trying," I informed her. She shifted to snuggle closer. "Don't you worry at all."

She chatted to me about missing her dad, about being scared of the dark, about never having seen a bed or looked into a mirror before. All things I take for granted. She told me that the bed didn't smell right but the floor did.

For everything I'd been through in the last two weeks, in the last two months, since getting here, it was kind of nice just to sit on a floor and to comfort a homesick little girl. It was more than an hour before I realized that she'd fallen asleep, and another before I was willing to put her into her bed. I tucked her in, then padded quietly out of the room without closing the door.

I crossed the parlor and opened the door. The Wolf Soldier guards snapped to attention. I recognized the sergeant.

"Send two men to the Lady's garden," I ordered him. "There are a couple of potted trees, one on other side of the door. Bring them. Be quiet about it."

In another half of an hour I had a sapling at either end of her bed. As I set down the second one, she roused, looked up and saw the tree leaves over her head, reached out and stroked them, then looked at me, smiled and went back to sleep. I waited for a while, then slipped back into my own room, into my own warm bed with my slave girl.

She slipped into my arms, telling me she hadn't been asleep, or at least not very asleep. I didn't see her checking in on us but that didn't mean much.

At least I wasn't a monster, or at least not much of a monster yet.

Chapter Fifteen

Party People

I *wish* I could have gotten away with one day of feasting and celebration for the inauguration. People who traveled for days or more to get here didn't want to show up for a few hours and go home, especially when they could find so many useful things to do now that we'd all come together, and I'd made myself a captive audience.

The palace had a gigantic ballroom with blue-veined marble floors and white, fluted pillars reaching up to the arched ceiling fifty feet above us. Huge bay windows opened up onto the bay, paned in real glass. Buffet tables lined the walls and a troupe of musicians played. The next day there would be dancing, and the day after that the players from the Theatre au Thera would be performing.

"Slave," the Confluni princess said, a flick of her wrist indicating the direction of the kitchens, "fetch us chilled wine, would you?"

Shela's eyes widened. The Confluni princess an exquisite creature, barely five feet tall with straight, jet-black hair and a willowy body. She dressed in long white silken robes with a red silk sash that trailed behind her. Three girls stood in her attendance, images of her, and ensured that no one stepped on her clothes.

"Um, we have servants who'll bring you what you want," I informed her. "Shela attends me."

She stepped in close to me, parking her body under my nose, making sure I got a good whiff of her perfume. She looked up into my eyes; hers warm and brown like some vulnerable predator.

"Perhaps I could attend you for now," she offered, "and we can give the slave a break."

The storm that crossed Shela's face was a terrifying thing to see.

"I admire you so for bringing back the institution," the princess informed me, her hand casually touching the front of my tunic. "Some are simply born to serve."

I couldn't help thinking that this chic would be dead in five minutes and then I would have hell to pay in a war between Conflu and Eldador.

But what to do? Shela *was* a slave, not a free woman. Lee as my daughter wouldn't succeed me – in fact, a son had no guarantee of that, either. That made me, in fact, the *single* King of Eldador, and what did I expect other nations to do *but* ply me with their daughters?

This wasn't the first one, either. A Volkhydran warlord had sent me a woman who spent an hour fascinated with my description of economics. Not to be exceeded, two Andaron warlords had sent their daughters on mares for me to deflower in exchange for Blizzard's services.

I couldn't help thinking that going after the horse was pretty low – but it *had* worked in the past.

"Shela, attend your father," I ordered her.

"Your majesty?" she asked me. It was a comment on her resolve that she was able to sputter that out.

"Now," I informed her. The princess would piss her off because she could, and something bad would surely happen. Shela was no shrinking violet. She wouldn't put up with that forever, slave or not.

"By your leave," she informed me with a nod, her eyes as cold as ice. The princess watched her leave, looking over her shoulder in order to ensure that her breasts remained pointed at me, shooting an, "It is good to discipline them," after the unfortunate Andaron while she remained in earshot.

Sparks dripped from Shela's clenched fist, down at her side. I put my back to my angry slave girl and shifted the princess on the other side of me. I didn't know if I could protect her that way, but it provided the only chance she had, and in fact she didn't burst into flame.

The reception dragged on. When I managed to excuse myself from one of these women, another found me. Once the foreigners finished with me, the locals started. Groff had a niece, Hectar a sister (seems his father had felt some surge of energy just before death) and the Lady Jameen of Angador a twin. She, an equestrian like Shela, sported a shocking head of red hair and a gigantic rack that she seemed very proud of. She wore a dress cut down half way to her navel and if they hadn't invented glue then the thing held onto her with either magic or pure faith. Tartan saw her and actually walked into a pillar.

"Your majesty," Rennin addressed me during a lull, Ceberro and Hectar in tow with him, Nantar and his wife right behind.

I pasted on a smile and took a drink from my bowl of mead. I felt bloated, halfway drunk, my feet ached and my head hurt. "Your Graces," I said, inclining my head.

I saw the two Andaron girls sizing me up for another pass – they'd parked themselves by the buffet tables. If I could get the Dukes to get me to the door, I could make a run for it and hide in my rooms.

"Enjoying yourself?" Ceberro asked me. The smirk on his face told me that he knew the answer. His lips and eyes weren't puffy anymore but there were purple marks. He'd been quite the topic of conversation – apparently it turned out to be a real honor for me to put your lights out.

"Tell me that one of our cities is under attack," I ordered him.

"All peaceful," Hectar informed me. His wife had sparked up a polite conversation with the Confluni princess when I had stupidly strayed into a corner. If she hadn't, I would probably still be there, getting felt up.

"Who would attack the Conqueror?" Rennin asked me. "You're invincible, you know."

"No, I'm not, I swear," I said. "Get the word out."

Nantar laughed his laugh. I don't know what it is about him, but you can't be too upset with Nantar there.

"Glennen used to hate this, too," Ceberro informed me. "One of the reasons he loved Alekanna so much I think is that she rescued him from the daughters, the sisters and hangers-on."

"And that happened when Eldador was a backwater," Hectar said. He swept the grand ballroom with a predator gaze, his eyes picking targets.

"Eldador is a major force of Fovea now," Nantar noted. "It's worth a daughter to make it hard for you to attack someone."

"Seems that the Andarons feel this way," Ceberro said, indicating the two girls with his chin.

Kills With a Glance joined us. I looked for Shela and she had left him. For a panicked moment, I couldn't find the Confluni princess.

"Your majesty," he said, inclining his head. "You were wise to send my daughter to me."

"Oh, oh," Nantar's wife, Lanette, said. "Oh, she must be furious."

"She has no place to be," Kills informed them. "She is a slave, fairly traded. She had to know that someday there would be other women."

"Thorn's father has three wives," Nantar added. "And a concubine as well. The concubine is Thorn's mother."

"A wise man," Kills noted.

Rennin grinned to himself. "Why can't I imagine Shela serving another wife?"

"Just think about the most violent thing you ever saw," Nantar said, "and then multiply it by... the next most violent thing you ever saw."

"Ha!" I told him. "Maybe to start."

"No," Kills informed us. "My daughter will follow her man as I raised her. She might not like it, but she knows full well who she is."

Thing is, Shela *did* know full well who she was, and that made her the love of my life, and I didn't *want* anyone else.

"There is no way to just... marry her?" I asked Kills.

He regarded me, then shook his head.

"It speaks well of you that you consider her," he informed me, "but you can't. Andarons marry only Andarons, and to do otherwise would shame her tribe."

"And I don't see you taking a few years off to be accepted by an Andaron tribe," Rennin told me, flatly. "I know something of the rituals."

"Seems to me that kings get to decree stuff like this," I said. "I mean – why be a king if I don't get to just change the laws at will?"

"You aren't the king of Andoron," Kills told me, and I could see him becoming irritated. "Andoron has no king. If you aren't an Andaron and you aren't accepted as an Andaron by one of its tribes, then no matter her love for you, she won't marry you and, if she tried, it would shame all of us."

I sighed. This was intolerable. It was also distracting, unfortunately, and it hadn't occurred to me that talking to Kills for this long was a perfect invitation to the two Andaron girls to swoop in, and of course they took advantage of it.

"Your Majesty," one said. She was 'Sings Softly' of the Wet Belly tribe – a large, southern tribe from the south of Andoron. Like Shela, her hair ran black down past her shoulders, olive skinned with big, brown eyes. She'd dressed out in a simple ball gown compared to the intricate, colorful outfits some of the other women were wearing. Her friend, from another southern tribe called the Drifters, was called 'Little Bird,' and other than being a couple inches shorter than Sings Softly with a rounder face and wider eyes, they could have been sisters.

Both were built like Shela. I guess the Andarons had decided what I liked.

I inclined my head to them. "My Ladies," I answered them.

Ceberro and Rennin exchanged a look, both smirking. Kills regarded both girls, clearly lingering on their breasts. The dresses didn't show much cleavage but both clearly were designed with cleavage in mind.

"We wanted to admire your command of our Andaron language," Little Bird said, her voice so soft that I really had to pay close attention in order to hear her. I think that might have been her goal.

"And we wondered," Sings Softly added, "if you shared an interest in our oral tradition."

Nantar rolled his eyes. Well... Thorn was his good friend, so I'm sure there was some joke or innuendo here I'd missed.

"Shela shares it with me all the time," I informed them. "I really enjoy it."

Kills shook his head and took his brow between his thumb and forefinger.

"I was admiring your mares," Rennin informed them, stepping in for me. "Those from the south or Andoron aren't like those from the north, are they?"

"No, your Grace," Sings Softly answered him, her eyes flickering between he and I, clearly wanting to be sure that I didn't escape while he occupied her. "The south is more prone to rain, the southern horses are wider of hoof, heavier."

"Slower," Ceberro chipped in.

"Little advantage to speed in the mud," Nantar said, "if your horse is mired or slipping."

All of the other men nodded. Yeah – no one's hunting you guys!

I felt a stroke on my arm and turned to see the Volkhydran woman had circled in from the left and flanked me. This one also had dark hair past her shoulders and a heaving bosom, on display in some kind of wrap-around, red thing which didn't reveal much skin, but looked like it revealed a *lot* of skin.

Rather than long and straight, this daughter of Volkhydro kept her hair kinky and wild – untamed like her people, I couldn't help but thinking. Aileen's had been blonde but wild like that, too. It occurred to me that I hadn't thought of Aileen in a long time.

She turned her head up to me with big, doe eyes and asked, "Are you discussing horses, your Majesty?"

Oh, sweet baby Jesus. Of course, I don't know that thinking that meant anything here.

"We are discussing the history of the Andarons," Sings Softly informed her, *just* stiff enough so that the rest of us caught it. "I don't suppose you've been educated?"

"Not in that," the Volkhydran girl – Neveratta, I believe, of Ulef, Kark's daughter – informed us all. "What – what would be the point?"

The Volkhydrans bristled, Nantar barked a laugh.

What a nightmare!

The two Andarons squared off on the Volkhydran girl. I faded back, cut behind Ceberro and made a beeline for the exit. Wolf Soldiers may or may not have cut off anyone coming after me – I didn't know and I didn't care. If Shela was as upset as I thought she'd be, then she'd go to the stables, and that's where I beat a hasty retreat to.

The best part about the stables was that the palace offered about a dozen ways to get there, all of them different. I swept through the halls, my hard-soled boots banging on the stone floors, past Uman servants who either bowed or curtsied in surprise, not expecting me to be in the back ways of the palace, especially not without a Wolf Soldier entourage.

I emerged through a side entrance that cut past the Heir's rooms, now vacant, and emerged from a little-known entrance where the stables cozied up against the palace walls. I stepped past an overfull hay cart, two wheeled and its tongue braced against the ground with the harness still attached.

I stopped next to it – that wasn't right! Leave the leather harness attached and the weather would get at it and ruin it, or stiffen it so that the animal pulling it would be miserable.

I shook my head and smiled. Here I was, the King of friggin' Eldador, and I was sweating the treatment of a harness that probably cost less than my boots.

"There's a rare sight from his Majesty," I heard from ahead of me.

I reached for my sword and then found the source of the statement, the red-haired sister of Ceberro's lady-friend, Jameen. She'd changed her gown with the plunging neckline to skin-tight trousers, black leather riding boots and a white cotton top with a plunging neckline. She'd wrapped her hair into a thick braid woven with baby's breath, and draped it over her left shoulder.

Her green eyes sparkled like Genna's had, and I immediately felt the same hunted feeling that Genna had inspired in me. I had to assume she was younger than Genna, although older than Shela. Closer to my own age or maybe just turned twenty.

"I mean you no harm," she purred, raising her hands up behind her head, of course accenting her figure. It wasn't lost on me.

I sheathed the sword. "My apologies, my Lady Shellene," I informed her, much as I wasn't supposed to apologize to anyone for anything as a king.

"Mine," she countered me, slowly lowering her hands. She moved gracefully, I had to give her that. Every motion seemed choreographed, as if we were all in some play and she was the only one who knew the lines.

I stepped past the cart to the aisle between the stalls and extended my left elbow for her to latch on to. She did so with a wide, toothy smile, making sure to rub her breast on my forearm. I couldn't help thinking, "Wow, Shela is going to see this and kill you dead."

We walked arm-in-arm past the stabled war horses to the paddocks where only Blizzard could be. We'd put mares around him but he shunned them. I couldn't help but notice that those two

Andaron mares were here now, one on either side of him, as I approached.

Blizzard saw me and shook his head, pawing the straw beneath him with an iron-shod hoof. I felt glad to see that a mandate of mine – that fresh carrots be left in leather bags throughout the stables – had been followed, and I reached into one and pulled him out a huge one.

"Oh, may I, your Majesty?" Shellene begged me, meeting my eyes and rubbing my forearm again. "I admire him so."

I shrugged. "He probably won't take it," I warned her, handing her the carrot, "but he bites, so be careful."

"I promise," she said, snatching away the carrot and approaching the steel gate to Blizzard's stall. Like any valuable horse, he was housed in a stall which had an outer, gated arena, or paddock, to let him stretch his legs while he was put up. Larger than most draft horses, Blizzard's stall was made from two smaller ones, and his paddock measured about fifteen feet by twenty-four, which is very large.

Blizzard took one look at Shellene, then one at me, and then pawed the ground and mule-kicked the outer wall to his stall. The mares on either side of him started circling in their own, smaller paddocks with their tails raised, trying to find out what had agitated the stallion, and the boom from his hooves against the double-reinforced wall rang through the stables.

"I'd better –" I began, not wanting her to whip him up into a frenzy and have him jump the paddock fence. He'd proven before that he was capable of it.

"A moment, if I may, your Majesty," she begged me, and I stopped. She reached into a pouch on her wide, brown leather belt and pulled out a clear vial with some green liquid in it. I immediately recognized wintergreen oil.

I smiled. "Where did you get that?" I asked her.

"There is a brotherhood of woodsmen," she informed me, as she dabbed a little of the oil on her pale, freckled left wrist, "who now collect this where they can find it. They are friends of your Free Legion ally, Arath, I am informed."

I nodded. Arath had spilled the secret. Aileen had been right – I needed to watch that kind of thing.

She rubbed her wrists together and she tucked the vial back away, then she reached her hand out again to the stallion with the carrot pointed at him.

The stallion snorted and pawed, then pranced over and sniffed at her. He craned his neck as far as it would go, trying to reach the carrot.

When he almost had it, his lips reaching the last few inches, Shellene withdrew the carrot ever-so-slowly, back to herself, bringing in the stallion with it, until he was in petting distance, and she let him have the top fourth of the carrot.

He clipped the carrot; she stroked the stallion's mane, grown out long enough again where it folded over to his left. He sought the rest of the carrot but he didn't pull away, his nostrils flaring, taking in as much of the wintergreen oil as he could.

"Clever, clever," I informed her.

She didn't look away, which impressed me. A stallion is a precocious beast, and right when you think you've made a friend he'll get it into his head that maybe he should kick you, or stomp you, or bite. A breeze could change and he might get a whiff of estrus, and then tear apart everything between him and the source.

He took the rest of the carrot, and then retreated across the paddock back into the shadow of his stall. Shellene watched him for a moment longer, then returned her attention to me.

I stepped up to the steel gate and whistled for him. Blizzard trotted back over and immediately batted me with his giant head, trying to get me to hold him. I held his forehead against my chest and would scratch his ears, and he seemed to love it.

"And this is the terrible white beast whose very mention terrifies the Confluni," Shellene cajoled me.

I stroked the side of his nose. "This is the warhorse who charged ten thousand Confluni infantry with me on his back," I informed her. "The Confluni fear him because he's killed more of them than the most seasoned warriors you may know."

I guess the whole thing pissed me off a little. Shellene nodded with due deference and let me have my interpretation. For all the world, Blizzard was like a big puppy right then.

"And of course you're breeding him," she said.

"We're trying," I informed her. I had no idea why I was opening up to her at all. This woman had come here with Ceberro and she *clearly* had her own agenda.

"He doesn't seem interested in regular mares," I said.

She knitted her pencil-thin eyebrows. "Interesting," she informed me. "And yet, there was Shela's slave price – a price that those Andaron daughters are here to collect."

I smiled. I guess that *was* a pretty famous story at this point.

"That night was an exception," I informed her.

"If I might inquire," she pursued, stepping up closer to me, so that I could smell the wintergreen oil, "was that night your first time with your slave?"

I frowned. Her green eyes sparkled.

"I propose," she said, "that the stallion is incentivized, if not by the act itself but then by its connection to you."

Now, why the heck didn't I figure that out?

I nodded. "I appreciate that," I informed her. Even if it didn't work that way, I'm sure Shela would have no problem after today if I took her in the stall.

"I am here but to serve my King," Shellene informed me, and curtsied. Then she smiled, "Think of all of the work involved for poor Shela, if this turns out to be the solution."

I laughed. "Shela won't be bothered by that at all," I informed her.

"Fortunate girl," she said. She stepped back from me, regarded me as she would any other horse she might be bidding on and, crossing her arms under her breasts, said, "Your love for her is the stuff of legends, and yet you realize that you'll have to take another to wife."

I sighed. Here it came.

"I've been reminded of that a lot lately," I informed her.

"Duke Ceberro, of course, would have you find that woman in me," she informed me. "I supposed I'm a prime woman for you – my father is an Earl in Ceberro's fealty and, before arriving, my virginity was certified."

I raised an eyebrow. "Was it now?" I asked her.

I've said it before, and I'll say it again. It had to suck sometimes to be a girl.

She nodded. "And, of course, where the first King had eyes only for his Alekanna, I've been warned that I'd likely have to share you with this other woman."

"This other woman," I repeated, and then added, "who blew the gates off of Outpost IX, and shattered the ones at Katarran."

"And is jealous," Shellene said, pressing the issue. "One look at her as she watched you, and one knows her intent. There is actually wager on the life expectancy of Jing-Wei of Conflu."

I grinned and nodded. "I would give her about three more days if she doesn't watch herself."

"I don't see how she could watch her actual person," Shellene said, looking down. "Perhaps with mirrors – and I don't think this would confuse your Andaron slave girl."

It was just too hard to keep up with the slang misinterpretations sometimes, so I didn't correct her.

She turned her gaze back up to me, and let me have the full effect of the eyes and the cleavage and the wintergreen oil. "If you seek a woman who is understanding of your predicament, however," she informed me, "then it is me. I would want a child, of course – what woman would not? But that mission achieved, I would accommodate the two of you as needed."

And there it was – laid out like a business deal. I don't know if she realized it, but she'd told me a lot more than she thought she had.

Because that woman knew a *lot* more about me and what I liked than any normal person, and even most of my friends would have.

Also, someone should have put in an appearance by now, because this was the longest time that I as monarch had been allowed to my own devices, even if I *might* be chatting up some honey for a little extra-slavery affair.

"That is an exceptionally generous offer," I informed her.

Coming from the Bounty Hunters' Guild, I added in my head. Nothing else made sense. I had quite cleverly put myself alone with her, and if I wasn't mistaken they'd already diverted or removed any Wolf Soldier guards who might be protecting me.

Crap.

"In all honesty," she informed me, "there is a selfish aspect." She stepped up to me again and, just as Genna had before, put her fingernails on the front of my white cotton shirt.

"You *are* an attractive man," she continued, her eyes cast shyly down, "and there are worse unions than to a king."

Trying not to look like I was looking, I searched the stables for some sign of anyone else being there. Stalls, lofts, spare wagons and a few empty saddle stands – nothing. No Uman, Men or Dwarves, not another living soul in sight, and *that* was plain strange because the stables were one of the most popular places in the palace.

I only took a second or two to look, then returned my attention to Shellene, just in time to catch her looking back up at me. I needed an escape plan, and I needed it not to *look* like an escape plan, and I needed it about ten minutes ago.

"This is interesting to me," I informed her. I forced a little smile and made myself look over her head, toward the palace walls, as if I were imagining what she offered. "I'd be a liar if I were to say I'm not attracted to you."

The fact that I didn't burst into flames told me that Shela wasn't within earshot.

She kept tracing the front of my shirt. "And your slave girl?" she asked me. "I have no desire to be cleaned up with a dust pan."

Definitely a spy, I thought to myself, and not a very good one, unless she was specifically trying to light off my radar. Why dump so much information? Anyone would bite at that.

"How do you know about that?" I asked her, looking into her eyes. Her choice to cover up or to reveal herself; mine to pursue it or to accept what she said.

She didn't even blink. "Ceberro meets regularly with Rennin," she informed me, meeting my eyes, reading me. "Rennin tells that tale as well as others. Ceberro confides *everything* to my sister."

"Who shares with you what you need to know," I added.

"And so," she informed me, with a smile.

"Your parents did an excellent job with you two," I said with a smile. "Imagine, a Queen of intelligence, beauty *and* breeding."

She smiled back. "For now," she said, "just imagine the breeding."

I laughed. I had an exit now. "I've been long from the party," I informed her. "You've robbed me of the ride I wanted to take."

She smiled, turned sideways to me, and put her dainty white hands on the upper rail of the paddock's steel gate. "I beg forgiveness, your Majesty," she said, and batted her eyes up at me, opening them up wide.

Arching her back, she said, "I'm yours to discipline."

Yeah – that verified two things: she'd done her homework, and Shela was nowhere near here.

I turned as if to go, my left arm swinging naturally forward, and without warning, with my body at three quarters to hers, swung

my open hand down and gave her pert backside a resounding *smack*.
She yelped appreciatively. I continued walking, turned my head to
my left and said, without missing a step, "There will be games
tomorrow – I'd be disappointed if Ceberro didn't bring you to attend
me."

I heard her say, "Your Majesty," but didn't slow down until I
found my way back out of the stables and into a corridor in the palace
that I knew for a fact was safe.

From there I marched myself to my personal chambers, where
I found Shela in her rocker with tear-stained cheeks, holding Lee.
She just watched me as I fished the chamber pot out from under the
bed and blew my lunch into it.

That was pretty much as scared as I'd been since I got here.

***

"Five dead," J'her informed me, sitting at the round table in
my personal chambers with Shela, every member of the Free Legion
and Duke Hectar. Nina had Lee and they were scouting out a wing of
the palace which had been a nursery once when Glennen's kids were
young.

The two of them and fifty Wolf Soldier guards to watch over
them.

After puking and letting Shela know what had happened,
she'd contacted D'gattis and he'd rounded up the Free Legion with
Karel's help. I was leaning pretty heavily on Karel right now because
I had no clue how to handle this.

"Plan on there being five more," Karel informed him, "who've
been mixed in with the Wolf Soldier guard."

"I think the consequences of doing that are pretty well
known," I informed Karel.

The Scitai shook his head, Ancenon and D'gattis with him.
"What you did was clever once, but lucky as well, and they'll be
better able to resist you. Keep in mind, as well, that your Wolf
Soldiers are many more than they used to be. Even with the Green
One's and D'gattis' help, Shela could not check them all at the same
time."

Dilvesh had been calling himself, "The Green One," or
someone else had and he'd decided that he liked it, but that was his
go-by these days.

J'her shook his head. "It's more complicated than that now," he informed us. "After that day, I set up a system where squads have codes and check in more regularly with commanders who know them. If they've mixed in five, we'll have them before the day is out."

"Don't count on your regular Wolf Soldiers to be able to handle trained Bounty Hunters," Arath – Earl Arath - informed him.

"I do not, your Excellence," J'her said. "There is a whole protocol in place – trust that we have our means."

"A real problem is that we don't have enough magic to meet our needs," I said, scowling. "And don't have the means to get it."

"A real problem is that one of your Dukes would like very much to kill you," Ancenon countered.

D'gattis sniffed and, sitting next to Ancenon, he informed us, "The *real* problem, which all of you are aloof of, is that our good King Rancor is alive."

I shook my head – this was supposed to be past us.

Karel nodded. "He's right," the Scitai said, sitting across the table from D'gattis. "That's been bothering me, too."

"Perhaps I shall settle that for the two of you right now," Shela informed them. She'd not liked listening to the encounter with Shellene and wasn't in the best mood to begin with. She took threats against me pretty seriously.

Dilvesh – the Green One – reached across the table and touched the back of Shela's hand. "You misunderstand, in your duress, my friend," he said. "Surely, the Bounty Hunters must realize what we'd find out."

D'gattis gave us one of his rare smiles. "As your owner points out," he said, "the spy was not clever, yet the trap a success. If the Bounty Hunters had managed to have the King alone, and clearly seek his demise, then why allow him to depart the stables?"

"Indeed," Ancenon said. "If he were correct, then what better time and place to remove him."

"There *is* a clear path from the stables out of the city," Thorn said, sitting back. "That is a much better plan than their actual assassination plot."

"So what are you saying here?" I demanded. This made no sense to me at all.

It was Hectar who said, "There's a huge celebration going on, Black Lupus. There was no one at the stables because the entire staff has been pressed into other services. You didn't know anything about that because you're a King now and it's beneath you to know how your palace is run. In fact, I'd be surprised if you even know who's responsible for running it."

I shrugged. "I thought you were," I informed him. That got a general laugh.

"I run the city," he said. "I don't even know who manages the palace staff. In fact, I suspected that it might be the Lady Shela."

All eyes turned to her. She shook her head. "There's an Uman named O'spiree," she said. "I didn't even think to check with him, but I remember him complaining that he had more guests than servants for the first time since he'd come here."

"So… I'm worried about nothing?" I asked them.

That got a few heads down, thinking. I looked from face-to-face.

Nantar finally said, "I think that Bounty Hunters are planning some new way to get into your Wolf Soldier guard. I think they might even have been in the process of trying something when you ran from the stables.

"I also believe that someone spoke to Shellene, and prepared her with enough information to entice you. She might actually have confessed the truth to you – that her intelligence comes to her from her sister, who gets it from Ceberro."

"Ceberro asks more questions about you and your origins than I'm comfortable answering," Hectar admitted. "He's a fellow Duke – a peer and a friend, but he loved Glennen and if he's forgotten the beating you laid on him to win your position, then that's the fastest I've ever seen him release a debt."

"Ceberro may be a whole other issue for you," Dilvesh said, "and the incident in the stables, and your own paranoia, may have conveniently revealed a new plot by the Bounty Hunters."

"So all we know is that there are plots out there," I said. "We really don't know that much about them."

D'gattis stood, and in all seriousness said, "Today, I believe, you become a member of the nobility."

Chapter Sixteen

Dating

To the east of Eldador the Port, on a wide, flat field where armies could muster or fairs be set up or all sorts of other useful things, a bandstand had been erected and a field laid out for a competition at arms. Theran Lancers jousted; there were foot races and trials at arms, feats of strength as well as jugglers and acrobats and a play in the hottest part of the day which, considering this was the month of Order and a fall month, wasn't really that hot. To our north the port stayed busy with ship after ship entering and leaving with goods from and for the harvest. To the south, wagons rolled into the city as farmers brought their goods to market.

I sat in a huge wooden throne that a bunch of porters had lugged out here, and Shela sat on a skin at my feet, Nina behind her. The little Aschire had made it through the night on her own, this time with Lee in her room in a bassinet. I'd doubled the guard and, of course, we'd caught four of the five Bounty Hunters Karel had suspected, and just driven off the fifth.

I'd confirmed that O'spiree, a fat Uman man over one hundred years of age with long, white hair down past his shoulders and a nose like a beak, had taken the entire stable staff for the previous day's party, and I told him to stop doing that. I explained to him the practice of 'temp labor', and he'd considered it a revolutionary idea and immediately recruited fifty unemployed peasants from the city streets and put them to work in the palace.

Shela had needed to check them all, which had exhausted her, and she spent half of the day sleeping with her cheek on my calf, which was just as well.

Magic might be useful, but it wasn't to be relied on, I'd decided.

In a place of honor, much as there was one, in a smaller throne next to me, padded in red velvet, sat Lady Shellene, magnificent with an open-front gown in baby-blue with white-lace trim and tiny jewels sparkling throughout its fabric. She'd styled her hair loose and wild around her shoulders with baby's breath and some kind of tiny yellow flowers woven into it, and her hand continuously strayed to the top of mine.

Shellene would, in fact, make a very good queen of Eldador, I had to admit. She just *looked* like one. The commons seemed to love her – she'd spent the early morning hours in the city with a retinue (and a Wolf Soldier squad) administering to the poor, not because it was a tradition here but because it seemed to be what she liked to do. My wildly-popular edict of 'be good to each other now that Glennen's dead' had brought no less than 1,000 beggars into the city and our employing fifty of them hadn't made life any easier for the rest. Nobles and wealthy commons were dispensing what food they could afford but a lot of this was falling on the city, and that meant that some of them were not, if fact, getting fed.

One of my number one fears was that I was really going to suck at being a king, and Shellene seemed to know something about how to do it. It would be a relief to have that sort of council.

And I liked her. Not with the emotion I felt toward Shela, but I appreciated her company and her intelligence, and I knew from past experience that this was a precursor for me, on its way to a relationship.

The crowd cheered and it drew me from my musings. Lee pointed a chubby finger out at the field where one warrior had just dealt a devastating blow with a wooden sword to another, knocking him flat on his back. I'd set the prize for victory as one hundred gold Tabaars, and that had the combatants really going at it.

Karel suspected that the winner would be a reverse-Robin Hood, a Bounty Hunter who would use the victory to get within striking distance of me – so in fact Hectar was scheduled to deliver the prize.

"You're pensive, your Majesty," Shellene commented.

"Weight of the crown," I informed her.

She looked at the top of my head. They didn't use crowns here, and in the local language I'd just told her that the top of my head was heavy. I smiled and added, "Heavy thoughts."

She smiled. "How very clever a turn of phrase," she said.

"One tries to amuse a lady," I said, smiling back.

Her whole face lit up in an even greater smile. That had to be some kind of amazing compliment that I wasn't aware of, or she was showing off her looks again.

The warrior on the field raised his wooden sword in victory as the other slapped the ground, counting himself out. Shellene took one of the roses laid out before me and, without asking but with a significant glance at Shela, cast it out over the heads of the persons seated in honor spots below but before me, out onto the field. The warrior made a great show of bowing to me, then went to the rose, picked it up, smelled it as if to say, "Victory's smell is sweet," and departed the field. Two Uman porters in the green house livery ran out to help the fallen warrior to his feet. Technically they should be in my grey, but it took time and a lot of money to change them all, and we were all kind of still stuck on Glennen.

Two more warriors stepped out onto the field, bowed to me, and were commanded by Hectar to fight.

Shellene settled back down beside me. In the chairs behind me were the Volkhydran, Andaron and Confluni daughters who were her competition. I could almost feel the heat of their gazes on my arm when she took my hand again.

I had an appointment with Henekh Dragorson after two more bouts, and then with Kills with a Glance after that. I had a feeling that the topic of fair access might be on their mind. The Confluni was either thanking her lucky stars or favorite goddess or something that I wasn't interested, or she had her own plans.

I'd heard practically nothing from the Toorians. That had me kind of worried, too.

Shela snored softly and I gave a little chuckle. The poor girl worked her behind off around here. She didn't give me a lot of opportunity to forget to whom I owed my success and loyalty, not that I needed one.

Wooden swords cracked together. The crowd cheered and my blood-thirsty daughter gave a squeal of delight.

"No doubt the child's parentage," Shellene commented.

"None at all," I said. I noted that Lee's bebe was folded over the crook of her arm, and that she checked it once in a while, to make sure either that it was there, or that she had its attention.

No, I thought, that's my girl.

"Are you aware of the trend she's started?" Shellene asked me.

I turned my attention to her. Behind us, the four daughters leaned forward. "No," I said, "I am not."

"Bebe daughters," the Confluni princess intruded, drawing my attention. She wore the gossamer wrap I'd come to associate with her, her hair hanging loose, as with the rest of the prospects. Apparently they'd decided that's what I liked.

Sings Softly, the Andaron from the Wet Belly tribe, said, "They're the newest prize for wealthy daughters in your city."

"Not just your city," Neveratta added, not missing an opportunity to one-up the Andarons. "Potters are working through the night to export the first five score to my own nation. I've invested heavily in such futures."

That drew looks from all of the other girls. Women didn't usually get involved in business here, and 'invest in futures' wasn't a term I'd heard here before. I repeated it to Neveratta.

She smiled. "I'm giving six coppers now for dolls yet to be made, that they'll be consigned to me once produced. I expect that I shall sell them for between one and two silvers."

A pretty profit for a toy, I thought. But then, men complimented each other on how they indulged their daughters, not on the deals they got.

"That," I said, and paused to draw out their attention, as I'd seen Groff do, "impresses me."

Neveratta beamed. The rest frowned, especially Shellene. She'd started this conversation for her own benefit.

"I'm informed that you're meeting with my uncle, Henekh, in a short time," she informed me.

"I believe I am," I answered. "I'd expect you to attend, of course."

"As your Majesty wishes," she lowered her eyes demurely.

In the back of my mind, I wondered if there'd be a fist-fight with the other girls. In the same thought, I thought maybe that wouldn't be such a bad thing. Then none of them would want to see me.

The crowd cheered. I turned my attention to see another warrior on his back, the victor in Volkhydran furs raising a wooden representation of a battle axe over his head and shaking it in triumph. Lee was clapping her hands and Nina, holding her, was smiling.

Shela bit my calf. I didn't yelp but it wasn't much of a bite. I reached down to stroke her long, black hair. I felt her fingers on the inside of my thigh and had to smile.

"It's good ta be da king," I said, to no one in particular.

***

One of the towers in the palace is filled with guest rooms, and around the fifth floor a huge, wide room with balconies had clearly been intended for meetings but never used. It contained a big, long table surrounded by chairs, a set of tapestries, one of them a map of Fovea as it had been known at the time it was woven, and an actual chalkboard, which I'd added.

I met here with Henekh and his staff, mostly because this place had outer doors which could be opened for a cross wind, and Henekh kind of reeked.

He was still a giant of a man, probably heavier than I, sporting thick red hair on every exposed inch of his skin with the possible exception of his eyelids, his hair braided warrior-style around his shoulders.

His niece, Neveratta, attended with a couple non-descript Volkhydran ladies. She'd changed to a blouse and long skirt and made sure to unbutton enough of the blouse to reveal cleavage, probably based on Shellene's perceived success.

She wasn't stacked like Shellene but he had nothing to be ashamed of, either. Dark hair and dark eyes just like Shela, not as slender but a dagger on her hip in a wide, leather belt – this was a Volkhydran daughter, no denying it.

I'd made sure that Henekh got here before I did, so that I could make an entrance. D'gattis had helped me out with that little pointer, the idea behind it being that this put me in the power position. Hectar attended me with his son, along with Shela and thirty Wolf Soldiers.

Henekh had five of his own warriors in attendance. They eyed the Wolf Soldiers with a speculation that said they'd love it if something broke out and they could prove themselves.

Shela pulled a chair out for me to sit in, on the side of the table opposite that which Henekh had chosen and directly in the center, which put the sun behind him, but not directly. This wasn't Henekh's first rodeo, either. I could tell he'd moved the table to give himself this advantage but didn't say anything.

"How may Eldador be of service to you, Lord Henekh?" I asked him.

He made a face and I remembered D'gattis telling me that this sort of behavior didn't suit me. I didn't like it much when he was right, but it wouldn't be smart not to listen to him, just because of that.

"What do you need, Henekh?" I asked him, correcting myself.

It's not like I hadn't been to Volkhydro, either.

Neveratta stood and crossed behind her uncle. While she moved, he said, "What I need is a fighting chance for my niece," he informed me. "That red-haired bitch has been sitting next to you all day."

"And from what I'm told," Neveratta said, rounding the end of the table and progressing toward me, ignoring an almost-murderous look from Shela, "she had you all to herself yesterday, when you all but ran from the rest of us."

I couldn't hold back a smile. At least I had called this one. "How did you know about that?" I asked.

"We aren't without resources," one of Henekh's men informed me.

Neveratta took up a position behind me and put her hands on my shoulders. I felt her thumbs dig into my upper back and neck muscles. Shela actually bared her teeth, making it sort of look like a smile after a moment.

"You shouldn't allow yourself to be distracted from long-term opportunities," she informed me, leaning forward to make sure that her warm breath touched my ear, "by such short-term ones."

"And don't be fooled," Henekh informed me, "that girl is a short term opportunity. A marriage to her brings you nothing."

"Does it now?" I asked him. Shela shifted in her seat next to me, and I didn't need to look at her to know that this was already pushing her past where she wanted to go.

This had to be hard on her. She didn't want this – she had no ambitions to be the Queen of anything. She'd be just as happy with me if I were a peasant farmer – probably happier because then I wouldn't be chasing off suitors.

"She's the daughter to a vassal whose loyalty isn't in question," Henekh informed me. "And who will be a vassal tomorrow, regardless of your decision with her now."

"If you seek nothing more than an ample bosom, look no farther than your current slave," Neveratta added. "But then any woman should be so gifted after the birth of a child."

I think that was a compliment, and Shela didn't do more than squint her eyes, so I couldn't be sure how to react to it. The overall impression was that I'm a horn-dog, though, and that I could handle.

"So what you're informing me," I said, with a sideways look at Hectar and his son, Hectaro, who each sat with their hands folder one over the other on the table in front of them, "is that I have more to fear from Volkhydro."

That got a wide-eyed reaction from two of Henekh's warriors, although the warlord himself kept his cool. Neveratta kept rubbing my back, which I was good with, seeing as she was really, really skilled at it.

"Volkhydro has never been bested in any field of battle by Eldadorians," Henekh informed me. "You should not confuse your luck with the Confluni with victories against us."

Had to admit, that's the most artful, open-handed threat I'd received in both of my days as a King. It even earned Henekh sideways looks from his own warriors.

Hectaro just chuckled. Hectar even allowed himself a smile.

Neveratta moved her hands lower down my back.

"You know," I said, squinting my eyes and nodding, "that's probably true. I think it might diminish Eldador, that we've had no such victories."

"The Eldadorian Regulars stand ready at your command, your Majesty," Hectar informed me.

Henekh squinted at me – he wasn't doing what I wanted him to do yet, but he was close. Neveratta wasn't missing a beat – I might take her just to spite him, after all.

I had an idea that he was going just for that. It would be a Volkhydran thing to do.

"It took four thousand Wolf Soldiers to sack Outpost IX," I informed them. "So perhaps six thousand for Volkha, alongside ten thousand Eldadorian Regulars."

"You don't have enough ships –" Henekh said, smiling broadly.

"I have the resources of Free Legion shipping at my disposal," I countered him, "and I think if I were to ask, I could get help from the Confluni if I wanted it."

To any Volkhydran, that was a dire threat, and it wasn't lost on Henekh. Without thinking, his hand went for the short sword at his side, on his belt.

That was what I'd been waiting for. Neveratta's dagger coming out of its sheath behind me, however, was a total surprise.

To me, that is, not to Shela, who sprang from her chair like a tigress and took the Volkhydran girl's blindside from the right.

If you want to handle Volkhydrans, then you have to think like a Volkhydran, because they aren't like any other people, and in a world dominated by Uman-Chi and how *they* handled politics, it was easy to overlook what mattered to simple, brutish Volkhydrans.

I could have vaulted over the table, the Sword of War in my hand, and dealt with Henekh while my Wolf Soldiers tore apart his personal guard. I could have shipped their heads back to Volkhydro with Neveratta and thought, "Boy, did I teach them a lesson."

They'd have chewed on it for a long time, bided their time and struck sometime in the future when I wasn't ready for it. That's how a Volkhydran mind works.

I left the Sword of War in its sheath. While Shela dealt with Neveratta, I put both hands under the table, ten feet long, and picked up the edge.

It wasn't a light table – that was pretty much the point. I got the end up, stepped forward and turned my wrists and, from the center of the table, picked the whole thing up off of the ground.

The Volkhydrans scrambled backwards over their chairs, their eyes wide, as I pushed the whole thing up over my head, took one giant step forward, and then heaved it at them.

This was a mammoth act of pure brute power. The table bowled over all five of them and their warlord. One set of legs broke off and the table itself shattered at the center. It crushed four matching chairs under its weight, a couple Volkhydran arms and legs along with them.

Panting, I stood over the tangle of Men and furniture, my Wolf Soldiers flanked behind me, Hectar and Hectaro to my left, and Shela straddling Neveratta on the floor, her dagger knocked away.

The table edge had taken Henekh right in the chest. From the wheezing, I had to guess we'd broken a few ribs. He stood, using the shoulder of one his warriors for support, the latter on all fours with his head down, gasping for air and dripping blood on the floor from his mouth and nose. None of the rest of them was getting up any time soon.

He stood up, and he faced me, but he made a point of keeping his hand away from his sword.

"Neveratta may sit next to me for the afternoon's entertainment, if she so wishes," I informed him.

"She does," Neveratta grunted from floor, under Shela.

"Shellene was certified a virgin before she was sent here," Hectar added.

Wow.

"I'll bend her right over the table edge for you right now if that's what you want," Henekh growled. He wasn't happy but this wasn't about being happy. This was about being the meanest dog in the fight. That had everything to do with being Volkhydran.

"Do it," Shela said, stepping up off of the Volkhydran girl.

I turned on my heel and left. It wasn't right for the King of Eldador to be a party to that sort of thing, and in fact I had somewhere else to be.

I needed to meet with Kills, and the best place to do that was the stables. Everything about me that interested him was centered there.

This wasn't the sort of meeting to bring Shela to, based on what I was pretty sure he'd want to discuss, but a man likes to see his granddaughter and I'd already arranged for Nina to have Lee there with her Wolf Soldier guard.

So when I marched in with *my* Wolf Soldier guard, I expected a 'grandpa moment,' meaning Kills holding Lee and making a big fuss over her.

What I *didn't* expect was that he'd have her sitting on the back of one of those mares he brought, seeing if she could keep her balance.

Nina stood to one side with the Wolf Soldiers, looking ready to leap out of her own skin. If you knew Aschire then you knew what they did when they were unhappy, and Nina was balanced on the balls of her feet, her arms back, that ever-surprised look on her face darkened by dread as she watched Lee coo and kick her heels on the horse's back.

"For the love of Weather, Kills With a Glance, did you decide you have too many granddaughters?" I bellowed to him.

The mare did a start/stop in surprise, as horses will do, and he plucked Lee from her back, cradling her in one arm, smiling guiltily. Nina stepped up with her arms out, reaching for Lee's hands.

"I can barely have *any* fun with her, thanks to this bodyguard you've assigned her," Kills complained, pointing to Nina. Nina shot me a nervous look and let Lee take one index finger in either hand. Her bebe was stilled bent over one arm.

"More to Nina's credit," I answered him. As I covered the distance down the aisle where Blizzard's paddock lay, she shot me a look that showed me her concern, and managed to drag Lee out of Kills' hands.

The Andaron's retinue, also five warriors, were occupied in the other mare's stall, the two Andaron daughters with them. They were arguing in Andaron as to which of the mares was a better prospect for my stallion, not that I was supposed to know that. Most Men didn't speak Andaron.

"Have you tried to breed these mares yet?" Kills demanded of me.

"No," I said. "Not yet."

"More interested in that red-headed mare you've been sitting next to all day?" he pressed me, grinning.

I chuckled. "I don't think your daughter would like that," I said.

He sighed. "We've had that conversation," he told me. "You're doing no one any favors spoiling her. No woman likes to see her man with others, but if it's going to happen, you should get it over with."

I nodded. It seemed to be looking that way.

He indicated the two Andaron women with his thumb. "I'm told you haven't touched either of them yet."

"I'm not sure I want to take the offer," I informed him.

Kills frowned and took a step closer to me. "You know that the mare I bred to him went to foal?" he asked me.

I nodded. I'd heard that he had a filly from it from Two Spears. In fact, it occurred to me that I hadn't seen much of Two Spears since I'd made him a Duke.

"I can tell you that I have no interest in any of the other tribes getting to that blood line," he informed me. Then he put a hand on my shoulder, "But I have less in the Drifters or the Wet Bellies coming up from the south and raiding my tribe, either. In fact, I'm leaving tomorrow because of it."

The tribes might all kill each other over that horse, it's true, I thought to myself. It would be better to let more have access to the line, at least the large tribes.

"So how does that work?" I asked Kills.

He smiled wide. "Your daughter looks too much like you for you to ask that question," he informed me.

I laughed and shoved him with both hands. He recovered and punched me in the chest.

"What I meant to ask," I informed him, grinning wide, "is what form do I follow with this? Just take them when I want them? Does the second one lose coup to the first? What if there's a child?"

Kills nodded. Men and women in the tribe 'counted coup,' meaning that they gathered or lost honor by certain actions or the way others treated them. It would be a legitimate question, then, if the order mattered, and Kills as a tribal war lord would be responsible for knowing which way honor fell.

"The Wet Bellies and the Drifters, they are more like two separate parts of one tribe," he informed me, "both in the south of Andoron, a barrier to the Slee Nation. I believe you will give coup to both because you're the warrior who brought Blizzard to the people, but more coup to the first, surely."

"If one tribe was bigger, then I would take their daughter first and then coup would not be affected," I surmised.

Kills nodded again. "Now, you are clearly just showing your preference. These girls were not offered to you, so you give them back to the tribe, with child or without. I think there are men who will want them pregnant, because your son would probably be a good son."

Well, that's nice to know. The whole tribe raised an Andaron child, so their idea of parental responsibility wasn't like mine. I, however, had no desire to run around fathering children whom I couldn't then be responsible for. That just wasn't me.

Words Genna had spoken to me stung me once again.

"You could always barter to keep them, if you want," Kills added.

"Or just keep them," I said off-handedly.

"No," Kills said, more emphatically. "Drifters and Wet Bellies, these are proud tribes, White Wolf. Large tribes. They *will* make war on you if you shame these daughters."

"And then you could have their lands, if you wanted them," I said, "because that would be the last anyone ever saw of the Wet Bellies or the Drifters."

Kills shrugged. "Neither tribe will hesitate because of your Wolf Soldiers," he said. Now his warriors were approaching us, the girls with them, because the conversation was becoming heated. "Likely they don't know or care anything about them, and an Andaron on a horse is the equal of many on foot."

His warriors nodded. The two girls cast nervous glances around them.

"If you make war on my tribe," Sings Softly said, her voice lowered, "they will just join with the Drifters if you do them that much harm."

"And Drifters with the Wet Bellies," Little Bird added. They were dressed now more like Shela dressed when I met her – the one-piece skin worn over the shoulders and tied at the middle, decorated here and there with beads. I'd learned that the beads identified the tribe.

"So you'd just make a new tribe, and a new enemy," Kills informed me. "Maybe more new enemies, as men and women with no tribe came to join this new tribe while it was easy."

That got my attention. "They wouldn't have to go through all of the rituals?" I asked.

All of the Andarons shook their heads. "When a new tribe is formed, it will usually take whoever wants to join it, at least at first. Small tribes rarely last – they're raided because they're weak."

I held back a smile – these warriors were going to return to Andoron soon, and Andarons are the biggest gossips in the world.

I turned to one of the sergeants in the Wolf Soldier squads that attended me. They'd been waiting bored back at the entrance to this part of the stables, none of them native Andaron speakers as far as I knew.

"Sergeant," I called him, then recognized him as Chuckurr, a Volkhydran I'd liberated from Hydran jails after he'd gone on a killing spree in response to the city Duke, Dragor (a relative of Henekh's, named after his father), had ordered some family member executed for cowardice on the battle field.

"Chukurr," I said, when I had his attention. "Your squad can bring these women to my apartments and provide them with whatever they need to clean themselves up."

He nodded and his squad snapped to attention. With nervous looks to the other to the Andaron males, who ignored them, the two girls fell in with the Wolf Soldiers and the group left.

"This is the right thing," Kills informed me. "Now – we can help you bring in these mares…"

I cut him off. "Telling me how to run my herd, Kills?"

The stopped him dead in his tracks. Telling another Andaron how to run his horses, or insinuating that he couldn't, constituted a pretty dire insult.

"Of – of course not, White Wolf," he informed me, bowing his head a little and stepping back. I'd fought all of the toughest warriors in his tribe, including his own son, Two Spears, and beaten them all.

"We're done here," I said to them. The remaining Wolf Soldiers snapped to attention.

"We can bring these women and horses back for you –" Kills stated, but stopped when I shot him another look.

"I'll handle that," I informed him.

"I can't guarantee how Eldadorian troops will be welcomed among the tribes," Kills said, following after me as I exited the stables.

Without looking at him, I grinned.

"I can."

Returning to the palace from the stables, my Wolf Soldier guard both clearing the way for me and following up behind, I had just about enough time to catch the play that was being performed in my honor. I put a lot of stake in the power of the theater, but it wouldn't appear that way if I blew it off.

The back passages through the palace, which were faster, were also darker and more full of twists. When I used them I routinely scared the crap out of the occasional Uman servant or courtier who found some use or other in them – I suspected mostly plotting and fornication but I couldn't prove it.

When the Wolf Soldiers preceded me, they'd just clear the way. Most people were afraid of them, so when they said, "Make way for the King," that was usually the whole conversation.

Still, I wasn't surprised to hear a familiar voice say, "I *won't* clear the way – I have to speak with him."

I hadn't heard that voice in a long time.

"Kvitch," I shouted out to the Dwarf ambassador, "You better not be trying to get my sword back from me again!"

When I'd barely been on Fovea a week, I'd met the Dwarves just before the Dorkans tried to win a military engagement against them. I'd helped them to win 'the Battle of Two Mountains,' and they'd rewarded me with my armor, my horse's first saddle, his first barding, and by making me an honorary Dwarf.

We turned the corner and there stood the Dwarven ambassador, resolute as a stone, just as I remembered him. His long, grey and white beard had been tucked into his belt, and he wore the same gold amulet around his neck with two fists pointed at each other. He'd dressed out in finer clothes and even wore a short blue cape over his shoulders. A red leather belt around his ample waist had a ring for the mace I'd seen him fight with, but he didn't have the weapon.

"Pass him," I ordered the Wolf Soldier, M'den, an Uman whom I'd liberated after returning to Eldador. M'den stood aside grinning like a maniac, which is how he normally seemed to be. The world made M'den happy, and only he knew why.

Nothing made Kvitch happy – he always had an axe to grind.

"I suppose those two Andaron virgins preceding you are whom you're following so fast," he accused me reaching out his hand. We took each other by the wrist and I felt the dagger up his sleeve. Kvitch may be a diplomat but he was no fool. People didn't trust Dwarves and it wasn't uncommon to prey on them.

"Nah," I informed him, releasing his grip. It was like shaking hands with a fuzzy statue. He turned to walk beside me as the Wolf Soldiers picked up the pace again, a little slower to accommodate shorter legs. "Off to see the play."

"I'd heard you had people acting," Kvitch said. "I actually went to your Theatre au Thera. Saw a bunch Uman pretending they were crazy – or maybe they were? Who knows?"

I laughed. "And you came all this way to get your money back?" I asked him.

"Ha!" he countered me. "There was no need – I was well entertained. I came here to see the most famous Dwarf, J'ktak. In case you're wondering, that's you."

"And here I thought it was you," I said. J'ktak was my Dwarven name – it meant 'the good man.'

"Me?" Kvitch coughed. We exited the passage we'd been in and emerged into the throne room from a door disguised with the image of Alekanna. Kvitch opened his mouth to say something, then the pillars caught his eyes.

Glennen had ordered the bases carved in the images of Dwarves straining to hold the pillars, as if the ceiling were almost too heavy for them. He'd tried to hire Dwarves to do the work but the Dwarves had turned him down, and whether this was tribute or mockery of them was anyone's guess.

Kvitch wasn't guessing.

"What in the name of Earth's ass is *that*?" he demanded.

Before I could answer, he pushed past the Wolf Soldiers and up to the nearest base. It stood almost at my height, about a tenth of the way to the ceiling, the Dwarf grimacing for the apparent weight of his burden.

"I heard that Glennen had commissioned these," Kvitch grumbled, "but did he have to hire a duck? That's what it looks like! That's what it looks like to *me*! It looks like a chicken pecked this – it looks like –"

"Do you want to recarve them?" I asked him.

Dwarves called themselves The Simple People. It was often better just to give in to them when they wanted something.

"Is there a choice?" he demanded. He turned back to the pillar and he actually smacked it with his open hand. "Can we leave this – can we have people thinking that *Dwarves* did this?"

"That would be terrible," I said, nodding solemnly.

He just stood there, shaking his head. I'd always thought they were pretty good, actually, but I wasn't about to say so now.

"I'm going to guess that you didn't come here for this, either," I said to him when he didn't move away from the pillars that had offended him.

"What?" he demanded. He forced himself away from the pillar and waddled back to me. His fingers were flexing, he was so angry. I think that if he had a chisel and a hammer on him, he'd had started on the pillars right then.

"Why are you here?" I asked him again. I hadn't seen him in the throne room or at the stairs for the coronation. He wasn't here for that or, if he was, he had something on his mind now.

"Why I am I here?" he demanded. "Why – well, why do you think I'm here, J'ktak?

"I'm here to save you!"

Chapter Seventeen

A Bold New World

I made it in time to see the end of the play. The whole field stood and bowed to me, Wolf Soldiers and Eldadorian Regulars saluting, as I appeared beside my outdoor throne. I sat and gave them what I hope passed for a regal wave and they got about their business again.

Neveratta was sitting in the smaller, velvet-covered throne. Shellene was seated behind me, looking both regal and pissed off at the same time, and the Confluni girl sat next to her. The Andarons, of course, weren't coming, and Shela sat on the skin at my feet. Nina had followed me back with Lee, and Shela took her.

"How is my father, your Majesty?" Shela asked me.

"He's well," I informed her. "He's leaving in the morning – you should spend tonight with him."

She looked up into my eyes, held me for a moment, and I felt her do the sniffing around thing that she did with me sometimes. She nodded, looked down and attended to Lee.

Nina tried to say something to her, but Shela just waved her off.

The whole thing just sucked.

Neveratta laid her hand on mine to get my attention.

"I am officially certified, your Majesty," she said, "an it interest you."

At first I didn't remember what she was talking about, but one lingering look set me straight on that regard.

"That is, um, excellent," I informed her. She left her hand on mine.

"I appreciate that you removed yourself," she began, but I raised a hand and she quieted. I had a lot going through my mind right then and I needed to mull through it.

The afternoon dragged on. I find it hard to believe that Neveratta got her money's worth with me, although I distractedly allowed her an invitation to dinner that she would have been entitled to anyway, and complimented her when one of her Volkhydran kinsmen took the field as the best of the warriors. Of course, her enthusiasm was lessened when it was revealed that the warrior was now an Eldadorian citizen.

It seemed that Eldador had become a vampire sucking the lifeblood out of the Fovean region, keeping all of the best and brightest for itself.

When the competitions were all over I stood and dismissed the crowd, and my Wolf Soldier guard escorted me back to my personal chambers. Of course, by then, I'd forgotten what I had waiting there.

As Shela had on the night I'd taken her on the plains in Andoron, Sings Softly and Little Bird had cast aside their virgin clothes and were waiting naked for me in my chambers. I think that, if Shela had decided to come here before seeing her father, the place might have been a crime scene.

I was actually starting to fear her wrath. This whole marriage and ceremony thing was destroying my 'king' experience.

"We await you, as ordered, your Majesty," Little Bird informed me.

"And we trust that you've made arrangements for our mares," Sings Softly added.

I entered and closed the door behind me. A few of the Wolf Soldiers left in the parlor outside shot glances within but I didn't hear anyone saying anything. The Pack would be passing this news like wild-fire. People thought that women and housewives gossiped, but warriors were one hundred times worse.

"I understand the terms," I informed them.

"Shall we bathe you first, your Majesty?" Sings Softly asked me. Of the two, she seemed the more outgoing. Little Bird seemed more demure and secretive, always speaking barely loud enough to be heard.

"I think that would be nice," I said. I had time before we ate. In fact, being late would be a gift to the rest of the nobility, who would want to change and, of course, scheme, before dinner.

Glennen had either appreciated a bath, or Alekanna had, but adjoining the bedroom a separate bathroom with indoor facilities and a wide, deep tub had been installed. Normally it would take twenty servants to form a bucket brigade from the kitchen cauldrons to get hot water in here, and if you ended up with tepid you were doing well. Then you'd super-heat something like a big anvil and toss it in there to get the temperature back up.

Draining it involved more buckets and a line to the window.

I'd had at the palace with a team of engineers, under the guidance of two Uman who had worked with the Dwarves in Thera, and now we had indoor plumbing and an efficient way to move water to personal bathrooms like this one. Water tanks had been installed at top of each of the palace towers and could both collect rain water and have water pumped to them nightly by prison labor. Copper wasn't the best material to use for piping, but it was definitely the easiest and it wasn't like I had a lot of time to put together a manufacturing plant. A simple cast iron centrifuge, some molten copper and a steam-driven motor and we were spinning out pipe as fast as we could melt the copper ore.

No one used copper for much of anything and it was inexpensive to collect. I'd discreetly invested in copper mines near Steel City with my own funds.

In time the investment would grow to include a manufacturing plant and produce a magnificent return. For now it meant that I turned a simple valve and opened a drain, and water poured into the tub as if from nowhere, then seemed to become hot on its own. I closed the drain and the tub filled in just a few minutes.

"What magic is this?" Little Bird asked, touching the surface of the water with one finger as if afraid it might bite her. "I can think of no single spell…"

"You're a sorceress?" I asked her. Sings Softly simply slipped into the tub.

"I have some of the gifts," Little Bird answered me. "This was meant to honor you."

"Those who are barely gifted may not use them," Sings Softly informed me. "There is the black mind, after all."

"What's the black mind?" I asked.

Little bird began unbuttoning my shirt. Steam rose from the surface of the tub. Sings Softly rested her back against the side of the tub, her legs apart, facing me. Her pert, brown nipples peeked out just above the surface of the water.

I needed to invent bubble bath.

"The black mind is the price of using power that a woman cannot master," Little Bird informed me. She looked into my eyes, her voice as usual just above a whisper. "Or a man, I suppose."

"When a sorceress casts unready, or too much, it will destroy her mind," Sings Softly said. She bent her left leg and hugged it, resting her chin on her knee. Little Bird pushed my shirt off and ran her fingers across my chest and down my abdomen.

"They'll lie staring into the oblivion, never speaking, they'll even foul themselves," Little Bird said. "If you feed them, they'll eat. They'll live as long as you let them, but they'll never recover."

"Not ever," Sings Softly said. "So the barely gifted might study, even apprentice to a degree, but they do not cast."

"And for those that do," Little Bird informed me, kneeling down and taking one of my boots in her tiny hands, "the black mind."

That seemed like an incredible waste to me.

Sings Softly crossed to my side of the tub, rose up out of the water, steam rising from her breasts and shoulder, her hair lying wet against her skull and back. She reached out and stroked my upper arm. The water from her hands felt warm to my skin.

As Little Bird pulled my boots off, Sings softly drew me to the side of the tub and started to nibble at my ear.

Her fingers slid into my pants. The naked girl at my feet pulled off one boot, then the other, and set them to one side, then reached to free the laces at the front of my leather pants.

Sings already had a grip on me. When my pants slid off, she pulled me backwards into the tub.

Little Bird entered after me. There was enough room for this, but not too awful much.

The kissing and touching was wonderful. I lay back into the water, two mouths on me, soft skin pressed against mine. I didn't know how the girls felt about having to do this, but they were definitely applying themselves now.

I could see how powerful men could have this, come to enjoy it, and lose what matters to them in light of what they could have. Little Bird straddled me while Sings Softly kissed my ear and stroked my chest and then my behind as I arched my back.

Little Bird bit her lip and raised her hands up onto my shoulders. The water around us turned red.

She rode me while the other waited. Both watched me. When it came time for my climax and my breathing changed, Sings Softly covered my lips with hers, her tongue penetrating me, exploring my mouth. I exploded up into Little Bird, felt her clamp down on me as if she were greedy for my seed.

We slowed. Sings Softly slid away from me, watching the two of us, a smile on her face. I took Little Bird's breasts in my hands, kissed her wide, brown areola, bit her nipples.

"My gift to you, your Majesty," she informed me, her eyes cast down. I turned my face up to her and she kissed my lips.

Yes, powerful men could easily get used to this, and lose what mattered. Shela would know what I was doing and, on the off chance that she didn't, her father would tell her. I'd have to face her again. She wasn't a woman who gave up what she considered hers.

She wasn't a woman who liked it cast away, either.

"We should drain this thing," Sings Softly said. "It is not befitting you to be covered in a woman's blood."

Little Bird slid off of me, wincing. I stood. I'd been thinking that people rubbed themselves with linen cloths here, and another thing I needed to introduce was terry-cloth.

My mind always racing, always on to the next thing; perhaps my training as a Naval Nuclear Engineer, perhaps my fear of the god War, who'd commanded me to be successful. He'd be loving this.

They wiped me down and, with the pink towels, let the tub drain and then wiped its surface. Sings Softly offered to let me have her over the edge of the bed and, taking me by the hand, led me to the bedroom.

"Would you like to beat me first, your Majesty?" she asked me.

That was a surprise. "What?"

"Many men will strike a woman," Little Bird informed me, quietly. "We know you beat your Shela."

Sings Softly bent over the edge of the bed, laying down another linen cloth first, sinking into the high-piled quilts and down mattress. Her butt was firm, tan and round, she spread her legs to expose herself.

"Who told you that?" I demanded of them.

Sings Softly looked over her shoulder at me. "Shela," she said. "Women speak, passing on traditions. She knows what we are here for."

"You should enjoy this," Little Bird said. "You give a great gift – the seed of a mighty stallion. We are for your pleasure, your Majesty."

"In fact," Sings Softly said, smiling, "I'm curious to know what makes Shela love you like she does."

Little Bird put her tiny hands on my waist and turned me sideways to the other Andaron, then knelt down at my feet, putting her hands on me, stroking.

"Beat her," she told me. "When you're ready I will help you take her."

Sings Softly turned back around. Her long brown hair draped wet over her shoulders.

My hand met the curve of her butt with a *smack*. She whimpered, no differently than Shela. I spanked her again, and again.

Her behind warmed, then became a reddish tan. Little Bird had me ready more quickly than I would have thought possible, and then guided me to Sings Softly.

Where Little Bird had been quiet, Sings Softly cried out as I broke her hymen. I began to move, and she responded moaning, and clawing at the quilts. My second time in a short time, it took much longer with Sings Softly, and the other Andaron expressed herself with every moment of it. She also orgasmed at least three times that I caught, before I found my release inside of her.

When I withdrew from her, Little Bird cleaned me, stroking me at the same time. Sings Softly lay panting for several minutes, then rose up off of the bed, holding the bloody linen to her, and made her way to the bathroom.

I stood there, watching Little Bird, who stayed kneeling, her knees apart, her head down.

"What happens with you now?" I asked her.

She looked up at me. "Your Majesty?"

In the bathroom, the water started running.

"Is this great coup for you?" I asked.

She smiled and looked back down. "Great coup," she said. "If I bear a son, perhaps a war chief's son will want me. Even should I not quicken, men will fight for what White Wolf has had."

The water turned back off. I heard Sings Softly hiss in pain.

"Were you well pleased, your Majesty?" she asked me from the bathroom.

Little Bird looked up and then back down.

I sighed.

"You were sent here by your fathers, with your fathers' horses, because you thought this would get you time with my stallion?" I asked them.

Little Bird looked up alarmed, searching for my eyes. Sings Softly opened the drain in the bath and emerged back into the bedroom, her eyebrows knit over her pretty brown eyes.

"As Kills With a Glance did with She Runs Swiftly," she said, quoting Shela's former name.

"And what happened with that girl?" I asked them.

They exchanged a glance, then looked back at me.

If I didn't like the deal, I should have rejected the girls. It would have shamed them, but their fathers didn't offer me the right price, and no one could doubt it.

I had no doubt that, if I wanted to just keep them and send back the pregnant mares, then there would be no questions asked, no raiding party from Andoron come to challenge The Conqueror in his home, no matter what Kills might have thought. Daughters weren't that much of a prize to the Andarons.

This could have been settled more amicably, but that isn't what I needed to do.

***

I appeared at dinner, the four Oligarchs waiting with Tartan Stowe outside of the dining hall doors for me. I'd kept them waiting longer than they probably liked, but then I'm the King.

"Is all well, your Majesty?" Oligarch one asked me. Even Tartan looked concerned.

"Nah," I said. "It's pretty well screwed up now, but not a lot we can do about it."

"You're – you're serious?" Tartan stammered.

I looked Tartan in the eyes. "Did your father ever take you campaigning with him?" I asked him.

"Um – well," Tartan searched my eyes, looked down, then tried to find them again and looked down again.

I felt like real crap and I wasn't hiding it. The Oligarch I'd assigned to him – I'd already forgotten his name – came to his rescue.

"Glennen thought to," the old man said, "but Alekanna wouldn't have it. He's been trained to spar but he's never actually fought for his life."

I nodded. "I'm campaigning soon," I informed him. "You're coming with me."

"Of course, your Majesty," he said, and lowered his head.

"Find Shela in the morning and pick out a good warhorse with her," I said.

He nodded but didn't respond.

I sighed. Normally one of the Oligarchs would open the door, but I popped it open on my own and walked through, the rest of the entourage trailing after me.

The court barons were few in attendance. We had visiting dignitaries and of course the daughters. The Andarons were present – Kills and Two Spears and Shela sitting with them, looking away from me, Lee in a high chair beside her. Neveratta sat where Shela normally would be and Shellene next to her, beside Ceberro and her sister. I moved to my normal seat and Tartan took the Heir's position, although I hadn't declared him.

Let the world wonder.

I took my seat and the rest took theirs. I raised a bowl for mead so that the rest could start drinking.

Even the thought of the alcohol turned my stomach. I wanted Shela next to me, and I wanted the rest of them to be gone, but that wasn't going to happen. Glennen had worn the mantle and the weight had killed him, and I was seeing the tip of that giant iceberg right now.

I drank. Dignitaries around the table raised their bowls for mead. Servants scurried to serve them. Kvitch caught my eye down the table, his long grey eyebrows and flat nose peaking over the table edge. He didn't need a booster seat like Karel did, but he couldn't reach everything, either. There was a Toorian sitting next to him who was helping him out.

To my right, close to the corner, the Confluni contingent left their bowls on the table. The delicate Princess sat closest to me – it occurred to me that I hadn't learned her name. That wasn't good.

"Is the drink not to your liking?" I asked the Princess.

She lowered her eyes and smiled bashfully. The rest of the Confluni exchanged glances but didn't say anything. The other daughters straightened and watched.

"I do not drink, your Majesty," she informed me, throwing me a shy glance and then returning her gaze back to her plate. "It is unbecoming a lady."

I smiled. Not the ones I knew, but that was an interesting outlook.

"Then what can I have brought to you, gracious daughter, which is to your liking?" I asked her.

Glances were flying around the table now. This was screwing up everyone's logistics. The Volkhydran was sitting right next to me, after all, and the Confluni and the Volkhydrans *really* hated each other.

She smiled again. "Your fare is mostly red meat," she informed me. "I would enjoy something from Tren Bay, an' it please thee, your Majesty."

I nodded and made eye contact with O'spiree, who stood in a corner of the room next to the bay windows. He nodded and was out the door. As a port, Eldador's capitol didn't want for sea food.

"Your Majesty is an attentive host," Shellene noted. I smiled to her and raised my bowl. The Confluni entourage was picking at the beef and cooked vegetables.

Around the table, Uman and Men were stuffing themselves. The Uman-Chi at the far end of the table seemed to be immersed in their own conversations and ignoring the rest of us.

Not a huge surprise there.

Free Legion members were interspersed throughout the group. Thorn sat with the Andarons, Dilvesh oddly enough with the Confluni. Nantar sat among the Volkhydrans and had clearly already started them drinking – it didn't bug me much. They were still pretty banged up from this afternoon and one of Henekh's guardsmen was missing. The rest wore bandages and winced when they reached.

Karel of Stone had a seat among the Toorians like Kvitch. They hadn't plied me with a daughter. In fact, I still hadn't spoken to a Toorian, and that bugged me, too.

Kvitch had warned me that not just the Toorians, but the Dorkans were conspicuously disinterested in any sort of alliance with me, and were only here to make their presence known, not in support of me. I'd only been a King for a couple of days, but I'd royally pissed them off before this.

This was all really getting under my skin and that wasn't good. On a battlefield I could release the energy that was building up with the frustration. One might think that the sex I'd just had would alleviate some of this but in fact it made the situation worse, as I found myself barely able to look at Shela.

"Your Majesty seems contemplative," Neveratta said, arching a dark eyebrow at me. I had to smile.

"My apologies, my Lady," I told her. "It is not the company, I assure you."

"I noted that the Andaron women from the Drifters and the Wet Bellies tribes are not in attendance," she commented.

"They've served their purpose," I answered.

That got a few stares as well, but I wanted it to. This needed to happen in a way that earned a lot of attention.

She lowered her head and shot a glance at the Confluni Princess, who in turn looked sideways at Shellene. Forty percent of the competition had just been kicked off of the playing field, and they still had another day for games.

I wondered if I got to call in sick.

Dinner progressed as dinner would. There were comments on the competitors, and a few speculated that it would have been nice to honor the champion of the games today with a place at the table. Unless we were going to have a kiddy table or boot some of these people out, I don't see how that would have happened. I grinned to myself when I thought about kicking one of these lot out and replacing him or her with a sweaty athlete.

"Would you share your mirth, your Majesty?" Shellene asked me. She'd come in a really gorgeous, light blue dress cut down almost to her navel, ruffled at the shoulders and her hair done up with white and yellow spring flowers in order to accentuate her neck. If Tartan had looked any harder down her front, I think he might have lost a retina.

"I'm thinking that I'm wasting an opportunity," I informed her, loud enough for the rest of the room to hear. "In fact, I'm wasting an opportunity to get the information I need, from some of the most learned people in Fovea, in an effort to stop wasting *another* opportunity, and in that I am twice the fool.

That got even Shela's attention. She'd spent the meal speaking with her countrymen in Andaron and tending Lee.

"We are ever here to advise you, your Majesty," Avek Noir informed me from the far end of the table, his silver-on-silver eyes most likely directed at me. His other Uman-Chi brethren, Ancenon and D'gattis and a young woman I didn't know, all in white robes, seemed to point their silver eyes at me, too. Around the table a hush fell – it wasn't every day that The Conqueror went looking for outside opinions.

Much less the opportunity to advise the King of the up-and-coming Eldadorian nation.

"I learned this day," I said, "of people who are called, 'barely gifted,' who have some of magic's talents, but who aren't worth training."

D'gattis treated me to a little condescending smile. "Perhaps the term 'not worth training' is miss-used, your Majesty," he said. "Those with very slight talent are usually trained, but in doing so they are taught not to use their talents at all."

"This is true, White Wolf," Shela said, and her father next to her nodded. "The barely gifted are a threat to themselves and to the people around them. Most lack the power to control the spells, but not the power to invoke great magic."

"Think of a warrior," Henekh Dragorson said to me, his rusty red beard already awash with beer foam and food crumbs, his ribs wrapped in a clean white cloth under his skins, "who wields an axe too large for him. He can swing it, but not control it. Eventually he's as likely to hit a comrade."

"That is a very good analogy," Ancenon complemented the war lord.

Henekh smiled and nodded.

"And then there's the black mind," an Uman from Sental said. They'd come in a congregation, men and women dressed alike, deferring to each other. Sental existed as a collective, a union of workers who owned everything.

They formed the backbone of the Free Legion's army.

Another Uman, a woman sitting next to the one who spoke first, said, "I myself am barely gifted. I was taught as soon as my power showed itself to suppress it. It's like an echo of an empty space inside of me."

"How much have you experimented with it?" I asked her, leaning forward.

Neveratta touched my upper arm. "They cannot experiment, your Majesty," she said. "That is the danger – that is the point. Even a little is too much."

I focused my eyes on the Uman woman. Hers were brown, her hair green, dressed in a plain tan dress, a silver necklace on her slender neck. She looked politely away and then back at me; then away again and back at me, this time clearly alarmed that I hadn't also looked away.

I didn't have to be some great prosecutor to know she was lying.

"Once in a while…" she said.

The room gasped collectively.

"Lendeen, you know full well –", said the Uman sitting beside her.

Shela straightened. "The call is irresistible," she said, and then she looked at me.

"But you'd guessed this, hadn't you?"

I nodded. No one knew me like Shela, and probably no one ever would.

"This is punishable –" her companion was saying, but I raised my hand and he actually winced back, as if afraid I would strike him.

"I think that we are wasting the gifts of the barely gifted," I said. "I think we shouldn't be teaching the people who are barely gifted to be happy with smaller magix, leaving more complicated works to more capable wizards and sorceresses."

Ancenon and D'gattis both leaned forward. "How do you mean?" the latter asked.

"Truth saying, for example, seems to be something that wizards and sorceresses can do without much effort," I said.

The gifted looked around the table at each other. A fat Dorkan in a purple robe with gold hoops in his ears said, "I think that truth saying is barely magic at all. It is just a little tickle of power – more the experience of the Wizard, than anything else."

"And you think that this should be taught to the barely gifted?" Henekh asked me.

I nodded. Kills with a Glance shook his head.

"You say this, White Wolf, because you do not know these things," he told me. "The call of the magic is too great. You don't teach children to ride wild horses, you teach them to ride tame."

"But you *do* teach them to ride," I argued.

I looked back at Lendeen. "I think that there are thousands of barely gifted who practice in secret, and who learn to control their power and do simple spells."

"If you want to fund some sort of experimentation," one of the Oligarchs informed me, "that is certainly within your power. May I only ask that we do it in a place not close to anything – um – "

"Anything you don't want to lose," Henekh finished for him. "Volkhydrans don't play with this power at all, Lupus. You'd be wise not to either. The gods grant magic to control the rest of us – but for a few big snakes you can see, a lot of little ones can be hiding anywhere."

That was an interesting hypothesis and jibed with a lot of other things I'd seen since I'd come here. We spoke through dinner without coming to any real conclusions, but I resolved that, before I left on the campaign I'd promised Tartan, I was going to set up a school for the barely gifted.

Nowhere near the palace, of course.

Chapter Eighteen

The Party's Over

I returned to my rooms a little drunk and a little flustered. I admit it – I don't like it when people disagree with me, especially when I know I'm right. None of them were going to set up the kind of schools I planned to set up, and even my own people were going to resist it.

This wasn't something that I could do on my own, even if I had the time, which I didn't. I pushed the door open to my rooms, grateful to see that Shela's countrywomen had vacated them, and pulled my shirt over my head. I sat down on the divan and pulled my boots off, and then leaned back and wondered if I wanted one more drink before I crashed.

I hadn't slept alone in a long time and I wasn't looking forward to it.

I about jumped out of my skin when Nina trotted out of the bath room. She was wearing something like a sun dress that girls around the palace usually wore when it was warm. It was a light, white cotton with a black belt and straps. Nina still had a child's body and the outfit suited her.

"Where's Shela and Lee?" she asked me.

She crossed the room and jumped up on the divan next to me. By jump I mean three steps, a leap, a twist in mid-air and then landing on her behind six inches from me to my right. I was impressed but didn't say anything because to an Aschire, that was as normal as breathing.

"They're staying with the Andarons in a pavilion outside of the stables," I informed her.

She nodded. "Those ladies left," she informed me.

"They did, huh?"

Nina nodded. "They were crying and complaining to each other in Andaron. I don't know what they said but the Wolf Soldiers took them from the parlor and they both had a bunch of bloody linens with them."

My life is hell.

"Um, so, do you understand, I mean – do you know...?" I sputtered out.

Nina sighed. "I figured you did babies with them," she informed me.

As honest an assessment as I would have been capable of, anyway.

"What do you think of that?" I asked her.

Her people considered Nina a woman now. More importantly, adults tended to tell children what to think rather than get their opinions, and I think that made for a disservice for both parties.

Of course, I had no friggin' idea *what* to tell Nina to think, and that helped.

She screwed up her face and looked up at the ceiling for a moment. "I think you're going to make Shela mad with that," she said, finally. "Krell taught me how some Men have more than one wife, and that's fine, but Aschire only have one, and I think that's better."

I smiled. "I think that's better, too," I told her. "I think from now on it's just Shela and me."

"And me," she informed me, laying her little purple head on my forearm. My heart skipped a beat.

"I'm going to watch all the babies," she concluded.

Oh, thank you, whichever god straightened that out.

"I need to go to sleep," I informed her. "Have you picked out rooms in the wing you were looking at this week?"

She took my forearm in both hands without looking up at me. "Yes, but they aren't ready."

Nina did *not* like to sleep alone. "Do you want to bring in a pillow and a blanket and sleep on the divan?" I asked her.

She nodded, still not looking up at me.

"Ok," I informed her, and she was up off of the divan before I could change my mind. I shucked off my pants and jumped into the big, lonely bed before she could get back. When she returned, she made herself a nest on the divan, piling up the blanket and then curling up on it, the pillow against the edge of the divan. A maid would come in later and put out the lights.

"Good night, Lupus of the Free Legion," she said to me.

"Good night, Nina of the Aschire," I said back.

That was the last thing I remembered of that troubling day.

Shela woke me in the morning by throwing open the curtains to the unshuttered windows facing the bay, hitting me square in the face with bright sunlight.

"I see I've been replaced," she informed me, hands on her hips.

She wore one of her green palace dresses. The palace staff usually wore light blue or grey, as they transitioned from Glennen's colors to mine, so green was a safe color for any of the nobility. It was a tremendous mark of shame to dress like the staff when you weren't one of them.

I pushed myself up in the bed on one hand, rubbing my face with the other. I immediately sought out Nina on the divan – if Lee was going to pick a fight, she wasn't going to be in the middle of it.

She was gone.

I felt my eyebrows furrow and the scar under my eye twitch. Shela pointed to the other side of the bed, where Nina had decided she'd be more comfortable in the middle of the night. She'd made the same nest and bordered it with pillows, leaving me the one I slept on.

Shela was smiling. "I think she is too young for you," she informed me.

"I think she needs her own room," I answered. Her purple hair framed her face in that look of peace that only a child can adopt, and then only when sleeping.

"When she didn't seek me out last night I knew that she must be with you," Shela said, crossing the room and sitting on the edge of the bed, laying a hand on my lap through the covers. "Aschire don't like Andarons and I think so many of them were too much for one girl to approach."

That made sense to me.

"I didn't see Sings Softly or Little Bird," Shela commented, not looking at me.

"They're under Wolf Soldier guard," I informed her. Nina stirred in her nest, the talking rousing her. "We're going to return them personally."

"Shall I take care of breeding the mares?" Shela continued. She'd reconciled herself to what had happened. There wasn't a lot she could do about it, after all. She had a station in life as she saw it, and we'd had a beautiful dream for her, and I could tell without asking that she thought a part of it was over.

Andarons behaved this way.

"We aren't going to breed their mares," I said. "I didn't like the terms from the Drifters and the Wet Bellies."

Shela's dark eyes rose and sought mine out. She scanned my face and did that thing she did when she sniffed around in my thoughts. No one else that I knew of could do that with me, but then, no one else was Shela.

"White Wolf," she said, her expression as close to dread as I had ever seen it, "the Wet Bellies and the Drifters are *powerful* tribes..."

"So are Long Manes," I argued, "and when your father wanted Blizzard's stud service, he offered me a sorceress, and I kept her."

I took my slave girl's, my *wife's*, hand in mine, and I brought it to my lips, where my stubble could rub the back of it.

"And I told her that is the tradition of my people only to have one," I finished.

A tear rolled down her cheek, and she threw her arms around my neck, and crushed her lips to mine. Her tongue invaded me, her tears passing her lips, feeding me her passion.

"But *I* get to raise all of the babies," Nina informed us from her nest. "Lupus *promised*."

My best morning in a long time.

***

Breakfast that morning was pretty much the same people as had been at dinner the night before. Jing-Wei, the Confluni princess, whose name also meant 'Little Bird,' oddly, sat next to me, Tartan on the other side. The Andarons had already left and Shela sat next to Tartan with Lee, displacing one of the Oligarchs by one seat.

The vacancy had let Tom Kelgan, the Bounty Hunter, slink back in with a few of the court barons. As voraciously as the latter attacked the breakfast plates, I had to assume that if I didn't feed them, they didn't eat.

Another thing to fix around here.

"Did you sleep well, my Lady?" I asked the Confluni Princess.

She smiled bashfully. "Very," she informed me. "Your beds are wonderful and your staff well trained. We are well accommodated here."

"The Princess wonders," one of her entourage, an older warrior with a bald head and long, Fu-Manchu moustache, piped up, "if she might be returning, she enjoys your palace so much."

"Of course," I said, and cut into a thick ham-steak in front of me. "Or perhaps she might invite me to her own palace, and show me the greatness of Confluni architecture."

Glances passed among the Confluni and interest perked around the table. Everyone knew about the paranoia with which the Confluni guarded their borders. Everyone also knew that etiquette was important to them, too. How could they be so ungracious not to return this invitation, having just begged for one of their own?

"Of course," the old warrior said, "it is the Emperor, not his daughter, who must extend such an invitation."

Three younger men, all sitting to his left, nodded vigorously. The Princess looked down into her lap again and was clearly mortified. Her advisor had pretty much knee-capped her in front of a good deal of the important people in her world.

"Perhaps a trip to Toor would be more to your liking," one of the Toorian delegates informed me. They sat farther down the table, and usually just kept their own council. Karel and Kvitch were still among them.

This was Kvitch's doing. He'd warned me yesterday that, while the Dorkans would be perfectly happy to hate me and to plot against me, with the Bounty Hunter's guild or alone, the Toorians were likely to actually *do* something about their feelings, especially if they thought that his was a moment of weakness for the Eldadorian people.

Angador, the southern part of Eldador, had no one but Ceberro looking out for it, especially since he'd booted the Free Legion out, and Ceberro had stretched himself pretty thin.

"I believe that would be excellent," I informed him. "I don't think the Eldadorian nation has ever officially visited Toor, and I would be honored to go."

The tensions around the breakfast table were palpable now. No one had particularly good relations with the Toorians. Like the Aschire and the Scitai, they lived wild and they didn't build cities. Kvitch had informed me that strong tribes spoke for them as a nation, and it was common to see new faces among the delegates to the Fovean High Council as tribes fell in and out of favor.

One way for the tribes to stop killing each other was for them to unite and to start killing *me*, and I really didn't want that happening.

"We will extend a personal invitation for the *Bara Hindi*, my people," the Toorian said. He wore white robes thicker than the Uman-Chi, folded over down the sleeves and open at the chest. His hair was cut short but revealed some gray – he'd been a powerful warrior once by the muscle and the scars on him, but his day had past.

"I am embarrassed to admit," I informed him, "that not only do you I not know who is the leader of the Bara Hindi, I don't even know your name."

He smiled wide, and the other four men with him. "I am called Akasema Duu," he said. "My warlord is Eusi Mfupa. We appreciate that we are welcomed here – when we return, we will be certain to introduce ourselves."

Glances flew around the table. I might be new here, but I knew when I'd been slammed, and that was pretty blatant. The Oligarchs were all frowning and trying to catch my eye – they clearly wanted to handle this.

I turned to the one I usually referred to as 'One,' and said, "My Lord, if you would make the appropriate arrangements with Ambassador Duu for us to visit Toor?"

"Of course, your Majesty," he responded. "At your convenience, Akasema Duu."

The Toorian nodded.

Breakfast went on to accomplish what is accomplished at breakfast.

***

Two Spears and I walked the docks at the port of Eldador, where ships swayed pier side and workers from every Fovean nation scurried between the ships, the warehouses and the common market. Karel of Stone had met us here uninvited and, for his diminutive size, had no trouble keeping up as we hurried to the far end, east of the city, where a tall wall obscured one ship.

"How many keels are being set now in Thera?" I asked Two Spears.

"A dozen," he informed me. "And we have the resources for a dozen more. The Talen shipyards have another dozen already done, but they aren't *special*."

By special, he meant enchanted. I'd acquired a total of six Dorkan wizards, three Andaron shamen and could get Avek to show up if I needed him. Eldador had its own Wizards as well.

Wood working innovations that I'd introduced, such as the plane, had dramatically increased the speed and the quality of the ships these people could build. Iron fittings that I had thought of as commonplace were new here, and our smiths were turning out not just the fittings but the molds to mass-produce them. Dwarves had been contracted to teach our smiths, in return for learning the secrets that I shared here.

"That *thing* you wanted, that belches our steaming sea water, is almost done, as well," Karel informed me. "I don't know why you want it – you can't make anything from steam."

I laughed. No, you can't make much from steam, but with a steam plant, you can move a turbine. And with a turbine, you can turn pumps and saws and all sorts of useful things.

Ancenon had asked me once if I could remove the salt from sea water. Well, yes, I could do that, and I would, and then I could do a lot with it.

We approached the wall. Wolf Soldier guards protected the one entrance past it. No one was allowed near here, no one could see what I was creating. The wharves in Thera and Talen were impossible to protect, but the ships were going to be finalized here.

The Wolf Soldiers on duty were a pair I called 'the book ends.' Agtar and Belmar, two black-haired, heavily muscled Volkhydrans whom I'd saved from hanging in Ulep. They were both brilliant Men, competent warriors and knew it.

"What news?" I asked them as we approached.

Each made a fist over his heart in salute to me. "All quiet, Lupus," Agtar informed me. Like Belmar, his eyebrows met above his nose, forming a dark 'V'. "The masts are up and the Dorkans are chanting."

"Well, that's news then, isn't it?" Karel challenged him.

Belmar regarded the little spy. "No *other* news to report," he said.

Two Spears laughed. He pointed an accusatory finger at Karel, "One day, one of these warriors is going to skin you for that hide you wear," he said.

"What is it your King says?" Karel asked. "Many have threatened, but here I am, and where are they?"

"Many have threatened me," Agtar said, standing to one side to let us pass. A steel gate stood behind him, a single hole in the giant wall, and Belmar unlocked it with a key he wore around his neck, "and they're all dead, and I'm not."

"That was it," Karel said. He turned his face up toward me, his blue eyes sparkling. "My version is better."

"So you say," I informed him, leading the rest through the opened gate. Agtar closed it behind us and Belmar locked it.

"I could get past that security," Karel informed me.

"You're getting to see it anyway," I said.

He nodded. "I have some work to do here, though," he said. "When is Shela done with the young Earl?"

There had been a ceremony after breakfast, and we'd elevated Tartan and given him the captured lands from Angador. There had been a bunch of peace proclamations, and now all of the dignitaries were going home.

"They're picking out a horse," I said. "It shouldn't take long. She's got Yeral, Yerel's daughter, with her. Yeral knows horses almost as well as Shela."

Yerel was a Duke I'd displaced while still the Heir. I'd promised to foster his daughters and his son. Yeral had become one of Shela's attendant ladies.

"Shouldn't take all morning," I decided.

"I'll get him to help me with some resources I'll need," Karel said. "Him and that Hectaro boy, the Duke of Eldador's son."

I nodded. Karel knew more about that sort of thing than I did.

I knew more about this.

We entered the fitting yard, the final stop for ships completed for the new Eldadorian navy. I was introducing a whole new technology here, and I didn't want people knowing too much about it until we were ready.

Uman-Chi Tech-Ships were enchanted. They could sail against the wind, they could fire some kind of electrical charge, and they could do a couple other things I wasn't sure of. The only way to know for certain would be to take them on in combat, and no one did that.

Their ships were single-masted, because that's how they made ships here. They were *clinker-built*, meaning that they used overlapping boards, riveted together and tarred at the joints, for their hulls. While they could be rowed, they usually weren't unless they were ramming.

My ships were three-masted and nearly twice the size. They wouldn't be able to ram, but their sides were flat-planked and pressed with sheets of copper. This would give them the maneuverability that the clinker-built ships enjoyed without the leaking. They could put more sail to the wind so they could be larger and move faster.

With steam-powered saw mills and compressed-air nail guns which I had been working on, we could turn them out at close to five times the speed of any other nations. We could carry more warriors, out-sail our enemies and out-fight them.

Unless someone caught on to what we were doing and either stopped us or did it first. That's why we used the tight security. These ships came into port from the shipyards on a single mast and the local style of jib, clunky and lurching, slow and difficult to handle. They'd leave more agile.

This was one of the prototypes. We'd have to figure out the positioning of the sails, the proper way to support the masts, the right size for the rudders. I knew a lot about this because I'd worked at a marina and I'd studied it a little in learning history, but that hadn't made me an architect, and the Eldadorians whom I'd put to work on these when I'd become the Heir had balked at a lot of it. Even now, some of them weren't sure I could pull this off.

We'd see.

"You want me to create this in Thera?" Two Spears asked me.

I nodded. "And we need a place to keep them when we're done," I said. "I was hoping maybe the Scitai-occupied portion of the Silent Isle."

Karel turned his face up to me and frowned. "Not a good idea," he said. "We don't have shipyards, we couldn't hide them. If you moor them off of our coasts the Uman-Chi are going to see them, and they're going to get curious."

"You don't want the Trenboni with their resources to get their hands on one of these," Two Spears informed me.

I'd been afraid of that. "I can't close off more of this port," I said. "I could close off more of Thera, because I actually own it, but then Thera's going to take a hard hit in the purse."

The two of them looked at me like I was crazy. Slang again. "It would cost a lot of money to lose those wharves," I said.

Both nodded.

"I need a place to put these things, where I can test them and keep the region quiet about them. I need to be able to get there fast."

"How deep drafted are these?" Two Spears asked me. Local ships ran shallow – some of them as little as ten feet.

"We're guessing twenty-one feet forward, twenty-three feet aft," I said. "We haven't had one with a full crew, but that seems right. Estimate twenty-five feet to be sure."

"So deep!" Karel exclaimed. We'd walked to the ship's side, where Uman carpenters and ship-builders were working under the direction of Dorkan Wizards in Wolf Soldier greys. The Wizards would weave spells into the wood fiber, and the artisans would finish and seal the wood.

My ships could launch fire – more effective at sea against other wooden ships. They would be able to protect themselves from spell-casting and soak in the magical energy used against them and use it. Like the spell that had shielded me from arrows at the gates of Katarran, my ships could throw up invisible shields against arrow fire.

Their steel-shod keels could shock the water around them – that should be an interesting surprise for whoever tried to swim onboard them.

Two Spears was smiling. "If they're fast, and you're brave, then I think I know where they can go," he said. "And the best part is, you're going there anyway."

I looked sideways at Two Spears. He was smiling through his long mustachios. The scar on his face, the Mark of the Conqueror, was wrinkled in a smile.

Wow, I thought. It must be really irritating when I'm cryptic like that.

Chapter Nineteen

Son of War

My daughter had been born in Life. It was a month when battles ended and harvest begun. People thought of wheat and grain, not swords and blood.

So when two thousand Wolf Soldier lancers and three thousand foot landed in Andoron between Chatoos and Talen, it didn't raise a lot of eyebrows. People were busy with their lives – if Lupus the Conqueror came for the Andarons, he would have sought out their cities.

On this campaign I brought my slave, my child, my blood brother and young Tartan. If he wanted to be an earl of a frontier province like Angador, then let him see something of power and how to wield it.

We'd been ported here in three prototype ships, the one from Eldador's secret wharf and two others that had been rushed to readiness. I'd surrounded them with dozens of my own ships. We'd passed Eldadorian Tech-Ships but they hadn't tried to interfere with us.

Shela had been quiet for days now; the two Andaron women as well. Usually three Andarons would talk each other's ears off exchanging gossip in the oral tradition, telling and retelling the same stories, making them a part of the tribal memory.

Not this time. All of the women sat sidesaddle, an indication that they were expectant with child.

With Shela, I knew it to be fact. With the other two, more like wishful thinking. Little Bird and Sings Softly weren't real happy with me and had made no secret of it. Blizzard had snubbed their mares, and I hadn't been too kind about it, either. They'd also continued to offer themselves to me until Shela had warned them off, and that was just a slap in the face.

When you get right down to it, I'm not a real nice guy.

One of the girls came from the Wet Belly tribe, the other a Drifter. Both kept to the south of Andoron. That made it perfect – I wanted to check out an anomaly on the Fovean map and it could be found down there. We forced-marched for sixteen days, the weather becoming ever colder, seeking out these two tribes in the south.

My outriders located them – Wolf Soldiers who had once been Wet Bellies, cast-out from the tribe, thieves in a land where honor meant everything.

When news got around that I pressed south with that many warriors, tribes sent scouts to pick out our path and to get away from it. We ignored them. The Drifters and the Wet Bellies, once it became clear that I was bound for them, brought their resources together, their women miles south of the men, their herds to the west. They waited for us as the month of Life ended, a line across a sea of wheat, the cold wind blowing tufts of grain like a rolling sea before us.

"There must be over a thousand between them," Two Spears informed me. His sister rode next to him, quiet. "I had no idea these tribes were so huge."

"Supposedly they fight Slee all year round," I said. "Small tribes would have had to move."

Slee looked like a cross between a Man and a lizard. They can't talk but they do fight in groups, and they are vicious. They eat, among other things, the flesh of Men and Uman.

"They look ready," another of my majors, Dev Nevala, informed me. An Uman woman, she had been Sentalan, and stabbed her lover for cheating on her. She was faster with her sword than I was with mine – I really liked her.

"Let them be," I said. "Two Spears, order your men to pull bows and arrows. I want them in groups of twenty, to circle the enemy to the right and left. Spread out like they are it will take us all day to fight them, and then we'll be exhausted and they'll be fresh. If we can drive them together, we'll hold them against the foot, and then we can bring our lances to bear on them."

"Why not just charge them one-to-one," Tartan asked me. Shela had picked him out a spirited chestnut mare with a thick barrel, muscles on muscles in her hind quarters. He sat her next to Two Spears, on the other side from me. "We have lances, they have swords – they'll never touch us."

"They have bows, and they're deadly with them," I informed him. "Go one-to-one with them over a distance like this and we'll lose most of the horse and have to try to take them with the foot – in fact, we'll *never* catch them, and then we'll leave here with nothing."

"So, we break up…" Tartan tried to work it out.

"We make so many, smaller targets that their line becomes a liability," Two Spears informed him. "They'll break up on their own, and we'll draw them into the center where we can engage them."

Tartan nodded. That might happen if we fought, of course. There were no guarantees. Not in this business.

I kicked Blizzard's barrel and he started to trot forward. Shela followed with the two Andaron women, Tartan and twenty lancers. Two Spears and Dev held the troops as they unpacked their arrows. Our supply train, half empty now, trundled far to the rear, a token guard on it.

Twenty came out from their side, as well. They were bare-chested, their dark hair free on the wind. They bore scimitars unsheathed on their saddles and bows over their shoulders.

Two separated – they would be the chieftains of the Drifters and the Wet Bellies. The other men would ride behind them.

Both sides stopped when about twenty feet separated us. I sat Blizzard, looking the two Andarons over, waiting for them to talk. If it took all day, I didn't care.

There is an art to this.

"You bring back our daughters," one said. From what I knew of Andarons, he would be the Wet Belly. His long mustachios were shot with grey, his hair beaded at the ends as only they did.

"I'm done with them," I said.

That got an eyebrow up. "And the service of your stallion?"

I laughed. "For a night with your daughters? Not likely."

That pissed him off – good to see that it wasn't just a family trait of Kills'.

"You took the daughters and you didn't seed the mares?" the other, a Drifter, demanded. He was smaller, younger, his mustachios barely to his chin, his hair black as night and his nose like an eagle's beak.

"The daughters served to assuage me for the insult," I said. "Kills with a Glance of the Long Manes *gave* me his daughter."

"We are a much larger tribe than the Long Manes," the Wet Belly said.

"Maybe not after today," I said.

That got a nervous look at my army. Those were Wolf Soldiers. Normally there would be Aschire archers – one could only assume they lay hidden somewhere. The Aschire were invisible, and the Wolf Soldiers invincible.

They probably didn't kid themselves into thinking that they could beat me. They had fought Confluni, they were no stranger to running now to fight another day. They might not like it, but it sure beat being dead.

So the trick was to get them pissed off enough to do something stupid.

"If you want the daughters, you can have them," the Drifter informed me. That got a look from the Wet Belly. Two women, however, were a small price to pay, and I had been infamously decent to Shela.

"I don't want them," I said. "They're defiled."

That made for an insult.

The Drifter and half of their men had their scimitars out. "You city scum," he spat at me.

I really wanted the Wet Belly, but I would settle for the Drifter.

"You have the nerve to fight me?"

"I will bury you here," he informed me.

I kicked Blizzard in the ribs. He leapt forward. The Drifter reacted no slower, probably more experienced at fighting in the saddle, definitely less encumbered and a better equestrian than I.

He came at me from the left, thinking that it would make my lance useless. Its end whipped before him and peeled him from the saddle before he came within scimitar range. He *did* manage to hit the lance with his weapon – I had never seen anyone fast enough to do that before.

I rode over him with Blizzard, turned and leveled the lance at his body. I might as well not have bothered – he lay dead, his head crushed in by an iron-shod hoof..

One of the girls wailed. The other put a hand on her shoulder.

Half of the Andarons started forward, thinking combat must be on, and hesitated when the rest of the entourage did nothing.

"I'll claim half of his horse, and half of his cattle," I informed the rest of them.

The Wet Belly laughed. "If you can find them."

"You think you're leaving this field before I know where they are?"

I could see the look on his face – he would bolt and take his chances. He couldn't count on the Drifters now. They would likely take off and choose a new chief. A good portion of the men would split the tribe and head for his – I just made him a lot stronger and he knew it. He probably counted on taking those horse and cattle himself.

"You run and it will be a slaughter," I told him. "Those are Wolf Soldiers – you know what they do. We'll be raping your daughters before the sun sets."

That got me a look from Tartan. I'm sure that's not what he thought he came here to do.

"And if we give you the Drifters?" he asked me.

Andarons did that, too. If I raided and took their horse and their cattle, the Drifters would fight. What I offered him was a chance not to have to join in on it. He could peel off his horse, his women and his livestock and be gone.

That's what I offered him. He opened his mouth to betray his allies.

The scimitar that took him through the spine leapt out of his chest like vengeance. He spread his arms, and his horse bolted, smelling blood.

I charged the man, now weaponless, who had done it. It had been worth a try, anyway. At least there would be chaos as they figured out who lead them.

In a fight, I usually didn't worry that much about myself anymore. That first time, in the Great Northern Mountain Range, and then in Myr, I had been afraid that I might die, but the more times I didn't, the easier it became not to think about it.

Tartan was a different story – this would be his first fight, and I wanted him to engage, but I wanted him to live through it, too. Andarons are pretty tough, and the warriors he met would be blooded.

He charged after me, probably the right thing to do, and skewered the man next to the man whom I did in, who had killed the Wet Bellies chief.

His lance snapped, and he fumbled for his sword when two of them charged him. He didn't even realize that they had engaged him until he pulled his sword, looked up, and there they were.

I took one from behind. The other pinked his arm before he stabbed the man in the face. His horse bolted from the blood smell, and he ended up carving the guy's head like a pumpkin, trying to free his sword. He made the mistake of watching it happen and then he was puking his guts out down the side of his mare.

That was a *huge* mistake – never barf on your horse. The warm liquid makes the horse think that it's hit and it will take off, which is what happened. So here we had a battle, and Tartan heading east with his feet out of his stirrups.

"Shela," I commanded. I couldn't leave the field. She nodded and took off after him. He wore heavy armor, she didn't – she would catch him fast enough.

The two Andaron women took off for their tribes. Half of that line turned tail and headed south, about a quarter on both sides came for me, and the rest didn't know *what* to do.

Dev's foot actually double-timed it close enough to me where I could leap within our ranks before the Andarons could get to me. Two Spears had our lancers arcing out west in squads of horse, driving in deserters with arrow-fire and rounding up attackers. Just as the mounted Andarons engaged the foot, they found themselves surrounded by my lancers and crushed against our shield wall. Pikemen and swordsmen killed Andaron and horse alike, suffering minimal injury, as our lances ripped them apart.

It probably took two hours before we marched south again with most of our numbers, a herd of Andaron horses and an embarrassed former prince with a yellow discoloration on the breastplate of his armor.

***

"So what did I do?" I asked him. We'd made night camp in our small city. We had no wood for spears around the perimeter but had lined up our pikes along the outer wall. If the Andarons charged us they would lose their first two ranks before they met us.

"You killed one chief," Tartan informed me, trying to buff his breastplate, "and got the other to get himself killed, and then they had no —"

I shook my head. He didn't get it. That might be better – let him get it into his head that he didn't know everything.

"I picked a fight with the first one to get the second to desert on him," I said. "They're tribes – they feel a bond of honor within the tribe, but not much obligation between the tribes. The Wet Belly forgot that he had the people he was about to betray sitting right behind him, however. That was my mistake, too – I should have separated them first."

"So you wanted to leave one alive?" Tartan pressed me.

I nodded. "It will be easier in the long run this way, but I was afraid I would have a worse fight than I had. I didn't expect them all to run like that."

"We caught half of them," Two Spears informed me. "The rest will be heading for the women and the cattle. I have men following them – in the morning we'll take that, too."

"So we leave these people to starve?" Tartan asked me. I caught the look on his face. The Conqueror had been called a heartless monster, after all, who ate babies.

I shook my head. "I think you can guess what happens after that," I said.

"But it didn't go as you planned," he pressed me. He leaned forward, and for a moment I saw his father in him.

Two Spears laughed and clapped him on the shoulder. "Lad," he said, "it *never* goes as planned. If you want to be a good earl or a good general, you do it when your plans fail, and you aren't rattled and win anyway."

Tartan nodded. If he could get that, then he would be ok.

We had found their herds as I expected, and their women and old men, tending them. Two Spears and Shela both assured me that they had grouped their aurochs together for security. No one in Andoron had a herd *that* big.

Seven hundred head, an equal number of horse. This meant real wealth on the Andoron plains, the makings of a rogue tribe.

As Thorn had informed me a whole lifetime ago. Now I just waited for independents to come in and offer to run my herds, and that had been happening all day.

The tribes traded women and cattle all the time. Men usually stayed with the same tribe their whole life, unless that tribe was overrun or fell on hard times. Then it wasn't uncommon for a tribe to dissolve and its members ply for membership into another tribe.

They could marry in, or they could go through the ceremonies, depending on who they were and who they joined. Wet Bellies and Drifters existed so close to each other that they could be interchangeable.

My rogue tribe called itself the Wolf Riders, and I knew everyone in it, and had been accepted by them all, because they came to me. I can honestly say that the horses didn't seem to mind me, the aurochs remained ambivalent and the two bulls could care less, so long as I stayed away from them.

As far as anyone was concerned, that made me an Andaron.

Two Spears didn't plan to join my tribe, but he gave me permission to marry his sister, and that satisfied one of the two things I had come here for.

Shela stood next to me, our baby standing between us, looking out onto the natural lake where the Great Mid River met the Safe River.

"Daddy," Lee informed me, "it's pretty."

"Yes, it is," I agreed with her. Turning to Shela, I asked, "Does it have a name?"

Shela had her cheek pressed to my chest. "No name that I know," she said. "It's too turbulent for swimming, and tradition says the fish stay away from the shore. If someone sailed down here and went east, they would have to brave the Slee and the Swamp Devils."

No one did that.

Her tears felt wet on my shirtfront. She had been weepy this pregnancy. At first I thought it might be my deflowering of the Andaron girls, but she assured me that she could care less about that. She'd accepted a physical act that needed to be done.

"Ready to be a married lady?" I asked her.

"I lived very happily as a slave," she informed me, without looking up at me. The sun was setting in the west and this view looked really, really nice.

"Ooooo," Lee informed us, pointing at the pink colors.

"You can stay a slave, if you want," I informed her. "But it is –"

Her soft fingers closed my lips. She knew – no need to tell her. Stay a slave and I would eventually have to marry someone, and that would mean nothing but trouble. She knew I loved her. She might have seen it as weakness, it might have made her warm inside, she didn't feel ready for that talk and we had our whole lives to get to it.

Lee hugged her bebe and took a tenuous step toward the water. The beach mud lay ankle deep, and what child could resist that?

"Stay away from the water," Shela warned her, absently. I had tossed a stick in there and it had floated off to the south faster than I could have run to catch it.

My new ships, my *Sea Wolves*, were out there on that natural lake, crews testing them, plying the wind. One had snapped a mast before we got here, and another had nearly flipped over when a strong wind caught it broadside and all of its canvas had pulled it sideways. The ships that had born us here had brought extra wood, and we could pillage the Confluni forest if we had to. As far as I knew, they didn't come this far south.

One of the Eldadorian captains who were part of the test had told me how impressed he was with the whole thing, and how much he wanted to go forward with it now. Based on how I'd had to drag him kicking and screaming into the program, that was good news.

We could see the ships out there, the sun setting past the edge of the lake, turning the sky pink and orange. Water lapped at the black mud at our feet, the smell of Men and horses washed over us from the camp when the wind changed and took Shela's black hair.

We'd go back to Eldador the Port when the testing completed and update how we built the ships. This sort of testing is invaluable when you're breaking new ground. I had a general idea of how wooden three-masters worked but I couldn't do the job of an architect and I didn't know enough about it to explain it effectively to someone who could.

Meanwhile, I had other things to do here.

***

I sat Blizzard on the plains to the east of a village I'd been calling 'Wisex,' on the shores of a lake with no name, with Shela to my left and Two Spears to my right, both mounted, and Tartan Stowe on a horse behind me. A dozen lancers flanked us, most of them Andarons in Wolf Soldier greys, the wind catching their long, black hair and the dour expressions on all of their faces.

A lot of the lancers were Andaron and most of them weren't too happy about this new tribe. They saw it as an outsider intruding on their ways, which were sacred to them no matter where they lived. We were facing three tribal war chiefs right now, all on horses and each with no less than a dozen warriors behind them, and none of them looked too ecstatic, either.

"What are you doing on our land?" the first among them asked me. An exceptionally fat Andaron sitting a stallion more draft than Andaron, his mustachios hung down to his chest but his head shone bald and glistening in the sun. He led the Sure Foot tribe from the center of Andoron – the largest and the oldest of all of the tribes. He'd been appropriately named, "Hungry as a Bull."

My first instinct was to tell him, "Whatever the hell I want to," but no good came from that angle. Instead, I said, "This isn't your land," which was about as neutral as I could be, considering the situation. The warriors around me stirred. There was barely a tribe on these plains that couldn't go far back and say that they were related somehow to the Sure Foot. Hungry as a Bull, literally, carried a lot of weight.

His wife was a sorceress like Shela, and Shela was clearly afraid of her.

"We think you need to go back to Eldador, Rancor Mordetur," he informed me. The other two chieftains, Angry Lion of Thorn's Hunter tribe and Black Hawk of the Bear tribe, nodded. Their warriors shifted on their horses behind them.

Not 'White Wolf,' I noted, as most Andarons referred to me. They didn't want me thinking that I belonged here.

"And what of the *Waya Agiladia*?" I asked them, using the Andaron for my Wolf Rider tribe.

"There are none," spat Angry Lion, a tall, thin Andaron in his late thirties with a bare chest and hair down past his arm pits. His mustachios weren't past his chin – he hadn't been a chieftain long.

"They can be Wet Bellies or Drifters," Black Hawk, a sturdy looking man with hair shot with grey, wearing a leather breast guard, his arms poking out muscular from its sides.

"Or they can be dead," a warrior from behind him commented.

None of the chieftains reacted to him. I wouldn't have put up with that from one of my warriors personally, but there you go.

"I've recognized this tribe," Two Spears informed them, putting his hands on his saddle's horn, leaning forward so that his long hair touched his horse's mane. "I've given him permission to marry my sister."

"You live in Eldador," Hungry informed him, his heavy-set face bland. "You don't speak for your father's tribe."

"Or you do, and they can die, too," the same warrior said from behind the chieftains.

I had my opening. "Who is this yapping dog, who speaks for you?" I demanded, pointing at the Andaron on his horse.

Two of these men had been chieftains a long time, and didn't bite like I'd hoped they would. "He's no concern of yours," Angry Lion said.

"Then tell him to shut up, so I don't have to hear him," I said.

To my surprise, Black Hawk turned and told the man, "Quiet yourself." He frowned deeply but he didn't say anything. I'd hoped I could pick a fight with him and then distract the rest from this confrontation.

That wasn't going to happen.

"These people pledged themselves to me to protect them," I told him. "I can't let you attack them."

I pointed at the one I'd singled out. "I can't let warriors like that prey on them, either."

"That isn't your concern," Angry Lion informed me. "You're not Andaron, you're not using them to call yourself Andaron, or to call your children Andaron. You're not bringing your Eldadorian nation here."

The Pequot and the Mohicans and the Cherokee probably said the same thing to English settlers at one point.

It didn't work out well for them.

"You think you can stop me?" I asked them. "Three tribes?"

"You're weak from fighting the Drifters and the Wet Bellies," Hungry informed me. "Your warriors still bleed. The tribe you call 'Wolf Riders,' they have few men left in them, just old ones and children – they can't help you."

"We can call twenty tribes," Angry added. "No one wants you here, Rancor Mordetur. We'll let you and your Wolf Soldiers leave now, but we won't let them leave tomorrow."

That wasn't much time to decide.

Chapter Twenty

The Bully On the Block

Being alone and outnumbered didn't bother me that much. I'd had plenty of time to get used to it. I also held a piece of ground that the lake bordered on three sides. Unless they learned how to fly, they weren't coming after me except dead on, and I could hold more than twice my numbers dead on.

Still, the elders in my new tribe had moved the aurochs and the horse herd to the south of us. I was actually surprised at how few of the Andarons who'd come to this tribe had bailed on me. Either they were more afraid of what was going to happen to them for joining me than of what would happen for staying with me, or I was a better leader than I gave myself credit for.

I'd sent a portion of my fleet home and just left the Sea Wolves here. The sailors weren't going to be a lot of help in the conflict but seeing the ships leave might make the Andarons think I'd turned tail and run. They'd come to investigate, and that would give me a few days to dig in better and to put my defenses up. Preparation takes time and I didn't have a lot of it.

Two Spears looked to the east and shook his head when the sun came up the next morning.

"They will ride straight in," he informed me. "A few warriors from each of the tribes. Already they have five, and twenty more are coming."

Even more tribes than Hungry as a Bull had hoped for, I thought to myself. Tartan stood next to us, saying nothing, and Shela had set up a tent with 'the people.' As the resident holy woman, she had the task of healing the sick, and we didn't want for them.

"When do you think they'll come after us?" I asked him.

Two Spears shook his head, his mustachios wagging under his chin. "Not today," he said. "Tomorrow morning I think. Early. They'll have eight tribes by then. They'll start riding by and firing arrows – make your people panic, maybe run. If your people run, they'll think you'll leave and they won't have to fight you."

"Which isn't going to happen," I informed him. "But they don't know that."

The Andaron turned to face me. "I could ride out with a few warriors, get my people, maybe a few tribes…" he offered.

I frowned. "You'd never make it over the horizon," I said. "If you did, I don't think your father would risk his people, much less get here in time."

Two Spears nodded and turned back to the east. "I think this will be a bloody fight," he said.

I had to agree with him on that. I might have bitten off more than I could chew this time.

***

Throughout history, people in the military looked at civilians as a liability and almost counter-productive to the war effort. Or they used them to hide among, to force the enemy to kill the innocent to get at their true target, in hope they wouldn't do it.

Neither way usually worked out well for the civilians. I knew that if I sent my new Wolf Riders away, the other tribes would slaughter them to get rid of me. The Wolf Riders only existed so that I had a legitimate claim on this part of Andoron, but that didn't mean I was willing to let them be cut down for no other reason.

War expected certain things of me, but I just didn't want to believe that slaughtering innocents was one of them. If it was, He was going to have to communicate that to me directly.

So rather than send the civilians away or hide among them, I put shovels in their hands and set them out onto the plains between this little village and the open stretches of Andoron. While my warriors slept and recovered their strength, women, children and old men turned the soil under the cover of darkness. I maintained a few squads of horsemen farther out on the plains to keep the curious out of eyeshot, not that I needed to. No one did anything at night in Andoron.

Tartan Stowe led them, and I rode out onto the plains an hour before dawn to check on him. I could see his surprise when I turned up on Blizzard out of the dark.

He kept a lance with a solid green pennon on it couched in his stirrup. His eyes were a little red from being up late, but that was to be expected. He'd had a long night.

"Your Majesty," he greeted me.

"Your Excellence," I returned. "Anything to report from the night guard?"

"Nothing," he said. "I'm surprised – I mean, I didn't expect, um…"

"What the hell am I doing here?" I asked him, grinning. The false dawn was cresting the horizon to the East. Behind me the Andarons were collecting their shovels and picks and returning exhausted to the village we called 'Wisex.'

Tartan looked away from me and then back into my eyes. "Yeah," he informed me.

"Better to surprise your watch," I informed him, "than to let them surprise you. You'll be a leader some day, and you'll appreciate the value of the night watch. Keeping them sharp is worth an hour's sleep."

He'd been trained by Glennen's advisors and he knew how many battles had begun with surprising the watch and getting past them. He knew why I'd done this.

Good for him, I thought. Never good to let anyone working for you get too comfortable in their position.

"Bring your troops in," I informed him. "Two Spears is going to put out some fast riders to warn us before their tribes roll in. See if you can grab some sleep."

He nodded his head. "Your Majesty," he said.

I trotted out past him. Shela had wanted to come with me, but she'd worked hard yesterday and she needed to be fresh if Hungry decided to risk bringing his wife. I also usually maintained a Wolf Soldier guard, but if I actually came across anything out here, it would be really, really useful to be able to outrun it. This was one of those times when it was better to go alone.

I'd been missing those times without realizing it.

Blizzard's hooves beat the soft earth beneath us, the light wind from the temperature change at dawn pulled at his mane. I rode without thinking of it, but aware of him at the same time. Blizzard changed my life in so many ways – more than Shela sometimes, though I'd never say that to her.

I didn't see anyone from any of the tribes, but that didn't mean that they weren't out here. I could just *feel* that I had eyes on me, in a way that made my flesh crawl.

Still, it came as a complete surprise when a tiny figure sprung up out of the long grass behind me, sprinted up behind Blizzard and, before the stallion could react, leapt up onto his butt, thin but strong arms wrapping themselves around my middle, heels seating themselves at the horse's midsection.

Blizzard reared in surprise and anger. I leaned forward and grabbed his mane in my left hand, instinctively leaving my sword arm free. A rearing horse is a very dangerous thing – the animal could flip over backwards and his saddle could break his spine. He could crush his rider or impale him on a saddle's pommel. An inexperienced rider could lean backwards and fall over and be stomped, or trip the horse, or haul back on the reins and pull the horse down on top of him.

I just swore – I think in three languages.

Blizzard settled and didn't try to buck us both off. I turned in my saddle, as much as my armor would let me, and found the mischievous grey eyes of the Aschire girl who wasn't supposed to be here – at least, not yet.

I couldn't say that she wasn't welcome.

An hour past the true dawn, the first of the Andarons trotted their horses up over the horizon to our east. One hundred fifty of them by my best count, though they mulled around and changed directions quite often, and that made it hard to be sure.

Nearly two hundred squads of Wolf Soldier infantry aligned themselves on the plains between them and the growing village called Wisex. Their formation resembled a backwards 'C', strong on the flanks and less in the middle in preparation for the sort of sweeping attacks I'd expect from light cavalry.

Within the 'C', one thousand eight hundred lancers sat their horses, pennons snapping on the ends of their weapons. Many of them were Andaron and knew exactly what to expect.

The Andarons shot an arrow into the air. It caught fire after it took flight – a signal that they wanted to speak before the fought.

And that they'd brought a Sorceress. Sitting Blizzard, I turned my head to where Shela sat on a stretched hide with two young girls who were serving her as apprentices. She'd surrounded herself with various pots and piles of things she needed for more challenging spell casting, or at least that's what I guessed she'd use them for. She didn't turn her face up to the sky, but then I had to assume she'd known before the rest of us that Hungry as a Bull had brought his wife to face her.

I sighed. Negotiating was pointless. I wasn't leaving and neither were they. Two Spears sat an Andaron stallion to my left and I said to him without turning, "Hold the line, and don't charge no matter what happens. They might be trying just to kill me to throw you off."

"You think then maybe you shouldn't go?" Tartan voiced his opinion from my other side. I smiled – about time he started acting like a teen ager.

I turned to him. "You want to go instead?" I asked him.

He straightened, turned his face to the East, and kicked his horse.

"Whoa, whoa, whoa!" I shouted after him, and gave Blizzard a kick to catch up with him. Fifty mounted Wolf Soldiers followed after us. He didn't stop so I caught him up.

"You got brave," I commented as we trotted out together.

He didn't turn to face me. "I'm tired of this," he said. "All the posturing, all the threats. They want to fight, let's just get it over with."

I smiled again. A new development in his education – his father the tactician was coming out in him, and that was a good thing. His father, though, was a 'jump in and fight them' kind of guy, and that wasn't going to necessarily win the day here.

"Let's see what they have to say first," I informed him. That got his attention. "They know I'm not going to move if I haven't already, and they haven't attacked yet. I have no problem with no more of my men dying."

Tartan shook his head. We followed what was becoming a beaten path down the center of the little peninsula we were guarding. It had grown wide enough for three horses to ride abreast, so we progressed down it double-file, my riders behind us. The enemy had arrows and they were good with them – there was no point in me hiding in the middle.

Tartan stayed quiet and we crossed the distance to the Andarons in a few more minutes, the clip-clop of our horses' steel-shod hooves on hard-packed dirt our only accompaniment.

Angry Lion and Black Hawk sat their own horses at the head of a few hundred Andarons. From the looks of things I'd gotten the number right. They formed a half-circle in front of us with the two chieftains at the center, right in front of us. My lancers formed up in a triangle behind me.

I couldn't keep out of my head the idea that there existed a lot of geometry in all of this. If I ever got back to my own Earth, I owed my old math teacher an apology.

Hungry was nowhere to be seen. Neither was his wife. I stopped my horse just within their half-circle, holding up my hand to halt the riders behind me. Both sides stood quiet, staring at the other. As I'd said before, there exists a science to this, and I wasn't going to be the first one to speak, even if the sun went down behind me.

I didn't have to wait that long. "You aren't going to leave?" Angry asked me, more of an accusation than a question. The heavier Black Hawk folded his arms in front of himself.

Beyond him, past a natural rise in the terrain, were the collected tribes they'd rallied, dozens of tribes collected together in a patchwork that stretched back over the horizon, thousands of warriors.

Now they had me thinking of Custer at Little Bighorn. Custer also went looking for a fight, as I recalled it.

The air should be filled with dust from their movement, but it wasn't. They moved in each others' tracks to minimize their signature. They were clever and disciplined.

I looked Angry in the eyes and I said, "I don't run."

"You *do* bleed," Black Hawk informed me, his face flat. "And you *will* die."

I allowed myself a little smile. "A lot of people have said that to me," I informed him. "They're all dead, and I'm not."

"Take your people, your Andarons included, and walk to Eldador," Angry ordered me. "No one will bother you. You can leave here."

I shook my head and folded my own arms over my breastplate in imitation of him. I needed this place. I could leave and come back with more warriors, but they'd do the same, and maybe then I'd have the Fovean High Council involved. They'd love an opportunity to come after me, especially away from home.

"Go back and die with your 'Wolf Riders,' Black Hawk told me. He wanted this fight. He might be the older warrior, the grey in his hair telling, but he was the one with the temper, not the younger Angry Lion.

He was my 'in.'

"I'll be looking for you, Black Hawk," I said, pointing at him. "I'll find you on the battle field, and you'll wish you'd stayed out of my way."

Black Hawk straightened and dropped his hands to his side.

"If you have the courage, then, little man," I challenged him.

Three of the warriors behind him gave a whoop but Angry Lion held up his hand. I heard my warriors shift behind me. It was too close for them to take advantage of their arrows and too far from their tribes to guarantee they'd get away against our lances. Angry Lion knew that I could stop the fight right now if I could kill these two leaders, which is likely why we didn't see Hungry anywhere.

"Go back to your people," he informed me. "We will come for you there."

I waited for Black Hawk to make a move but he wasn't going to oblige me. His warriors weren't happy. It had been worth a shot.

"On the battle field, then," I said to him. "Where you have better men to hide behind."

He started but Angry put a hand in front of him. No, this wasn't going to happen. I laughed and I turned Blizzard around, Tartan next to me. I led my warriors back down the trail to the little village we'd made, my mind racing.

To get at me, they were going to have to charge down the peninsula. They'd come in firing arrows from horseback, trying to keep us down. Then they'd engage us with their greater numbers at close quarters, where the peninsula would work against me. I needed to be able to move around against a light horse advance and I'd given that up for the inability to be surrounded.

My archers were the old men and younger children who were part of my 'tribe.' Historically speaking, they'd been the archers throughout history once warfare started trying to be 'modern.' You put a lot of arrows in the air in the direction of your enemy and let them run into them – being an expert might be more impressive but in fact it works against you in the long run. Better to put ten barely-trained archers in place than one who took you years to train and years to replace.

Say what you will – missiles take the grace out of combat, and turn it into a numbers game. I'd lose a numbers game pretty easily here.

"Ware!" a Wolf Soldier shouted to me. It wasn't J'her – I had left him to hold Eldador the Port. Dev Nevala held my left side, and Two Spears the right. I'd taken the horse – this was going to boil down to them.

All eyes turned east and we saw a dust cloud and a wall of Andarons come trotting up over the horizon. They moved like a dark wave, warriors and horses together, not whooping and building up their own courage but angry and serious, knowing what they were riding into, knowing that the ones whom we were looking at right now were likely dead men, the first wave of the attack doomed to fall to whatever I had planned for them, and they were coming anyway.

Warriors who'd rather be dead than give in to me.

"All hands," I shouted, turning my head left and right, mounted on Blizzard as I had been for most of the morning.

Wolf Soldiers mounted up or took their places on our battlements. We'd improvised a little on the 'small city,' and created an earth wall with a ditch in front of it, which was going to be hell for them to get their horses over. I'd managed to port some wood over from the Confluni side of the lake we were on, using my new ships. We had spears that they wouldn't be expecting, as well as extra arrows and bows and some other useful things.

The ground started to shake a little as they got themselves moving. Wolf Soldiers were exchanging glances as they noticed it. Blizzard and some of the other horses snorted and stamped. My stallion likely knew what he was in for – this wasn't his first rodeo.

The wave came forward and we could hear a few war whoops from the middle – Andarons who thought that maybe they wouldn't die. I could see the bows and the arrows now. Most were held down to conserve the elasticity of the wood. Some were cocked and ready, the warriors standing in their saddles, waiting for the command to fire.

"Archers!" I shouted. My own Andarons pulled back, a few hundred of them. We'd given them some basic instruction on how to do this from my veterans.

I waited for the Andarons to pass a couple flags I'd planted in the ground out past the battlements – the outer range of our bows. Likely they either didn't notice them or didn't care. I wanted the first rank to get past them, and shoot for the warriors right behind.

My breath quickened. There was no sure outcome here – this was one of those fights that I might lose.

They crossed the flags, one rank, two, three…

"Loose!" I commanded.

The air filled with the twang of the bow strings, the whistle of the arrows through the air. They arced gracefully over our heads, a few flying off the side useless, released improperly from children who barely knew one end from the other. Life was harder on the Andaron plains and kids learned to do these things earlier, but a kid is still a kid, and they knew what happened to conquered tribes.

Several arrows flew back in return, warriors firing before the order was given. Their archers essentially used the same bows as we did – they would start firing as a group as soon as they realized that these arrows landed within our midst.

Our arrows fell like rain into the front portion of their advancing army, past the first rows as I'd hoped. Theirs fell among us. I heard a few angry grunts. Other warriors scrambled for their shields on Dev and Two Spears' orders. No point in just taking their fire.

The Andarons picked up their pace and their arrows started coming sporadically. I waited. I wanted another few rows of Andarons to get past.

"Pull!" I shouted, as the arrows started to patter down on our shields. More and more of them filled the air, landing among us and then against the front of our battlements, fired too early.

"Loose!" I shouted, and our arrows flew out again, fewer mistakes this time.

I'd had workers out digging in those plains. What I'd arranged for them was going to start happening soon.

Arrows were hitting the ground about 100 feet in front of our own archers. I was going to get another shot in before I pulled them back. I had lined the horse up behind them.

"Pull!" I shouted. There was clear fear and dissention in the archer ranks. They were starting to think I was going to let them take fire, and they would break. They weren't warriors, they were civilians who'd come to me because they had nowhere else to go.

The Andarons were picking up their pace now. Their arrows were raining down on the warriors in the battlements. I was starting to lose troops.

"Loose!" I commanded. The arrows flew out again – some of them off to the side. Their fear was getting to them.

"Archers, retreat!" I ordered. They dropped their bows, turned and ran. I heard swearing from among the lancers. Who knew what they could be thinking- they'd just lost whatever means they had to defend themselves if the Wolf Soldiers failed.

The Andaron riders were moving in at a gallop now, pummeling us with arrows. They'd reach the horse soon if something didn't stop them.

That's when they hit the first trench in the ground outside of the ramparts.

For three nights in a row, we'd trucked out our civilians to dig long, shallow trenches, and then fill them back with sod in order that they look like nothing more than an anomaly in the plains. When the Andaron front lines hit the unnatural dip in the ground, their horses stumbled both on the loose sod and the unexpected drop, becoming worse when the horses' weight pushed the loose soil even farther down.

It wasn't a deep ditch – they'd have noticed that. It was just enough to surprise a running horse and a rider standing in his stirrups, firing arrows.

Hundreds stumbled, and the line following behind them at a sizeable gap both crashed into them, or stopped in time and were themselves crashed into the riders behind them. The whole situation repeated itself behind, where the force of the charge folded in on itself, or ahead, where those who managed to push through hit another dip in the ground, and the whole thing happened again to a smaller degree.

"Charge!" I ordered my Wolf Soldiers, driving my heels into Blizzard's sides. The white stallion leapt forward, the lancers behind me following. Our front lines opened up at the center where we'd built a wall of half cut timbers that my front line could push out over the ditch just outside of our ramparts. Shela used her magic to strengthen this make-shift bridge as we thundered over it three at-a-time, into the churning mass which had been a well-instituted charge by the Andarons.

The hardship for my lancers was to face Andaron mounted archers. That advantage was gone now. My Wolf soldier foot began to pick up and throw spears we'd cut from the Confluni timber we'd ported from the other side of the lake. Warriors and horses screamed as we rode out and met them, still outnumbered as many as five-to-one.

The lance under my right arm jumped backwards as it engaged the breastbone of the first Andaron who got in my way. It shattered against the second. Thundering to the left of the Andaron mass, I pulled Blizzard to the outside of the three columns of lancers which flowed out of Wisex. Another lancer replaced me and struck another Andaron, and another, and then a third before his lance also shattered and he pulled to the outside beside me, replaced by another lancer. Down the column as we wrapped the Andarons from the left, the lancers followed suit. Strike from the inside of the charging column until your lance broke, and then pull out and let another warrior replace you. Meanwhile we pressed the perimeter, closing in on the Andarons, adding to their confusion as some tried to engage us and some tried to get out of our way. I and the lancers around me all without our lances now, we pressed on with our swords out, slashing the Andarons as we passed, killing them and their horses as they began to get their mounts under control and small groups of them tried to rally.

Lightening crackled in the air above us. Fireballs arched out from behind the Andaron lines.

Shela met them from our own. I didn't know how long she could hold out, how badly outnumbered she might be. In the rest of Fovea her style of magic came as a complete surprise. Here is where she learned it; here were the people who'd taught her what she knew. I'd told her not to try to fight them, just conserve her energy and block what they try to do. It's much easier to disrupt a magical attack than to originate one.

The lightening discharged harmlessly above us. The fireballs fell as ash.

We'd wrapped a fourth of the Andarons and my lancers were still pouring out of our 'gate'. The Andarons themselves were pulling back or simply dying on our lancers where we'd stopped them at the second ditch in the ground. We were having to move farther and farther forward to find fresh targets for them.

Dev Nevala's foot soldiers pressed forward over the ramparts, engaging the Andarons on the right hand side before they could prepare for us. They moved forward in classic squads, shields in front and pikes bristling from behind, swords stabbing at the Andaron horse that came too close. Dev's troops became a wall to push the Andarons against.

In front of me an entire tribe of Andarons had managed to break off from the mass and their leader could be seen rallying them, lining them up to face the continuing charge. Hundreds strong, they'd seen what we were doing and knew they had to stop us before we could get half way around the Andaron main force and then turn and press them on two sides. That would force their warriors to meet us one-to-one while their own front lines kept the mass of their numbers from engaging.

"Wolf Soldiers to the 'fore!" I commanded, slowing Blizzard's charge. The lancers around me spread out into a line, first three across, then six, then twelve, increasing in number and being supplied by the charging Wolf Soldier lancers behind us.

I ordered one of Two Spears' lieutenants to hold back and siphon off 200 for my uses, but to keep the mainstay of our forces encircling the Andarons. It wouldn't help us to have a break here, or to leave the main force of the enemy alone to recollect themselves. Even now, most of them couldn't decide whether to attack the lancers, to pull back or to just wait for orders.

My lancers were 50 across and two ranks deep when I ordered them forward. By then the Andarons were moving as well, some with arrows but most not. Very few of my own riders had their lances intact – this was going to be a bloody hand-to-hand with a veteran opponent which outnumbered me. My troops stretched almost to the beach at the edge of the peninsula, and almost to the line of charging lancers emanating from our battlements. At least the enemy had to face me one-to-one and would have a hard time flanking me.

They started to scream and whoop and fire arrows. A horse went down right next to Blizzard with an arrow in his throat. Another arrow pinged off of the front of my armor.

Blizzard put his head down and stretched his legs, outdistancing the other horses. As I drew closer, I couldn't recognize the tribe except to say that I didn't think it was the Bears. I wouldn't be meeting Black Hawk here.

Too bad.

Our warriors clashed. My sword decapitated one man and cut the arm from another. A scimitar screeched across my mid-section but didn't get to me. Blizzard shouldered another stallion facing him to one side and I straight-armed his rider with my left hand, knocking him to the ground where the warriors behind me likely trampled him.

I didn't check to be sure. Before I would have thought possible I was through their lines and emerging from the other side, wheeling the stallion to the left to line him up for another pass.

About half of my lancers had made it with me. We wheeled and started trotting back toward the enemy. Thanks to Two Spears' training, every warrior wheeled to the left, minimizing our recovery for the second pass. All of them did it at about the same time. The back row became the front, the group of us, though depleted, worked as a unit.

The Andarons facing us had lost far more warriors than we had, and now they were in a tangle. As soon as a few of them realized that we were charging again they turned their horses toward us while most tried to collect themselves. Horses bumped each other, reared and fought their riders. Their leader screamed orders in shrill Andaron as we picked up a canter.

We rode down the few riders who'd come out to meet us and then hit the rest of them at least as hard as before. Horses screamed and warriors swore and died. Once again modern warfare, the time spent training the warriors who engaged each other, prevailed. Where archers could get by just putting missiles in the air, the horse moving as one delivered unimaginable punishment to the unready enemy.

When we passed through them this time it took longer. When we found ourselves on the other side, we met another hundred fresh riders lined up as we had been, and we outnumbered our enemy, a good portion of whom threw down their weapons and headed for the plains.

Back at the main battle, we were nearly half way around the Andarons, who had begun to collect themselves. Half of Two Spears' infantry were marching out to support us, many of them carrying bundles of fresh lances. Dev's warriors were taking a beating on the far side of Andaron mass but where holding, which was all I needed them to do. A wave of pure flame flowed off of the plains toward us and evaporated before it reached our lines. The earth shook and then stopped.

My riders were beginning to disengage the enemy and line up in two files facing the Andarons, waiting for their lances. Very soon we'd begin a final charge into their midst.

I saw Angry Lion at the center of them now. He was screaming at his warriors and telling them to line up like we were, to meet us ready and to fire their arrows. Other tribal leaders were shouting contradicting orders and, just as the first of my Wolf Soldiers began handing out the first of the fresh lances, an entire section of Andarons, over one hundred strong, turned East and departed as fast as they could.

My orders were to let them go. I wasn't here to slaughter, just to survive.

When the desertions started the Andaron confidence started to shake. They still outnumbered me by at least three to one. I'd lost warriors as well, but their dead littered the ground and actually limited where they could move easily.

Andarons were starting to take Angry Lion's orders and to line themselves up toward us. Another chieftain or some important Andaron was pulling troops away from Dev's front in order to focus more on us. As I had done so many times, they'd realized that it was better to fight two smaller enemies than to address them both at the same time.

I pulled the collapsible bow from my thigh – the one I'd taken from Genna what seemed so long ago – and I pointed it into the air. It fired, arcing over the Andarons, and then it burst into green flame. Shela has placed a simple enchantment on it before the battle began.

Almost no one on the Andaron side reacted to it.

Then arrows by the hundreds flew out of the swaying plains grass to the southeast. Nina had gone back to her people and told them that I might need them on the plains, even before I'd fought my first battle here. Krell had responded as soon as he could. Fortunately, as Nina had told me when I rode out onto the plains that night and she'd leaped up onto Blizzard's butt, it had been soon enough.

The Andarons were taken completely by surprise by the Aschire archers. More to the point, when they recognized whom they were up against, a third of them turned tail and ran for the east, leaving the rest to face me on three fronts.

I reached down and accepted a lance from a grinning Wolf Soldier, my warriors with me.

All that was left to do now was to call the advance.

Chapter Twenty-One

Empire

Very few battles are ever fought to the last warrior, although I'd certainly seen my share. At some point, even the worst commander or whoever outlived him realizes that all hope is lost and it's time to run and fight another day.

By the time the Andarons came to that conclusion, I clearly outnumbered them. The Andaron war chiefs may have thought that the first skirmish should have been perfunctory – just a 'getting to know you' battle where we felt out each others' weaknesses. This would give their tribes the opportunity to learn to work together and their chieftains time to argue over the things that were important to them.

Me hitting them so hard on the first pass had caught them by surprise, but then when you think about it, that's a pretty important thing to do if you want to survive the kind of crazy crap that I did.

I couldn't have done it without the help of the Aschire. Once again, my purple-haired allies had come to my rescue when I needed them, not that they needed a lot of prodding to come after the Andarons who raided their forest for wood.

I rode out into the plains on the night after the battle, where scavengers were eating dead horses and dead warriors from both sides. The place stank of rotting flesh and excrement, of blood and urine and wet steel. I pushed Blizzard through this, past the occasional Andaron family looking for a familiar body, and out into the open where the Aschire were camped.

Once again, I sensed rather than heard small, running feet from behind me, and then Nina vaulted up onto Blizzard's butt, her arms wrapping around my armored waist.

Once again, the stallion reared in surprise. I took hold of his mane and leaned forward until he settled.

"He's going to bite you if you keep doing that," I informed her, turning in the saddle.

She smiled wide. "I'm too fast for him," she informed me.

"I never thought I'd see my daughter on a Man's horse," Krell informed me, rising up out of the plains grass. Others popped up behind him. "These are not good days."

I couldn't see his face well in the darkness, and an Aschire is hard to read, anyway. I hoped he was kidding but I couldn't be sure.

"Part of her training," I said to him, smiling as wide as I could.

He nodded. I didn't reach down to take his hand because the Aschire didn't do that. He stared up at me, his head to one side.

"You beat a lot of Andarons," he stated.

I nodded. "I couldn't have done it without you," I said.

He looked around him on the plains. "Don't know how I feel about that," he said. Then he looked back up at me.

"Why do you want to fight for this place?"

Krell was one of my Dukes now, so he deserved an answer, however even a trusted ally could know too much about you.

I also didn't know how much I could spill in front of his people, not that they were likely to talk to anyone.

"I need the lake," I answered, honestly. "I'm going to build a city on it."

"I've never been to the lake," he said. "I don't think it even has a name."

"Maybe I'll name it," I said, smiling again.

He nodded. "Well," he said, "I hope the lake brings you happiness."

"Thank you, Krell," I said.

"Your Grace," he answered me.

"Pardon?"

"You call your Dukes, 'Your Grace,'" he corrected me. "You should call me that."

I nodded. "My apologies," I said. "I didn't think you wanted me to, when we are alone."

Krell considered that. "I didn't think I'd like it," he said, finally, "but it seems that other Aschire consider me to be part a Man now, and a leader among our people, for bringing them to you. If that is true, then I can be a Duke, and you can call me, 'your Grace.'"

"My thanks to your people, and you, your Grace," I said to him.

"Our pleasure, your Majesty," Krell answered and, to my surprise, made a fist over his heart. I felt Nina give me a squeeze.

I didn't know if this was a case of power corrupting, or Krell coming into his own, or Aschire getting a taste for the combat I kept exposing them to from the winning side. Whatever it was, the Aschire were probably not going to be the same anymore.

I felt that this was an example of one of those things War wanted. Whatever it was, it had been added to the price of this excursion into Andoron.

***

In the beginning of the month of Power, with seasonal storms not uncommon on the Andaron plains and a giant graveyard freshly dug both for my warriors and theirs standing to our north, I crossed a wide, beaten plain where the last battle had been fought. This is where thousands had died, where the land had been scored and the long grass ripped away. Errant breezes pulled the bloody dust across the ground and here and there a bird would land to pick at nothing. I sat Blizzard once again in front of a delegation of Andaron tribes, facing Hungry as a Bull, Angry Lion and Black Hawk again, Tartan stood his mare at my left and Two Spears his stallion at my right, and Shela on her gelding behind me.

This time an older, fat Andaron woman had been brought on a litter; her black hair was streaked with grey and tied into a ponytail behind her head. Her face was leathery and deeply tanned, her crooked nose on its way to meeting her chin. She wore a tan dress that resembled a bag more than anything else, clinging to a round stomach.

This was Hungry as a Bull's sorceress wife – the one whom Shela had held at bay during the battle. She didn't look up at us, she held a strand of beads in her hands and she seemed focused on that.

They'd brought a few dozen warriors with them – most of them showing scars from battle. I'd brought my same fifty, none of them injured, though most of them with banged-up armor.

It had occurred to me that the first improvement that my new city needed was a forge.

"We appreciate that you buried our dead alongside your own," Hungry as a Bull informed me. His horse was a draft almost the size of Blizzard, brown with white socks. He rode it with a saddle, where a large majority of his warriors were bareback.

I nodded, not saying anything. Tartan looked straight ahead beside me. He'd supposedly done his share of fighting from among the lancers, and it had left him a little grimmer. I heard a little chuckle from Two Spears.

"We would like to see you leave this place," Black Hawk spoke up. That got him a sideways look from Angry Lion and Hungry. "You know you don't belong here."

"Seems to me like I do," I answered him. "At least, it doesn't look like you can do much about it."

Hungry opened up his mouth, but his wife spoke instead. Without looking up, she said, "Shela, it looks to me like these men are wanting to fight each other again."

"Yes, Strong Spirit," Shela answered in Andoron, her attention focused on the old woman. "It seems that way to me, too."

"I have enough to heal among the Sure Foot," Strong Spirit continued. I hadn't been introduced to her – they didn't bother introducing the women unless there was a reason. "Are there so few among the Wolf Riders?"

This was the first person outside of the tribe who'd acknowledged us, other than Two Spears.

"My tents are full of sick and injured," Shela responded. She shot me a glance. "I have alcohol to treat them, but it still takes time."

Strong looked up at Shela on her horse. Shela wore her regular Andaron garb, the leather halter and skirt split up the side. The faint stretch marks on her stomach were becoming more noticeable as her pregnancy was starting to show. The light breeze pulled at her long, black hair.

"My people have no alcohol," she said. "We know that yours use this, and you save many lives. I have hundreds sick with fever. Even if I had alcohol, I wouldn't know how to use it."

"If my tribe were friends with the Sure Foot," I said, interrupting them, "then I would have to share my alcohol, and show my friends how to use it, and how to make it for themselves."

Hungry exchanged glances with Angry and Black Hawk. It looked to me like the latter wasn't ready to forgive me yet, but before the days when surgeons realized that germs spread disease and sickness, and that they could be killed with alcohol, more warriors died after a battle from infection than during it from lethal wounds.

The secret of alcohol would make a huge difference to the Andaron people, where the tribes fought frequently.

"If you would do this," Angry Lion said, "then you would be a friend to my people."

"And mine," Hungry added.

The two turned to Black Lion. He stared straight at me.

"I would take it as a bribe not to attack you," he said, finally.

Good enough.

***

Until the month of Desire, the Wolf Riders traded with the Sure Foot and the Hunters. In that time my Sea Wolves set sail for Eldador and returned with stocks of raw alcohol and witch hazel extract, building materials and tools, artisans and experts, as well as wealthy commons looking to invest in the new enterprise, the city I would call Wisex, which would rise up from the lake bed.

A cavalcade of Dwarves arrived as well, only one of whom I knew. I'd sent messengers back to the north to ask for more help in designing a new city, and twenty had responded.

Kvitch waddled down the gang plank from one my newest ships, "The Stallion." She was more in the design of a cutter than a warship, meant for speed, a scout ship to precede an armada.

"Dwarves do *not* like ships!" the ambassador of the Simple People informed me, taking my forearm in his. Once again he wore that golden sunburst amulet that I'd seen on him when last we parted. Other Dwarves were already poking around the dirt and staring out into the lake, probably looking for the island that they'd come to work on. They all dressed in rough brown pants closer to canvas than cloth, white homespun shirts with wide collars and green capes over their shoulders. Their beards were brown and red and black all streaked with grey. These were older Dwarves more experienced in what they did.

"Well, you've a few more trips on them in front of you," I informed him. "We're going out onto the lake tomorrow and raise up that island you'll be working on."

"And you believe your wife – your queen – can do this?" he asked me.

"She believes it," I said.

"I don't know of any Uman-Chi who could do something like that," he informed me, his eyebrows twitching skeptically. "Your wife is very self-confident."

"I might be able to help with that," another said, a white-robed figure in a brown cowl. We both turned and watched Dilvesh, my Druid ally from the Free Legion, descend down the gang plank from the same ship as the Dwarves. I'd sent for him, too – Shela felt sure that she could raise the island on her own, but this was more of Dilvesh's thing.

I felt a smile spread across my face as I stepped forward and reached out a hand to Dilvesh. He returned the gesture, reaching out to me and smiling from under a mob of green, curly hair. He threw back the brown cowl and opened up his out robes to reveal the green question mark, turned upside-down on his white inner robes. I gripped his forearm in mine as the Dwarf looked on.

"This is the returning Druid that we've heard about in the North?" the Dwarf asked.

Dilvesh regarded him. He'd probably staid dark and hidden on the ship while it sailed – that was more the Druid's way. No one had known they still existed a year ago and that wasn't a habit he'd be quick to break.

Not Dilvesh, anyway.

"Your idea interests me," he admitted. "This idea of creating a city on a lake where no island exists, starting with the island."

"I thought you'd like it," I answered him.

"You've seen that there's lots of good land here," Kvitch commented.

I pointed out onto the plains at the end of the peninsula, where the beaten down plains stood out between us and where the winter hay blew wild; where horse bones could still be seen. "This land is vulnerable," I said. "I don't want something where I can defend myself; I want something where I don't have to."

"That idea worked for the Uman-Chi," Dilvesh noted.

"Until you came along," Kvitch added, smiling through his beard. "Or had you not noticed that, either?"

I chuckled. "This time I won't have to conquer it," I said.

"Not what all of those graves to your north are telling me," Kvitch said.

Now I squared off on the little man. He'd managed to find a sore spot that I felt like I shouldn't have. "If you're not up to the task," I informed him, "then these ships can take you right to Sental."

Kvitch frowned. "Oh, if Men can think of it, then Dwarves can make it real," he assured me. "If your wife can call an island up out of this lake, then we'll reinforce it, build a bridge to it if we have to – we'll do what is needed for whatever you want to build."

He turned his back on us, and looked out over the lake's black water, where the currents ran fast and crazy and a swimmer could be swept away five feet from the muddy banks.

"I'll give you your first step to an Eldadorian Empire," he said. "But you're the one who will do the rest of the walking."

"He's right, you know," Dilvesh informed me.

He, Shela and I were sitting in the pavilion that had been Shela's and my home since we'd come here. I'd thought it might be nice to switch to the Sea Wolves once they got here, but Shela had grown up living this way and she'd come to miss it. Our warriors and civilians had been inter-mingling a good bit, the Andarons teaching my Wolf Soldiers their ways, and one thing they'd done is to skin all of the dead horses from the battle. There were horse-hide tents and clothing all over the place now, and uncounted implements made from horse bones.

My Wolf Riders were looking more like a tribe every day; however they'd harvested wood from the Confluni forests and built stables, warehouses, even a few homes. This tribe wouldn't roam the plains when the weather changed, they'd be staying here.

"Right about what?" Shela asked him. She'd cooked us a dinner of wild herbs and venison. Nina had helped her. Now she and Lee were playing a game with Lee's bebe in a corner of the tent.

"Kvitch said that this was the start of an Eldadorian Empire," I said to her. "Wisex is a colony on Andaron soil; the Wolf Riders are my colonists."

"He's right," Dilvesh repeated.

"It takes more than one colony to turn a kingdom into an empire," I informed the Druid. "It takes a lust to grow, to collect more power, to absorb other people and cultures."

The Druid looked me square in the eye.

He drove me crazy sometimes.

"What if this *is* the start of an Eldadorian Empire?" Shela challenged us. She leaned forward on her collapsible canvas chair – we travelled with these, made of leather and bone, because they were easy to move and somewhat comfortable. "What if Eldador expands to other lands, if that is the gods' will?"

"That all depends on which gods," Dilvesh said, leaning back. His eyes wandered the canvas top of the pavilion. "Certainly Law and Order don't seek for Eldador to spread its power."

I was more concerned with War, Shela with Power, but neither of us said so.

"This needs to happen, regardless," I said. "If Eldador is now an empire, then the rest of Fovea is going to have to live with it. Conflu is an Empire and no one seems to mind."

"Accept for us when we're killing them," Dilvesh said, not looking away from the ceiling.

Dilvesh knew what he was talking about – this I had to remind myself of. Dilvesh had revealed more to me at the Battle of Tamaran Glen than he'd intended. I hadn't shared that secret, even with Shela, because it wasn't mine to share and because Dilvesh would know instantly if I did.

And because I needed Dilvesh, and Dilvesh knew that, too.

***

Everyone was up the next day with the sun, on the 15th day of Power, and stood looking out at the lake. We still hadn't given it a name, not that we hadn't tried. Nothing seemed to fit.

I'd have liked to have D'gattis here, but I wasn't sure how to lay hands on him and it seemed to me he was probably still angry enough with me that he'd just do his nay-sayer thing until we threw up our hands in frustration.

As I'd said so many times, this needed to happen. Wisex fit into my future plans on almost every level.

"There's enough rock in the lake bottom to do what you want," Kvitch informed us. "This probably wasn't here before the Blast, and the two rivers parted because something like a set of hills parted them."

That made no sense to me – there Mid River flowed right out of Conflu. Even if the Safe River were created by the Blast, it didn't flow up backwards to a tributary and then start and then correct itself. He knew more about this sort of thing than I did, so I kept my mouth shut.

"I can sense the collection of hard stone," Dilvesh informed the Dwarves and Shela. They stood just where the black beach began to meet the water, myself and a couple squads of Wolf Soldier guards behind them. Nina held Lee in her arms and bounced her, while my daughter, hugging her bebe, did her best to go back to sleep.

"So if I can raise that up, you can keep it all together?" Shela asked him.

"Molding it all into one piece shouldn't be a problem," Dilvesh answered, "but that's a *lot* of rock. I don't see how you can –"

"His plans," Shela cut him off. "My power derives from what others desire. The stronger the desire – "

"But he's only one man," Dilvesh argued.

"He isn't the only one who wants it," she said. "If he's right then I become the avatar for a million unheard voices."

"And if he's wrong?" the pessimistic Dwarf asked her.

She turned her head to look down on Kvitch. "Then a lot of my countrymen just died for nothing."

The little Dwarf said nothing to that, and Shela didn't expand on it. She and Dilvesh moved right out to the water's edge, and they began to chant.

It occurred to me both that they'd worked together several times now to combine their magic, and that Shela had informed D'gattis once that, if she weren't with me, then she'd be with him. I suppressed a little ripple of jealousy right then, and focused on what I wanted.

What I believed my god wanted. What I had to think Shela's god, Power, wanted as well.

I felt something move through, kind of like a flush. I shuddered but I couldn't shake it off. People from the tribe I'd created and the Wolf Soldiers gathered around behind us to see what we were doing.

Shela raised her hand before her, her long, black leather raider cloak falling off of her shoulders. She took a step to the side as if she were getting a better stance to lift something.

Maybe she was?

Lee cooed from Nina's arms and she lifted up one hand like her mother. Dilvesh spread both hands before him.

The lake began to churn. People were pointing and commenting behind us. Shela began to incant, the strain clear in her voice. Dilvesh did the same beside her. Lee began to make nonsense sounds in imitation of her mother.

The churning increased. A shelf of black rock peeked up out of the center of the lake, a sheet of water flowing off of it. More rose around it, then started to level off. They were creating a huge shelf, I couldn't tell yet how wide. The rock stood out as black as the water around it- the color from the lake might be taken from the bottom, I thought.

Lee was shouting now in her self-made baby-language. Nina was bouncing her. The level from the lake didn't change as this rock was simply a rearrangement of the lake's bottom.

This was going to create even more crazy channels in the lake's currents, and probably dump a ton of silt into the swamp downstream.

I might be dealing with a lot of angry Slee.

All at once, Shela stopped her chanting. Dilvesh continued for a little while longer, then he stopped, too. They both stared out at what they'd created for a minute or two afterwards, and then they both turned to face me.

Shela looked exhausted and Dilvesh could barely stand. They approached me and Wolf Soldiers ran out to support them both. Shela almost fell into my arms from theirs.

We took them to the pavilion and laid them down to sleep. Nina entered after us with Lee in her arms, and laid the baby down next to her mother on a mat on the floor, her bebe next to her.

"Did you see that?" Nina asked me.

"I was right there next to you," I informed her.

Outside of the pavilion, the Wolf Soldiers and the Andarons were chattering about the amazing thing they'd seen. I could hear Kvitch arguing with a captain of one of my Sea Wolves that he needed to go out and inspect this new island right away, and the captain was saying that he wanted some time to study the new currents.

Nina clucked her tongue at me.

"I meant Lee, Lupus," she said to me, in that exasperated way kids have. "Did you see Lee?"

"Yes," I said. I squatted down next to my sleeping girls and pulled a blanket over them. Shela would likely sleep through the day. Lee was anyone's guess, and Dilvesh pretty much did what he wanted to.

"That was very funny," I said.

Nina actually smacked me. I turned to look over my shoulder into her angry grey eyes.

"She joined in the *spell*," Nina informed me. "I can't even do that."

I felt my eyebrows drop and my scar twitch.

"Your daughter's a sorceress," the little Aschire girl informed me.

Chapter Twenty-Two

Reconstruction

I stood on a wide field of stone, miles across, the surface rough and uneven and black, in the middle of a lake where the current twisted like a tangle of snakes and the sun beat down in the autumnal month of Power, sacred to my woman's god.

It would be winter here. Supposedly the Andaron plains were always temperate, but this had turned into a cold month. On 'the rock,' as I'd been calling it in my mind, it seemed pretty warm to me.

"We can use this," Kvitch informed me. Other Dwarves were nodding. "This is a good base – we can build your city on this, if you want it."

It wouldn't have happened without my daughter's interference. She wasn't just a sorceress, she showed the raw abilities to be a powerful sorceress. Shela and Dilvesh were wracking their minds to try to figure out where her power came from, while the Dwarves were doing the same thing in regard to this lump of rock we'd given them.

"Of course, you're going to have to defend it before we're finished with it," one of the Dwarves said. Her name was Grellia – a red-bearded Dwarf with fine fingers and long eyebrows. "The currents dumped a ton of silt into the Mid River and the Slee who live there aren't going to put up with that for long. They're going to come looking for a reason why, and if what I've heard of them is true, they're not going to like the reason."

What was scary was how right they were.

"If the Slee can weaken you, then the Andarons will sweep in right behind them," Two Spears informed me. "My people have made peace with you, but they did it because they had to, not because they want anything to do with you."

More good news.

"So my question, thin-brained Man," Kvitch asked me, crossing his arms over his stomach and looking up at me with those soulful brown eyes, "is, 'Do you want it?'"

Daughter whose powers were going to exceed her abilities and endanger us all, enemies on every front, most of whom I'd gone out of my way to piss off, expense uncertain and future unclear; hell, yeah, I wanted it, and I said so.

"Build it," I informed him. "Make it tough enough to withstand the combined Fovean armies if it has to. Whatever you need, just tell me."

I turned on my heel and started back to the barge that would take me to the Sea Wolf, that would take me to the shore. The currents were too crazy for it to be trusted to go too far – in fact, the Sea Wolf would have to push itself into a position to block that current for the four strong Men who rowed the barge to move it from the stone shore to the ship's side. We'd already lost a rowboat down the Great Mid River and two squads of fast horses hadn't been able to get to it before it bore its occupants down into the Slee swamp. Nothing came out of there alive.

It was all creeping over me, I admitted to myself. It was becoming too much. Being a monarch, being a warlord, being a husband, a father; keeping it all together. I couldn't move ahead anymore, I was just fighting how much farther I fell behind.

If this kept up, I was going to crash, and I didn't do anything small.

If you went upstream of the Black Lake, as we were calling it, into Confluni territory, you came to a mountain range that sat as an escarpment to the north of the Great Mid River. The Dwarves claimed that the rock from there was good enough for what they wanted to do.

Before they left, Aschire scouts verified that there were no Confluni patrols in that part of their territory. No one came to this part of Andoron, and so the Confluni saw no point in guarding it.

We pillaged the forest, we'd pillage the rock escarpment. We could build a city out of nothing and call it 'Wisex.'

I don't even know where I came up with the name.

I left on a Sea Wolf back to Eldador the Port with my wife, Nina, Tartan and our horses. The Wolf Soldier contingent and associated Theran Lancers were going to winter here, and then I'd make a decision on how many stayed through the summer based on the city's progress and how many Andarons I attracted.

Two Spears would stay in command for a while. He'd met a girl he liked, a short brunette named 'Soft Eyes,' whom Shela had sent his way. Sisters named their brothers in Andaron culture and picked out their wives, and despite everything else that might be going on, Shela tended her men and performed her duties as an Andaron woman.

She kept it all together *way* better than I did.

Dilvesh actually absented himself before we realized it. The next morning he just wasn't there. He'd brought that big horse of his, and it was gone, too; I had to assume that, whatever Druids did, he was off doing it.

We pulled in to Eldador's busy port on the twelfth day of Desire, after a long and arduous sea journey. The wind blew cold over Tren Bay and it was misery to man the rigging of a Sea Wolf. Barefoot sailors crunched across swaying decks sometimes slick with ice, or through freezing rain, with a strength I wasn't sure I possessed.

There wasn't much of a crowd to greet us – the weather didn't lend itself to cheering crowds and we hadn't announced the arrival. We pulled directly into a slip next to the part of the wharves I'd walled off, and only did that because another Sea Wolf was being finished in that place.

We'd construct a temporary wall here if we had to, however it was fast-becoming pointless now. We could point to five Sea Wolves now and we'd double that before the spring. I couldn't keep them all in the Black Lake, even if I wanted to.

I walked Blizzard off of the ship and led him down the wharves with his tack on his back, because it was too slick and dangerous to ride him. Shela did the same with her gelding. Nina carried Lee, whom we'd dressed in a fox-fur parka. Of course, her bebe had to have one, too.

J'her met us half way down the wharves with fifty Wolf Soldiers. He wasn't smiling.

"How bad?" I asked him.

That got a little smirk from him. "Bad enough," he informed me, turning so that he could walk next to me. The Wolf Soldiers formed up around us. Blizzard stomped and snorted at them, not liking to feel hemmed in.

Sea travel was always hard on him.

"The Andarons have complained that you illegally invaded their nation," J'her said, "and they've called an emergency session of the Fovean High Council. You've got a week to respond, but Dorkan is already pledging two thousand warriors to the conflict, and the Confluni and the Toorians are willing to support them, magic aid included."

"That was fast," I commented.

"You supposedly killed a lot of people and left a sizable army behind you," he said. "There's also a rumor that you made the lake down there even more impassable, and now the Toorians are saying you've ruined irrigation systems that took them decades to build."

I felt my scar twitch. "I didn't know they did that?" he said.

J'her shook his head. "No one did," he said. "No one goes to Toor. No one knows what they do down there, and I didn't think that you could do *anything* that far upstream of them that could affect their nation.

In fact, I *did* know that silt could travel for hundreds of miles downstream of a disturbance like the one we'd created. I'd been worried that we'd create natural dams that would raise that lake's level and overrun the island, but apparently that's not what happened.

"We have to be in Outpost IX in a week?" Shela asked J'her.

The Uman nodded. "That's what we're informed," he said, "however I think you'd be crazy to go."

We were passing through the market place and approaching the city gates. They'd been constructed of wrapped timbers which had proved difficult to maintain and which always looked like they were about to come apart. I needed to have them remade.

Hitler worried how he'd widen the streets of Berlin so that it could function as the capitol of the world, as his troops fell back on every front, too.

"You think that the Uman-Chi will arrest him the second he puts a foot down on Trenboni soil," Shela said, looking sideways at me.

"I would," J'her agreed.

I wouldn't, but I don't act like most of the people here.

"If I don't go, then they'll try to invade me before I make that place too strong to invade," I said. "I guess this isn't something that the delegates I employ can handle for me?"

"That's a question better asked of Duke Hectar," J'her said, looking straight forward. "He's been running the actual government while you were away."

"How's *he* been doing?" I asked.

J'her shrugged inside of his armor. My officers wore scalloped steel sleeves and tooled steel greaves outside of their grey tunics, with their breastplates underneath, while the regular enlisted just wore tunics over leather or steel with single-piece, plain covers on their lower legs and upper arms. "He's had a lot of practice so he's good at it. He wouldn't complain to me, if he had any."

I sensed some tension there but it wasn't worth pursuing. I could let them work it out and intervene if one of them asked me. There were just some things here that I had to let go, and this was one of them.

We walked the rest of the way in silence, until we found ourselves inside of the city proper. J'her had a big, black carriage waiting with six black horses to pull it. Everyone but me climbed in – I knew Blizzard wouldn't trail behind it so I rode him in its wake.

Sitting atop him, I saw passersby recognize me and wave. I waved back as much as I could. I'd dressed out in my armor because the padding kept me really warm, a few of the braver people, mostly Men though some Uman, too, actually approached me and knocked on it. I'd been told before that knocking on a warrior's armor was a wish for him to have good luck in combat.

I had to order the Wolf Soldier guards to let them pass, of course. I think most of them would have bashed some heads, had they had their way. They took my safety pretty seriously and an attempt on my life by the Bounty Hunters' Guild was still fresh in their minds.

I reached down and let some of the commons touch my gauntlet. Some of the women would take it and kiss it. A few of the kids tried to touch Blizzard but I warned them off – he didn't have a friendly reputation. The Wolf Soldiers had to step in a few times on that account.

It took an hour but we made it to the palace. No one got hurt. That's pretty good for me.

I clipped my helmet to my belt and I entered the throne room while court was still in session. Hectar was listening to some fat guy with no hair describing his need for tax relief from the State. The Duke looked for all the world like he'd rather be hanging by his thumbnails in the dungeon than sitting where he was. His face expanded in a smile when he saw me and I could almost hear him saying, "Good – you do this now!"

"His Majesty," the court crier, an older Uman whose baritone had gotten him the job, called from next to the gallery, "Rancor the First, of the House Mordetur, King of Eldador."

"King of Eldador," I corrected him, striding down the length of the throne room as guests and subjects rose, "and of the city state of Wisex on Black Lake."

"Wisex on Black Lake, your Majesty?" Hectar asked me. "I do not know this part of Fovea."

"Black Lake is the joining of the Great Mid River and the Safe River," I said, "and Wisex is the Andaron village next to it, as well as the name of the island at the center of it. Both are claimed by the Wolf Rider clan, of which I am chieftain."

"My congratulations, your Imperial Majesty," Hectar said, standing. "Although I believe that the Fovean High Council may well have an opinion as to Eldador's expansion."

I trotted up the steps to the stone throne and took Hectar's forearm in mine. He stepped down a step and I stepped up, turned and sat in my throne.

The court sat as well. The old, fat guy at the foot of the stairs to the throne just stood there trying to smile, and probably wondering if he'd have to repeat his whole story again.

"How do We interest this gentleman?" I asked Hectaro.

Hectar smiled a political smile and said, "This Baron of the town of Jellith is justifying to me why we should forgive him his taxes. He'd also like to rename his village to *Lee's Hope*, after your daughter."

I smiled despite myself. That was pretty creative. If I allowed it, then half of the country would be named after my family before the year was out, and I didn't like looking like that sort of narcissist.

But I like to reward creativity.

"First," I said, "I don't want any other cities, towns, villages, hamlets, by-ways or what-have-you's named after my family," I said to him. The murmur was already flowing through the gallery.

"Second, why do you need tax relief?"

"Our little town is located to the south of Eldador the Port," the fat man informed me. "We have only farming to support us, and most of our population has lived in Eldador for less than a year."

I shrugged inside of my armor. I don't know if he could tell. "More than half of the villages in the country can say the same thing," I said.

"We seek to build a marketplace," he continued, oblivious. "In this, we can consolidate the products of our neighboring – "

"No," I informed him. That one was easy.

He turned his chubby cheeks up toward me, dumbfounded. "Your – your Majesty?" he asked me.

"Markets will grow up where people need them," I informed him. I remembered this much from college economics before they kicked me out. "Giving you a tax break to create one won't make people want to come to it – it just means we'll be supporting it forever. You'll be here in a year complaining that the market just needs a little more investment, and the year after that saying, for all of the money we've put into it, we can't let it fail now.

"No," I said. "If your little town needs a market, rest assured the people there will start one. You're not getting one from me."

I didn't mean to come off so harsh to him, but it had been a pretty screwed up month and I didn't know what to do about the Fovean High Council. I hadn't counted on the Andarons running crying to them, and that was a mistake.

I didn't like making mistakes.

The Baron nodded and withdrew. There were a few other courtiers but most of them didn't even try with me – I guess they all wanted money, too.

Court ended early and I left down the normal passageways with Hectar and the ever-present Wolf Soldier entourage. Shela and Nina had taken off together after the stables and I had no idea where Tartan had gotten to.

"I'm told it was quite a battle in Andaron," Hectar commented. I just grunted at him.

"The troubadours are calling it, 'Battle of the New Emperor,' whatever that means."

I gave him a sideways glance but didn't slow down. "It probably means that they don't like me leaving a few thousand warriors and a powerful Duke in Andoron after wiping out two of its most powerful tribes," I said.

Hectar nodded. "The Fovean High Council was rather impressed with that, as well," he said.

"I heard," I said.

We turned down a passage to the right on our way to the royal chambers. The kitchens were along the way and I felt like grabbing something to eat. Me showing up in the kitchen usually freaked out the staff, but I was hungry and, frankly, I didn't care.

These mood swings weren't helping me, I knew.

"This is more than your delegates can take care of for you," he informed me, looking straight forward. "You've pushed the High Council too far, and given them too many arrows to point against you. The Dorkans, the Confluni, the Trenboni and now the Andarons – all of them will benefit from your downfall now."

"What do you think they'll want?" I asked him.

Hectar was quiet for a moment, marching on next to me, giving me his profile. I didn't like this. I wanted to be the guy with the answers, not the questions. I don't know why I thought that taking on the mantle of King would give me the one without the other, but I realized then that I'd thought exactly that.

"The Fovean High Council can't depose a leader," he said, as we turned another corner. Now I could smell the kitchens – beef browning over an open fire, steam from soup or broth, maybe. "However, they can order an attack against another nation, and they can limit trade, although they've never done so. I think that all of the other Fovean nations would love to hear that Eldadorian products are going to have to stay in Eldador, and not come to their shores at prices too low for their merchants to compete with. I think that the Uman-Chi have seen a way to limit your power without lifting a sword."

That hadn't occurred to me at all, and I couldn't help thinking that this was the *first* thing that should have come to mind. Foveans weren't stupid. They'd found a way to adapt to what I was doing.

I was playing in a new ball field now. I needed to step up my game.

Chapter Twenty-Three

Education

A week and two days later, on the 21st day of the month of Desire, I stood once again at the podium before the assembled delegates of the Fovean High Council. This time every stone seat in the place had someone's behind in it, and a crowd had assembled outside, where criers were repeating what was said in here. I'd heard that they'd even found a big, blonde Volkhydran to represent me.

I hadn't donned my armor. I dressed in royal finery – white shirt with a ruffled front and blousy, fashionable blue pants of some kind of wool, black boots shined to a high polish and a purple over coat like a blazer but with tails, a red cape dragging from its shoulders to the floor. I still had the gold headpiece holding back my long, blonde hair.

Shela had scrubbed it until my scalp bled. She sat to one side of me with D'gattis and Ancenon, both of them wearing the question-mark, turned upside-down, of the Free Legion.

I bore that mark as well on an armband, over the wolf's head which marked the Wolf Soldiers. I also wore the Sword of War at my hip. I'd come here on three of my new Sea Wolves and three hundred warriors.

Three hundred wouldn't save me if a fight broke out, but they wouldn't hurt if some of the locals got froggy. You could still see the damage I'd done here, and no one applauded me as I walked from the docks to the coliseum.

We'd left the baby at home with Nina and Karel of Stone, who wanted to start the Aschire's training. Arath, Nantar and Thorn were laying the foundations of a city to be called 'Metz' in the center of the Andurin peninsula, and Hectar sat my throne.

He'd advised me I should come back soon. I wasn't making any promises.

One of the Uman-Chi stood to address me. I didn't recognize him. He wore the white robes of a delegate. "Your Majesty, King Rancor Mordetur, you are charged with the illegal invasion of the south of Andoron, of seizing land there, of an unprovoked attack on several of the tribes there, resulting in loss to the nation of Andoron and strife to the people therein."

All of the Andarons were nodding, the Dorkans and the Confluni with them. I took a breath and put my hands on the podium.

"How do you respond to these charges, your Majesty?" the Uman-Chi asked me.

"Delegate," I said. I didn't call him 'Sir' like last time, because I ranked him now, "I am a chieftain of the Wolf Rider tribe, and I ask that you address me accordingly."

The Uman-Chi smiled and looked down, hiding his face in his long, green hair while he collected himself. I'd have been surprised if they *hadn't* guessed I'd pull this. The Fovean High Council had no power to intervene in an internal matter.

The Uman-Chi raised his face and turned back to me, letting me see his sharp, angular nose and high-arched brows. "Yonega Waya," he said to me in Andaron, calling me 'White Wolf,' "when you invaded, you were not yet an Andaron, but acting in the auspices of the Eldadorian state, for which you are liable, and for which the Eldadorian state is liable."

"And which means that we address you as an Eldadorian, not an Andaron," a Dorkan said, standing. He was a fat bald man wearing purple robes under those of delegate white and big, gold hoop earrings dangling from his lobes. Despite the cold Desire air, he was sweating.

"Don't you try to confuse these issues, Rancor Mordetur!" he warned me.

I felt my eyebrows rise. "So I'm to be addressed as a common here?" I asked the collected delegates. "This is the etiquette of a Fovean High Council?"

In fact, it didn't bug me, but being able to play offended didn't hurt me, either. If I could get them squabbling among themselves as to how to treat me, this could all fall apart.

Another Dorkan, a woman with long, straight brown hair and chubby cheeks, stood up next to the first and put a hand on his shoulder. "We apologize, your Ma – Yonega Waya," she said. "My compatriot here is somewhat distressed, in that you murdered his brother."

"And a lot of other brothers!" an Andaron said, standing.

"And some very good friends," a Sentalan shouted from their delegation.

Now more of the delegates stood and started shouting at me. A storm of white robes shook on the floor of the coliseum below me as those wearing them started to vent their feelings about what I'd done, to whom, and what they thought about it.

I took a step back and acted surprised. The Uman-Chi were shouting to the other delegates for order and being ignored. I allowed myself a sideways glance at Ancenon, D'gattis and Shela and, while the two Uman-Chi were scowling in exasperation, Shela was grinning fiercely.

In the stadium seats, those watching were clearly enjoying the show. I'm sure we weren't quite as good as gladiators, but more entertaining than the regular evening in a winter month. I saw Uman, Uman-Chi, Men and even some Scitai in attendance.

No Xinto. It would be a bad day for Xinto, if I found him here.

"Delegates, delegates, *please*," the flustered Uman-Chi called out over his peers, making a pushing-down motion with his hands. "All of these grievances can be addressed –"

"No," I said, in my best battle-field voice, "I have to say I think that they cannot."

That got a few curious looks, so I pushed on.

"People of Fovea," I said, "I hate to be the one to tell you this, but this 'High Council' of yours is a morass, and if you can't even control yourselves, then I can't imagine how you plan to hold me accountable to whatever it is you imagine that I did."

"You invaded our nation!" an Andaron shouted back at me, standing and almost sputtering. From the beads sewn into the leather pants and jacket that he wore, I could tell he'd come here from the city of Chatoos.

"I returned two Andarons to their home tribe, and they attacked me," I said, shaking my head. "Did I push my advantage after that? Yes, I did, but now I'm your buffer against the Slee."

"We didn't *need* a buffer against the Slee until you wiped out the Drifters and the Wet Bellies," the Andaron shouted. Others of their delegation stood.

Other nations' delegates quieted a little but the Dorkans were still shouting and the Uman-Chi were still trying to shush them.

"Then better for you if they hadn't attacked me," I informed him. That was purely argumentative, however I wanted the argument.

I didn't want an embargo against Eldador. We could be self-sufficient if we had to be – we certainly had enough citizens to consume all of our own wares, however I wanted to pursue these new interests in the Black Lake as well as my own projects at home, and I needed to be able to tax to do that.

I didn't want to drain my people dry. I needed foreign trade, and that meant that I didn't want an embargo.

"Better still if we attack you again," the Andaron threatened. "Don't underestimate our power, and your few thousand are far from home."

There it was. The Uman-Chi's mouth dropped open. Probably smarter than I am, he saw where I was going right then.

"You mean to declare war on my tribe?" I demanded, gripping the podium's top with both hands and leaning forward.

"We'll kill your warriors and take your herds," he swore to me. "Your women will only be available to the lowest among us, so your children will shame you."

Shela straightened. That had to be a serious oath.

"And we will stand with the Andarons," the fat Dorkan swore, speaking for his country.

"Then I declare the Andoron nation in civil war!" I shouted, and slammed a hand down on the top of the podium. "And I call on the Fovean High Council to protect our borders from those who would exploit this situation."

"You can't request that –" the Dorkan began, but he caught himself.

I couldn't request that as an Eldadorian, but I *definitely* could as an Andaron chieftain.

And the Uman-Chi had all but recognized me. Certainly close enough for me to make my case.

"The Andaron people, then," the Andaron delegate declared, "demand protection for Eldadorian intervention in this civil war."

"The Dorkans second," the Dorkan woman said, standing. Her fat friend was still spluttering and probably wondering what was going on.

"From this day forward," I said still holding the podium but leaning back, "I declare for the Eldadorian nation as an Empire, the Black Lake and the city and the village of Wisex as a protectorate, and myself as an Emperor."

I had no idea if I could do that, however this was as good a time as any to find out.

"Eldador as an empire is outside of the charter of the Fovean High Council," the Uman-Chi informed me.

"As the only admitted, and not founding, member of the High Council," a Confluni said, standing, "I believe that Eldador is not within the charter of the Fovean High Council at all."

This came as a complete surprise to me. The little yellow-skinned man, his grey and black hair down past his shoulders, had his face turned up toward me, but his eyes unfocused. I couldn't tell if this was support, or a delegate who felt honor-bound to state a fact.

"It *is* true," the Uman-Chi said, drawing out his words, "that Eldador is entered on the rolls only as 'Eldador,' while Conflu is actually entered as the Confluni Empire and Trenbon as the nation-state of Trenbon."

"And Andoron," Ancenon said, standing up behind me, "as 'the tribes of Andoron in unison, albeit individually sovereign."

The grin on his face was unmistakable. The collective Andaron delegates turned to each other in alarm. If Eldador could carve out a tribe and then demand a portion of their nation, then why couldn't anyone else?

I think the Confluni were thinking the same thing.

Now the Uman-Chi were in a pickle. They had to recognize their own charter, but they had to keep me out of Andoron, or they'd be dealing with the rest of Fovea carving it up and a return to the open warfare that had made the Fovean High Council necessary.

"Volkhydro recognizes Eldador as an Empire, and the Emperor Rancor The First, of the House Mordetur," a Volkhydran said, rising.

I recognized Count Tezzen of Myr. His hair looked a little longer and a little greyer. His body still kept the muscle that I'd associated with him, and his eyes the same hard calculation that keeps a warrior alive on a battle field.

Henekh had asked me what my plans were, and I'd warned him not to be the first to get in my way. I had to think that he'd had a conversation with his countrymen.

"Conflu seconds," that same Confluni delegate called out.

"Protection *must* be granted to Andoron until we can decide what happens with this *Wolf Rider* tribe," another Andaron delegate demanded, standing. He'd also dressed out in the leathers that Andarons wore in the winter, with beads identifying him as being from Chatoos.

A Toorian stood, sighing. He wasn't anyone I recognized from the coronation. His hair was completely grey and his deep-brown face lined with age wrinkles. "Toor will recognize this Eldadorian Empire," he said. "Let the Fovean High Council defend Andoron until this civil war is settled."

"Rest assured that the Dorkan nation will pay close attention to this civil war," the fat Dorkan delegate informed us all, sitting.

"I leave the task of working out these details to my Eldadorian delegates," I informed the group of them. My delegates were busy loading their robes with their own sweat while all of this had been going on. I had to think that the best news they'd had all day was that I'd be leaving right now.

The silver-on-silver eyes of an angry Uman-Chi delegate seemed to find mine. I couldn't differentiate the cornea from the iris at this distance, but the irritation was unmistakable.

"This Fovean High Council dismisses this Emperor of Eldador, with our thanks," he said.

I nodded, swept the collected delegates with a glare, and turned on my heel. Shela ran up beside me and took my arm in both of hers. Ancenon and D'gattis lined up behind me and we all exited the podium area for the tunnel that lead out of the coliseum of the High Council.

I held my face plain but I wanted to be grinning like an idiot. *Victory!* I couldn't help thinking. Beat them *again!* The Fovean-friggin' High Council and haughty Uman-Chi were choking on my dust *again*.

I stepped out into the cold crisp air outside of the coliseum, finding a crown of mostly-Uman waiting for me, behind a barrier of warriors in Trenboni livery whose job it was to control the crowd and keep their common hands off of my royal person.

One of them, an Uman-Chi in military red-and-blues of the Trenboni High Guard with a golden star burst on an epaulette on his left shoulder, stepped forward and regarded me with a hand on the hilt of the sword on his hip. Behind him, I could see three Uman-Chi in the white robes of their 'Casters,' or Wizards.

Shela stopped dead in her tracks, even her face frozen in an expression of surprise. D'gattis and Ancenon both leapt to one side. Three hundred Wolf Soldier guards stood at attention to one side of the entrance to the coliseum, but they had a whole crowd between them and me.

"What is *this?*" I demanded.

"Your Imperial Majesty, Rancor Mordetur of Eldador, we present to take custody and possession of the common Andaron woman, Shela, for her war crimes against the sovereign nation of Trenbon, sedition of the Scitai people and her personal attack on Outpost IX," he informed me.

I pulled the Sword of War. He leapt back, and the three Wizards each raised a right hand white with power. Shela stood where she was, but I recognized a commander's voice among the Wolf Soldiers calling them to ready.

This was going to be bloody. Really bloody. We were both outnumbered and separated from our troops, and rest-assured that the locals were going to chime in.

I felt a hand on my shoulder. I turned to see D'gattis regarding me. This time, I *could* see the cornea of his silver-on-silver eyes.

"There is no victory here," the Uman-Chi informed me. "Black Lupus, you must accede to this noble warrior and relinquish your slave girl."

"My *wife*," I said to him. "The Empress of —"

"No," Ancenon said, stepping forward. "You've had no ceremony and the Trenboni government recognizes no slave. She is a free common the moment her foot touches the Silent Isle, and as such she is responsible for her own actions and her own crimes."

My eyes flicked back between the one ally and the other. I could feel my scar twitch. "They'll kill her," I hissed.

"They'll do that now," Ancenon informed me. "I am still a Duke of Trenbon, from an important house, and I think you have no small friendship in Avek Noir, the Heir. I'll speak to her safety, and where I might fail, I'm certain he shall not."

D'gattis gripped my shoulder harder. "I'll fight beside you," he informed me, "but we'll lose. You see three casters but don't see thirty more. I believe you told me once about existing for another day of combat."

"Live to fight another day," I corrected him. I turned away and faced the Uman-Chi commander.

"Harm her in any way," I informed him, looking into his eyes now, "scratch her skin, bruise her flesh, do anything, and it will be my life's work, not just to hunt you down, but to find everyone you love, and everyone you've *ever* loved, and visit horror on them that you couldn't imagine if you live another thousand years."

"Not wise to threaten a Commander of the High Guard," the Uman-Chi informed me, seeming unimpressed.

I stepped into his personal space and almost touched the end of my nose to his. "A threat is something that I might not do," I informed him. "I *vow* to you, unto the god War, one bloody massacre after the next visited on your friends and family if she comes to any harm."

The Uman-Chi met my stare and nodded. He ordered four of his warriors to pick Shela up off of the ground, and they carried her past their warriors and mine toward the palace at Outpost IX.

D'gattis kept his hand on my shoulder the entire time. The Major commanding the Wolf Soldier guard kept trying to catch my eye but I looked right through him.

This had turned into a really *not* good day.

***

While a noble might own a property in a foreign land and stay there, the Eldadorian nation did not, in fact, have an embassy to Trenbon and there was no concept here of embassies being sacrosanct within another nation's boundaries.

I could buy land here and have something built, but that would take years. I could have had Shela raise something but that really wasn't her thing, and bellied the actual problem that she was in a dungeon somewhere, where her magic was likely negated.

So I was pacing the captain's cabin of one of the Sea Wolves I'd brought here, and trying to rely on Karel of Stone's spies whom we employed in Trenbon, through what I remembered him telling me about them, which wasn't much.

I didn't want to tip my hand and actually expose one of them, because I didn't want it in the head of whoever ran this city that they had a real security problem. I didn't want to go running around the city, either, because I had to think that the Bounty Hunter's Guild had wind of what had happened here by now, and they'd said a lot of times that, if not for Shela, they'd have had me.

D'gattis had already taken off for the palace in Eldador, but I had no idea how long that was going to take him, and I *did* know that he wouldn't miss Shela if something happened to her.

A lot of people would like her out of their way. This had been a pretty smart move on the Uman-Chi's part and I should have thought of it beforehand. Taking Shela out was definitely a way to limit me, and even my own god wanted her out of my life.

"Someone is going to die for this," I swore again, my steel heels clanking on the cabin's floor boards. I'd put my armor on the moment I got back onboard.

"Strike out against the Trenboni and I promise you that your wife will die before you accomplish anything," Ancenon informed me. He sat on a padded stool in a dark corner of the cabin away from the door. "Angron Aurelias is no fool, Black Lupus. If there isn't a warrior with a knife at Shela's throat at all times, then it's because they thought ahead and rigged a whole portion of the royal dungeons to fall on her in a moment's notice.

"You are no stranger here, and there are no doubts as to your wrath."

Yeah, that all served me *real* well, I thought to myself.

I'd left these people nowhere to go and a lot to fear about me. I'd kept throwing their own rules back in their faces and never guessed that they'd just start ignoring them. Kick a man who's down enough times, and if it doesn't kill him, he'll get back up no matter what the odds.

"Lupus?" a Wolf Soldier guard said, poking his head in through the cabin's door.

"What?" I snapped at him.

"A Scitai to see you," he said.

I half expected it to be Xinto, but the woman who walked in had red hair and a white blouse and black skirt with a rapier at her hip. She looked up at me with sea-green eyes and I thought immediately of Genna.

Genna would be loving this.

"Lupus the Conqueror?" the woman asked me, looking up from less than three feet of height.

"One name for me," I said. "Who the hell are you?"

She smiled a wicked smile. "She's Tara the Red," Ancenon informed me, not rising. "A pirate on the Forgotten Seas. She's a friend of Karel of Stone's."

"Well, more than a friend," she informed us. She sauntered in and leapt up on a cot next to Ancenon, casually brushing her rapier out of her way. She turned and regarded me, looking me up and down like a stallion she might put down a bid on.

"Karel had a big opinion of you," she informed me. "I don't see it."

"You're probably not as smart as he is, then," I informed her. I usually liked banter like this, but I usually wasn't worrying that my wife was being tortured. "Maybe I should send you back to him in pieces?"

That got a wide-eyed look from her. She wasn't intimidated, though – had to give her that. She kicked her feet, looked away from me and then looked back.

"Just business, then?" she asked me.

"Probably safer for both of us, yes," I said.

"Very well," she said, then looked to Ancenon, and then to me. "You both know that the Uman-Chi have her locked up tight and naked in a cell in the deepest part of their dungeons, with a dozen wards on her and a few hundred guards, as well as a bunch of other crap that would take too long to tell you about."

"You heard this?" I asked her.

"I saw it myself," she answered. "Wasn't easy, either. They're working with the Bounty Hunter's Guild, and those people aren't stupid. If you're working your courage up to go take your woman back, then you're wasting your time because you're not getting in there, and she's not getting out."

I felt this overwhelming urge to strangle the life out of the little red-head but I suppressed it. I'd let myself get caught, that wasn't her fault. The Uman-Chi were taking no chances, and that wasn't her fault, either.

"They'll charge her tomorrow," Tara continued on. "A lot more guards, a lot fewer wards. They won't parade her out of there naked, and a sorceress can make a spell out of anything, at least a good one can, and I'm told she's very good."

"So you think I should take her back tomorrow before they have time –" I began.

"Oh, no, no, no!" she said, waving her hands in front of her. "That's what they want you to do – that's what they're counting on. Then they can swoop in and destroy these ships of yours, which they're afraid of, and then they can let the Bounty Hunters pile on you, who're they're even more afraid of.

"No, Lupus the Conqueror," the little Scitai woman informed me. "You do *not* want to rescue her tomorrow. You don't want to even be here tomorrow. You don't want to be here *now*."

"What?" I demanded of her, pacing the cabin and throwing up my hands. "I should leave her? More fish in the sea? More Andarons where that one came from? Get on with my life?"

"Are you asking me?" Tara asked, her eyes wide. "Because I have to tell you, in my experience, that's what males do, especially the powerful ones."

I turned before I realized it and took either side of the outer rail of the cot she sat on in hand, and placed my face about an inch from hers. She had a dagger out at my throat but I didn't care.

"Well I'm not like that, and if I have to die to save her, than plan the funeral because I guess I'm going to die," I informed her.

Even as I said the words, I realized that this would make Lee an orphan, and there was no way to guarantee her life without me. The dynasty was too new – I didn't have enough allies who'd pledge themselves to her wellbeing.

I stood, and I felt my eyes well up. This was all out of hand. I'd pushed too far, too fast, and I might now pay for it, but my girls might.

"Looked to me like your girl friend has been putting on some weight," Tara informed me.

I turned back to face her. I saw Ancenon straighten. "What?"

"A little swelly in the belly?" Tara said, grinning. "Getting ready for a weight gain, then a sudden loss?"

"She's pregnant," I said, wondering where she was going with this.

"Oh," Ancenon said, and then grinned wide.

"What?" I demanded.

Ancenon looked sideways at Tara and then back at me. "A woman with child is sacrosanct among my people," he said. "No matter her crimes, she cannot be convicted, she cannot even be tried while pregnant. She'll be charged tomorrow, but then she'll declare herself or be found pregnant, and she'll be tended properly in her cell for the duration of her pregnancy."

"And then they'll find her guilty and they'll kill her in one day, don't be mistaken," Tara said. "But they'll even send you back your child, male or female. A child is an innocent to the Uman-Chi."

I remembered the stone statue I'd received from Aniquen the Uman-Chi, so many months ago. It was still in Lee's bedroom. She'd dressed it up in her clothes once.

"So no matter what, she's safe for about seven months," I said.

They both nodded.

"Hmmmm," I said, nodding with them.

"Seven months is a long time."

Chapter Twenty-Four

Pretty Much Why No One Likes Me

A week later I was back in Eldador the Port. People found out Shela wasn't with me, and they were pissed.

Apparently the palace staff really loved her. The common people did, too. I actually had a common woman, an old, Uman great-grandmother with a flock of children in tow, pushed her way past my Wolf Soldier guards to throw her hands around my shoulders and weep against my breast when I went out to the common market on the day before All Gods' Day.

"You get them, your Majesty," she said to me, looking up into my face through teary eyes. "You get them–you get them all for this. Eveave will forgive you–she's a mother, too."

I thanked her and pressed a couple gold Tabaars into her hands. Seeing as the Wolf Soldiers were about to brain her and I actually had to hand-signal them not to, she made out better than she could have imagined. Other commons called out from beyond the Wolf Soldier guards, "Adriam be with you, your Majesty," and "We're praying for you." I nodded and waved, and then called the Wolf Soldier sergeant to my side.

"You know the Bounty Hunters' Guild are after me, right?" I asked him, a big, rough Volkhydran named Erok whom I'd recruited after the Battle of Tamaran Glen.

"My apologies, Lupus," he said. "She moved too fast–"

I caught his eye. "Too fast? She had to weigh as much as I do, and she's five feet tall. If she's too fast for you, maybe you're in the wrong job,"

"It won't happen again," he promised me.

Another person in his guard, a busty Uman woman with dark hair, cut short, named D'leer, was shaking her head. She stopped when I caught her doing it.

"You," I said, pointing to her. I remembered her–a Trenboni whore who'd stabbed a noble. "Think you can do a better job?"

She looked me right in the eye. "Yep," she informed me.

I nodded. "You're sergeant now. You," I said to Erok, "are reassigned to the barracks. Send someone there to replace you here. You can keep your rank–for now."

D'leer was grinning fiercely. "Don't let it go to your head," I informed her. "Screw up and I'll demote you to the Regulars."

Both Wolf Soldiers made a fist over their hands in salute to me. The other Wolf Soldiers in my personal guard were shooting glances between each other and at D'leer. She'd make her way and earn their respect, or she wouldn't–that's how things worked in the Pack.

That's how things worked in life, or so I was learning.

A couple years ago I'd been in the market place of Eldador the Port on the day before All Gods' Day, and it had been practically deserted. Now I came here and it was packed–people from all nations trading goods that once had rarely been seen in this part of Fovea. Winter crops from southern Toor, steel from Volkhydro, winter wheat from Sental.

And horses from Andoron, because Eldador had a huge appetite for horses. I found these traders, city men from Talen, staring daggers at me because they knew what I'd done in their southern nation.

I walked right up to them, my Wolf Soldiers lined up behind me.

One inclined his head, dressed in his native leathers with beads sewn into the cuffs and shoulders.

"Your Majesty," he said to me, spitting out the words.

"You know what's happened to Shela, my woman?" I asked him in Andaron.

"I know what happened to her, because of her association with you," he informed me. "Don't think you have allies here, White Wolf, because the Uman-Chi took your slave."

"That slave would be my wife," I informed him. I tried to look him in the eye but he wouldn't have it. "That woman bears my child in her belly."

"More a comment on you," another of the Andaron traders informed me. They kept a small corral with a few mares in it–solid and large, the makings of a draft breed which the Andarons would have little use for, but which Eldadorian farms would want.

There were five of them, and I had all of their attention now. City dwellers in Andoron tended to keep clean faces, and these had no mustachios like Two Spears.

"Those children are going to be raised by me," I informed them all. "No matter what happens to Shela, the children will have an Andaron mother and live with me."

"So?" the first one demanded. He didn't like me–I couldn't blame him.

I inhaled and sighed. I didn't know if I was giving up something here, because I knew my wife and I knew her beliefs, however most people, especially most Andarons, didn't know how deeply I regarded her.

"Those children can be raised in the Andaron tradition," I said. "They can be raised to consider themselves Andaron, not Eldadorian."

The traders regarded me, then exchanged glances with each other. Using merchants to pass messages wasn't uncommon in Earth's Middle Ages and according to my Oligarchs it was pretty normal here.

"A son will rule Eldador one day," I said them. "An Eldadorian Emperor who considers himself an Andaron would be a useful ally."

"Emperor?" one asked.

"Pass the word," I informed them all, looking from face to face. "All I want any Andaron to do is nothing. I can take care of my own, but not if I'm fending off the tribes."

"You have more to worry about than Andoron," the second one informed me. Another reason people used merchants as emissaries–they tended to hear a lot, so they tended to know a lot more than anyone would think.

"I can deal with the rest of Fovea," I informed him.

"Pass my word on to Andoron."

They all nodded. I turned on my heel and I walked away.

One down and a lot to go.

***

J'her met with me on the morning of All Gods' Day. I was sitting alone with Lee in the dining room, probably to the anger of a lot of hungry palace barons and three needy Oligarchs. The fourth (or, actually, the second–already forgot his name) had left for Angador with Tartan. J'her just sauntered in with a Wolf Soldier squad in attendance of him, walked the length of the dining hall on the window side and pulled out a chair for himself.

"Unca Chair!" Lee said to him, smiling wide. He reached out, grabbed her nose and shook it.

From a corner of the room behind both of us, Nina of the Aschire arched an already-arched eyebrow but said nothing. Shela's loss had hit her hard, but she hadn't been talking about it. Instead she'd clamped down on Lee's security. Even Wolf Soldiers couldn't get near her without Nina wanting to back them off.

She also always carried a dagger on each thigh now. Karel had shown her how to use them and from what I'd heard the lessons had been a rousing success.

Lee was working on some porridge with an oversized wooden spoon, and went back to it. I had ham and eggs sitting in front of me but they tasted like wax. This was yet another morning when I would have liked a cup of coffee.

J'her seated himself. "Hectar has been asking me if it's safe to approach you yet," he said.

"Told him, 'No'?" I asked, not looking at the Uman.

His mouth curled into a smile below his aquiline nose. "Yeah," he said. "I told him to try tomorrow. Holy days are hard when you lose someone."

"I have to remind myself you know that better than I," I informed him.

J'her had lost his whole family when Rennin had taken his land.

"I also need you today, and I know you don't want to talk about your new ships in front of Rennin yet."

"And?" I said to him. Like he said–holy days are harder when your wife is missing.

"And we can have about thirty of them ready by the War months," he informed me. "That involves the ports in Andurin, Eldador and Thera. You're going to have to go visit Groff yourself, though, and explain to him what's going on."

"What have you had to tell him?" I asked.

"I haven't told him anything," J'her said. A serving girl had come in and set a tray down before him with food like mine. He drank some of the tea and made a face.

"How do you drink that?" he asked me.

"You get used to it," I informed him. He was already on my nerves and J'her practically never got on my nerves. Lee banged her wooden spoon on the table in front of her, and I reached out and put two fingers on her wrist to quiet her.

"A two year old is a ruler," J'her said, smiling at Lee. It was something locals said, like I'd said, "Terrible two's."

I sighed.

"Two Spears was speaking with Groff," J'her said, mercifully. "Groff wants to rent his wharf space, but he doesn't like not knowing what's going on. Two Spears would just do that thing he does where he makes you laugh at your own worries. I can't do that."

"I can't do that either," I said. Not that I'd want to. "I'll have to tell him what's going on."

"You should talk to Hectar first," J'her said, "or, better, bring Hectar with you when you see him. Groff doesn't like things to change, and this is a lot of change."

I nodded.

"Dispatch a troop of Eldadorian Regulars to the Aschire forest, to Duke Krell," I told him.

"Eldadorian Regulars don't answer to me," J'her informed me.

"Just pass the word for me," I told him. "Tell Daggonin to pick the warriors – he's a junior officer in the Regulars. Have him see me before he sends them and I'll have a message for them to bring."

J'her shrugged.

"That all?" I asked him.

J'her regarded me with a raised eyebrow. "I guess so," he said. "Am I dismissed?"

J'her had a relationship with me as the second in command of the Wolf Soldier guard. He considered me a friend as well as a leader. He didn't answer to me as the King or Emperor of Eldador. He answered to me as a man.

I owed him better than to just dismiss him. I needed J'her. I'd been doing too much on my own, and J'her was one of the people who could be trusted to help.

I needed to pull my shit together, get focused and do what I had to do to get my woman back; I knew it and I believed it.

"Yeah," I said. "You're dismissed."

He stood and made a fist over his heart in salute to me. He turned on his heel and he left.

It was starting to come apart. I was watching it happen. They'd taken Shela from me, and it rattled me.

I was starting to think I knew how Glennen felt, and I didn't want to know that much about those feelings at all.

All Gods' Day passed. When I slept, I kept Lee in her bassinette in the corner of my room, and Nina made her usual nest of pillows on some part of my bed. If a servant came in, as they did during the night, she was always awake with a dagger in her hand before I was roused at all.

I wasn't drinking anything but milk and water because the thought of Glennen's fate terrified me. I was waiting for War's booming voice to show up in my head to tell me to go get another woman, and I was dreading it.

However I handled this had to ameliorate War as well as get Shela back. I'd noted I'd started thinking that way, anyway.

When you know your own god's will, you start to act the way He wants you to feel as if that's the way you want to be. You also start caring a lot less about whom it hurts. I could argue there was probably a diplomatic solution to the situation with Trenbon, and in fact that's what they likely wanted from me. They were already getting their city rebuilt–they probably wanted reparations from me, or some sort of trade consideration.

Uman-Chi don't think of short term gain – I'd made that observation a dozen times. In the long term, they were going to outlive me. They might only ask that I pick someone beside Lee to succeed me when my reign ended.

That wasn't going to make War happy, and it wasn't going to make me feel any better. I didn't just need Shela back, I needed to make it clear that doing this to me was a really *bad* idea.

I thought about this on the first day of the month of Adriam, sitting the throne, listening to another Baron begging for money from the state. His name was Jahon, and he ruled the peninsula of Britt, which extended from Eldador the Port out onto Tren Bay. He was a thin, angular man who dressed in light blue tunic and hose, with brown boots that wrinkled on his legs and his long, brown hair actually hanging in a pony tail over one shoulder. His brown eyes searched whatever he looked at, myself included. He'd been on a battlefield, I thought, and it hadn't gone well for him.

I had information this man was in communication with the Dorkans. We'd been suspicious of him since the coronation, and Karel had informed me that, yes, he'd been talking to Dorkans through intermediaries.

"And so," he informed me, "with the generosity of the Kingdom, I believe I can return two-fold your very short-term investment."

"Of the Kingdom," I parroted him. I stroked my chin, felt the stubble. "Tell me, Baron. Which Kingdom is that?"

He blinked. "My – my Lord, your Majesty?"

I leaned forward. "Which Kingdom?" I asked him again. "Would that be my Kingdom, Eldador, or would that be the Dorkan nation and whatever passes for leadership there?"

His eyes shifted to the left and right, as if he thought there were Wolf Soldier guards sneaking up on him, or some ally who would set this right. "The Dorkans, your Majesty?" he asked.

I leaned back, felt the stone throne behind me against my shoulders. "Well," I said to him, "you do entertain a lot of Dorkan emissaries, after all."

"Is this forbidden?" he asked me. I found myself frowning before I realized it. I definitely didn't expect this tack from him.

"Speaking with enemies of the Eldadorian state, members of other nations seeking against Us before the Fovean High Council?" I asked him. "Well, perhaps more inadvisable than illegal."

His back straightened. "King Glennen allowed us to speak with whom we would, your Majesty," he informed me.

"I see," I said. That came across as a slap to me, kind of like a kid saying to his mother's new husband, "My real dad lets me do it."

"Well," I continued, "I can certainly send you to a place where you can answer to him."

His eyes widened. I think right then he might have realized what he'd said to me.

"Your Majesty, I meant no offense," he said.

"I wonder what you might have said, had you meant to offend me," I said.

"My apologies, of course, your Majesty," he said, lowering his head. His brown eyes found mine for a moment, then the floor.

If I went killing or demoting my barons, I'd alienate the ones I left standing. I'd already suffered unanticipated consequences with Yerel in Uman City. I didn't want to double-down on that.

At the same time, I had to let it be known that this sort of behavior wasn't tolerable.

"If you prefer their company, then you might as well be useful to the state," I said to him, steepling my fingers before me. He raised his head and straightened again, searching my face. "Eldador needs an ambassador to Dorkan, I'm naming you."

He smiled and bowed to me. "Your Majesty," he said.

Got you, you son of a bitch, I thought.

"In your absence, I'll appoint a baron of the court to manage your estates," I informed him. "He will maintain no title, merely ensure your properties are maintained and your subjects cared for in your absence."

He went back to searching my face. "Your Majesty is too kind," he informed me.

"Tom Kalgan, a bounty hunter and friend of the court, shall be assigned to you for your protection," I informed him, finally. "Your person is too valuable to jeopardize."

He didn't respond to that. I think he realized at this point that he'd stepped in something, and he didn't realize what.

"You shall leave with the morning tide on one of our new Sea Wolves," I informed him.

"Leave…in the morning, your Majesty?"

"There is no time to waste," I informed him. I also wasn't planning to give him time to get his affairs in order. I wanted him to have time to get off some emergency messages and that's all.

In fact, I was counting on those messages.

His ship set sail on the second day of Adriam, in the 83rd year of the Fovean High Council, with a minimum crew which included the Wolf Soldier guard whom I'd demoted from my personal squads in favor of D'leer.

I received news a week later it had been sunk trying to cross the Straights of Deception by the Dorkans. They'd gotten their confidence back now that I was in hot water with the Fovean High Council.

So at least that went according to plan.

Chapter Twenty-Five

Getting Back to Business

There's a purpose to a fleet having a flagship. It's a point of pride to the fleet. It establishes the idea that 'this is the best,' that there's a standard among the sailors, that it can be aspired to, and it can be rewarded by performing one's duties among others who excel.

The flagship of the Eldadorian fleet had been just another ship. Now it was three-master 250 feet long and a width just under fifty feet. Other Sea Wolves had copper pressed into their sides to make them more limber in combat with clinker-built one-masters which were the standard on Tren Bay and the Forgotten Sea. These were ships in the fashion of ancient Greek triremes and Viking raiders; mine were patterned after the USS Constitution, a heavy frigate which sported as many as 50 guns, except mine had a thin sheet of steel coated with tar that crossed her waterline on either side.

She didn't have 32 pounders like an early American frigate, but in fact she had other things going for her. In fact, ol' Ironsides didn't have iron sides–copper sheathing was used to prevent 'shipworm,' or water born creatures like barnacles boring into her wooden hull. Doing the same thing with iron was actually quite a trick, but ships rammed each other here and I wanted more than average protection from it.

They didn't break a bottle of Champagne over the bow of new ships here. Volkhydrans would sometimes drag a Confluni from the stern of a new ship until he drowned, but I had enough troubles.

Two weeks into the month of Adriam she slid into the ice-cold waves of Tren Bay, under the name I'd picked out personally for her, "*The Bitch of Eldador*."

"Is that in fact a wise name?" D'gattis asked me, standing next to me on the pier she slipped from.

Ancenon and Dilvesh stood next to him. On my other side Avek Noir and his new pal, Aniquen, were in attendance, along with a troop of Trenboni Uman who'd come to talk to me about my pregnant wife.

"I think it is," I informed him. I had fifty Wolf Soldier guards, a couple Dorkan Wizards from the Wolf Soldiers, and Hectar with me.

They'd wanted to come see me in the royal court but I wasn't having it. Not if they were sending frigging Aniquen again.

The ship hit the water with a splash, only the mains'l and the jib unfurled. She flew the Eldadorian flag, white stripes on a green background, over my Wolf's Head on her main mast.

"I'm surprised it floats," Aniquen commented as it drifted into the open bay. Her captain could be heard shouting orders to the crew, to unfurl more sail and turn the rudder. She was already moving to port.

"I bet you are," I said to the open air without looking at him.

The Uman-Chi were here to ask for whatever they wanted from me to give me back my woman alive. They were well aware of the loss of one of these ships already, as well as my Dorkan Ambassador. If I'd whacked Jahon it would have weighed against me, if the Dorkans did it, after the Baron I'd sent to his properties started gossiping about all of the gold coins minted in Dorkan that he'd found there, then it served as a statement that there was no reward there.

The Uman-Chi tended to be very sensitive about sea power or, more to the point, bay power. Their spies were also probably better or at least as good as mine. They knew what I was doing on the Black Lake, they knew about the shipyards cranking out these ships.

I hoped they didn't know the ship that had been sunk was one of the prototypes from the Black Lake that had mast problems. I didn't like sending men and women to their deaths, but warriors die some times.

"I sense strong magic in this vessel," Aniquen continued. "You must miss your woman sorely."

I turned and looked into his silver-on-silver eyes.

"You must want another ass-whipping," I informed him.

"Then you admit to a first?" he countered.

"A first what?" I countered. "I referred to the one handed to you by the Dorkans. Are you saying you lied about that?"

He smiled the kind of smile that cocky, young guys have when they think they have a handle on the world.

I laid my hand on the pommel of the Sword of War at my hip.

Avek reached out and laid his own hand on my shoulder. "I think violence against an emissary and a favorite of the King who holds your wife is inadvisable, your Majesty," he said.

"Bringing this clown here was an even bigger mistake," I informed him. "I think he needs to go home in a box."

"What silliness is this?" Aniquen demanded. "You would bolt me into some crate? To what end?"

"He means that he'd like to kill you, young Aniquen," D'gattis informed him with a sigh. "By the way you're baiting him; I'm surprised he's not done so already. He's not notoriously even-tempered, and we do hold the woman he loves."

"To that end," Avek said, "we can negotiate the conditions of her return."

The *Bitch* dropped another sail, and the warship picked up some speed, moving past our wharves and toward the breakwater. From there she'd enter the open bay for her maiden voyage.

I'd have loved to have been on her, but there was simply too much to do.

"Which are?" I asked him, turning my body to face him.

"Your *Majesty*," Hectaro exclaimed. The idea of negotiating with someone who'd taken custody of my woman spoke of weakness. Arguably, the idea they'd come to me when they held what should have been considered a very strong hand tended to say they were the ones with something to fear, but I didn't need to dwell on that.

I wanted my wife back.

"First of all, the production of these ships must cease," Avek said. "Trenbon is the sea power on Tren Bay. We will brook no challenge to that claim."

"Not that this pittance of ships could accomplish that," Aniquen added.

"And?" I asked Avek, ignoring the other. I caught Ancenon leaning forward to whisper into the younger Uman-Chi's ear as Avek continued.

"Damages by the Eldadorian state must be acknowledged and, of course, paid for," Avek said.

"I thought they were being paid for?" I said to him.

I'd set Avek up with the gold being used to fix the damage done to Outpost IX. In return, he was essentially my man by sacred oath. This had gotten him the title of Heir to the Trenboni throne, displacing Ancenon, my ally.

I'd be more than surprised if anyone important among the Uman-Chi wasn't fully aware of that by now.

"Paid for by the Eldadorian state," Avek corrected me.

"For the unprovoked attack on Outpost IX," Aniquen added.

The back of my hand against the side of Aniquen's head made a hollow sound. With close to a one hundred pound weight advantage on him, I actually knocked him off of his feet before he hit the ground.

The Uman-Chi remained stone-faced in their white robes. Dilvesh knelt at the Uman-Chi's side. His pressed a hand to the side of the fallen man's head, and then that head glowed white.

Aniquen moaned. Dilvesh stood.

"You nearly killed him," he informed me, looking into my eyes. A fine sheen of sweat glistened on his forehead in the cold air, under his mop of curly green hair.

"Maybe next time," I said. I turned to Avek.

"What else?" I asked him.

"Perhaps we should convene when you are less distressed," he offered.

"Not going to happen," I told him. "What else?"

"Your Majesty…" he said.

"I'm not asking again, Avek," I informed him.

I should have called him, "Highness." Uman-Chi hang on protocols. Avek knew me well enough where he knew that I knew better.

"Very well," he said, "we shall foster your first son."

That actually made me take a step back.

"It is an honor," Ancenon informed me. "Fovean royals have in the past paid a warrior's weight in gold for their children—"

He went on, but I wasn't listening to him. I couldn't. They wanted to get their hands on one of my kids. They wanted to do that so they could influence how he was raised. They figured that, if they couldn't get to me, they'd settle for one of mine.

"You were wise to bring D'gattis and Ancenon," I informed Avek, interrupting my Free Legion ally.

"And why is that, your Majesty," Avek answered me.

"Because you will be leaving here alive," I said, looking Avek right in the eyes.

I wouldn't do anything to Avek, and he knew it. I also knew this wasn't his idea. He acted as the Heir, reflecting the will of his King, whether he agreed with it or not. I'd actually had to do this, and Avek's King wasn't a drunk, he was a genius, and I had to imagine he kept a tighter rein on his Heir.

Still, Avek straightened.

"You have until the commencement of her trial," he informed me, as stiff as I'd ever seen an Uman-Chi. "That trial will not last long. Once begun, I have to believe that, with the overwhelming evidence against her, your woman will be found guilty and punished for her actions against Trenbon and the crown. From there we shall brook no negotiation."

I nodded. "You can find your way back to your ship?" I asked him.

He nodded.

I turned and left, my Duke, my warriors and Dilvesh with me.

***

The next day I was at what I was calling 'my lab' in the tunnels beneath the Eldadorian palace. I'd developed my laughing gas here, as well as the centrifuge where I'd spun my first copper pipe. That was done at a factory now, and that factory used a steam engine to drive its spinning parts.

I kept a smaller one down here, powered by coal. A dwarf had cut the ventilation for the place so the fumes didn't kill me. People who warmed themselves with wood stoves and who lived underground were experts in carbon monoxide.

Dilvesh was here with me, along with D'gattis and Ancenon, J'her and Hectar. I had several vats here with different stuff in them. One which was stinking up the place was crude oil, alongside a container of apatite, another of sulfur and vat of common pine resin.

"Are you going to make more people laugh?" D'gattis asked me.

"After his behavior for the Heir, that would be a feat of magic past his wife's capabilities," Ancenon commented.

"Don't start him swinging his fists again," Dilvesh warned. "That healing was draining."

"In fact, I thought poor Aniquen dead," Ancenon said.

"As did I," said Hectar.

"Not that the boy didn't deserve his treatment," D'gattis said, "but in fact he is the King's favorite among the gifted."

"He acts like it," I said, "and no, this isn't going to make anyone laugh."

"Perhaps gag," Dilvesh said, indicating the pot of crude oil. "What is that vile stuff?"

"Naptha," Hectar said. "It is commonly used in warfare."

The ancients of my own world called petroleum 'naptha.' I actually hadn't pieced that together until I got a look at it here at the black lake. Now we had something very close to an oil derrick pumping the stuff from around the black lake and shipping it here.

"And this other material?" D'gattis asked me, plucking a green and white lump of apatite from the black steel canister that held it.

"Common rock among your people," I said. "I intend to smash some of them and use the white powder, but after I smash one of them, I need to heat it."

"And for this you need us?" Ancenon asked me.

I reached out my hand to D'gattis for the lump of apatite and he handed it to me. On my planet it wasn't common and wasn't rare. Here they tended to find lots of it near their best iron mines. The stuff was streaked with white and was sometimes used for cheap jewelry.

It was rich in phosphorous. I needed it for that.

"There's an element in this I want to make exceptionally hot," I said. "Once it's that hot, hot enough to make it into a gas, I need to keep it like that and pump it through that naptha. Then I need to combine the naptha with the other elements here, and contain it in cast iron containers which I can make air tight."

Ancenon looked at me skeptically. "Why?" he asked me.

I took a moment. Hectar walked to the vat of sulfur and poked at it.

"This burns, you know," he said absently.

"Yes," I said. "I know."

"The poor will sometimes use it, but it stinks. We call it dragon's breath."

That seemed appropriate.

"I've shown you chemistry a few times," I said to them.

They all nodded. Hectar moved to the other vats and canisters.

"I'm going to make a liquid developed by a people we called 'the Byzantines'," I said. "They could use this to defend themselves."

"I'd think the stink of it alone would keep enemies away," D'gattis said to me.

"Something like that," I said.

"And you'll show us how to use this *chem-stree*," Dilvesh asked me.

I didn't want to do that. It was more than just the idea of only me having it – this stuff was dangerous as hell to make or even to handle, and when the Byzantines used it they took themselves out as often as they got their enemies.

At the same time, once word got around that they had it; their enemies would retreat if they even saw sign of it. Their secret of it died, and their empire died soon after.

In fact, I was pretty sure I knew how to make it, and I was pretty sure other people did as well. Once you figured it out, it wasn't the kind of thing you shared, because you could take out a battleship with enough of the stuff.

"I will share it with you as my allies," I said, "if you will promise not to try to make it on your own, from what I tell you."

"Because you don't want to face it," D'gattis conjectured.

"Because you don't want to live in a world where the secret of this is out," I said. "If just anyone could do what we're about to do, well–you know how you don't want to teach the barely gifted serious magic?"

"Yes," D'gattis said.

"Imagine if everyone were barely gifted," I said, "and imagine them all trying to use their gifts whenever the mood struck them, every time something didn't go their way."

Things progressed quietly from there.

***

On the first day of Eveave, while sitting my throne in the now-imperial throne room during court, explaining to a few collected Earls what it meant now that we were an Empire, I was informed by the captain of the Wolf Soldier guard they'd caught a bounty hunter trying to get at Lee. He wanted to take me with his squad of Wolf Soldiers to where they'd hidden her, and I nearly went with them. J'her had intervened with fifty Wolf Soldiers of his own and after a bloodbath in the throne room that got about thirty people killed, in addition to three of my Earls, I found out that, in fact, these Wolf Soldiers were the bounty hunters and they'd wanted to take me to one side and assassinate me.

As this was going on, another bounty hunter actually did go after Lee, and Nina took him out. Not bad for a girl pushing eleven years old – she'd used a spell to slow him down and then stabbed him with her daggers.

That night another Bounty Hunter tried to climb into my room through the open window and Karel of Stone had taken him out from the roof of one of the other towers in the palace. I had no idea what he was doing there and, when he didn't want to tell me, I had a really hard time pressing the issue.

The Bounty Hunters' Guild had claimed the only reason they couldn't get at me was because of Shela. In fact, I had more allies than that. For me to say I was in so far over my head I could only dream of the sky was an understatement. There were a lot of people keeping me alive, and I was having a harder and harder time justifying why they were doing it.

So in the middle of Eveave, leaving Hectar behind me and taking Dilvesh and a thousand Wolf Soldiers with me, I jumped up on Blizzard's back and rode out toward Andurin, via the new city of Metz. I left Lee and Nina under Hectar and Karel's care, and actually prayed to War for their safety.

My god had been oddly silent. I had to think the crap I pulled was exactly what he expected of me, or he needed to see me humbled. I could believe either one at this point.

Blizzard hadn't gotten a good ride for too long and he was almost unmanageable now. I had to break away from the main army a few times and just let him cut loose, which really freaked out the Wolf Soldier guard, but there was nothing for it. Pounding the earth on my giant stallion did a lot to clear my head and resurrect my thinking, and I know he enjoyed it.

On the sixth day of the month of Weather we rode in to Andurin at the head of a full millennium of Wolf Soldiers, Arath and Nantar beside me and Dilvesh left behind at Metz. I wasn't surprised to learn a Druid could really speed the construction of a city, and I leant the Free Legion some of my more experienced Uman cutters, trained by Dwarves. The former were fully engaged in the construction of Wisex now, and a report by fast ships and then fast riders let me know that, since I'd spoken with the Andaron merchants four months ago. Of course, the report was a month old, and the message couldn't have been delivered before the middle of Adriam's month, so in fact Wisex could be a pile of smoking bodies and I wouldn't know any better right now, however one did what one could with the tools one has.

In the here and now, a mile from the gates of Andurin, Groff met me with none other than Ceberro on horseback and a retinue of one hundred Eldadorian Regulars. Kind of large for a personal guard and pathetically small to stand up to one thousand Wolf Soldiers, however I wasn't here to depose him and, if he didn't know that, I didn't know Groff.

Ceberro's presence was anyone's guess. The Duke eyed me from the back of a white stallion about a hand shorter than mine. It snorted and pawed the earth on sight of mine, but that wasn't uncommon. Blizzard, being Blizzard, ignored him.

"Your Grace," I said, and nodded to Groff, then turned to Ceberro. "Your Grace," I said again.

"Your Imperial Majesty," Groff said to me – the first one, actually. Ceberro grinned what I almost wanted to call evilly and repeated the title, bowing in the saddle.

"Word precedes me," I said to them. Nantar chuckled at my side.

"Earl Arath of Metz!" Groff said, a grin splitting the narrow features of his face. "I was not expecting you! How goes our latest stronghold."

"Better now," Arath said, looking sideways at me. "I've gained a Druid and a dozen Dwarf-trained Uman. My city could be habitable in two years."

"So soon!" Ceberro exclaimed. "Angador under young Tartan won't have more than a garrison for three more years."

Arath turned to me. "I could part with the Uman if they train more like themselves. Maybe…six months?"

"Do it," I said, then turned to Groff. "You should send your own men as well to learn from them."

"Your Imperial Majesty is ever gracious with his knowledge," the Duke said. "In keeping with that, I welcome you and your... significant military might to my humble city."

I smiled. "These warriors are here to take command of the Sea Wolves under construction in your wharves," I said. "A few of them are what I call Construction Builders, or Sea Bees, and will spend their time under your command, building a steam plant."

"We've heard of this magic," Ceberro said. The sun glistened on his bald scalp. His helmet had been clipped to his belt and he wore his armor tight in the warming spring day. "You've trained your own warriors to work it?"

"It isn't–" I began, but really, what's the point? They were convinced this was magic and they weren't going to understand it any other way.

"It's what you call, 'chem-stree,'" I said. "Apply heat to water and you can do a lot of things with it."

"Like make tea," Groff said, nodding.

"Like make tea," I agreed. "When you're ready, I am."

Groff eyed the Millennium behind me. "I'm not sure–well, I mean, your Imperial Majesty..."

That was as nervous as I'd ever seen the Duke. Hospitality was taken very seriously by Eldadorian nobles–you were never supposed to be unable to put up someone from the peerage. I got my first Earldom because of that.

"These warriors need to toughen up," I said. I turned to Nantar. "Scarlet Nantar, would you take command and have this Millennium construct our 'small city' on the plains, a safe distance from the city."

"Good luck," Ceberro said. I turned to him, as did everyone else. "The moment the commons see the famous Wolf Soldiers, they'll flock to your barricades."

Groff agreed with a wince. "It's true, your Imperial Majesty," he said. "People are bored at the end of the winter months. With the first plantings still weeks away, they'll come running to see Wolf Soldiers."

"A series of parades, then?" Arath suggested. "Perhaps some war games?"

"I could have my Sarandi here in a week," Nantar drawled, a smile curling under his beard.

Nantar had become very proud of his own elite troops, and he was dying to match them against mine.

Normally I'd be itching to do the same, but there just wasn't time. "The parades are a good idea," I said, "but the Sea Bees have work to do and the rest will be supporting them. As well, we're going to be outfitting ships.

"Next time," Nantar assured me. He'd learned that expression from me.

He pulled the reins on his horse and gave her a kick, and he was off to the Major in charge of the Millennium. Groff and Ceberro turned their horses around and his Regulars lined up around us.

We marched into the city, to an actual cheering crowd. Blizzard started picking up his hooves as if he knew what was going on. A few threw spring flowers or bits of parchment with 'He Conquers!' written on them, and those who could get close enough, which were surprisingly many, rapped our armor with a closed fist.

A Bounty Hunter didn't try to kill me, so I guess that's good news.

Chapter Twenty-Six

Negotiations

Groff's throne room looked a lot like my own, meaning it looked like any other throne room on Fovea, as the Cheyak had designed them more than a thousand years before.

A long hall, a gallery on the right hand side, an elevated throne at one end and double doors bound in brass on the other with a deep, blue carpet running down the center. His floor was some kind of polished granite which looked really nice but was hard to walk across without slipping, and the pillars running down the center alongside the carpet were plain, not groaning Dwarves like mine.

Where I had a platform to one side for my Oligarchs, he had one for his son and Alekennen, who was already married to Groff's son.

"Well, look at this young lady!" I said as I greeted her. She did a perfect curtsy and then took the back of my hand in hers and kissed it. I'd never seen anyone do that before. She pressed the back of my hand to her cheek and looked into my eyes.

"A nation grieves that you are separated from your Shela, your Imperial Majesty," she informed me. "Your love for her is the stuff of legends, of songs."

Groff ran a much more formal court than mine. It was rubbing off on Alekennen already. I'd worry for her except for the look in her husband's eyes when they followed her. Young love is unmistakable, and he wasn't trying to hide it. Groff saw me watching them and smiled but didn't say anything.

The Lady Jameen sat in attendance in the gallery, her eyes never leaving Ceberro. I didn't see Shellene anywhere, but then again that didn't mean she wasn't here.

Groff conducted a long, droning court. Every single decree was a speech, every single question took minutes to ask and longer to answer. A few of the plaintiffs seeking either justice or favors looked furtively to me, but probably because they knew I was richer.

It took all morning and a good part of the afternoon. From there we went to an early meal because we were all starving. After feeding mostly on preserved fruits and vegetables and fish, we finally convened in Groff's approximation of my war room.

He'd picked a round room, not rectangular. He'd lined the walls with cork and then covered the cork with black slate chalk boards like mine, as well. He'd set a main and a subsidiary table, and his idea was that idea began at the subsidiary table and could be percolated up to the main table.

Wow. I was surprised once again this guy didn't click when he walked. He'd never met a bureaucracy he didn't embrace.

We sat down on our second day here with Nantar and Arath, Groff and his son, and Ceberro, all crowded around the main table, with no one at the second table. A map was held down with weights on the corners in front of us, facing Groff. I sat opposite him.

"We convene this meeting in order that we might discuss the advance and the activities of his Imperial Majesty's projects in our wharves," Groff began, looking one after the other of us in the eye.

Ceberro grinned a wry grin and caught my eyes with his. I felt my scar twitch. If he was going to go on like this, Groff was going to drive me crazy and I think the other Duke knew it. Arath sighed and leaned back in his chair, I leaned forward in mine.

"If we could dispense with the formalities, your Grace?" I asked him.

Groff's face took on an expression of complete surprise. I could only think that even Glennen had always indulged him in his own city.

He opened up his hands before him. "You have all of our attention, your Imperial Majesty," he said.

This time I couldn't miss the air of contempt woven into the words. Congratulations, bone-head. You pissed off another Duke.

Ceberro must be loving this.

"It's my fault," Arath said, coming to my rescue. "I must return to my city, now that I have the Uman artisans from the capitol."

"Of course, your Excellence," Groff said, then his eyes squinted as he added, "with my own artisans, of course, as promised."

"Of course, your Grace," he said. "But, for right now, the ships in the wharves…"

"The ship builders in your wharves," I said, trying to take back the meeting, "should be able to produce seven hulls before the month of War."

"We used to say 'seven masts,'" Ceberro chimed in, "but it appears you've changed that, your Grace."

"Your ships take a long time to build, and a lot of wood to build them," Groff complained. "We're buying timber both from the south of Sental and Angador, and using it almost as quickly as we can turn out boards."

"The steam plant will help with that," I informed him. "In a month you'll have high-speed saws that can reduce a tree to a pile of boards in a few minutes."

"That would be something to see," Ceberro said, "however a kiln can still only cure a board at one speed. Won't we simply be transferring the backlog from saw mill to the kiln?"

"I can build more kilns," Groff said. "However, when this project is over, their sitting idle doesn't serve me. At least, not well."

"A central location for our kilns makes more sense," Nantar chimed in.

All eyes turned to Arath.

He sighed. "I see no problem with more kilns being built in Metz," he said. "Adriam knows I have the room and peasants who can use the work."

"They are not inexpensive," Ceberro commented.

Nantar grinned into his beard, Arath and I with him. This project was on the Outpost X payroll, and Outpost X was doing fine.

"Is the wealth of the Free Legion that extensive?" Groff asked the three of us.

I forced my face back to being plain. "We've had some very good years," Nantar said.

"The war between Sental and Volkhydro had to have benefitted you," Ceberro commented, not looking at any of us.

You have no idea, I thought.

"And your Wolf Soldiers will man these ships?" Groff got back on track.

"Yes," I informed him. "I wouldn't strip your garrison for the Navy. A training team will be here from Eldador the Port by week's end. You may deduct the cost of housing them from your taxes to the State."

Groff lowered his head. "Your Imperial Majesty is too kind," he said.

"Glennen would make us pay for his troops in our cities ourselves, even when he was just moving them," Ceberro commented.

Wish I'd know that. Too late now, though.

"How many warriors to a ship?" Arath asked me. He'd clearly done the math.

"One hundred, with room for one hundred more," I informed him.

Several eyebrows rose. By local standards, that was a hell of a compliment. The biggest merchant ships they had now could move fifty if they didn't have to go too far. It took the whole fishing fleet out of Tonkin to move my Wolf Soldiers one time from Eldador to the Silent Isle, and the whole Fovean Shipping Company to move them back with the Trenboni on our tails.

"Based on these ships' performance of late," Ceberro said, referring to the defeat of the prototype ship on the Straights of Deception, "I fail to see the justification in gold and lives."

I nodded. "That will become clear, your Grace," I assured him. "One other thing, if you don't mind."

"You have all of our attention," Groff assured me.

"I'll be sending what will seem to you to be a very strange, brass fitting for some of these ships," I informed him. "Along with this will come vats of cast iron which will be sealed. You will want to examine these."

Groff and Ceberro exchanged glances.

I leaned forward. "You must not, not for any reason, not under any circumstances. Not for a moment, not a quick look, nothing."

"Your *Imperial Majesty*!" Groff exclaimed

"This *is* extremely irregular," Ceberro assured me.

Even Arath looked concerned. Of course, he had his own city now.

"This is irregular," I assured them. "However, it is imperative to my – to Shela's safety that we have these fittings and these containers onboard these ships, and if you open one of these containers, even for a moment, then what is inside it will kill you and, very likely, destroy the city."

Now Groff looked truly concerned.

"More of your *chem-stree*?" Ceberro asked me.

"For lack of a better term," I informed him. "Think of it as the full force of my '*chem-stree*.'"

They didn't like it, but they were vassals, not citizens. If I wanted them to think or behave a certain way, they were beholden at least to try. Of course, vassals had an uncomfortable habit of doing things like revolting and overthrowing the new guy if he was weak, too oppressive or both.

As we stood and took each others' wrists in congratulations to our ability to have a simple meeting, I didn't think I was perceived as weak, or as overly oppressive. Groff had jumped onboard the Empire train a little quick for my tastes, and I had no idea where Ceberro was coming from, but I think I had their curiosity enough to keep them watching until they saw what I did with these Sea Wolves.

If that failed, quite frankly, whatever they wanted to do to me had nothing on what I'd likely do to myself.

***

My rooms in the palace at Andurin included a large bed, a sitting room with books and overstuffed chairs and a thick-piled rug, a side room for eating and a tub for bathing if I wanted it. I smelled pretty bad so I'd ordered hot water brought up, and I was thinking about which book I wanted to look into while I soaked and brooded.

A knock at the door was answered by one of my over-alert Wolf Soldier personal guards. A trip outside of the capitol was a perfect opportunity for the Bounty Hunters to get at me, and of course no Wolf Soldier wanted that to happen on their watch. D'leer had been pretty happy to tell anyone who'd listen that the sergeant whose job she'd taken was on that ship that sank, and no one wanted to be on the next mission like that.

D'leer was actually assigned to Lee now. A Man from Volkhydro named Greggor opened the door, a hand on his sword, and the rest of his squad poised to strike if he told them to.

In trooped a caravan of Uman bearing steaming buckets on yokes across their shoulders, from the door to the bathing tub, a few of them slopping water on the carpet.

Greggor shot me a look. Did I want them to stay in the room when I bathed? Foveans were notoriously free displaying their bodies, especially among subordinates, and I was just as notoriously shy about stripping for a crowd.

A jerked my head at the door and went back to looking for the right book. Mostly Groff had treatises on theories like how to invest a copper and get back a silver, or why peasants can't run their own lives, and other stuff that I'd consider if I wanted to fall asleep, but not if I wanted to get my mind off of my troubles.

I heard the door close. I could smell evergreen oil, which is what passed for the local shampoo.

"Your bath is ready, your Imperial Majesty," a woman's voice purred.

I almost ripped my sword from its sheath. Greggor would not leave the room empty of Wolf Soldiers with another person in here. That meant she'd sneaked in, and I knew what that meant.

Shellene stood in front of the entrance to the bed chamber, dressed in a white robe with her red hair long and free around her shoulders, an unstoppered bottle in her hand and a smile on her lips. Her hunting green eyes reminded me of Genna's, although as far as I could tell she didn't have a weapon on her.

I had the idea she would let me search her if I wanted to.

I felt my eyebrows knit over my eyes. "How did you get in here?" I demanded.

She sighed. "Groff's palace is full of back doors and tunnels between the walls. They aren't hard to find if you know where to look."

I placed my feet apart. "And how did you learn where to look?" I asked her.

She looked over her shoulder and back at me. "Your bath is getting cold," she informed me.

"So's my mood," I answered.

She wanted to cross the room to me; her body kept making little moves forward. However she had to know I'd be on edge and she didn't want to press me.

I had a strong suspicion this woman was either a Bounty Hunter or worked with them. If she wanted me dead I think I'd be dead twice over now. If she wanted to help someone to kill me then she didn't want to let me know how easy it was for them to come after me.

"My Lord," she said, "if you will let me bathe you, then in gratitude I will tell you what you need to know, as well as a few things I think you'd like to know."

She had an agenda, and likely it was Ceberro's. I didn't trust him either. In fact my list of people whom I felt like I could trust was getting shorter all the time.

This had all seemed easy once.

She must have seen my shoulders relax or something, because she crossed the room and took my hand in hers. Shela's hands were soft but strong – you knew she handled leather reins and did her own cooking. Shellene's skin had never known anything harsher than silk, I think, and her skin's caress was like a whisper.

I wasn't wearing my armor or my boots so once she brought me into the bedroom she had my clothes off pretty quickly. I sank down into the tub and into the hot water, room enough for one if I bent my knees. She took a position behind me and I saw her white robe fly across the room and land by the doorway.

The memory of what I'd done to the Andaron girls was like a crow that haunted my mood and pecked at it, become more bold in Shela's absence. While I was sure there were men and especially nobles who would welcome a dalliance when their wife or woman wasn't available, I wasn't one of them.

She dipped a copper pitcher into the water between my legs, leaning over my shoulder to ensure that her breast stroked the side of my cheek, then leaned back, dripping water on my chest and face, and poured it into my long, blonde hair.

A flow of water and dirt flowed down my chest and stomach.

"You're a long time between bathing, my Lord," she informed me.

"Life on the road," I said.

I felt the evergreen oil as she dribbled it onto my scalp. "Was I a pleasant part of your coronation?" she asked.

"I enjoyed getting to know you," I answered.

"I'm happy," she said, and began to work my scalp with her fingernails. "I dared to believe you would take advantage of my offer."

"I considered it seriously," I said. "I didn't think you were the kind of woman who should be treated that way."

Her fingers stopped in my scalp. "Your Ma–your Imperial Majesty?" she said.

I leaned back and looked up at her from the tub. I could see the undersides of her firm breasts and her nipples, and her curious eyes and delicate nose past them.

"You're too amazing not to have a man whose heart is all yours," I said to her.

Okay, that was pretty much a line, and as a line, it was a pretty obvious one. But at the same time, when a woman has to justify the idea she was thrown over for another woman, especially one who is in no way her social equal and arguably no prettier, a line can be a good thing to hear, not because she fell for it, but because the man who jilted her had class enough at least to come up with it.

Her eyes actually welled up and she pushed my head forward, rubbing my scalp and hair. I sat quiet for a moment, letting her fingers work on my skin.

The water around me was already tinted by the dirt from my body.

"You know the Bounty Hunter's Guild is here," she said to me, finally. There was a catch in her voice, but just a tiny one.

"They've been pretty hot after me," I said. "I had to think they'd be here."

"I work with them from time to time," she said. She dipped the copper pitcher again and poured it over my hair. Once again, she made sure her breasts rubbed my face and shoulder.

She smelled like green apples. I didn't know if that was perfume or just her.

"I'm not one of them," she said. "I don't have the skills; I certainly don't have the will to do what they do."

"So how do you?" I began to ask, but she interrupted me.

"I do things, I know things, my father is an influential man, as is Ceberro," she said. "A woman in a society that trades women for power does well to know where the power is. Bounty Hunters have a lot."

That made sense. I think Shela thought that way, even if she didn't say it.

"They will not be making further attempts on your daughter," Shellene continued. "Of this I'm sure. It isn't that the idea is beneath them, because it's not. There is a general consensus that you're under considerable stress from the loss of your wife, and if the loss of your daughter were added to that, then you would go insane."

I barked a laugh. She dipped the pitcher again from over my shoulder.

"And here I thought they wanted to drive me crazy," I said.

"They want you off balance," Shellene said, and pushed my head farther forward so she could get at my back. I felt the water spill across my shoulders. "But Fovea knows the Ballad of the Battle of Tamaran Glen. The insanity that drove you when you thought your wife fallen – no one wants that directed at them, with the resources you have now."

I frowned. This was good to know. "So…no crazy," I said.

She chuckled. She circled around the tub to face me, put a foot on the edge of the tub across from me, and reached out her hands. I took them and she pulled me to my feet, standing naked before each other, me dripping wet and her with water droplets across her breasts and abdomen.

She squatted down, picked up a wash cloth and a bar of soap, and dipped both in the water. She stood and rubbed them together, saying, "No crazy, my Lord," she agreed. "Better to kill you than to invoke you."

"Any idea how that's going to be done?" I asked her.

She rubbed the cloth on my chest. This wasn't the regular lye soap that most people used; this was something gentler that smelled like roses. It lathered up like the soaps I'd used on my own Earth.

"I've no idea," she said. "I would recommend you guard the secret entrances to this room and others you might go to. Keep men close to you whom you know."

So, nothing. But at least I knew something was coming.

"I don't suppose you can tell me why you're telling me this," I asked her. She looked up into my eyes. "I can't say I've earned it from you, you've made it plain you have to seek your own sources of power. You could have kept quiet and whether I live or die, you'd be in a better bargaining position."

She dipped the copper pitcher again and poured the water over me. The water ran up past my ankles, grey and brown with bubbles in it now.

She smiled and looked down. "I don't suppose I could ask for a night of your favor?" she said, rubbing the wash cloth with the soap again. "An illegitimate heir might still have a bright future whether you live or die."

She wasn't shy, that's for sure. I frowned at her. It was bad enough we were doing this.

"I thought not," she sighed. She squatted down and started rubbing my stomach and legs.

"However, and while this is no less mercenary, one must deal with a real world," she said, still not looking me in the eyes. "There is the possibility your Shela will not survive her incarceration. The Uman-Chi will execute her, given the chance."

"They've already offered me terms for her return," I informed her.

She chuckled. "Stripped of her power–did they mention that?" she said. "Her will broken, all excusable by her frequent attempts to escape of course, though her story will be different."

"She's pregnant," I said. Shellene looked up at me. "I'm told they won't do anything that would endanger an unborn child."

She rubbed the wash cloth up the inside of my leg. "So the stories of them say," she agreed. "And that may save her some of their abuses, but not the binding of her powers once the child is born. And what could you say, Shela returned to you weakened and broken? Would you say that this is not your woman? Would decry a Shela not a sorceress is not the Shela of your heart's desire?"

No, I thought, as she reached for the pitcher again. It would break Shela's heart. And yet, Shela without her power would be like a flower clipped from its root. She'd die. She'd look at me and think she was a burden on me, and she would wither away.

The rage that washed over me scared me. Shellene poured the water over my mid section in quiet.

"Your mind races," she said. "You know the truth of my words."

"And if that happens, and if she dies," I said.

"I'd have her place beside you, for my loyalty," she said.

"I have to think, then, that you've plenty more to barter with," I said to her.

She chuckled, turned and walked to one of the overstuffed chairs in the bedroom, where a pile of linen towels had been laid. She grabbed up a few of them, threw one of them by the side of tub, then crossed back to the tub and took my hand in hers.

She looked up into my eyes. "Your Imperial Majesty," she said, "consider me a wellspring of more than information."

She pulled me out of the tub and I stood on the linen towel. She rubbed me down with the towels, tossing them into the tub when she was finished with each. When I was dry, she rubbed herself down, and then without warning she pressed herself against me, her breasts against my chest, her hand in my hair, right at the roots.

She raised her chin as if she would kiss me, and she said, "Have we struck a deal, my Lord?"

I sighed. She didn't just make a persuasive argument, she gave a brilliant presentation. Who in their right mind wouldn't want a woman like this?

How would things be different, if I'd met this one first?

How, that is, except if I'd met her as a wandering sword for hire and I'd done so much as look at her cross-eyed, she'd likely have had me flogged. Different in that, if my fortunes evaporated and I went back to being that sword for hire, she'd forget she'd ever met me.

This whole act was supposed to make me lust for her, but she didn't know me. This same line, these same promises, are what had made Genna such a turn-off.

Like any good huckster, she knew when she'd lost the mark. She pushed herself away from me, she looked me up and down, with her hand still on my chest, and then she turned, crossed the room and scooped up her robe.

Next to the bed there was a book stand. Putting the robe back on, she crossed the room again, touched a book on the stand, and caused part of the wall to slide into the passage beyond it. Without a look over her shoulder she slipped inside and the passage closed behind her.

I stood naked in a room suddenly grown remarkably cold.

Chapter Twenty-Seven

A Matter of Deceptions

I left Andurin a week later, on the 14th day of Weather, after I received another status report from Wisex that it still existed and a detailed analysis from Two Spears on how the aurochs were calving. He'd picked me out a sub-chief to run things for me while I wasn't there, and he'd be returning to Thera with his woman, Soft Eyes, whom he'd taken as his own.

He wasn't real happy about what was going on with his sister, but technically Andoron was in civil war, and during a civil war you didn't want to go raiding the impenetrable city of Outpost IX. In fact a couple of tribes had turned on each other in the vicinity of the part of Andoron we claimed, but it really didn't affect us.

When I arrived in Metz again, a week later, I learned further that the Fovean High Council wanted to declare an end to the Andoron Civil War, and would be meeting on the first week of the month of War. It wasn't the sort of meeting I was supposed to attend and I didn't plan to – my delegates could handle the idea that we were back to where we'd pretended to have started from.

I and one hundred mounted Wolf Soldiers managed to get back into the gates of Eldador the Port by the 4th day of Earth's month, taking the commons entirely by surprise. People actually stood open-mouthed when Blizzard high-stepped in through the heavy wooden gates, now under reconstruction, with five columns of Wolf Soldiers behind him.

"*He Conquers!*" someone cheered. "*The Emperor*! *The Emperor*!" cried another.

"*Death to Trenbon!*" another roared, much to the shock and consternation of a few Uman merchants presumably from the Silent Isle. It wouldn't be uncommon for nationalist sentiment to spill over into action against the merchants of another country, and it wasn't likely to turn out well for those merchants.

One of the Wolf Soldiers, a Man whom I remembered as the disgraced son of a baron out of Rennin's duchy, waved to the crowd. That wasn't the kind of thing I usually liked to see in my warriors, but I didn't get an opportunity to say anything about it because an arrow took him under the arm, knocking him from his saddle.

"*Dammit!*" I swore, and put heels to Blizzard. The stallion reared and pawed the air above the cobbled street to the palace.

The problem, however, is that Earth's month is when the market place really came alive, and the space after the gates inside the main city was clogged with people come from every nation. While Blizzard could in fact ride them down if I pushed him, it's really a bad idea to go killing your own people and your sought-after guests while you ran like a coward from a fight. However a man on horseback is no match for archers he can't see.

People started screaming, and of course started milling around. My Wolf Soldiers tried to surge forward to protect me with their bodies, but there's only so much you can do when the guy you're protecting is on the back of a horse a hand and a half taller than the next largest one around him, and that guy is taller than all of the other riders and decked out in Dwarfish armor.

Three arrows stopped dead on my breast plate and another rang my helmet. I'd put Blizzard's barding on him and it was a good thing, because another arrow rang from that and ended up in a peasant's shoulder.

That person, and an Uman man in a brown tunic and hose, screamed, and then the crowd just went nuts.

The sound of arrows whipping through the air filled my ears. Horses were spinning on their back legs and neighing, my warriors were cursing and fighting to control their mounts, a few of the commons were trampled as they were pushed in front of us by the swirling crowd.

But there wasn't another arrow falling amongst us, and that was strange.

"Aschire!" someone screamed. "Aschire at the gates! *Aschire attacking the city walls!*"

A few of my warriors pulled their swords, but the veterans just smiled and knew better. Three months ago I'd sent word to Krell of the Aschire that I needed archers for my Sea Wolves.

Apparently they'd come.

***

In the Imperial stables (so very much like the Royal stables), I pulled Blizzard's saddle from his back, my Wolf Soldiers around me doing the same thing.

Krell and Nina stood just outside of the stallion's stall, Lee in Nina's arms. She was already bigger than I remembered her, her black hair down past her shoulders with a piece of birch bark braided into it as a gift from Krell.

"Once again, we've saved you from this Bounty Hunter's guild," Krell informed me, as if he had to.

They'd arrived two weeks ago, and they'd taken up the wall guard again. It suited them because they liked the height, they liked looking down on the rest of us and they didn't like mixing with people who would invariably touch them.

The Bounty Hunters had spent three months infiltrating the Regulars who also patrolled the walls. When the Imperial entourage was spotted, they'd insisted the Aschire leave the walls 'for security reasons,' and that had tipped Krell off. No one in Eldador the Port didn't want Aschire on the walls.

So they went outside and they waited, and they were right.

"I don't keep you around for your good looks," I countered Krell. There was a long, red line down Blizzard's whither. It wouldn't need to be stitched but it did need to be salved. I called the stableman.

He turned to his daughter. "He likes men?"

She shook her head. "It's something he says," she informed him. "Their kind are strange."

He nodded.

I turned to Krell. "I thank you, again, your Grace," I informed him. "The Aschire are my closest allies and among my best friends, yourself and your daughter especially."

Nina smiled. Lee kissed her.

"And now you want us out on the water," he asked me. You could see the skepticism on the surprised-looking face if you knew them well enough. The arched eyebrows were furrowed, the thin lips turned down in a frown.

"On to the water and into danger," I said, doubling-down on it. "Against forces aligned against us, which would otherwise show you no ill-will."

Krell considered. "It is not the nature of the Aschire to go looking for enemies," he said. He kept his eyes right on me, gaging me. "We come to defend you, we even helped you avenge your Queen, but it is not for the Aschire to seek an enemy."

"I know this," I said. "It is not in your nature to come to an Andaron's aid, either, however Shela is held captive, and the price of her freedom might be not just her powers, but the child that she carries."

"They'd take her baby?" Nina asked. She couldn't believe it. She'd also already claimed all of the babies as her own.

I looked her in the eyes, and then her father. Both of them were the only grey-eyed Aschire that I knew of.

"That's what the Uman-Chi tell me," I said. "And I have allies who agree."

I don't know how Krell felt about Shela. I had no history of them ever having any sort of relationship. When Krell or the Aschire showed up, they dealt with me, and Shela normally found something else to do.

I know how Krell feels about kids.

"Then they must die," he informed me.

***

In the last week of Earth, the thirtieth of the new Sea Wolves left the used-to-be-secret section of my personal wharves. There were twelve in the capitol port, eight in Andurin and ten in Thera.

Four of the ones in each port had a long, brass tube down the side. This tube ran from the stern, where a black steel pump could be connected to feed into it, to twelve feet past the bow, extending like a sword out over the waves.

It had been pointed out that this end was vulnerable to passing ships in close combat. In fact, we'd refit them later to let the end be detachable and replaceable.

For now, there was only so much time.

Karel of Stone stood beside me on the pier as I watched the last of the new ships creeping down the wharves. He'd overseen a lot of the formulation of the new weapon I'd been brewing in my lab beneath the city. This kind of thing suited him, as it needed to be done in secret, and tested in secret, and you had to be pretty intelligent to make the adjustments necessary to get the mix right.

Like almost everything else I did, I formulated the idea and then others more qualified run with it. Another thing Karel brought to the table was the ability to find local alchemists – persons who sufficed for chemists in Fovea – to handle the mixing. It wasn't everyone who could get their mind around the idea you could heat a substance you found in a rock and turn it into a gas.

Fortunately the whole premise for making laughing gas had set the foundation for a lot of this. There was a good business going in turning sheep-dung into ammonia and selling it as a cleaning agent. There were no words for how that elated a whole crop of shepherds.

And, of course, Eldador ran a huge business providing alcohol from wheat, so we knew no shortage of distillers, either. All-in-all we had the tools to make what I was calling 'Eldadorian Fire.'

"That stuff we're making blows up easily," Karel informed me.

"Kind of the point of it," I said.

"You were right to warn us that water won't put out the fire," he said. "If you bury it in sand for a few days it will cool down enough to dispose of, but even then we had a peasant farmer uncover it and die in a blaze two nights after one experiment."

"Did we take care of his family?" I asked.

The wind picked up on the wharf. The new Sea Wolf, *The Green Dragon*, picked up speed and put more canvas to the wind. She'd sail once around the Bay of Eldador, which was the space west of the peninsula of Britt, as her shakedown cruise.

Only one of these had seen combat, and it had lost. The entire Navy was volunteer onboard these ships, mostly Wolf Soldiers, meaning the house guard of 2,000 and the Theran Lancers were the only Wolf Soldier troops I didn't have committed to this endeavor. If I got my ass handed to me, I was going to be weak enough someone would likely come after me.

I was actually surprised the Confluni hadn't attacked already.

"Ten gold Tabaars," Karel said. He looked up at me. "Kind of generous, if you ask me."

"Would you let someone kill you for ten gold Tabaars?" I asked him.

He grinned that grin of his. I really don't like Karel of Stone. He just…bugs me. But he has skills and I need them.

"How did you know how to make that stuff?" he asked me.

The Green Dragon was tacking to starboard. She'd pull out of the port for the breakwater soon.

A Wolf Soldier from my personal guard coughed behind me. People milled around us, kept at a safe distance by the Wolf Soldiers, on a busy port. Our Sea Wolves held the outermost berths, eleven ships bobbing with the waves.

"I guessed," I informed him, honestly.

"Seriously?" he asked me.

There were Tech Ships out there. The Uman-Chi were pissed as hell I was still making these vessels. After the predictable complaint that I'd nearly punched Aniquen's head off of his shoulders, there'd been another that cited a limit of fifty ships of war being the maximum allowed any Fovean nation, and that with our existing Navy, we had eighty by their counting. I'd immediately retired forty of the older-style ships, selling them at a discount to our growing merchant fleet.

They had to go to Talen to have them refitted, because there wasn't an inch of available wharf space in Eldador. Even Ceberro was getting in on the act and had commissioned two dozen hulls. I'd sent him a couple Wizards who were familiar with the spells we wove into our vessels.

"Yeah," I informed Karel.

He turned back toward the Sea Wolf pulling out onto the bay.

"Good guess."

On the 24th day of Earth, in the 83rd year of the Fovean High Council, ten Sea Wolves set sail from Thera for Eldador the Port. On the first day of War, my dozen from the capitol of the Eldadorian Empire met them at sea and turned east.

We meant to take the Straights of Deception and to hold the southern passages through it in the name of the Eldadorian Empire. Under the treaty of the Fovean High Council, no one actually owned any part of the Straights, even though the Dorkans preyed on any ship that tried to cross it. Of course, they didn't bother Trenboni ships, because no one wanted to contest Trenbon's advantages as a sea power.

I don't think the Dorkans were particularly worried about twenty-two ships headed at the same time for that part of the Bay. First of all, you could barely cross three ships at a time through the Straights. They were a maze of jagged rocks encrusted with barnacles and coral from a foot above the waterline to yards below it, and a single bad turn could rip your ship apart. In fact there were masts visible throughout the Straights as evidence of sailors who'd lost their way and paid the price.

Second, the currents were barely predictable, which is why sailors on Tren Bay still embraced oared ships. You could be on the right path through the Straights and the wind could change or the tide could shift, and you could be dragged across rocks you couldn't see before you realized you were in trouble.

So assuming I wanted to risk my ships, the Dorkans likely felt the Straights could do their work for them.

The Trenboni were another matter. They weren't about to cede the only path out of Tren Bay for the Forgotten Sea to Eldador, especially when they felt they had the upper hand, holding my wife and all.

Dilvesh was left conspicuously in Metz. The rest of the Free Legion was busily getting ready for the War months, which weren't looking at being that busy because of the Andoron civil war and the fear I was going to go berserk over the capture of my woman. However none of them were with me now.

On the fifth day of the month of War, as my ships approached the Straights of Deception, we were greeted by a line of Trenboni Tech Ships sixty strong, with their backs to the East. One ship out front bore an Admiral's four stars under the Trenboni eagle.

I stood on the wheel deck of my flagship, *The Bitch of Eldador*, next to the captain of the vessel, Jaspar, a Man of Eldador who'd grown up in Kor as a pirate and whom Groff had wanted to torture to death for his obscenities against prisoners. He died his hair green for some reason and wore it long. He'd risen quickly among the Wolf Soldiers and been a natural choice for this job.

"That's *Her Lady's Lovely Way*," he informed me, pointing to the Admiral's ship. "The flag of the Tech fleet, under Geledar Taboorin, High Admiral of Trenbon."

His voice was almost gravelly; his brown eyes squinted in a look of pure hate. Jaspar was a drinker, this I knew, but he was built like a brick right down to a smashed, flat nose. His thick lips were parted, his teeth showing, all of his focus on the Tech Ship.

"I guess you don't like him much," I said.

Jaspar barked a laugh. "No," he said. "That ship has sunk me on more than one occasion, Lupus. There's a lot of pirates as would like to be where I am now, much as them as aren't dead."

I nodded.

I'd been a sailor. I knew what it meant to hate another ship and the people on it. I saw that in him now.

The Tech Ship raised a red flag with a white star, then another with blue and white stripes, and another yellow, also with a star. At sea, signalmen could communicate between ships this way—with one set of flags which were communications between ships of different nations, in a language that rarely changed, and another set for ships of the same fleet, which changed all the time. My Sea Wolves used colored lights instead of flags, because they were faster and because no one did it this way here.

"They're asking us if we plan to turn around, or engage them," Jaspar informed me, as more flags travelled up a line between the flag ship's bow and the top of its one mast. "They warn that if we fight, they will give no quarter."

"Confident," I commented.

Jaspar didn't turn away from me. "They never lose," he said.

"Let's see what we can do about that," I said. "Specials to the fore!"

Signalmen from my own ship stood at either side of the wheel deck, the open-air space where the ship's wheel and command crew were located. Some ships in my fleet enclosed this and some did not—I hadn't committed to which style was better yet. I'd find out today.

Balls of different colors sat under metal cans on the rails. Signalmen raised the cans, counted to different numbers and lowered them. The color and the time exposed meant different messages to others in the fleet, which would pass them on.

Eight ships, including *The Bitch*, each with the long, brass tube down its starboard side, glided forward while the other fourteen hung back. We had the wind behind us – I'd managed to arrive with the sun three hours from setting behind us. The Trenboni didn't mind giving up the advantage because their ships were equally fast against the wind.

Probably never a good idea to hand an advantage to your enemy, even if you don't need it, but there you go.

"Load the tubes!" I commanded.

The brass tubes were the key to delivering Eldadorian Fire, which had been known as Byzantine Fire or, if you watched the wrong movie, Greek Fire, around 400 to 700 AD. The liquid was poured into the tube; the tubes were pressurized with hand-pumps, and could then be discharged out across the water. Supposedly the Byzantines used something more like a water cannon, but it had limited range and wasn't useful in rough seas or tight quarters.

Also, you then have a guy standing there, manning it, and if the wind changed he was going to get blow-back, as was his ship. Out to sea, that was simply not a good idea.

Valves were turned onboard *The Bitch*, as well as on our other 'specials,' I had to assume. I'd shown the artisans who'd built the canisters how to put a glass tube in the metal wall, so the tube could be filled with the liquid inside and then show when a canister was empty. We didn't want to have to be popping canisters open during combat when everything was wet, because water would ignite the contents.

"The flag ship is sending a new message," Jaspar informed me. "A last chance to retreat."

"They didn't think we'd be a match for them in Outpost IX," I said. "They aren't going to make that mistake again."

The ship slipped forward. The thump of the hand-driven pumps moved fluid into the brass tube alongside of the ship. The tube was filled with baffles, most of them just holding chambers, some of them heated. Heating the fluid activated the diphosphorus I'd bled into the naptha as a gas. This was the common denominator about Byzantine Fire that no one got, because you had to get white phosphorus up over 1,000 degrees Kelvin to make this P2, and then it wasn't stable if it became a liquid or a solid.

Unless you used a catalyst, like petroleum and pine resin. Combine that with sulfur and you essential mixed the dynamite with the blasting cap.

"All pipes are full, Lupus," the Wolf Soldier signalman informed me.

"Charge all pipes," I ordered him.

Another benefit of the baffle system was that we could squeeze off a few shots per tube, rather than spilling it all at the same time. Below decks we maintained bottles of compressed nitrogen–

another benefit of our sheep-dung enterprises–which were used to pressurized different baffles, forcing the fluid down the pipe.

And the brass could withstand the salt-water of Tren Bay. Steel would be safer, but it would rust.

"All pipes are charged," the signalman informed me.

I couldn't hold back a smile.

The Trenboni fleet began to move forward at almost three times our numbers. Behind them, eight more Sea Wolves were approaching the other side of the Straights.

It never hurts to have a backup plan.

The wind rippled our canvas sails. We had about ten times their sheets to the wind. They plowed straight forward, wanting to get into the range of their magical weapons, their oars rising and lowering in the water. They wouldn't be ramming if they were coming against the wind, so they kept their masts up. They counted on their superior speed to let them engage when they were ready.

"Full sails!" I ordered.

Had to take that away as well.

Sails don't work like engines–you don't suddenly lurch forward unless something really weird happens with the wind. However you can run your sails at half and then drop them to full all-of-a-sudden, all at the same time, and get something close.

That's what we did. The masts creaked, the decks shifted just a little bit. With the wind behind us, our ships didn't quite leap out of the water, but they all rose higher on the waves.

We closed the distance at a speed that had to be faster than an Admiral trying to coordinate sixty ships was ready for. I know this because we were inside their weapons range, and then inside of ours, before their flag ship let us have it.

With a scream like tearing metal, a ragged bolt of pure energy much like the ones I'd faced in the Battle of Two Mountains with the Dwarves ripped the air between the bow of their flagship and the sails in ours. As Forn has warned me years ago, a peppery bitch who could fire a bolt up your arse, if she had a mind.

The bolt struck our mast. Our mast absorbed it as if nothing had happened. In fact, our ship's weapons worked on something similar to a 'magic battery,' a giant, enchanted, ceramic capacitor in the hold of the ship. Magic attacks engaged our defensive spells, which simply absorbed the energy in order to reuse it.

I'd suspected this and Shela and I had worked it out with some of our Wizards. It was all just energy, no matter what the form, no matter what the intent. As they taught us in Nuclear Power School, it's all just 'trons.

You can store electrons, if you know how.

I smiled. Some of the sailors were staring in wonder at the mast that should be lying as kindling around the ship.

"Fire!" I ordered.

Their flag ship banked hard to port. Our brass tube discharged a thick black liquid like a lance through the air. It left the brass tube alongside the ship, flew through the air and through the space where *Her Lady's Lovely Way* should have been, and plastered the ship behind it.

The front of that ship exploded in flame. From seven other ships to either side the same thing happened. Four other Tech Ships caught fire, in two places puddles of the liquid burned on the surface of the Bay, spreading out as the petroleum mix, lighter than water, covered the surface.

200 yards off of our port side, one of my own ships exploded. Pieces flew past our rigging, burning liquid sank beneath the surface of Tren Bay and then and rose back to the top, a boiling black mass of foul smelling steam that cooked the crewmen from that ship alive.

"Forward attack formation!" I ordered. The fourteen ships behind us had been warned not to sail through the burning oil or the remains of our own ships because Eldadorian Fire burned on water. The Trenboni had not been so informed.

Three of their ships sailed too close to the Fire burning on the Bay's surface and exploded into flames. Our seven remaining Sea Wolves turned thirty degrees to starboard and let loose again, spraying burning liquid on more new ships and into the Bay around them.

Less maneuverable and fighting the wind, the Trenboni ships fought to get out of the line of fire of this new threat. Uman screams and the crackle of fire filled our ears, rank black smoke our nostrils. More lightening crackled across the waves and into the rigging of our Sea Wolves, doing nothing but making us more powerful.

Our plan was for the forward ships to break to starboard, the ships behind to port. Some had to pick their way around the burning refuse of our lost Sea Wolf. Their confusion opened up a space for the enemy flag ship, and that ship spun around on the effort of her oarsmen, flying new orders for the assembled Trenboni.

Another problem with flags is that flags are a physical thing. You can affect flags. Lights can be put out or misinterpreted, but you can't change red to green and alter the message.

One of the fourteen 'regular' Sea Wolves found its way into arrow range of the flag ship, and Aschire arrows flew out from her side. Most were focused on the crew, a few picked flags from the message line down the front of the ship.

This changed the message to her fleet. I didn't know the flag signals, so I didn't know from what to what, however I saw the Tech Ships break their formation, some almost bumping in to each other, as our 'special' ships fired again.

Now our fleet was passing through theirs, and more than twenty of their hulls were burning.

Arrow fire pin-cushioned the deck and sides of *The Bitch*, killing several of the sailors in the rigging. The 'special' ships didn't have Aschire archers. Jaspar ordered return fire and what Uman archers we still had took up position at the gunwales.

"Engage the jewel!" Jaspar ordered, looking to the crow's nest, or the highest point on the middle or 'missen' mast.

The jewel was the firing point for our own enchanted weapons. They used lightening, we employed both fire and a heat sink spell with sucked the kinetic energy out of whatever it hit, essentially a 'cold ray.' Creating this had required long conversations with exceptionally skeptical Wizards, however the result was something that could freeze the surface of the Bay like a scene from a Batman movie.

Our ship fired to starboard and froze a passing Tech Ship's oars in the water. The ship, passing us, turned hard to starboard itself, right toward us, as the rowers on one side became a drag on the ship and the ones on the other rowed free.

Their ship bumped the side of ours. The ship shook and started spinning to port side. The jewel fired again to the other side, at another Tech Ship, as we fought to right ourselves.

The Bitch spun one hundred eighty degrees, her main weapon now pointing at the encumbered ship.

"Fire the main!" Jaspar shouted.

We sprayed down her side, the unlucky ship exploding in flame and black smoke. Past our personal battle I could see our fleet was passing through theirs. We'd lost at least one other ship, overwhelmed by their archers and then rammed by a Tech Ship who'd shattered her mast in the process. Past that I thought I could see where another of my Sea Wolves was burning.

"Hard to port! Hard to port!" Jaspar shouted. Sailors scrambled through the rigging, turning the sails on the mast, bringing the great ship to heel.

More arrows peppered the deck. One whizzed by my ear.

To port one of the Sea Wolves launched fire from her mast into the rigging of a Tech Ship. Not protected like ours, the main sail burst into flame. *The Bitch* righted herself and began pressing through the enemy fleet again.

"Main Watch! Report sails!" Jaspar ordered. Some of the arrows he'd taken were burning and several of the archers had dropped their bows and picked up buckets. There were a dozen dead or severely wounded sailors I could see.

Standing there, observing, not taking charge, was the hardest thing I'd ever done. But a ship can't have two captains, and this was Jaspar's command. I didn't agree with everything he was doing but I'd make it worse, not better, if I interfered.

Finally we were through the enemy fleet and each of our ships, once clear of the others, began tacking to port.

"Eighteen of ours, twenty-four of theirs," someone called down from the Crow's Nest.

Jaspar turned to me and grinned.

On the other side of the Straights, I could see there were Dorkan ships engaging the fleet out of Andurin. I'm sure they thought they'd beaten this type of ship once and would have no trouble. A quick count showed maybe six of the Dorkans, and three of those were already on fire.

Groff could be said to be 'doing better' than I was. I'm sure he'd like that.

Our ships were lining up again. Their flag ship now finished a row all the way to port of their fleet. She was running flags up on the other side of more than thirty burning hulls, through a haze of reeking black smoke that hung low and oily between us.

"They'll use the smoke," I said to Jaspar. "They'll line up on the other side of the thickest of it and try to engage us with their archers and their rams."

"Your orders, Lupus?" Jaspar asked me.

"All sails to port," I said. "Leave *The House of Stowe* behind to search for survivors. We'll come around the burning ships and then hold the enemy against them."

Jaspar nodded. *The House of Stowe* wasn't a 'special' ship. Our ships started to tack sideways to the wind, pushing around the wreckage.

Our tacking to port would put us on the opposite side of their fleet as their flagship. With some luck they wouldn't realize what was going on until we started to trap them.

A set of stairs led from the wheel deck to the lower main deck, or poop. I dropped down to where some of the sailors who'd been injured were laying.

I'd done triage in the Navy, I did that now. I worked with two other sailors to bind wounds and make those who couldn't be helped comfortable. It was better than watching good men die.

One was an Uman woman with white hair. I thought she might be an old woman when, in fact, she turned out to be a youngish girl.

"Lupus," she said, and licked her lips. "Lupus, I'm dying."

An arrow was buried in her gut. She lay in a puddle of her own blood.

"The hell you are," I said through gritted teeth. I turned her half way over and could see the arrow hadn't come out the other side. It was probably buried in some internal organ she needed, like her bowels.

She smiled and closed her eyes. I hated this. I hated having to pay this price. People had to die for me to do what I wanted. People who'd come to me to have a better life. You can make an argument that some things are worth dying for, but those things tend to change in value when you're the one doing the dying.

"Thank–thank you," she said to me. She reached up, and she stroked the side of my face with a bloody hand.

"Thank you," she repeated. I looked into her eyes.

"All I wanted," she sighed, and looked away from me, "was to get one chance to fight back."

And then she was gone, and Jaspar was calling to me. The enemy fleet had spotted us coming 'round the burning hulls, but we'd already engaged a few with our Eldadorian Fire.

Thank you wasn't something I was used to hearing.

Chapter Twenty-Eight

Sea Power

We lost six ships in the Battle of the Deceptions, as it was being called. The Trenboni lost fifty before they withdrew.

Their flag ship accounted for two of ours, one a special, in her escape. I could have run her down if I wanted. Our ships were bigger and a lot faster. I didn't want him, though. I had other issues.

On the 9th day of the month of War, my entire fleet of Sea Wolves, twenty-four strong, pulled in to the empty wharves of Outpost IX, where the gates were closed and the city walls were manned with archers, some of them Scitai.

Friends can be fickle, but then, who knew what they'd do once the fighting started.

Groff and one of his sons, Grak, stood beside me on my wheel deck with Jaspar. Grak stood tall and thin like his father, maybe a little more meat on him but not much. He pony-tailed his black hair like mine, but he already showed a widow's peak. He's commanded a ship in the fleet, one of the specials, and he'd supposedly done a good job of it.

"Looks like they heard what happened at the Straights," Grak said to me, a smile on his lips. Another way he was unlike his father.

Groff just nodded. I turned to Jaspar.

"Let them know we want to talk, before we decide whether we want to fight," I said to him.

"We don't have flags like that," Jaspar informed me, but as I opened my mouth, he added, "but I'll get them out here, if they'll come."

He went down to the signalman. Flags flew up our missen mast.

We waited.

Ten minutes later, they dipped the pennons flying over the city gates. These were some kind of bird or something–every house among the Uman-Chi claimed some part of the city and had their pennons over that part.

"They'll talk," Jaspar said.

"Make port, just the flag ship," I said to Jaspar. To the signalman, I shouted, "To the fleet–stand ready. If they attack us, set pipes for long range and assault the city gate and walls."

The signalman began to raise and lower the covers over our communication lights.

"Another attack on Outpost IX?" Grak asked me.

"Your Imperial Majesty," Groff corrected him.

Grak turned to Groff. "His troops call him by familiar," he said.

"And will you be joining the ranks of his Wolf Soldiers?" Groff scowled. "I'm sure they'll take you."

Grak swallowed and bowed to me. "Your Imperial Majesty," he said.

What a family.

We pulled into port, and an Uman-Chi in a white robe, surrounded by Uman warriors, was waiting. I don't know how he got there and at this point I didn't care.

Groff and Grak and I went down to meet him with twenty Wolf Soldiers. He stood at the edge of the pier, watching us as we approached.

When we stopped he inclined his head.

"Your Imperial Majesty," he said to me. His hair was white and his skin showed signs of aging. He had a big belly and the usual silver-on-silver eyes, and seemed to want to grin.

"I've never had the pleasure," I said.

He looked dumb-founded. "Your Imperial Majesty?" he said, not understanding me.

I sighed. "The pleasure of meeting you," I said. "Therefore, I don't know your name."

He did smile then. "Ah," he said. "I am Chaheff Tamulin, of the house Tamulin, which are merchants. And yet, I am a Caster."

"You know where I've come from?" I asked him.

He lost his smile. "You managed to leave a caster or two alive, so yes; I know where you've come from, and what you've done."

"Then you know why I'm here," I said.

"You probably believe we'll give you back your wife," he said, "or your woman, or whatever she is.

"I think that would be a good idea, yes," I informed him.

"I could also just kill you right now," Chaheff informed me. "That might also be a 'good idea.'"

I frowned and nodded. "It would," I agreed, "except then those ships in your harbor will turn their weapons on your city, and they will burn it in its entirety to the ground."

Chaheff smiled again. "Burn stone?" he said. "I think you were a poor student of the sciences."

"Make stone hot enough and it will crack," I informed him. "This burns very, very hot, Sirrah. I assure you; they will either destroy your city or leave it uninhabitable."

'Sirrah' was something Uman-Chi called other people. It didn't denote respect, more acknowledgement that without some title, feelings would be hurt. Chaheff seemed a little surprised I would use it now.

"Where I to give you your woman," he said, and I think he was trying to look me in the eye, though it was hard to tell, "what then would keep you from attacking us anyway?"

"If I have my woman," I said, "I will have everything from Trenbon that I could want. I won't care enough about you to attack you.

"You would be," I said, and I leaned closer, and looked into his silver-on-silver eyes, "insignificant to me."

Not something I think the multi-centurial Uman-Chi were accustomed to hearing, I'm sure. But I'd just whacked their fleet. This was their number one claim to fame on Tren Bay. They probably already knew their magic wasn't working on my Sea Wolves, whether or not they knew it made them stronger, so they were probably doing more biting than they could do chewing right about now.

An hour later Shela rode side-saddle out the main gate of Outpost IX dressed in a red velvet robe and blue satin slippers, a troop of Uman surrounding her. Whether that was to protect her baby or her person from the new crop of widows I'd just generated from Trenbon was anyone's guess.

***

We sat in the dark, in the captain's cabin onboard *The Bitch of Eldador*. Shela and I–she'd shucked the red robes as soon as she'd entered the cabin, saying she'd rather be naked than wear anything from the Uman-Chi.

She hadn't commented on the ship's name, but she had other things on her mind.

After more than an hour, she said, "They didn't hurt me."

"Then I won't kill all of them," I said to her.

"You shouldn't go after them at all," she told me. I couldn't see her face in the dark. I couldn't guess at what she'd been through, but it couldn't have been too pleasant. I'm sure they made no secret of their plans for her.

"Well, too late for that," I said.

She inhaled sharply. "What did you do?" she asked me.

"You know how they used to have the largest fleet on Tren Bay with sixty ships?" I asked her.

"You sank them all?"

"All but ten," I said.

"Those new ships of yours."

"Yeah."

She slid closer to me in the dark. We were both sitting on the captain's bed. It could be big enough for two, even two and a half, as we clearly were now. Shela would be delivering some time in Chaos, I thought.

I felt her hands on my neck and shoulders.

"Who was the girl?" she asked me.

Like an ice pick in my heart. I slid my hand around her waist.

"Shellene, that friend of Ceberro's, made an offer," I informed her. "She thought you'd come back broken if you came back at all, and she wanted to replace you."

Shela chuckled. "Foolish girl," she said. No one knew me better than Shela. "Proud of her body though?"

"Oh, yeah," I said. "Gave me the whole view when she snuck into my chambers in Andurin and washed my hair."

Her fingers stiffened on me. "She bathed you?"

"Yeah," I said. "Made her pitch."

"Did she…"

I squeezed her. "Couldn't even stomach the idea," I informed her. "I told you–it's my people's tradition to have only one. I guess you figured out by now that one is you."

She was quiet for a while after that. The ship rocked from side to side. I felt her cheek on my shoulder.

"How many," she began, and then I heard her swallow.

"How many had to die?" she asked me finally.

"Thousands," I informed her. "I lost six ships, sank fifty of theirs. If you want to get technical about this, then chalk up the dead from Andoron. That was what sparked this off, and I had to do it if I wanted to marry you."

I could feel the wetness on my shoulder from her tears.

"Once, a long time ago, I think, I held you in my arms," she said to me. "In a tent in Conflu, you wept for your dead, for the people whom you had to kill, and you lamented that there was no reason, that you could have just lived your life and left them to live theirs."

"And now I'm holding you," I said to her.

"You are holding me, and now I weep, for my pride, because I wouldn't be a concubine. Because I wouldn't share you, couldn't stand a simple thing, another wife, another woman in your bed."

"That's an important thing," I said.

"It's not," she hissed. She took my face in her hands; I felt her breath on my lips as she spoke. "My mother was a second wife. My father took another after her. So why am I so proud? Why can I not share a powerful man?"

"I never wanted you to–"

She smothered my mouth with hers, her tongue against mine, her hands in my hair. I stroked her back, her belly, her hips in the dark. I didn't know what she wanted from me, so I didn't know what I should do with her.

She broke the kiss, and she said, "I didn't know your sadness then. I think that I do now. In the months I sat alone in a cell, naked, nothing to do but think, I thought about the man you are, the man were, the man you are becoming."

She sobbed. "I am destroying you, White Wolf," she said. "The things you do now, the things you do for me, these are not good things. My selfishness, my greed, it drives you, it makes of you a monster that others fear."

"No," I said. "No, no–not you. Not ever you."

"Of course me," she said, and sniffed. "How many did you kill at the Battle of Tamaran Glen? How many in the south of Andoron? How many now? For me, White Wolf. For me."

"The sack of Outpost IX," I said. "The Battle of Thera. That wasn't you."

"But afterward," she told me, "after those battles, you did not cry. Your own people dead around you, and you did not cry."

I didn't know what to say. It's true–it had started to bother me less. I'd have burned Outpost IX to the ground; I'd sent my own warriors to be killed for a tactical advantage. I did what I had to do, and no, it didn't bother me as much as it used to.

But that wasn't Shela's fault. I was doing War's will. I knew the consequences of displeasing Him. Perhaps a faithful man would have still wept, but not one with *proof.*

"Let's go," she said to me. She took my hands in hers. "Let's leave for Wisex. You can be the chieftain of the Wolf Riders, you can have your magic city on the lake. Let Tartan Stowe have back his father's kingdom, let the Foveans have their stupid wars."

I could almost see her eyes glistening in the dark. I didn't need my eyes to see her. I knew every curve of her face. I knew every hair on her head. I could almost name them. I knew how her eyes looked when she cried for me.

"The Bounty Hunter's Guild would love that," I informed her. "We have done a lot of things no one can forgive, my love. The last thing we can do is weaken ourselves and then dare them to come after us.

"The Uman-Chi have long memories. The Andarons can smell weakness. The Confluni would love to have that city on Black Lake."

She took me in her eyes and she sobbed. She'd been a captive, all alone, for a long time. She had only her thoughts to comfort her. Finally, those things turned against her as well.

It's hard to turn into an object, when you were raised to be a woman. I could tell that now.

***

We were back in Eldador the Port in three days. Eight ships, the full compliment, returned to Andurin across the Straights of Deception. Eight more returned to Thera, the rest to Eldador the Port. I stood at the bow of *The Bitch of Eldador* with Shela beside me in a flowing white dress she'd conjured from her possessions in the capitol. It accentuated the swell of her belly. Her black hair flew free behind her.

More than a thousand stood cheering on the pier. The Regulars were hard-pressed to contain them. Fifty squads of Wolf Soldier home guard under J'her's personal command lined the pier where *The Bitch* would pull in. People threw flowers in the water in front of the ship.

Shela waved to them. They cheered louder. She smiled wide – it's hard not to like being adored.

I knew what was going on in her heart.

We exited the ship on a gang plank for the solid wooden wharves beside her. Sailors made the flagship fast and my corps of engineers were already scrambling to assess her damage. The brass end of her fire pipe was scored and cracked and it appeared these would have to be re-engineered.

It still bothered me that one of the 'specials' had blown up the first time she tried to use her weapon.

Hectar and his son approached me through the line of Regulars keeping the crowd back, marching past the lines of Wolf Soldier waiting to escort us back to the palace.

"Well met, your Imperial Majesties," he said. He took my forearm in his and then kissed the back of Shela's hand.

"You are radiant, my Lady," he said. "Resplendent! In your glory."

"My feet hurt," she informed him, leaning close, "and I need to pee."

He blanched, but it wasn't like he didn't have kids of his own.

He turned and walked between us down the pier, his son behind us, the Wolf Soldiers falling in before and behind us all in their squads. "I've got the big carriage waiting for us at the end of the pier," he said. "And of course Blizzard for The Conqueror."

I nodded. "Anything going on I need to know about?" I asked.

He shrugged. "Nothing from the Bounty Hunter's guild," he said. "I'm told Duke Ceberro has broken his engagement with that red-head. I didn't think it would last."

I had my own thoughts on that.

"How do you like being the inspiration for a war vessel?" he asked Shela.

Shela made a face. "Your pardon, your Grace?"

He pointed at the stern of my flagship, where her name was spelled out in great, bold letters.

Shela's jaw dropped.

Her eyes flew to the stern of the flagship, and then back to me.

"Really?" she said.

"What?"

"Not The Lady of Eldador, or The Andaron or She Sails Swiftly?" she demanded.

"For the flag ship?" I returned. "A flag ship has to be terrifying."

"I'll show you terrifying," she informed me.

"Well, it's bad luck to rename a ship," I said.

She turned to Hectar. So did I.

He knew where his bread was buttered.

"The worst of luck," he said. "Some men won't even serve on one."

"I think *The Bitch* is more terrifying than She Sails Swiftly," Hectaro chimed in from behind us. "And people are commenting on it already, how much the Emperor loves you, his contempt for his enemies, that he would turn a slur against you into something that will kill them."

Smart kid. I had to give him something.

Shela was nodding and frowning appreciatively, then her face broke into a wide smile.

"The first time I heard that was on the Silent Isle, and her first battle was with the Uman-Chi," she said. "I guess that's proper, then."

We walked down the pier and to the carriage. Blizzard was stomping and snorting and he nuzzled me as soon as I got close to him. Someone had managed to get his saddle on him, but his bridle was over the saddle horn, and I had to feed his bit to him.

Shela entered the carriage, waved to the crowd from the open door, and disappeared inside. I heard, "My darling!" and had to assume Nina and Lee were inside.

The trip back to the palace seemed to take forever, but that was okay with me.

I slept with my wife that night, for the first time in five months. We exhausted ourselves beforehand, much as the geometry of sex with a pregnant woman is a precarious thing. Where there was a will, there was a way, and if Shela was anything she was willing.

Nina and a few hundred Wolf Soldiers slept in a nursery wing of the palace which had been renovated. Well, the Wolf Soldiers were probably not sleeping. When Shela had found out there'd been an attempt on Lee, she went ballistic and proceeded on a witch hunt for any other Bounty Hunters who might be lingering. If there were any, and they had a brain in their head, they were still running for the border.

I drifted off to sleep with Shela's head tucked under my chin. I dreamt of riding Blizzard once again, across a wide plain of grass, from nowhere to nowhere. His hooves pounded the grass, filling my nose with the good smell of crushed grass and horse sweat.

Even as I dreamt, I thought, "I need to do this."

A familiar voice rang ominous in my mind, "So now you've wrested sea and land power."

I pulled Blizzard up short. He snorted and stomped the ground. He wanted to run, and I wanted to run with him.

"Does that please you, Lord?" I asked the god War.

"It suits My purpose," He said. "Glennen is disposed of, his family no threat to you. While your enemies are lined up against you, your victories are clear. My followers grow."

That had to be important to a god. I didn't know if it was safe to ask Him about that and I couldn't think of a thing I would gain for knowing, so I didn't.

"The enemies are more than I thought there would be," I admitted instead.

"They are all the world," War told me. "The swelling power of a new nation terrifies them, and now you command the seas. Conflu especially looks seriously to the East."

Conflu would not like to see a united Fovea under me. They would have a very hard time keeping us out of their nation.

"Even now your mind leaps ahead," War said. "And this pleases me."

"I appreciate…" I said, and then had to choke back the emotions. "I appreciate that You answered my prayer, that You let me keep my family."

The sense of satisfaction that filled me flowed off of my god. It left me feeling enriched and dirty at the same time.

These were dangerous games I played.

"I come to you now for Wisex," He said. "Your woman thinks you fought that battle for her, but I know the truth of this.

"The greatness of a people is like the greatness of a man, and that is in knowledge," He said. "And I know you plan to build a great city in Wisex, patterned after what you saw in your old world, and to fill it with the knowledge you will scavenge from the Cheyak."

My ultimate dream. War always stripped me to my most basic self. It was true–I was glad this gave me the ability to marry my Andaron plains girl, but in fact the purpose was to build a stronghold for the knowledge I planned to gather.

What was the empire of Alexander best known for, if not the lost library of Alexandria? What was the first great thing the United States had to offer, if not the Library of Congress?

When Genghis Khan conquered the steppe, he gathered every written word he could find and sent it back to Samarkand. When the Romans crushed the Greeks, they robbed the libraries and maintained the scholars.

Knowledge is power. The greatness of a people isn't just in its military; it's in its library. Everything arose from there.

Every step I'd taken, since I'd realized what War wanted of me, had been toward this. The Free Legion, then expanding into the Eldadorian peerage when that opportunity presented itself, taking over the monarchy and now hammering the Trenboni–it set one thing in motion:

I had to go after all of the lost Outposts, and I had to rob their libraries, bring them back here and fill this place with scholars whom I could trust, who would take that knowledge and build on it.

War had brought me here not just because I could 'break the rule,' not just because He could talk to me. War brought a history buff and a mechanic here. War wanted someone who could learn His lesson:

Those who ignored the past may be doomed to repeat it, but those who learned from it – who expanded on it – they could get something that the whole world craved.

A do over.

Chapter Twenty-Nine

Report Card

The essence of the god War, with Chaos and Power beside him, observed the wonderful fruits of his labors.

"This suits us well," Power agreed.

Chaos for a moment burned hotter than the sun, then became freezing cold, then reverted to nothing but the smell of oranges.

"It thinks it has found its way," War said to them. "Without knowing how it serves me, it serves me well."

"I worried about the interference of the Andaron female," Power said. "I had no desire to enter again into your machinations. But now that she is involved, I approve. The tidal wave becomes a tsunami."

Chaos rained down on them as water, then exploded and reformed itself as a little girl with a puppy. Then it devoured the puppy.

"And you have heard nothing from Adriam, or Eveave?" Power asked.

War became a darker color. "The universe is full of nothing but the word of Adriam and Eveave," he said. "It is Life's interference that concerns me."

"Life," Power said, growing dark as well. Chaos became a beautiful woman with high, full breasts, dressed in gossamer, and licked its lips lasciviously at the other gods, as it melted like hot wax into a puddle.

"The Almadain makes no sense," War said. "It must oppose me—Life would never side with War, however it supports my instrument in all things, and gives him heart when he has none. I think I might have lost it in Conflu, had it not been for the Almadain."

"Then that concerns me," Power said. "Have you attempted to remove the Almadain?"

"My instrument cherishes it," War said. "Yours as well, to some degree. It will prove difficult to remove from him now, and prior I did not expect it to live long. I sent minions to take it and they failed."

"Then your victories are not complete," Power said.

Chaos formed up from the puddle into a slavering demon, clutching at them with wicked claws and whipping its spiked tale back and forth. "Not complete, not complete!" it snarled.

Beneath them, the instrument and his woman plotted for an Eldadorian Empire. Other nations moved like the pieces of a board game, like the parts of one of the instrument's beloved machines. Cause and effect, action and reaction. The Eldadorians built ships, the ports throughout Fovea built walls. Spies sought the formula for Eldadorian Fire, other spies sought out the spies.

Eveave's favorites, the Bounty Hunters, sought out the instrument. His allies sought out the Bounty Hunters.

Cause and effect. Attack and retaliation. These are the properties of the god War.

This was how they worshipped Him.

"My victories," War said, "pile up around me. My instrument strikes fear in the hearts of the followers of other gods. They dare not stand before him."

"But they will," Power said. "The whole of Fovea will turn on your tool before he is done."

"Before he is done," War said. "He will have turned on them. Clearly you can see where he is going."

"I can," Power said.

"Then you can see what he will do," War said.

Chaos evaporated into a cloud of steam, exploded and was gone. The other gods waited for him to return, but he did not.

By then, the instrument's woman had given him a son. It wasn't in the nature of the Eldadorian nation for a child of the ruler to be the heir.   In fact, throughout Fovea, dynasties were rare. The children of the instrument, however, were as unique as he.

Many seasons passed. The Instrument's seed grew rich on Earth, although he didn't realize it. A mortal's life and vision are both brief, unlike those of a god.

Power glowed a satisfied purple and regarded War.

"It begins," he said.